DILATION

by

TRAVIS STECHER

MULTICOSM PUBLISHING
LOS ANGELES, CA

Published in the United States by Multicosm Publishing
www.MulticosmPublishing.com

Printed by IngramSpark

Library of Congress Control Number: 2022900104

ISBN: 978-1-73-726661-7 (paperback)
ISBN: 978-1-73-726662-4 (hardcover)
ISBN: 978-1-73-726660-0 (ebook)

Second edition 2025

*This book is dedicated to my parents—Sunni and David Stecher,
for always being in my corner.*

CONTENTS

IMPORTED CREW MANIFESTS//

SALVATION//
D/ 2030

CONWAY, ▮LFRED
FOWLER, ISAAC

KAHLIL, BRODY

SHARAB▮, MAYA
SHINO, TEEGAN

WALKER, DENIS▮

S.R.▮ HOURGLASS//
D/ 2130

HATEM, EMILEE

NABOK▮V, VEEKTOR
PHILLIPS, RONAL▮

VIOLET SHIFT//
D/ 3180

BOUCHET▮ MARQUIS
DRAGER, KIHON

KENTWOOD, ALITA

MORR▮SON, ANTON

▮AYNOR, NADIA

RETRIBUTION ARK//
D/ 46▮▮

DECEASED

DECEASED

DECEASED
TIAN E.

BRAND Q.
DECEASED

O'KEETE B.

G▮▮▮▮

DECEASED

DECEASED

DECEASED

LOST ▮▮E IV//
D/ 7609

LYRS, MINSKO

▮\\▮\ERROR▮\▮\\

EXPORTED CREW MANIFESTS//

STRIKE TEAM: DISSENT//
D/ 12596

ALEJANDRA	TSEELA	B. 8122	ALBINO FIRE
DORINGO	DOMA	B. 3389	TERRA.VERRA
FOWLER	ISAAC	B. 1997	SALVATION
LEKKETT	SLADIE	B.10578	XT5260
LOCKHEART	AZA	B. 7754	SOL40E
MACTEAL	LORA	B. 5277	APEXIONAIRE
NABOKOV	VEEKTOR	B. 2097	S.R.A. HOURGLASS
ROVASATTI	KRANDEN	B. 9101	PREBORN 12

ZENAUT TECHNOLOGIES
Arvonia, VA

CHIEF EXECUTIVE	G. SUTHERLAND
DIRECTOR OF CHEMISTRY	M. DIAZ
DIRECTOR OF COMP. SCI.	I. MONROE
DIRECTOR OF BIOLOGY	D. WALKER
DIRECTOR OF PHYSICS	B. KAHLIL
DIRECTOR OF ENGINEERING	T. PLUM
DIRECTOR OF SECURITY	T.B.D.

Contact Team

Dennis Lauer	DoD
Kelly Ditka	DARPA
Leonard Sconi	DIA
Isaac Fowler	DIA
Douglas Pierson	DIA
~~Mandy Atherton~~	~~USAF~~
Theodore Plum	NASA
Jeremy Dobbs	CDC

~~Brody Kahlil~~	~~Kentucky~~
~~Cameron Lennon?~~	~~Bama~~
Denise Walker?	Duke
~~Richard deRusso?~~	~~USF~~

0

12595 A.D.

The courtyard was nearly silent in the midday heat, surrounded by low, metallic buildings. Four blocks of soldiers, each sixty people wide and twenty rows deep, formed a perfect square with their front lines.

In the center of that square stood General Teckann, as much of a stranger to them as they were to each other. He donned an identical black and grey uniform—theirs, a recent upgrade from their new military. It provided a deceptively cohesive air to what was an otherwise disparate group of combatants.

Nadia Raynor stood towards the side of her block. Her eyes wandered to the shambly-looking buildings at the edge of the courtyard, their curved, sheer roofs generating far more power than the occupants inside would use. Aesthetically, the half-cylinder shacks were more like sheds made of sheet metal—shoddy in comparison to the other buildings on the large base.

Over the past month, Starling Base had taken in about six thousand people, including non-military personnel like scientists and engineers. It was an impressive display of administrative coordination, with hundreds of quarantines and thousands of briefings. Raynor had spent her recent weeks being shuffled from person to person while the site tried to figure out who she was, where she needed to go, and what they needed to give her—mostly inoculations.

Her gaze snapped forward as General Teckann began speaking, though it was unlikely he could see her in the back half of her block. Teckann was a squat man in his fifties, with wide shoulders and a crooked jaw. As a natural-born citizen, he was younger than their entire lot. And by no small means. To Raynor's estimation, she was about ninety-four hundred years Teckann's senior.

Biologically, she was just over thirty, though when it came time to celebrate her thirty-first birthday, she'd need to consult a physicist to be certain. For the past few years of their respective lives, every person in the courtyard ranks had been traveling through the emptiest reaches of space as close to the speed of light as possible.

Their destination—right where they started.

It hadn't been a "where," but a "when"—12,595 A.D. Thousands of ships from across the millennia had successfully met up within a few weeks of each other, the pure harmony of which made Raynor's head spin. But if there was ever a cause to function harmoniously for, it was this one. They came for the most important, glorified, romanticized purpose anyone could be sold on: defending the human race from extinction.

Or rather, from extermination.

Teckann continued briefing the pristine rectangles of pseudo time-travelers. He stood straight, his arms folded behind his back, rotating ninety degrees every few moments to face a different block.

"We have at least a couple of years to acclimate you to life in the 126th century," he said. "Technology, interfaces, conventions, weapons, recent events..." He turned to the group on Raynor's right. "Enlisted CAF personnel will retain their ranks. The rest of you will be enlisted as cadets."

Raynor's translator got bogged down by expletives in so many languages, but its effort was moot. The uproar throughout the courtyard eclipsed all barriers of culture and time. Raynor had suspected they would start from the bottom, though the timing of that information seemed poor. They were all hot, tired, anxious, and many were recovering from extreme cases of cabin fever. Even after preparing for five years to land in the future, the future hit like an iron glove.

Unfolding his arms from behind his back, Teckann's wide shoulders sank. Raynor assumed his mannerisms were calculated. The challenge of wrangling people from so many eras who all thought they were the hottest shit in the universe couldn't be understated.

"I understand, believe me," he consoled. "But no matter how exceptional your training may have been, there is no modern equivalent for most of it."

The disconnect between Teckann's mouth and words became more apparent as he addressed Raynor's block, allowing her to appreciate the fluidity of it. Often enough, it happened without any noticeable delay, perfectly capturing the speaker's pitch, tone, and inflection. If Teckann were to learn her language, he would probably be indistinguishable from the device.

While Raynor got lost in admiration of everyday technology, the clamor of her peers ended. She trained her focus back to Teckann, his arms returning to their folded position behind his back.

"...removed all regular criteria for advancement. You'll be undergoing rigorous training in a wide variety of tools and technologies, and your ranks will increase as deemed appropriate by your mastery. I assure you, your skills will not go to waste. We can't afford for them to." He raised his crooked chin, gazing across the four blocks. "It will be a genuine honor to help you find your place in the CAF and see you in action. Coming to fight for our species has earned you both my respect and appreciation. I know you've all traveled far to be here. Some for over ten thousand years..."

Several eyes shifted to a man in the next block over. Raynor didn't have to follow them to know who. Isaac Fowler, born just after the invention of space travel, was the oldest person in their ranks, and one of the most famous people in many cultures' histories. In a haze of faces ripped straight out of grade school texts—Raynor's included—Fowler's stood out.

And while she hadn't stolen a glance at Fowler, Rynor's gaze veered nonetheless. Starling Base's site administrator had been watching the briefing from afar, hiding from the heat in a small sliver of shade offered by one of the seemingly flimsy buildings. Another woman had appeared at the edge of the courtyard to join her. She was strikingly familiar, maybe fifteen years older than Raynor, her wiry brunette hair streaked with silver. She struck up a casual conversation with the site administrator as they watched.

Then it clicked. Raynor had learned a number of the names and faces surrounding her while catching up on nine thousand years of missed history, but the woman in the shade wasn't one of them. She was yet another figure from Raynor's childhood, a face she had seen in early grade school.

Raynor was staring at the mother of xenobiology, Dr. Denise Walker. The woman who made first contact with alien life, who performed the first autopsies ten thousand years before.

Everyone else was looking at the man who killed them.

DILATION

1

WALKER

In an uproar of heavy debate, Denise Walker's biology class broke into a controlled chaos. It was two weeks into the 2023 summer semester, and Walker was already enjoying it more than the regular academic year. Her students were lively and engaged. The course, Comparative Physiology of Marine Animals, fulfilled requirements for a few majors. Any student enrolled in the grueling Monday through Friday class during their summer break did so because they either wanted to or desperately needed to.

This summer marked the completion of Walker's eighth year at Duke University. Joining right after obtaining her doctorate from Berkeley, her focus was ecological biology: the interactions between organisms. Her first years at Duke had involved far more publishing than recent ones—the University had encouraged it—but over the past few years, she'd slowly increased her course load. Her new aim was to correct the issues she'd experienced in the greater academic community by teaching the next generation of scientists.

The sound of squabbling students amused Walker while she observed invisibly from the front of the small classroom. Unlike the larger introductory courses that took place in massive lecture halls, this course had a minuscule enrollment list, and much of the class took place in the field or in labs. On days they did have a lecture, it was in a normal-sized classroom with thirty desks facing a chalkboard. Students who took the class usually found the prospect of dirtying their hands appealing. They wanted to walk around in the marshes and examine aquatic life. They wanted to experience real science. And nothing was more real than a roaring argument amongst thirty people with just enough information to have an opinion.

The prompt she'd given them was: "Did octopodes have arms or tentacles?"

"They're obviously tentacles!" said a boy whose name Walker had yet to learn. "She just wants us to overthink it."

In her large lectures, she never bothered trying to learn names; she'd eventually learn the ones who participated. For the small summer class, she was making a concerted effort to learn them all, but it was only Wednesday of their second week.

"Why would she even ask, then?" a girl in the front immediately countered. "Maybe the way their tentacles are structured makes them *not* tentacles?"

Walker waited to see if anyone didn't fall into those two camps. After a moment of silence, she finally asked, "I take it nobody read ahead?" She smiled as some of the students' faces warped at the suggestion. During the regular semester, there were always a few students who read ahead and spearheaded the discussions. For the compact schedule, Walked was just hoping they would keep up. "You don't have to," she added, "*but*…it means you'll have to wait until tomorrow's lab for your answer."

Groans emitted from the bunch of young adults. Walker often ended lectures with a discussion for them to engage in. It made days in the classroom less monotonous and kept the students interested.

The students gathered their things. Walker picked up the chalkboard eraser and slid it in giant, swooping arcs across the terms she'd written.

"Um…Professor Walker?" a tiny voice piped from behind her. She turned to find a short girl in a yellow tank-top, dirty blonde hair tied in a ponytail, tan book bag slung over her shoulder. Walker might actually know her name already…

"Courtney, right?"

"Yeah!" the girl said louder.

"What can I do for you?"

Courtney shifted her book bag. "Is the lab just in chapter three, or should we also look at four?"

"A very small part of three," Walker said. "Mostly the second section. But all of the information you'll need will be included in the lab."

Walker suspected there was more to their interaction. Courtney lingered a moment, her body language telling. Early in her career, Walker had been a minor celebrity among the biological community. The majority of her students came and went without knowing otherwise, but she could see the signs.

"I read your paper!" Courtney blurted. A faint rose color fled to her cheeks. "I mean, when it first came out."

As vague a statement as it was, Walker didn't need to ask which paper Courtney was referring to. In the summer of her third year at Duke, she wrote a paper on taxonomic classification that had been read more than all of the rest combined. Not for the content, unfortunately, but for the controversy in its wake. She'd criticized the taxonomy system and proposed modern, genetic-based alternatives, outlining several problematic examples in the current system that would be solved. The purpose was to display the unrivaled flexibility of a 21st-century system of organic classification, one that could adapt to new biological data without room for ambiguity.

Several members of the zoological community slammed it, calling her naive and unrealistic. Her academic critics pointed to hypothetical examples in order to paint her body of evidence as flimsy, even though her cited proof was grounded, thorough, and plentiful. They said she was trying to gain attention by being radical, labeling her as too young despite her being over thirty at the time.

Those critics all happened to be elderly men.

The result was a nationwide argument about sexism in STEM fields: science, technology, engineering, and mathematics. Several peers came to her defense and ratified her methods, but the debate had overshadowed the content of her paper, and it ultimately vanished into a political void. In Walker's eye, her adversaries had won. Their goal had been to bury her proposal, and they'd succeeded. It cost many of them their already piss-poor reputations, which seemed like an appalling level of schadenfreude.

At least, that *was* her perspective until she started receiving emails from young girls across the country whom she'd inspired to pursue science despite being told they couldn't. From parents thanking her for being a role model. Even from talk shows asking to interview her.

Duke loved it, sporting a 30% increase in female STEM applicants from their highest previous year. Not to mention great press. Walker's course load was removed in lieu of individual seminars, allowing her to continue publishing while satisfying the increasing demand for public appearances. The conversation moved onto major news networks, where Walker was the default expert, introduced as "Professor at Duke University." She even delivered seminars at other institutions in the hopes of providing a similar boost to Duke's post-graduate programs.

With her hectic schedule, successive publications weren't up to the quality she wanted. It forced her to tackle easier topics, and for all of the discourse, the scientific community was still problematic. Every paper she wrote was assumed ignorant regardless of methodology. After years of repeatedly punching the same brick wall, she became exhausted with it and stopped publishing. Then, a year ago, she stopped doing appearances altogether.

In the time since, Walker had been doing some light research that piqued her interest, but didn't have any plans to write about it. Not unless she stumbled onto a result worth publishing.

Walker's full return to teaching had also served to humble her. For all of the emails she'd received from inspired children, none of her students had so much as heard her name. Teenagers didn't watch academic gender debates on CNN. Denise Walker was the scientific equivalent of a famous blogger...back when those still existed.

And without that shift in drive, Walker wouldn't be standing before this future biologist in the yellow tank top. Courtney would have been fourteen or fifteen when that paper was published.

"That's very impressive," Walker told her. "It was a fairly dense read for high school."

"There was a lot I didn't understand the first time," she said. "But it was the reason I got into biology."

All of the crap teachers say about this being why they do it...this is why Walker did it.

"That's wonderful to hear!" she said. "Hopefully I'm able to teach you something valuable this summer."

A loud, guttural laugh burst from the once-shy girl, as if the idea she could learn anything less than lifelong wisdom was preposterous. She collected herself with a snort, crimson returning to her cheeks, and wished Walker a good day.

With the rest of the afternoon free, Walker sequestered herself to her small office. Soft, golden light bathed a desk overcrowded with books about reptiles and biochemistry. With the desk and file cabinet, there was enough standing room for a few people at most. Until this year, she had spent minimal time in the workspace.

For the past few days, she had been struggling to find quality data surrounding the manufacturing of antivenin. At this stage, it was barely more than a curiosity. She was interested to see what the most common difficulties were in creating it, and whether genetic similarities in the animals played a significant role in the manufacturing.

Creating antivenin—also called antivenom—was not the routine process people assumed. Antidotes weren't created from the venom itself. Small doses were given to animals sporting natural resistances, and the host's antibodies were synthesized to make the antidote.

The initial problem with this process was that the host animal often died as a result of the venom doing its job. Tough animals like horses were safer bets, but it wasn't enough for them to simply endure the venom. Different animals created different antibodies, which may be harder to utilize.

Worse still, some venoms were too tricky to combat with these methods. It wasn't until 2019 that a proper antivenin was discovered for the box jellyfish. At the time, it was one of the most dangerous venoms on the planet. Applying it to any animal killed the host outright without the creation of antibodies, making the venom impossible to combat.

The solution was finally discovered in the same location as all of the world's top antivenins: Australia. Researchers at Sydney identified the pathway through which the venom moved, noticed it required a certain type of cholesterol to function, and used existing drugs to block the flow of venom rather than synthesize an antidote.

Walker was interested to see how similar the final process was for venoms of genetically similar animals. It harkened back to her dissertation—the inspiration for the paper she published in '18—but truthfully, she was just curious.

Rubbing her fists into her eyes, Walker leaned back from her desk. The sun had dropped behind some buildings across the walkway, darkening the blue sky. She glanced up at the analog clock on the opposite wall. It was almost seven; time had slipped away from her.

She got up and stretched, looking across the desk to decide what materials she wanted to take home for the night, if any. A soft knock came from the door, followed promptly by the airy voice of one of her newest colleagues, Katrina Stein.

Stein was another biologist, finishing her first year as an associate professor. She was taller than Walker, as most people were. Her brown eyes were set into a pale, round face, framed by shoulder-length brunette hair. Stein had been an undergrad during Walker's bout with fame, later referencing one of Walker's publications for her graduate thesis. Over the past year, the two had become friends outside of work. It was hard to tell if Walker had turned Stein into a protégé, or if Stein had made Walker her mentor, but that's essentially what had happened.

"Hello?" Stein said as she opened the door. She wore a red polo and tan slacks underneath a white lab coat covered in some sort of dried gunk. "What are you still doing here?"

"Just reading about neurotoxins," Walker said. She smiled. "And staying clean, apparently. Busy day?"

Stein looked down at herself. "Oh…we did anatomy labs today," she said indifferently. She'd been teaching a couple of general biology courses for the summer. "I forgot I had slime on my gloves. Is there still any in my hair?"

Walker stifled a laugh. "A little, yeah."

"I texted you a little while ago. Is your phone off?"

"No. It must have died," Walker said. She pulled the black rectangle from her pocket and looked at its reflective surface. "I wasn't expecting to stay this late."

"I was going to see if you were up for getting a drink when I was done, but probably not now." She gestured to the gastrointestinal fluids crusted in her hair.

Walking to the staff parking lot, they discussed the beginnings of their summer courses. Walker had done little lecturing compared to most professors, so she never had great advice on it. But when Stein was ready to publish hew own research, Walker would happily list off every problem she should expect, but there was no point in scaring her this early on.

* * *

Walker made the quick drive home to her small, three-bedroom house in Durham. She lived in a semi-rural area. There were was some space between lots while only being a few blocks from town. The taqueria on the corner of the turnoff caught her eye, and Walker became suddenly aware that she hadn't eaten since lunch. Deciding against eating out, she soon pulled her electric sedan into the long, narrow driveway of her home.

She stepped out into the chilly evening air. Like most houses on the quiet street, hers was surrounded by a number of trees. The blue-grey paint of the exterior was contrasted by red brick at the corners. A few of the tiles on the roof were peeling, but it wouldn't be a concern until the end of summer.

With a thud, she dropped her bag of books next to the coat rack and shed her coat, never fully stopping as she made her way to the kitchen. Long shadows fell over her indoor spice garden from the trees in her backyard.

Gardening had never been an interest for Walker, but after spending so much time traveling during her career, she had been blindsided by her sudden domestication. Spending most of her time at home had kick-started some primal urge to grow her own parsley, so her backyard was now home to a growing vegetable garden complete with dead tomato plants.

After staring vacantly into the fridge for a minute, Walker grabbed a carton of cherry yogurt to tide her over while she contemplated how much cooking she was willing to do. The evening news had already started when she sank into the couch and flicked the TV on. She ate her yogurt, half-listening to the end of a report about a test pilot in Georgia—he survived. Her coat still held her cell phone, but as she looked towards the coat rack, it felt much too far. Anyone important could reach her at home.

Like every old soul, Walker had a landline.

She reached to the end table and checked the answering machine for messages. She took her empty carton back to the kitchen as they played, deciding on simplicity for her dinner. Back-to-back messages from robo-dialers blended with the news, now discussing primary candidates for the 2024 election, a mere seventeen months away.

With her chef's knife halfway through a stalk of broccoli, the third message gave Walker pause.

"Dr. Walker, this is Defense Secretary Dennis Lauer," the machine reverberated. Walker set the knife down, returned to the living room, and shut the TV off before restarting the message.

"Dr. Walker, this is Defense Secretary Dennis Lauer. We're in need of your expertise in an urgent matter and short on time—"

Her brow furrowed as the message played. Why would the secretary of defense call her? Could it be someone from the university playing a prank? In eight years at Duke, Walker had never been pranked by a student. Not to her knowledge, anyway.

The number was listed as blocked, and she had no idea what the current Secretary of Defense sounded like. She was only vaguely sure his name was Lauer.

"We'll try your work and cell again," the voice said. "When you get this message, please remain at home. I'm sending two agents with a car and will be able to give you more information in person."

If this was a joke, it was a confusing one. The message continued while Walker fetched her cell phone and threw it on a charger. "I know this is inconvenient, and I apologize that I can't explain more, but I assure you the defense of our nation is at stake."

"Ha!" Walker laughed audibly. It was too much to be taken seriously. She stared at the answering machine in silence while her cell juiced up.

Sure enough, her notifications showed a pair of texts from Stein and a new voicemail from a blocked number left half an hour prior. Same person, same content.

"...head home as soon as possible and wait there. I'm sending two agents with a car..."

The doorbell rang.

Walker paused.

Someone was actually here…

This all felt too elaborate to be a prank, now, but it also didn't make sense otherwise. In what scenario was her expertise needed for national defense? *Urgently?*

She went to the door, rising to the tips of her toes to look through the peephole, hoping to find a college kid having a laugh.

Nope. Not a kid.

She opened the door. On the porch stood a suited man, a bit younger than Walker but certainly past college age. He was average height, standing with excellent posture. His dark face was cleanly shaven, his black hair buzzed closely to the scalp.

If his general appearance didn't make him look like a federal agent, the suit and sunglasses sold the image. He looked *overly* like a fed. Like he was auditioning for the role of *Federal Agent* in a cheesy TV show.

"Dr. Denise Walker?" he asked, though he clearly knew the answer. From his inside pocket, he removed a badge in a small folding booklet, the letters *DIA* printed in block letters in the background. "Defense Intelligence Agency. You were told to expect us."

She glanced over his shoulder. A black Escalade with tinted windows sat backed into the driveway behind her car.

"Did I do something?" she asked, trying to get a read on the man behind the shades. He was like stone.

"No ma'am, your assistance is requested by the Department of Defense," he said formally. Something still felt off about the whole thing.

"May I see your badge again?" Walker asked. Without reaction, the man removed his badge again and held it up closer. She leaned in to get a good look, her sharp nose nearly touching the plastic cover. She had absolutely no idea what a DIA badge was supposed to look like, let alone what a *fake* one would look like, but she had already committed to inspecting it. It looked as official as any other government identification she'd seen.

Given the suspicious nature of their encounter, Walker also hadn't decided whether being a real federal agent made the man more or less trustworthy than a jerk student. She tried again to get a read on the agent's inanimate, sunglass-hidden face. If he found her prolonged inspection annoying, he didn't show it.

She looked back at the badge to get a name, printed in bold letters on top of layers of microprinting and watermarks.

FOWLER, ISAAC.

2

FOWLER

Isaac Fowler's morning had been mundane, but they all were these days. Not that he was complaining—he had seen enough action for a lifetime—but his three years at the Defense Intelligence Agency had not been as originally described.

Before the DIA, he'd been an Army Ranger, and a damn good one. He was smart, skilled, and professional. Just the kind of man to load up with a few million dollars of equipment and send into dangerous territory. Then, Russian-American tensions hit a boiling point, and rather than waging all-out war while North Korea was still at the table, both sides regressed to tactics utilized for several decades in the 20th century.

Begin the Second Cold War, dubbed "CW2" by media outlets in their typical push for sensationalism and antiquated trendiness. As far as Fowler was concerned, there was no war. If the original conflict had been cold, its sequel was frozen solid. There had been threats, sanctions, tariffs, and some light spying…nothing new.

Of course, Fowler hadn't known that would be the outcome when the Pentagon first came to him with a job offer. It wasn't a hard sell: no more crawling in the mud, no more MREs…throw on a suit, make more money, and enjoy the freedom of operating as a federal agent. Fowler's country needed an intelligence asset, and the DIA wanted to utilize his skills in small-team combat to neutralize Russian assets on domestic soil.

None of that had happened. If there had been any downed surveillance craft or neutralized spies, the information never made it down to Fowler.

Not until this evening, that is. Just as Fowler was about to call it a day, every intelligence agency went into a frenzy. Reports shot hastily through the agencies that the Russians had new spytech over American soil, putting everyone on high alert. Flurries of disparate information trickled down the ranks: the plane had been spotted, but no one could track it; Canada didn't see it cross their airspace. Even after the craft was finally located, nobody could keep tabs on it.

Fowler overheard a frantic conversation between his superiors about the apparent technology gap, but the discussion was otherwise above his pay grade, and while his section of the DIA—Defense Clandestine Services—*was* responsible for intelligence-gathering assets, Fowler was not one. He was there to intercept uncooperative spies, which meant he would be stuck at Rivanna Station until further notice.

Trying not to get sucked into speculative discussions by the civilian personnel, Fowler sat around his desk talking about the current baseball season with one of the other agents. Leonard Sconi was another Army veteran, joining the DIA one year before Fowler. Neither of them were avid followers of baseball, but they also weren't prone to gossiping. It was just a means of killing time until they were either assigned to a task or sent home.

Just after six, both men were called into a briefing. No additional chairs had been brought into the small conference room, but the walls felt even closer than usual. The blinds were closed, and a projector sat in the center of the dark conference table, shining an image onto the far wall.

The Director of the DIA stood across the table, a round man with a receding black hairline atop a square head. Fowler liked him enough; he was good at filtering bureaucratic bullshit and pretty relaxed for his pay grade. Tonight, though, he was stern—tense. Fowler had no reason to think he and Sconi were in trouble, but that was the vibe in the room: somebody was in trouble.

A third agent arrived behind them, Doug Pierson. Since most intelligence work didn't require military training, the personnel of their rural Charlottesville outpost were primarily civilian. Fowler, Sconi, and Pierson were all special ops veterans.

Looks like they're shooting the plane down…

"This information is TS/SCI," the director said without so much as a welcome. The acronym stood for Top Secret: Sensitive Compartmented Information, reserved for specific groupings of information otherwise inaccessible to those with top-secret clearance. It was the formal shorthand for "need-to-know."

The agents acknowledged silently, and the projector image blinked. Defense Secretary Lauer appeared as he sat down. Fowler had been on details with Lauer a few times over the past three years. He was a politician to the core, though perhaps slightly less crooked than the average one.

Lauer proceeded to verify most of the gossip that had trickled within earshot of Fowler and Sconi over the past hour. The Russians denied ownership of the unidentified ship, but no one knew who else it could belong to. We threatened to blow it out of the sky if Russia didn't remove it. They told us to go ahead.

"We hit it with a couple of 150s," Lauer said, "and the craft went down intact."

The Raytheon AIM-150 was one of America's biggest flexes in Cold War II, designed to destroy Russian MiGs more efficiently than the Swedish Meteor. The 150 was easily the most destructive air-to-air missile on the planet, and it didn't leave planes intact.

It was unusual to send in a small team once the military was already involved, but it turned out that American intelligence operatives in Russia had since confirmed the country's story. The three DIA agents weren't being tasked to capture a spy at all. They were detailing Lauer. The secretary was heading to Georgia, himself, and they were readily-available DoD assets able to adapt in the field. Nobody knew what they would find at the crash site, but it wouldn't be a Russian pilot.

The DoD paved their way, with a small plane ready for them at Albemarle Airport, near Rivanna Station along the Blue Ridge Mountains. It was probably a noteworthy story for the staff of the small airport. Fowler didn't know how common it was for the Pentagon to call one and demand airspace and a plane.

Flying into Raleigh-Durham, Fowler and Pierson made a stop in North Carolina to pick up some biologist. Given the specifics of their orders—the person they were picking up, the man Sconi was getting, and the woman Lauer was bringing—it was difficult for Fowler to stop his mind from wandering to some truly insane theories.

Remaining vigilant, Fowler walked up the driveway to the house of Dr. Denise Walker. No one had gotten a hold of her, and for all Fowler knew, she might be in danger. He scanned the trees next to the driveway, eyes darting up to the branches, then to the eastern neighbor a hundred yards away. None of it was particularly important; he just wanted to remain focused on the present. Not about what *might* be waiting for them in Georgia.

A tinge of relief hit Fowler when the biologist opened the door. She was a bit older than him—short and thin with wiry, brunette hair. He waited patiently during her prolonged badge inspection. She obviously had no idea what was going on, so he couldn't fault her suspicion even though they needed to get moving quickly.

Eventually, she pulled her head back from the small booklet.

"Why does the Department of Defense need me?" she asked. Understandably, sensitive details couldn't be left for her over voicemail, but it was a bit annoying how little information she'd been given. Somebody at the Pentagon had expected her to readily hop in a tinted Escalade with two strangers; somebody who had never done fieldwork. As if moving six people across three states in two hours was simple or routine.

"Apologies, ma'am, but I'm not authorized to divulge details. The defense secretary has requested you for your expertise."

Her eyebrows raised, "My expertise?"

"Yes, ma'am."

She thought to herself for a moment. "Is there anything you *can* tell me?" she asked, "so I know what sort of references or notes I might need?"

"Bring anything you'd need overnight," he said. Her eyes widened at the word *overnight*, so he added, "Just in case…"

The professor went back inside for a couple of minutes, leaving Fowler waiting at the door. He passively surveyed the inside of her living room: lab coat, couch, TV, sliding glass door, garden. It was surprisingly cathartic. Just…standing there. The past hour had felt like a day, and there would be several more just like it ahead of them. But right now, his only job was to wait. The air had started cooling; the sky was vibrant orange. It was placid.

Pierson's head popped out the SUV's window and looked back. Radio static cued into Fowler's ear.

"Is she coming?" he asked, a slight echo as his voice traveled across the driveway and through the radio.

"A-firm," Fowler droned.

"Tell her to hurry. This sucks."

"I actually told her you would get antsy. She said she didn't care."

"What an ass," Pierson said, and his head disappeared back into the car. The informality was unusual, but so was the evening, and they were the only agents in the area.

Walker reappeared at the door with a small blue duffel bag printed with the Duke logo and a laptop bag slung over her shoulder. Fowler walked briskly to the SUV, opening the back hatch for her bags and the side door for her. Like a chauffeur. He jumped into the passenger seat, barely able to get the door closed before Pierson took off. Introduced the other agent lazily while he buckled his seatbelt.

Walker leaned up towards the front seats. "Where are we meeting the defense secretary?" she asked.

"The CDC," Fowler said, holding the handrail above the window as Pierson took a sharp turn towards the freeway.

"In Atlanta?"

"Yup."

"Why?"

Fowler gave a heavy sigh and leaned back against the headrest. "Ma'am, I really wish I knew."

In all honesty, he really didn't.

Traffic was light along the 147 freeway. It took barely over ten minutes to return to Raleigh-Durham International. The black SUV careened around the off-ramp loop, hastily following signs to the airport. Walker hated navigating RDU, but the agent driving seemed to know where he was going. He pulled the car off the main road for departures, drove around the parking structure, and arrived at a small, single-room building beside a ten-foot-high gate.

All four tinted windows were lowered as the vehicle pulled to a stop. Out of the building lumbered a puffy-faced man in a blue windbreaker labeled "TSA." He began walking towards the car; the agent behind the wheel leaned out his window.

"It's us."

The man continued moving slowly, not seeming to care about the DIA agent's perceived rush. He peered in the window at Walker like she might be a giant bag of drugs disguised as a woman. Pierson quickly became impatient, tapping his hand on the wheel. "We told you we were picking up another passenger."

"I know," the man droned. "Is she bringing any packages onto the property?"

"Yes, and their contents are classified, so let's go. We're in a hurry."

Glaring lethargically at Pierson, the TSA agent shuffled back into the building at his leisurely pace. A moment later, the gate began opening, and the SUV started forward.

"Not sure if her bags fall under 'top secret,'" Fowler said casually as he looked towards a small commercial jet off to the side.

"Fuuuck him," Pierson said. "Transit dick. You know they fail 80% of their tests to detect weapons? I'm not letting one of them hold us up so they can pretend like they do their jobs for a minute."

"I think it's down to 70."

"Oh, well in that case…"

Cool air rushed into the open windows as the Escalade took a sweeping turn towards the small plane.

"Why aren't we using a military airport?" Walker shouted over the noise of the wind and distant jet engines.

"This one's closer," Fowler said back without elaborating. Walker didn't press further. If they were flying to Atlanta on this plane, she'd have at least an hour to pry for information.

At the bottom of the mobile staircase stood a man in brown slacks and a light blue button-up shirt. As they walked up, Pierson handed over the Escalade's keys and trotted up the stairs. The man didn't so much as look at Walker, but shook Fowler's hand when he hiked by.

The plane was only four seats wide, split into pairs by a narrow walkway. As soon as Fowler got inside, the pilot closed the hatch and headed into the cockpit. He did not seem happy about the arrangement. They settled into three aisle seats near the front. The engines were already firing up as she clicked her seatbelt in, apparently last used by a giant.

With the sun almost setting, both agents removed their sunglasses. Walker felt like she was seeing them for the first time. Fowler appeared concerned, deep in thought across the aisle from her. In front of him, Pierson looked intense—almost angry. It made Walker a bit uneasy. She almost preferred it when they were robots.

"Is this a commandeering?" Walker asked, only partially joking. Fowler seemed to have an internal debate before answering.

"I suppose."

"All to save twenty minutes of travel time?"

"That sounds about right."

Walker laughed in disbelief. "Wonderful to see our taxes being used efficiently...a private plane for the good of the commonwealth."

"Better safe than sorry," he said dismissively. Even with his glasses off, the DIA agent was stoic, and the cryptic nature of the situation was becoming an annoyance. Walker recognized that these two might not be allowed to explain much—hell, they might actually not know anything—but somebody did, and that person owed her an explanation. *They* requested *her*.

She tried to hold back her frustration. "I forgot how many lives can be lost every minute an ecological biology professor isn't around. The Pentagon understands I don't study diseases, right?"

"Yes."

"Then *what*? I refuse to believe the safety of our nation depends on my knowledge of vultures or alligators."

"You've never been to Georgia, then."

"I've—" Walker paused, caught off guard by the reserved agent's bout of sarcasm. He reclined his chair and closed his eyes.

"Your name was on a list of people to contact," he added. Walker sat back as well, staring blankly at the seat in front of her as the plane took off, her mind reeling.

A list?

The paper Walker wrote on taxonomic classification would likely have caused some backlash even without the political spectacle. Linnaean taxonomy—named after Swedish biologist Carl Linnaeus —was almost three hundred years old, and due for an overhaul.

Every plant and animal was given a classification of increasingly specific size down to the exact species. These names were typically Latin, such as *felis catus*—a domesticated cat. *Felis* refers to a genus of small cats, and *catus* differentiates them from their wild counterparts like the jungle cat. Moving into larger groups, the animals get less similar. Family *felidae* includes all cats, big and small, from tabby to lion, continuing up to the kingdom, *animalia*, and more recently, the cellular domain of *eukarya*.

It was nothing more than an administrative convenience. The jungle cat was also commonly called a reed cat or swamp cat, but their taxonomy ensures they're never confused scientifically. The system was well ahead of its time, predating the concept of genetics by 124 years, and as a result, it was far from perfect. Scientists used sloppy methods to identify animals that were already classified— what was referred to as "parallel nomenclature." It resulted in a wide range of issues, one of the most famous ones surrounding the African spitting cobra.

As the name suggested, spitting cobras were dangerous. The venom might only cause permanent blindness when spat into a victim's eyes, but bites were lethal—a danger only amplified by having them classified in two different genera. African spitting cobras were in the subgenus *Afronaja*, near other spitting cobras, as well as a separate genus—*Spracklandus*.

Thankfully, *Afronaja* wasn't a famous example due to a plague of medical mishaps, but rather because the research was regarded to have been stolen—an increasingly common issue. Many so-called scientists built their entire careers on naming animals; some named thousands. None of them were out in the wild discovering each species. They were thieves specializing in clerical formalities.

Real biologists would spend years tracking an individual animal —called the holotype—collecting data and building documentation. Before they were done, someone would steal the partially-completed work to name the species. It was as juvenile as it sounded. Many researchers stopped publishing their findings entirely.

The act was more recent, fueled by the internet and systemically enabled within the industry. Scientific publications were done through a formal process including a thorough peer review, but taxonomy was not. It was governed by a specific entity—the International Commission of Zoological Nomenclature, and their guidelines contained no significant methods of validation, allowing taxonomy vandals to publish through their own websites without review. Walker mentioned some of the vandals and ICZN by name, outlining potential systems in detail that would remove both issues, among others. That same year marked the launch of the Earth BioGenome Project, which aimed to map every complex lifeform on the planet. Genetic classification was inevitable; the only question was whether they wanted to get ahead of the tide.

In effect, they would use the holotype as a genetic marker, with percentages of variance for levels of classification inside a Linnaean-style hierarchy. There was more to it, but it allowed for adaptation, holding together in the most extreme of situations—fragmented DNA, a species evolving out of its existing classification, even the incorporation of extraterrestrial organisms with the same level of accuracy. Mars was a hot topic in the years leading up to her paper, with evidence suggesting it had once contained life. It wasn't the focus of her paper by any means, just an example—what if we found an alien bacterium with genetic similarities to terrestrial life? Instead of using incomplete knowledge to build the taxonomy, the very act of classification would help scientists define their knowledge.

The taxonomy vandals locked onto it. Then came the fallout, sexism in STEM fields, bountiful press, Oprah…all of it.

One of the numerous PR events Walker did revolved around space exploration. The presidential administration of the time was considered anti-space by many, so they did a few media grabs to appear more cosmos-friendly. One of those displays involved compiling a list of top scientists to consult in the event of extraterrestrial contact. It was an idle version of the Voyager golden record, which was placed on the spacecraft to play Earth sounds for aliens. It was a cute idea, but ultimately a stunt. Prominent researchers in a wide range of fields were added. Given the spotlight on her and the surrounding conversation, Walker was included as a "trailblazer in the future study of extraterrestrial biology."

It was worth a good laugh, which was exactly what she'd had. It was one of the least-noteworthy events of her career.

Mild turbulence rocked the small airliner back and forth. Walker turned slowly to Fowler.

"Agent, you said I was on some government list?"

His eyes remained closed. "Mhm."

"It's not a black list, is it?"

He smiled. "No."

"It was a list of researchers from various fields?"

"That's right."

Walker tried to think of other possibilities. She didn't want to sound crazy, but with the secrecy, the DIA involvement, commandeering the plane...if it were an animal-spread disease of some kind, she certainly would have heard about it through her circles, if not on...

The news.

She stared intently at Fowler, looking for any sort of reaction. "I saw a report about a plane crash. A test pilot in Georgia—we're heading to Georgia."

"That we are."

"It wasn't a test pilot, was it?" She waited for the likely response —that he wouldn't be able to discuss the details of any military activity. He sat up to respond, but Walker cut him off. "Are we heading to a possible...alien crash site?"

With his mouth already open to speak, he inhaled a little heavier than usual. He also didn't laugh, which was perhaps more revealing. Pierson turned back from the seat in front.

"Dr. Walker, we're not allowed to tell you anything we know, which is very little. The secretary of defense will be briefing you with us. Okay?"

Her head was spinning. If this were simply a UFO—a likely spy craft—there wouldn't be all of the red carpet. The execution of this operation required some level of certainty.

Walker didn't ask anything else for the duration of the flight. She didn't know what research to prep; her only exposure to the topic was a tongue-in-cheek demonstration of a genetic classification system she'd proposed five years ago that wasn't even adopted.

She was completely unqualified for this.

3

THE CDC

Each barracks housed around two hundred soldiers. They were only temporary, but far roomier than any housing Raynor had received in the militia. Eventually, they'd all be moved into apartment-like rooms in three large dormitories, but during the interim, the barracks were available; Starling Base wasn't currently in use as a defense station.

The non-military time-skippers were moving into the towers first, knowing more or less what sort of work they'd be doing. The soldiers had less clarity, but they'd have a better idea tonight. Their regimens were coming in, which would outline specific courses over the coming months. It would clarify a bit of confusion as they began moving into long-term domiciles.

Despite her curiosity, Raynor fought the impulse to bother Fowler. The man sleeping a dozen beds away was portrayed quite unfavorably during her time, which seemed to be the case for many.

Many, but not all. Some cultures had no public knowledge of the invasion. A large chunk of them didn't know aliens existed at all, and even in societies that outlined Fowler as the responsible party, there were those who lauded him. Their mismatched group came to this century to kill monsters from space. Who better to befriend than the Cain of aliens? The reverence seemed to make Fowler uncomfortable, which Raynor thought was peculiar.

A captain she'd never met called them from the front of the barracks. "Attention, cadets. Your initial training schedules are ready. Since most of you aren't familiar with jewels and data terminals, we're supplying you with physical, non-interactive copies." Two corporals started moving along the rows with small tablets— thin, rigid tiles in their recipient's native language. "You'll all surely have questions about the types of training you're being assigned, but these are just the first months. Many of your job classes are outdated, so you're being introduced to specialities related to your experience. The most common are combat pilots, which we don't have—"

Raynor's stomach twisted in her gut. She'd been flying since before she was old enough to have a license. It was the entire reason she was here at all. She figured human pilots would be less common, but had assumed there would still be some sort of remote piloting.

She took a deep breath. Intermittent chatter from the corporals fell beneath the captain's crisp voice as she outlined job classes that relied on skills honed through piloting.

"—and drone modulators are far more effective when they have advanced piloting skills."

Drone modulators…

When war first took to the stars—not long before Raynor's own time—one of the first limitations had been signal delays. Some operations took place hours away as light traveled, so those squadrons either had to be trained for complete autonomy, or be drones. Most were simple, stupid machines able to carry out basic chores without oversight; mechanical soldier ants designed to complete one or two specific tasks.

Advanced drone ships with full combat capabilities had been in production during the revolution. The expensive ships were controlled from afar by remote operators similar to pilots, which is what Raynor had expected the future to hold. She'd flown beside some, but they were even more plagued by the complications of signal delay than pilots. Now, it seemed autonomous ships had become smart enough to erase pilots from existence entirely.

Still, she was here. There was no going back. Raynor hadn't been born a pilot; she became one through years of practice.

She would adapt—it's what humans did.

The night sky was clear as they touched down at DeKalb-Peachtree Airport in Chamblee, just north of Atlanta. With the sun completely set, the air was still and cold. Back when Walker was traveling frequently, she had gone to Atlanta a few times, but always flew directly into the city. Chamblee reminded her a lot of Durham. She didn't get a chance to truly appreciate the town as it sped by her window on the way to the Centers for Disease Control. Rural roads quickly turned to town roads, then to city streets, and before long, they were at the edge of the CDC campus.

A small, 1950s-style firehouse sat at the front of the property, but the grounds featured several buildings exceeding a dozen floors. Handfuls of business-casual men and women strolled along the sidewalks and a few cars scattered the parking lots. Pierson pulled up to a smaller, four-floor office building, which they promptly took an elevator to the third floor of.

The hallway was dimly lit; each office they walked by was closed and dark. Towards the end of the corridor, a single door sat open, the light from within streaking across the ground. The nameplate on the open door read: JEREMY DOBBS, Ph.D. Rounding the edge of the door, Walker saw a young man sitting at a clean, minimalist desk. To one side was a tall, four-drawer file cabinet. On the other stood a large bookshelf packed full of reference books, many of which overlapped with Walker's field: polymorphism, apoptosis, cellular metabolism…

The rest of the office was fairly open. A couple of canvas hangings of landscapes adorned the walls, along with a poster of an

MMA fighter Walker had never heard of. At the edge of the room, a small brown couch sat next to a white mini-fridge, and a pull-up bar hung on the inside of the doorway. It looked a bit like a frat boy's room—albeit a clean one who was studying some seriously advanced biochemistry.

As Walker took in the scene, Pierson got Dobbs' attention. It seemed the young man was expecting them. He dynamically jumped up from his desk to shake their hands, repeating each of their names as he did so. He towered over Walker, eye-to-eye with Pierson plus an extra twenty pounds of muscle. He could easily have been a football player, and for all Walker knew, he recently was. He looked grad school age.

"Welcome to the CDC!" Dobbs boomed with a handsome smile. "I'd give you a tour, but I assume the rest will be here soon. Please, help yourselves," he gestured to the mini-fridge. "I've got water, vitamin water…there's also beer, but given the circumstances, we probably shouldn't."

"What exactly *are* the circumstances?" Walker sank into the couch. Dobbs' energy was refreshing, and she might actually be able to get some answers from him. The DIA agents remained by the door, far from relaxed as Dobbs sat back down in his desk chair.

"You mean you don't *know?*" he asked.

"I've put some pieces together."

"Riiight. None of us 'knows,' but with the information at hand… we pretty much do."

"I haven't been given any information."

The exuberant smile faded from the man's face. He glanced at Fowler and Pierson. "You didn't tell her?"

"Lauer was unable to speak with her directly," Fowler said coolly. "We're not authorized to divulge any information."

"Can *I* tell her?"

"As I said—"

Dobbs raised an eyebrow suspiciously. "Okay…well, if I go to Gitmo, I'm taking the Wi-Fi password with me." His eyes lit up as he turned back to Walker. "We're gonna go find *aliens!*"

For the first time all night, she laughed. He said it like they all won a trip to Six Flags. "How much of that has been confirmed?"

"Not much," he admitted. "But at the very least, it's an alien ship. The CDC has a small group setting up a medical quarantine right now, but it's all legit. An engineer from NASA tracked it back up to space and out of Earth's gravitational pull—it screwed up a bunch of private satellites."

"Where is it?"

"It crashed up north in Chattahoochee National Forest; a great hiking spot, also really fun to say."

"And it's definitely an alien ship?" Walker asked, trying to veil her suspicion. "Not a foreign satellite or something?"

"Or *something.*"

"Do you know who else is going?"

Dobbs started listing people off on his fingers, "The secretary of defense; another one of *these* guys," he gestured to the DIA agents. "A code-cracker from DARPA, and the guy from NASA: Plum—a man I can only hope is a professor somewhere."

"That's decently rounded," Walker said. She wanted to ask Dobbs why he was included, but wasn't sure if it would sound rude. "What sort of research do you do?"

"Well, I started in pharma making new antibiotics, and that caught the CDC's attention, so for the last five years, I've been working on reducing antimicrobial resistance here."

"Really? You look so young."

"I am. I was twenty-two when I got my doctorate."

"Wow." It was the only response she could think of. "So, your work doesn't have any theoretical overlap with extraterrestrial biochemistry?"

The room vibrated from the deep echoes of his laugh. "Aha! No. I think you proved well enough that our community doesn't handle that well." Walker must have made a face of some kind. Dobbs' smile faded. "Sorry, Dr. Walker. I didn't mean anything by that. I loved your paper."

"You read it?"

"Of course, how could I not? It was this whole thing."

"It wasn't exactly an essay on xenobiology, was it?"

"No. And they only added me because I was young and the CDC had just picked me up. Talk about lucky, right? I mean, who knew *that* would be the greatest thing to happen to my career?" He leaned forward on his desk. "Granted, this whole operation seems ass-backwards, doesn't it?" He turned to the DIA agents by the door. "No offense, fellas."

"You're fine," Fowler said motionlessly.

"I'm honestly surprised we could put together a quarantine team—quaran-team…trademarked. None of them have any clue what to do or expect. They're mainly just going to sterilize every-thing and collect samples. I think someone in D.C. grabbed the first piece of paper resembling procedure and started dialing anyone near Georgia."

"You got that feeling too?" she said.

"Still, this is a once-in-a-lifetime opportunity!" Dobbs' excite-ment was infectious. Regardless of how the government decided to do things, Walker would be seeing something tonight that no human had ever laid eyes on before.

Fowler cut in abruptly. "Is there a larger room we can use? Secretary Lauer is on his way up."

Faint, green scribbles from some sort of chemistry formula were partially erased on the whiteboard of the small meeting room. An oval table sat in the center, surrounded by chairs of the same design. It would do. Fowler didn't imagine they'd be here long.

After a couple of minutes, Sconi arrived with Secretary Lauer and the other two specialists. Lauer had a narrow, stern face with piercing eyes, his hair in the standard military high-and-tight. His suit was expensive, accessorized with a red power tie that mostly covered a small gut.

Fowler had never met the other two contracted experts. The woman, Kelly Ditka, worked at DARPA: the Defense Advanced Research Projects Agency. She was in her late twenties, with short brunette hair and light freckles that gave her face a much friendlier appearance than her demeanor, which was entirely Washington D.C. She developed some sort of intelligent program to identify Russian communications—a linguist turned codebreaker.

The other stranger was Dr. Theodore Plum, an astronautical engineer from the UK. Judging by the Liverpool Football Club jacket worn over his NASA polo…probably from Liverpool. He'd worked at Lockheed, applying to NASA after passing his citizenship test.

Lauer gave a half-hearted greeting before speaking with Walker off to the side. Probably the typical political garb…thanks for coming, sorry about missing you on the phone, I'm about to explain everything, and so on.

They were greeted with small manila folders this time. The corner bore the Department of Defense seal and the word CLASSI-FIED was stamped in red block letters across the front. The folder didn't contain much—official timelines of the night's events and maps piecing together the UFO's flight path. There were some impressive satellite images of the craft just before it was shot down. It looked sort of like a pointed oval, with light coming out of a band along the top and bottom. It was a bit hard to tell from so far up.

The first half of the briefing was old news for Fowler—a polished regurgitation of the information they'd received at Rivanna. It meant he no longer had to walk on eggshells around the civilians, though, which had required a lot more attention than he wanted to give to it.

"We'll head up in both cars," Lauer continued. "Agent Fowler, take Doctors Walker, Dobbs, and Plum in one. Pierson, you'll be driving myself, Ms. Ditka, and Agent Sconi in the other. Our military quarantine was in place around 1854. Nothing left the area prior to that point; we suspect any intelligent life is deceased. Once through the military quarantine, we'll arrive at the CDC's. They have protective and examination equipment there.

"It must be reiterated that the dispersal of any information pertaining to this mission will be tried as treason. All research and notes will be collected on government-issued devices. Your phones and computers won't be allowed through quarantine, and you won't be able to publish anything you learn—especially not in wartime."

"You mean that thing with Russia?" Dobbs joked. The secretary either didn't notice the tone or chose to ignore it. He nodded and continued without losing step.

"Should the need arise to release the information, you'll be appropriately accredited, but assume it will remain classified until long after we're dead." He gave a slight chortle. "This is usually where I explain that having official ties to classified government research is more beneficial than publishing. People tend to jump to more extreme assumptions than the reality, but I don't think that will be the case this time around. These are the terms for your councils. If anyone prefers to not be involved, this is the time to say it. We'll arrange your trip home and monitor you going forward."

Monitoring was probably unnecessary. Anyone they told would think they were nuts. Fowler half-expected to see at least one of the civilians duck out, but none of them did. The secretary proceeded to list off areas of concern for the Pentagon—toxic chemicals in the alloys of the ship and the bodies on board. A mobile lab was being set up beside the medical quarantine for more extensive tests.

Lauer turned to the three DIA agents. They habitually stood slightly more upright. "Your primary task is to be three extra sets of eyes. In the unlikely event we find living creatures—sentient or otherwise—you are not authorized to fire unless given a direct order from me."

"Yes, sir," they said in unison. The instruction didn't shock Fowler in the least. As far as the DoD was concerned, every person on this team was expendable. If there was a live alien on the ship, it was more valuable than all eight of them combined. He and Sconi exchanged a glance that substituted a full conversation—their priority was safety, even at the cost of their careers.

Just before 2100 hours, they locked their phones in Dobbs' office, an unprecedented tension hanging over them as they walked down the dim hallway to the elevator.

4

CHATTAHOOCHEE

City lights became sparse as Fowler sped behind the other vehicle on their way to the forest. Upon seeing the two black SUVs parked side by side, Dobbs had asked if the Department of Defense got a bulk discount on tinted Escalades. Nobody had answered, but honestly—they probably did.

All three scientists rode in silence along the freeway, which eventually hit I-19. The concrete buildings were soon replaced by trees, some of which stretched ten to fifteen stories tall. Fowler stared absently at the vehicle in front of him. His mind often looped through worst-case scenarios before he deployed, but this was different. There was so much unpredictability here…they didn't even know what any potentially living creatures might look like. If a gelatinous blob tried to absorb the Secretary of Defense, what the fuck could Fowler do about it? Let it happen? Pray to whichever god came to mind first that shooting would stop it?

Fowler wondered how God felt about aliens. When he was growing up, his mother made him go to church every week. It had been a sort of spiritual recovery for her after losing his father, but she kept it up to this day. Fowler never paid much attention, or even wanted to go, but from what he remembered, aliens weren't—

"Hey, look!" Plum pointed through the windshield at a green exit sign illuminated by four lights at the base. It was for the westbound 170 to Roswell. "Brilliant."

"That explains it," Dobbs said. "Once per century, the aliens crash a ship near a town called Roswell."

"I think if there were a seventy-year-old alien research facility in New Mexico, none of us would have been called."

"Someone look up how many Roswells there are—oh wait…I forgot, we *can't*. Too risky…we might post pictures of mutilated alien corpses on our dating profiles. Well, all of us except Kelly Ditka."

"Her computer's already government property," Fowler said dully. He was surprised he hadn't thought about Area 51 until now. It seemed unlikely there had been an alien crash in New Mexico, based on tonight's disorganization and confusion.

Walker caught his eye in the rearview mirror. "Do Lauer and Ditka work together often?"

"They have in the past. She does a lot of intelligence work."

"The other car is only defense personnel. Is there a reason for that?"

"Most likely." The vehicle split was a bit concerning to Fowler. Lauer was likely discussing defense concerns in the SUV ahead—a conversation Fowler would like to have heard.

"Uh oh, did you get in trouble?" Dobbs poked. The boyish attitude was getting on Fowler's nerves, though no one else seemed bothered by it. Academia was a very different world.

"I'm the only one good enough to babysit you solo," Fowler said. Dobbs scoffed.

"We won't need any sitters, let alone three."

"You don't think we're going to find intelligent life?" asked Walker.

"Do you?"

"I don't know what we'll find."

"Sure, but we know they're not alive."

"How do you figure?"

"The amount of work done on the ship when it crashed would be so extreme that any surviving life would have to be microscopic."

"It went down intact, though," said Fowler. He was invested now.

"And?"

"And…it should have been a five-mile-long scrapyard."

"That's true," said Plum. "The amount of damage done to the craft—or lack of damage, rather—is beyond explanation. It's safe to say, we have no idea how much force was experienced inside the cabin."

"Or how much pressure any organisms on board can handle," said Walker. "Some species can withstand incredible forces; tardigrades can survive out in the vacuum of space."

"I know, Denise," Dobbs said. "I know *how* they do it, and it's only possible because they're microscopic. That's what I'm saying."

"What are these things?" asked Fowler.

"They're commonly called water bears," Walker explained, "because they're often found in lakes and resemble eight-legged bears under a microscope. They've also been found frozen solid in mountains and boiling in hot springs. Their livable temperature is something like -200 to 150 degrees Celsius."

"-330 to 300 Fahrenheit," Dobbs clarified.

"Scientists started testing every unnatural boundary they could think of. Water bears can live without oxygen. They can withstand six thousand grays of radiation, where five grays will kill a person. And more to the point, they can handle six thousand times the pressure of our atmosphere. Someone eventually shot a whole batch of them into space—no protection, no radiation shielding, nothing. They were brought back ten days later, still able to reproduce."

"Then there are the gritty details," said Dobbs. "Those feats are accomplished by suspending themselves in a sort of stasis—a *tun*—that drops their metabolism a thousand times below normal. Other functions change depending on the stimulus to ensure survival. If they're freezing, the tun prevents crystal formation on cells. If they're suffocating, it relaxes their muscles. They're practically dead, but they revive once they're thrown back into water, even a century later. Larger lifeforms can't do the same. A human dies when less than half of the brain's oxygen supply is cut. Tardigrade brains don't do anything."

"Right, but these hypothetical aliens only need to handle some extra force. There are large, complex lifeforms at the bottom of the Mariana Trench living in a thousand times our atmospheric pressure."

Dobbs thought for a moment before letting out a huge, thunderous laugh. He slapped his hand down on his leg.

"I'm convinced!" he cheered. "Live aliens it is."

"If there is life on board, they traveled quite far," Plum said. "Unless the species is immortal or has some form of hyperspace travel, they'd have to fly near the speed of light to make the trip without dying of old age. Withstanding larger forces would allow them to reach the required speeds far more easily."

"How significant would that be?" asked Walker.

"Very. Ignoring energy consumption, for a human being to accelerate to those speeds and brake…it would take a few years. Not to mention the time spent at the maximum speed. Would you be willing to cram yourself in a small ship for six years?"

"Never."

"What if it were only one?"

"Still, no," Walker said. "But I see your point. They'd be more inclined to accept interstellar travel."

"Broad-stroke speculation."

"Sure."

Dobbs clicked on the roof light behind Fowler, browsing over the contents of his manila folder.

"We're not talking about a light sail pulling a camera at a quarter of the speed of light, here. This ship weighs several kilotons, at least, and would need to travel within a fraction of a percent of the speed of light. It's an unfathomable amount of energy."

"Right you are," Plum said, smiling in the moonlight beside Fowler. "However they got here, it will change engineering as we know it."

Intermittent light from street lamps dissipated as the freeway became a highway. Not long after, they crawled along a narrow, unpaved road with only Pierson's taillights guiding their way. Shortleaf pines and southern red oaks tightly enclosed the unlit path, blocking the stars as they delved further into the park. For fifteen minutes, they wound along the narrow road, long past the signs for recreational spots, tourists, and hikers.

"A bit off the reservation, aren't we?" mulled Plum.

"This is the beginning of the Appalachian Trail," Dobbs said. "So…no."

A reflection from up ahead caught Fowler's eye as the other car's headlights passed over a military vehicle. The checkpoint consisted of two armed guards dressed in forest camouflage and an unhappy Forest Ranger. After a brief pat-down and scan of their vehicle, they were back on the trail, hitting the end of the road a couple of minutes later.

The last eighty feet of packed dirt were home to three tents. Each was adorned with a small light to help find it, but looked more like stars peeking through the canopy from afar. Fowler pulled their SUV beside the other, and the four hastily made their way into the CDC quarantine.

On her way into the first tent, Walker struggled to keep her eyes open. It was barely visible from the outside and illuminated like a lab on the inside. Three people from the CDC were already setting up the interior equipment. Monitors covered a desk beside them, all of which faced away from Walker. To the right of the entrance were a couple of lockers and a table with boxes of radio equipment.

The far half of the tent was sectioned off by a clear plastic wall, the inside of which was split again into two sections. Pale, orange hazmat suits hung on the wall in the right half. They weren't quite as bulky as the ones Walker had seen in the past. The front half of the helmet consisted of a large viewing section—as if someone had cut a plastic sphere in half.

The other half of the partition was empty aside from an exit flap and a grid of piping along the top with half a dozen sprinklers poking down. The tubing connected to a couple of sleek, white drums on the other side of the main divider.

Secretary Lauer introduced the three doctors, none of whom Dobbs seemed to know.

"Welcome to base camp," said the woman running the show, introduced as Doctor Chandler. "This tent is primarily for surveillance and decontamination. The other two tents are being set up for sample analysis."

They didn't get a tour of the other tents. Instead, Chandler directed them to put on radios and hazmat suits, promptly leaving with Lauer to check on the progress of the pop-up labs. The secretary turned back briefly, looking between the three DIA agents as if he were picking sandwich bread at the deli.

"Oh, ah—Fowler's on point."

Without waiting for a response, he ducked through the entrance flap. As the group gravitated towards the radio, Walker looked towards the two remaining researchers.

"Has anyone gone out to look at the site?"

"Yes," said one. She didn't elaborate, continuing to check connections between the machines.

"And how long ago was that?"

"About an hour," said the other. His CDC badge showed his name as Xi. "We've been monitoring from a distance. No one's been within four hundred meters of the craft—that's where we set up the stationary cameras."

Both researchers seemed frazzled. Walker assumed they would inform the contact team if something were seen on the cameras, but at this point, it was hard to tell if that was true. She watched the other researcher dig through a box of wires for a moment before making her way over to the lockers with the others.

Fowler really didn't want to take point on this. Not that he felt incapable, he just didn't want to. As soon as Lauer exited the tent, the three intelligence agents met together, speaking quietly so only they could hear.

"You feeling good, Iffy?" Sconi asked. Fowler never cared much for the nickname, but it had stuck years before. He shook his head, watching the odd group of doctorates scratch their heads trying to figure out the radio equipment.

"Not really. I hate going in this blind. We don't even know what to look for if things take a bad turn."

"It's bad if they start firing lasers at us," Pierson said.

"Noted."

"Sharpen up then," Sconi said, "because you're making the calls."

"No, Lauer's making the calls. I'm just the first one into the ship."

"I thought you and I were on the same page about this? You gave me the look and everything. Lauer hasn't been in a combat situation since the nineties. He's sure as hell not going to prioritize these people's lives."

"He'll prioritize his own, though," said Pierson.

"After he realizes he's in danger. I'm just saying we're responsible for their safety, and I trust Isaac's judgement more, so we do this like the Richmond standoff. If he pulls the trigger, so do I."

"Same," Pierson said.

"*Only* if everything is fucked..."

"No shit."

Sconi looked back to the lockers. Ditka was placing her laptop inside one while Dobbs struggled with radio wires.

"Point-man, we're gonna need hip holsters," Sconi said, eyeing the orange hazmat suits. He handed Fowler a set of keys. "There's some in the back of our van. Grab us a few."

"Why can't you do it?"

"I'm gonna help these poor bastards get mic'd up. We also brought some extra equipment. If you're going in first, you get to lug it around."

Fowler begrudgingly left the tent, waiting for a few seconds as his eyes adjusted to the canopy-shrouded night. Once he made the outline of the two black SUVs, he opened the one Pierson had driven and sifted through a bag of tactical straps. He finally dug three hip holsters out of the dark nylon coil, but the rest of the vehicle was empty. Twice he went through it without any luck, and just as he was about to close the back and head in, he realized the bag was on top of a large gun case that took up the entire width of the trunk.

Flicking the locks off, he found an M4A1 carbine with a suppressor and infrared sight. Far more than Fowler thought was necessary, but as the saying went, it was better to have it and not need it. Still, reentering the tent with an automatic weapon slung over his shoulder gave everyone pause.

Moving into the first partition, the group started putting on the faded, tangerine suits. The large helmet offered outstanding visibility, with the transparent half encompassing most of Fowler's field of vision. When he turned his head to the side, he saw the edge of the sideways dome in his peripheral, along with a small camera fastened on the inside of the helmet.

Dobbs checked each tank's airflow with what little range of motion he had, the top half of his suit clinging tight against his chest while the bottom dangled loosely. Plum discovered the switch on his belt for the headlamps—they were sufficiently bright.

Fowler needed some help getting the rifle to rest comfortably on his back beside the air tank. The agents struggled to fasten their holsters around their hazmat suits. Drawing and holstering his pistol a couple of times, Pierson grunted.

"These gloves are clumsy. I can't even get my finger through the trigger guard," he said, trying to squeeze his index finger through the small loop of metal designed to prevent the gun from accidentally being fired.

"I don't think the CDC uses hazmat suits with tactical gloves," Fowler said. He handed his sidearm to Pierson. It had a wider trigger guard, and the rifle's was even bigger. "Plus, if you have to use it, tearing the glove will be the least of your concerns."

As they finished sealing up their hazmat suits, Lauer returned with Dr. Chandler, who beckoned them all back into the main partition to outfit them before their hike to the ship.

"Those suits are tough, but not armored," Chandler explained to the seven orange silhouettes. Her voice was muffled by the plastic dome and partially obscured by the light hiss of air. "Try not to block the camera, watch where you step, and more importantly, be careful what you brush up against. The suit *can* tear. In the event of a tear, radio us immediately and return to the decontamination chamber alone."

A small collection of gadgets strewed the table to Walker's left—a Geiger counter, a spectrum analyzer, an aerosol impaction mechanism. Dobbs started filling the pockets of his suit with smaller objects—the kind of items that would certainly come in handy at some point before they returned. Walker did the same, lining herself with sample cases and litmus testing kits. What she really needed was a camera or tablet…something to document and take notes.

"This is all of the handheld equipment the Department of Defense has authorized us to use," Xi told them with mild irritation. "If you need something else, I'll see if I can find a suitable replacement. The labs will be more extensive, so this should suffice for anything that can't be brought back."

A small assortment of power tools sat amongst the sensors. It gave Walker an uneasy feeling for some reason. Maybe it was just the idea of taking apart something from the ship. It felt wrong—like disturbing a nest.

The concern faded as Ditka joined them at the table, carrying portable speakers and some rolled-up posters. Walker hadn't had a chance to speak to the DARPA woman since they'd first met. It was hard to tell if she was austere or simply quiet. Walker's voice almost seemed to startle her.

"What are those?"

"Oh!" Ditka said quietly. "Auditory and visual stimuli. I had to produce an assortment of potential communication materials…in case there's a living being on board. These two mediums were deemed safest."

She unrolled the posters partway. They contained images of people and animals: a family, a person hugging a dog, a woman talking to a parrot perched on her arm. The last few were landscapes and buildings—a beach, a meadow, the Parthenon, the New York skyline.

"I want to show them what we look like, show us interacting positively with other species, and hear what we sound like." She held up the speakers. "It also has animal sounds for the images, but primarily, I want to play classical music. It's mathematical in foundation, so they may be able to feel or hear the patterns to know it was designed."

"How thoughtful," Walker smiled. She had been thinking about communication during part of the drive up. Animals communicated in so many different ways, and many of them are easy to perceive as hostile. Tactile communication was out of the question entirely. Pheromones and other aerosols could be easily considered aggressive, not that any live aliens would breathe the air, anyway.

Lauer returned in a hazmat suit of his own. Walker couldn't help but be impressed by the secretary of defense's willingness to go with the first contact group. For all she knew, the president was making him, but it made her feel a bit more at ease. Dobbs checked the small air tank on Lauer's back, giving him the thumbs up as the octet moved into the decontamination room. Different solutions alternated from the sprinklers above for a minute, washing their own bacteria off before finally rinsing them free of the chemical cocktail.

"You're clear to leave," Xi's voice came digitally through the radio. One by one, the contact team left the tent, hiking north into the night forest.

Headlamps illuminated their way as Fowler led the team through the Chattahoochee forest. Xi was monitoring their cameras, giving Fowler brief directions as they trekked along. The ground had a slight upward slope, but ample room to move between the trees. None of the conifers had the giant trunks you'd imagine when thinking of a forest. They were thin, like an unorganized orchard.

He could hear the doctors organizing equipment among heavy breaths behind him as they walked uphill. Ditka was looking for someone to hold up posters when she flipped through the audio clips and music. Dobbs quickly volunteered, despite being arrogantly certain not more than an hour ago that they'd never find live aliens.

"This one first..." Ditka explained. "Don't walk towards them, just hold it up at arm's length. Don't block your camera, though. Count to ten, then the next one. No—this one. They're already in order."

Fowler hadn't been actively searching for the stationary cameras set up by the CDC, but was a little disappointed in himself after discovering he'd missed them completely.

"We just picked you up on a stationary camera," Xi's voice came through the radio. "You should be able to see the craft once you round those two large trees at your eleven o'clock."

"Everyone drop the chatter," Fowler called into the radio. He listened carefully as he led the group up to the trees Xi mentioned. The ship must still be a good distance past them to be obstructed by the thin trunks. Then again, it was dark. The canopy sat about fifty feet above their heads, sufficiently blocking out all of the starlight. The only light came from their headlamps, and the only sound came from their feet. The forest was unnervingly still—not even the sounds of wildlife.

"What kind of animals are supposed to be out here?" Fowler asked.

"Oh shit," Walker said—not the response he wanted to hear. "Uh…there could be black bears, but we might be too far south. Keep an eye out."

"Wonderful…Anything else?"

"Just typical forest dwellers like birds and deer…maybe salamanders or garter snakes."

"Those aren't poisonous?" Pierson asked.

"Garter snakes? No."

Crunching through small twigs, Fowler rounded the two large ash trees, easily spotting the clearing two hundred yards away. Every tree in a seventy-five-yard radius was destroyed, surrounding the clearing with a barricade of large splinters. Unhindered moonlight brilliantly illuminated the scene like a spotlight from heaven, outlining a shallow crater of dark, freshly upturned dirt.

And in the center of the crater sat a spacecraft.

5

THE SHIP

For fake meat, the plate of food in front of Raynor was pretty good, though it dawned on her she'd never had a meat substitute before. There had been multiple types eaten by people on Earth, but Mars had no space for livestock. Without a strong palate for meat, there was no market for substitutes. If you didn't want to eat fish or fowl, you simply didn't.

The slab of unidentified brown tissue on the table before her wasn't really a substitute, though. It was meat, it just hadn't come from an animal. A machine constructed the food, molecularly identical, pulling nutrients from giant vats in the wall behind the interface. The chef operated just like a regular constructor, only instead of creating everyday objects like hats or cutlery, it built food. She imagined there was a similar market of schematics—recipes—sold by programmers with an affinity for cuisine.

Having only tried a few meals so far, she was impressed. It wasn't quite as good as a home-cooked meal, but the difference in flavor might have less to do with the means of creation and more to do with the nutritional content. Still, it beat every meal she'd had in the militia. Field rations were bricks of nutrients flavored to taste like bricks, and space rations were nutrient pastes flavored to taste like paste. Food on base had been better, but still mass-produced on a budget.

This was just…food.

The canteen spanned the second floors of all three dormitory buildings. Wide, lounge-like walkways interconnected the three buildings at the same level. Scattered throughout each of the rooms were tables of various sizes and shapes, many of which were empty now that most people's second meals were over. A haze of indistinguishable chatter filled the large cafeteria. Her translator managed to handle all of the nearby conversation, but after a certain number of voices, it just gave up. Raynor was tuning all of it out anyway. A clearer voice came from her left.

"May I sit?"

Raynor looked up to see a man with wide shoulders, his head shaved down. He wasn't quite as light-skinned as the old Europeans, but considerably more than most people on base.

"Sure." She gestured to the empty seats. He sat diagonally from her.

"Is the rest of your ship on a different schedule?" he asked.

Raynor blinked. "Some…a few already left. I think they're wandering around here." She didn't get along with most of her ship. Only one other person had been from Mars; the rest were her former subjugators. The man must have sensed her hesitation.

"I didn't mean to pry. I tend to see people sticking with those they traveled with."

Raynor looked around. She saw groups varying from two to twelve, which was as many as you could reasonably fit around the larger tables. She didn't notice any signs suggesting they were from the same ships.

"Where's the rest of your ship?" she asked.

"I don't have one," he said. "The last one left before I was born."

"So you're from here?" Raynor became suddenly intrigued. This man was training at Starling Base but had never gone into time dilation.

"Not here. I'm from Tannon, a nation on the other side of the planet." All of the time Raynor had been forced to spend learning geography in grade school, and it meant nothing.

"What did you do there?"

"How do you mean?" He stared blankly. "I did many things each day."

"In the military," she laughed. "What was your job?"

He rotated his shoulder, showing a badge with his rank symbol on it. "Specialist."

"And what was your specialty?"

"Sorry, cadet. I can't tell you that," he jested—almost sarcastically, like it was incredibly boring. Then again, if he was here, he must have done something noteworthy.

"Can you tell me your name, or is that classified?"

"Very much classified—but I'll tell you anyway. Eldon Rhyso."

"Nadia Raynor."

"I know. 'Procaine.'"

"Wow," she said. "You did your research."

Rhyso shrugged. "Just school. Most people know who you are."

After the first whispers of independence on Mars, Earth responded by heavily restricting trade. Supplies were only shipped to the red planet if deemed substandard, making Procaine the primary Martian anesthetic. Raynor operated a fighter like a precision instrument. Some people started calling her "The Surgeon of the Stars," and "Procaine" followed in suit.

Her callsign had also been restricted information, only spoken by a handful of pilots who all died several millennia ago. To her, it was recent, but children today grew up learning about it in school. It made Raynor feel strangely naked. A rush of surreal embarrassment washed over her. She recalled facts she'd learned about historical figures—details of their lives, what happened behind the scenes. There wasn't anything in particular she had to be embarrassed about, but the sudden transparency of her entire life was off-putting.

For the rest of her meal, she talked with Rhyso about the base. A handful of people from the modern era were included at Starling. They were all technical and scientific personnel, though. The broad man in front of her was the only soldier at Starling Base born in the last fifty years. And with his training still current, he was enjoying a bit of down time while the rest got caught up on the basics. He had gotten roped into doing some work during his leave. Apparently, Rhyso served under General Teckann back when Teckann was just a major. It wasn't the worst connection to have.

He asked her about details from "major battles" in history, hanging on her every word. It was a new experience. Missions she'd flown a few years ago were now significant events from ancient Martian history. Rhyso looked at them the same way she looked at battles from World War III.

"I didn't mean to keep you longer than you intended," he said after she finished her meal. "I guess I'm just a bit star-struck."

"Well, I'm flattered." She didn't think that was the right word, but there likely wasn't one for being a celebrity in the eyes of someone older than you who grew up learning about something you just did.

"Don't be," Rhyso laughed. "It happens every hour. I think I saw King Tutankhamun earlier, which arises many concerning questions."

Despite this new, strange sense of esteem, their brief conversation cured much of Raynor's culture shock. For as different as their two worlds were, they were more or less the same.

Technically, garter snakes were venomous, but Walker didn't think this was the appropriate time to split those hairs. They didn't have fangs, but they had a venom sac. The small snakes hunted like constrictors, allowing their venom to be delivered through their saliva, seeping into cuts made by their tiny little teeth. It was dangerous to a mouse, but rarely even caused localized swelling in humans. They were also one of the most docile serpents. Black bears were also fairly timid, but if they had cubs, it could be a problem.

Trailing behind Dobbs and Ditka, Walker couldn't see anything but their faded orange suits glowing brightly in her headlamps. She nearly ran into Dobbs when they stopped moving.

"Well, that's rather different from the first imaging, isn't it?" Plum said. Walker moved around the orange masses to get a glimpse of the ship, which was perfectly outlined in the distance by a beam of moonlight.

He was right. The ship didn't seem to have any specific orientation other than up. It wasn't exactly a flying saucer...more like a flying ice cream sandwich. The center of the ship was a ring with a concave edge, like a thin car wheel without a tire. Above and below the center wheel, the ship flared out slightly towards the edge, and on the very top, there was a circular dome. Had it not been lodged into the ground at an angle, there would be nothing to indicate a front of any kind.

"Dr. Plum," Lauer said slowly, as if trying not to startle the ship while they stared in awe. "Do you see anything coming from it?"

Plum gulped, holding the spectrum analyzer. "A strong microwave radio frequency is being broadcast from it."

"8.348 gigahertz?" Xi's voice cut in.

"That's it."

"We've been recording that, but so far it's nothing."

"8348—in billions," Ditka mused. "I wonder if that's significant..."

"It's in the range of frequencies that transmit exceptionally clearly from our planet," Plum said. "Anything below one gigahertz is muddled in the background noise of our galaxy, and anything above ten gets absorbed by Earth's atmosphere. It's called the microwave window."

"Funny," Lauer said. "Does that mean the signal is intentional?"

"Could be," Plum said in a way that, to Walker, sounded like, *How the hell should I know?*

"Eyes peeled," Fowler said as he started hiking toward the ship.

Running water sloshed faintly in the distance—probably a stream, but the fauna was silent. They trekked through the forest in no particular formation, short breaths puffing into their radios as the eight slowly closed their distance to the derelict craft. Carefully, so as not to tear the orange lining of their safety wear, they climbed over the ring of fallen tree trunks marking the perimeter of the clearing. Fresh dirt covered the arena-sized opening, the light from their headlamps bright even against the moonlight.

"Any movement?" Fowler asked.

"Negative," Pierson said.

"Contact—what's our time?"

Walker looked at the viewfinder of the camera, "Ten—I mean 2240 hours."

"2240," Chandler repeated over the radio. "Congratulations."

Fowler issued commands to sweep the area, but Walker didn't wait for the DIA agents to finish before approaching the downed ship. It was huge—a couple of stories tall and a hundred meters in diameter. Ditka methodically swept her light across the hull as Walker crouched down to collect samples of dirt disturbed by the craft. As she stood up and got a good look at the ship, she finally realized what it resembled.

"It looks like a yo-yo," she said. "Those pro kinds they tried to sell us in school."

"It does!" Dobbs laughed, his voice almost painful in her ear. "Hey, Theo, are you looking at the middle? The part you would wrap the string around?"

"The propulsion system," replied Plum.

Walker looked at the midsection of the ship. It was smooth, concave. It matched the rest of the ship in color, but looked almost like it was made of a different material. There were shallow, vertical seams every thirty or forty centimeters.

"You got that, too, eh? What do you make of it?"

"Our imaging showed the ship tilted on its side, which means some kind of energy emits from the band here. If each of these panels can thrust independently, it would explain the fragmented flight paths."

"Strange way to apply thrust to a ship…"

"Genius, probably. What's really strange is the rest of the ship."

Lauer turned to Plum, shining him in bright light. "Why?"

"It has no seams. Aside from the panels around the middle, the hull is either a single piece of material or perfectly fused." Everyone turned to look at the ship, bathing it in beams of light.

Xi keyed in his mic.

"Wait. Kelly, take a couple of steps to your right." The linguist stood about forty meters from Walker, counter-clockwise along the ship. She stepped to the side carefully, like she was avoiding a landmine. "There's a seam. It's hairline, but it shows on infrared. It might be a hatch."

"Should we knock?" Dobbs asked.

"If there are creatures still alive on the ship, it would be better to let them investigate us first," Ditka said. "If it's all right, Mr. Secretary, I'd like to start playing audio recordings."

"That's fine," Lauer said. "Fowler, post up on the north side. Pierson, southwest. Sconi, southeast. Fallback point is Agent Sconi."

Rifle in hand, Fowler marched into sight, joining Ditka at his new post. Walker started taking pictures of plants on the ground, collecting a few as samples. She wasn't looking for anything in particular, just documenting impacts on the existing ecosystem. Until she could see the bodies of an organism or their habitat, it was all she could really do.

The ship crashed towards the south, elevating the north end high above the ground. About fifteen meters underneath, there was a deeper indentation in the dirt—a fat X. Walker looked up at the underbelly of the ship, unable to find a source. It looked almost like a landing gear had been pushed out, but no gear was engaged. Whatever caused the imprint had happened after the crash.

She started to ask Plum to come and take a look, but only got out one syllable before a thunderous sound cut her off. In fear of being crushed by the massive vessel, Walker lunged out from underneath, landing face-down in the dirt. The noise hadn't come from the radio; it was from outside her suit…from the forest behind her.

Rifle pressed into his shoulder, Fowler frequently angled his head-lamps towards the edge of the clearing. He'd love nothing more than to look at the ship, but the aliens were a wild card—they could be dead, they could be hostile, they could be friendly. Bears were not friendly, and the complete lack of sound from the forest was spooky.

He saw Dr. Walker a little further along the hull, taking photos of the ground beneath the ship. He had just turned away from the perimeter when a loud sound disrupted the quiet. He jumped, rifle raised.

Four loud sounds.

Beethoven's 5th Symphony.

He chided himself for jumping—he had *watched* Ditka plug the portable speakers into a device. It had only made sense that she would ease into the volume, maybe start with something softer. From the edge of his helmet's glass dome, he saw Dobbs spin around quickly, shining his headlamps towards this end of the clearing. Walker dove back from the ship.

"A little warning, Kelly!" The resounding voice of Jeremy Dobbs was barely audible over the symphony. "I'd like to save my heart attack for later, thank you."

"I confirmed with Secretary Lauer on the open channel, *Jeremy.* Many would consider that a warning." The volume lowered slightly, though not much.

"Isn't this too intense?" Lauer asked nervously.

"They'll know it's communicative. This song is structured around the Fibonacci sequence."

"Really?" Dobbs asked.

"No, I'm playing it as a joke at the first-ever alien crash site."

"Well, look at you dishing it out…"

Walker's voice cut in. She'd returned to the same spot underneath the ship she had dove away from. "Hey, Theo, come and look at this. I think these might be indentations from a landing gear."

"I don't see any landing gear," Plum said.

"I know. The indentation is shallow, but it's inside the skid."

There was a long pause over the radio. Beethoven continued playing from Ditka's hand.

"That would mean it was both deployed and retracted after the ship crashed…"

"Correct."

"There could be an automatic protocol."

"Either that or one of them survived."

More silence. The opening four notes of the symphony repeated partway through the song. It didn't have the calming effect classical music was supposed to have on people.

"Let me take a look," Plum finally replied.

The ring around the center of the ship turned on. Nothing but white could be seen. The light was so bright, it blinded Fowler completely. He pulled Ditka to the ground as the radio erupted with shouting and cursing. Fowler wasn't sure if the ground was any safer, but it was the only thing he could think of to protect them.

Amidst the overlapping screams, he heard Xi say he lost visual. Plum said something about the engines, but for a few seconds, it was impossible to hear anyone clearly.

"It's just light," Sconi yelled. "Everyone back to my twenty! Southeast!"

There was no roar of engines. In fact, there was no noise at all besides the nine of them screaming on the radio. The portable speakers had gotten disconnected when Fowler pulled their owner to the ground. He turned to see if she was okay, but something pulled roughly on his right arm.

"Come on!" Walker yelled, trying to get him and Kelly off the ground. Her eyes were wide, her face lit up in dim orange by the reflection of the bright engine lights on their hazmat suits.

Fowler turned to Ditka. "Are you alright?"

"Yes," she said softly. "Just get off of me."

"Sorry." He got up, pulling her with him as the two followed Walker to the other side of the ship. Their shadows had nearly disappeared, the surrounding forest illuminated thirty yards from the clearing. They ran around the football field-sized craft, which felt a whole lot bigger now.

At the southeast edge of the clearing, Fowler moved towards the center of the group. All eight stared at the ship, eyes peeled.

On Fowler's right, he saw Pierson holding his pistol, then looked down at the M4 in his hands. He threw it over his shoulder, the sling pulling taut as the rifle fell beside his air tank.

"Holster your guns," he said quietly through the radio.

"No one draws unless ordered," Lauer added harshly before either agent could respond. Not a moment too soon. On the north side of the ship, a faint strip of light crawled along the well-lit ground as a hatch opened, soon blurred by shadows.

No one could speak. No gasps, no curses, no breaths. They just watched as time froze. Deep down, they'd all held onto a shred of doubt—foreign spies, rogue satellite, experimental craft. Even after they'd arrived at the crash site, there *could* have been some far-fetched explanation—an elaborate, expensive hoax. An *earthly* explanation.

Not anymore.

6

FIRST CONTACT

Three figures stood in front of the hatch on the far side of the space-craft, no more than a hundred meters away. One of the creatures squatted down.

"The speakers," Ditka whispered. "Jeremy, can you hand me the posters?"

"I dropped them…" Dobbs said in a trance.

Walker was locked onto the aliens, trying to spot details the moment they came into view. They were bipedal, like humans, standing upright, a little over a meter tall—just under four feet. Their legs moved fluidly, either from a lack of rigid bone joints or a plethora of them, extending down from narrow, cylindrical bodies. Each foot split into a long X with rounded toes, like the indentation of the landing gear.

From the upper half of their tube-like midsection sprouted four arms, forming their own X around the body with two in front and two in back. Like their legs, their arms seemed to move without major joint locations, flexing in different areas, sometimes uniform-ly. Three thick fingers branched at the end of the arms, with one opposing the other two.

The aliens came to a stop fifteen meters in front of them. They didn't have much of a neck area; the cylinder got slightly wider and came to a curved top like a microphone. They were wearing thin navy protective suits with a transparent window starting above their arms and ending below the top of their heads, around where the neck would be on a human. Towards the top of their faces was a single, visor-like lens that ran the entire circumference of their heads.

As they came to a stop, the first one turned towards the ship, its back facing the contact team. It didn't look any different from the second one, which turned towards them instead. The third stood perpendicular to the group, facing the other two. Walker suspected all three could see them just fine. It was both fascinating and creepy.

It was so…*alien*.

A surge of ideas flooded into Walker's head. An entire civilization of technology conceptualized with no front or back—like the ship they'd emerged from. There was no mouth visible in the clear portion of their suits—perhaps it was near their arms like a cephalopod, though she might only be thinking of squids because of her summer course. The prehensile limbs could just as easily be structured like a monkey tail, an elephant trunk, a snake body…

She was definitely missing her classes tomorrow.

Below the black, visor-like lens, the perpendicular creature had pale, purple skin, the other two more of a brownish-orange. On those, Walker could faintly see two small, vertical slits on the sides of their faces corresponding to their legs—perhaps noses or ears.

Suddenly, the visible skin of the middle alien changed. A vibrant line of royal blue appeared within the brownish-orange, running around the circumference of its face. As quickly as it had come, it was replaced by a vivid shade of green across the entire area.

Their skin—at least, the skin on their faces—was made up of chromatophores. Again, like a cephalopod. Each cell contained an elastic pigment sack, surrounded by muscles that could stretch it over a larger area. Different colored chromatophores sat side by side, and animals would stretch one while contracting the others to change their skin color. The cells could only be a few colors, though. These alien cells were much more advanced. For a species that could see in every direction, a complex, visual communication system would only be natural.

The creature's face returned to its original color as a strange sound emitted from one of them. A low, guttural clicking, like a slow croak. None of the humans had reacted to visual communication, so they were using sound.

Low sound would travel far underwater, though it didn't look like there was water in their suits, and no water had rushed out of the open hatch. Perhaps they more recently evolved out of the ocean. Maybe their planet had an extremely thick, swampy atmosphere.

Another one joined the first, the sound echoing through the trees.

"Jesus…" someone finally said. It sounded like Pierson.

"What should we do?" Sconi asked.

"Nothing," replied Lauer. "Everyone, keep still."

"Dr. Plum," Xi said from the tent. "Video, please."

"Right…" Plum slowly, carefully raised a video camera.

Faint crimson rapidly spread across the face of the leftmost alien in a wave. With one of its farther arms, the creature quickly pulled out a device, curling the prehensile appendage around its body to point it towards the NASA engineer. A narrow, pink beam emitted from the end, causing half of them to jump as a loud bang—like a gunshot—echoed off the hull.

Fowler's heart was racing, and the Predator-like clicking wasn't making it any better. He was backing Lauer's call completely—let these things do whatever they need to do, don't startle them. Like his mother told him when he was six and found a raccoon in the garbage, *"It's more afraid of you than you are of it."*

He watched in astonishment as their skin changed to a full spectrum of colors in various patterns. Some appeared rapidly, others held for a while. Like a chameleon, but instantly.

Fowler's vision started to fog when Plum lifted the camera. It felt dangerous. None of them had any clue what the aliens would do. One of the creatures pulled an object out from behind them…or in front of them. The jury was still out on that one. Fowler's hand tensed towards the rifle stock at his side. Light gasps came from the team as a flat, pink light came from the end of the device. According to every TV show Fowler had ever seen, it was doing a scan of some kind.

Then the slow, quiet scene was broken by a gunshot.

Oh no.

The legs of the creature went limp as it collapsed to the ground. Four arms lay at every odd angle. The helmet made it difficult for Fowler to tell exactly where the shot came from, but it was somewhere to his right.

God damnit, Pierson.

Fowler's skin grew cold. Secretary Lauer screamed again for everyone to hold fire, his voice cracking. What would the creatures do? Flee? Retaliate? Could this be salvaged if they all stayed still? Fowler didn't know what else to do, immediately disregarding his earlier conversation with Sconi. He didn't want to make any decisions for this.

Rapid patterns of different colors flashed across the remaining creatures' faces as they moved with frightening speed. The alien facing towards them dropped down to all fours, planting its two closest arms on the ground and leaving the other two free above its body. The top of the creature's head was angled towards Pierson like it was about to charge.

It didn't charge. During its drop to the ground, the alien had similarly retrieved a device with one of its free arms, now angled directly at Pierson. A high-pitched sound—a reversed zap that rapidly rose in pitch before silencing—was followed by a crack and a wet popping sound. The visor of Pierson's suit shattered as a crimson, liquid mist shot out of the hole. A thick trail of red slush covered the ground beside a flattened hazmat suit as Pierson was instantly pureed.

Fowler couldn't even say the reaction was excessive, but he also couldn't wait to see if the creatures continued down the line of people before drawing. He grabbed the jagged edge of the M4's collapsible stock, pulling it up to his shoulder in a motion he'd performed thousands of times. His right hand instantly found the grip of the carbine, pulling it tight to his body. He had a clear view of whatever you'd consider to be the animal's face, even as it rotated its body and arm towards Lauer.

By the time the secretary of defense started to give the order to fire, Fowler was already squeezing the trigger. The full motion had taken him no more than half a second, but it was still too slow.

"Fi—" was all Lauer managed to scream. With the same zap, crack, and pop, his partially-levigated body splashed through his helmet. The engine lights lit the splatter up in the brightest red Fowler had ever seen. As the remains of Lauer splashed across the ground, Fowler fired a burst of four rounds into the top of the creature's head, tearing through its suit and clanking against some sort of hard shell.

"Oh my god!" Ditka screamed as Jeremy Dobbs came bursting out of his helmet next to her. Before the hard-headed being had a chance to turn towards Fowler, he put half a dozen rounds through its face, splashing blueish-purple blood on the inside of the clear plastic mask.

The third alien had sprung away from the other two with impressive agility, landing in the same lowered position as the second had. Fowler swung his rifle towards it, waiting to see if it reached for a similar gizmo. As quickly as he turned his aim, the alien dove towards the dropped weapon. A trail of bullets kicked dirt into the air as Fowler swept the rifle behind it. With three thick fingers, the creature grabbed the futuristic pistol of its fallen comrade, rolling across the ground into yet again the same combat position.

Pattering rounds from the M4 caught up to the creature, hitting the top of its head. As before, they tore through the navy material of the suit, rattling against the hard shell underneath. Additional holes appeared in the synthetic fabric from Sconi's gun to the same effect.

A jointless, drunken arm angled the weapon towards Fowler. He dropped hard to his knee, pain shooting through his leg. A high-pitched *zapping* sound pierced through the night, followed by the *crunch* of a tree at the edge of the clearing behind him. The sudden burst of heat knocked Plum to the ground as fiery splinters showered the area. Small pieces of charred bark cascaded around Fowler, slapping against his back. He was only getting one more salvo before becoming strawberry jam.

The alien's face was just barely visible below the hardened dome. Pushing the barrel down slightly, Fowler let the last burst of rounds erupt from the assault rifle. The first one hit the ground behind the alien, the recoil dragging the barrel up. A line of bullets walked up the alien's neck, with the last puncturing downward through the circular lens of its eye.

He stopped firing, keeping his gun trained for a moment. None of the bodies moved. The light crackle of fire from the fragments of burning trees danced around him.

Walker was crouched down next to Sconi, who had a large piece of timber lodged clean through his thigh. Plum was still face-down on the ground, his chest slowly rising and falling. Ditka was either sobbing quietly or hyperventilating in the center of the three chunky red streaks, more than a little of which covered her once-orange hazmat suit. Had Fowler been thinking straight, he would have moved to cover them from the ship in case more of these things came out. He would have tried to put out the fires before they took down the forest, gotten Sconi away from the scene, now that his suit was torn.

But he wasn't thinking straight. His mind was in a loop. All Isaac Fowler could think was that he had just killed the first aliens ever to set foot on Earth…within a minute of their disembarkment.

Another glimpse of the liquified bodies turned his stomach. He doubled over, taking deep, slow breaths to avoid throwing up in the helmet of his air-tight suit.

"Agent Fowler…" Xi's voice came weakly through the earpiece. "What just happened?"

7

THE YO-YO

It was difficult for Fowler to focus while surrounded by three alien corpses and the mush of three humans. Sconi writhed on the ground nearby, a jagged stake impaled through his leg.

"Check on Leo," Fowler said to nobody in particular. His eyes darted across the hull of the ship, but he couldn't see anything beyond the blinding light emitted from the center ring. Dr. Xi's radio keyed in again, slightly more composed.

"Agent Fowler, we need you to—"

"Shut up," Fowler cut him off in a heavy whisper. He strained his ears, listening for commotion inside the ship—croaks from their visitors, movement near the hatch…anything.

"Isaac," Walker said calmly. "Agent Sconi needs to go to quarantine."

"Will everyone just be quiet for a minute?"

Bluish-purple blood flowed from the various bullet holes in the three alien bodies. The one Pierson killed was starting to dry in a darker shade near the edges. Lauer, Pierson, and Dobbs were still very undried, their bodies trailing back to their deflated hazmat suits. Fowler wretched again. Ditka now stood amidst the burning embers, her suit heaving while she inched away slowly from the three crimson puddles.

"Isaac," Walker said again, "he has an open wound, he needs to go *now*."

Fowler looked down at Sconi. His face was pale; a significant amount of blood was mixed into the dirt beneath him. "Can you walk?"

"With help, yeah."

"I don't feel too good…" Ditka said, her voice labored. Fowler started to ask Plum to check her for tears, but Dr. Xi was again trying to get his attention over the radio.

"*What?*" Fowler snapped at the CDC researcher.

"The signal changed drastically. It's much more complex, and over a much wider spectrum." It took Fowler a moment to figure out what Xi meant. The signal was being emitted from the ship, and something changed it.

"When did that start?"

"Just after the gunshots."

Fowler raised his rifle towards the open hatch on the north side of the ship. He tried to look through the infrared scope, made difficult by the large helmet. The engines didn't seem to be emitting much heat. That was a good thing.

"Theo, how are you with a gun?"

"Rubbish," said Plum.

"You and Denise take Leo and Kelly back to quarantine."

"You're not seriously staying out here by yourself, are you?"

"I'm not." Fowler walked steadily towards the opening in the hull, minding his step through Lauer and Pierson.

"Agent Fowler, come back and wait for Washington to make a decision." It was Chandler piping in at the eleventh hour.

"The Secretary of Defense is dead. I'm securing the area."

"I don't think you can make that decision."

"Watch me." Fowler would have turned the radio off if it didn't require removing part of his suit. He kept his sights trained as he continued towards the opening. A short ramp had folded out from the hull, leading up at a bizarre angle due to the ship's crashed orientation.

The incline ended at a dimly lit, hexagonal room. A clear wall covered the path to the remainder of the ship directly across from the hatch. Three of the four remaining walls were empty, housing the navy environmental suits worn by the aliens outside. The fourth suit was still there.

Fowler pushed on the clear wall, but it wouldn't budge. The room might be a mantrap, preventing the barricade from opening until the exterior door was closed. In that case, it would be best to wait outside and keep an eye on the exit. Then he noticed that part of the dark-grey wall beside the barricade was smoother than the rest and a bit lighter.

Why not?

He pushed on the wall.

It didn't recede, but the surface changed to a shade of steel blue before turning back. Nothing happened, so he pressed it once more. Again, the color changed. This time, to a different shade of blue, accompanied by an unnerving clicking sound. Puffs of gas shot from the walls, causing Fowler to jump. Some more clicking, then the transparent barrier slid up, causing a wave of heavy air to push him back.

A corridor of hexagonal rooms extended from the doorway, each small enough for one creature to interact with panels on all sides. Careful not to hit his head on the low ceilings, Fowler moved slowly through the hall until he reached a larger room. Two tables sat towards the far, wall and short, pointed statues scattered the floor. They could be chairs, but they would have to be the most uncomfortable ones designed. Power ran through panels by the tables, with lights silently flashing across the various interfaces. Another walkway exited the room to his right, so he started to edge his way towards the screens.

Clunk.

Reverberations came through the floor beneath him—something hit it. Fowler spun around, sweeping his rifle across the room, but it was as empty as when he arrived.

Clunk.

He couldn't tell which direction it came from—*damn helmet.* The thought briefly crossed his mind that the sound was part of the ship moving, but that notion was nixed quickly. The unmistakable sound of soft footsteps came into earshot, followed by a faint glow from around the corner.

At first, the academy was less like military training and more like school. Not without reason—most of the Starling cadets had the modern equivalent of a pre-teen education and the technological prowess of a toddler. They had at least two years to get caught up to speed and trained, but that meant a lot of education, which irritated the battle-hardened time-travelers. The pill was hard to swallow, but Starling was firm on it. No one would be given an energy weapon without an adolescent's understanding of its properties.

Raynor was excited. She never had the freedom to pursue higher education because of the war, and it seemed like the perfect way to get her bearings in this strange land before having to...well...go back to war.

Residents were split into groups based largely on their departure year. Military personnel were getting a slew of introductory courses followed by an evaluation to determine what informational gaps they had. Once they had a proper foundation, they'd include combat training with the same process, though considerably longer. At the end of it all, they'd get job assignments and focus on specialized training.

Judging by the schedule of Kihon Drager—the astrophysicist from Raynor's ship—scientific personnel were accelerating through most of that process. Aside from some modern essentials, they were moving straight towards their areas of expertise.

Drager had been the leading theorist on wormholes—a certifiable genius. He also had no real investment in the colonization of Mars, so Raynor got along with him well enough. Hearing him lament about his own regimen was disheartening. She generally assumed Drager knew everything about everything, but it seemed he would have known more if he'd simply grown up in the 126th century.

"I wonder if I can opt out of the assessment on *sub-atomic graviton manipulation*," he mumbled while gazing over his long-term program. "I don't even understand what that entails."

Raynor had two months of *basic tools*.

One of the most common pieces of technology was a thin rectangle of clear plastic called a jewel. It functioned like a touchscreen pad, but without any visible components or ports. The entire sheet was maybe two millimeters thick. Dragging your finger across the jewel created a bright line, glowing from the screen like a thin neon light. The surface seemed to know when it was being handled. During the half-hour Raynor spent playing with it, there was never an unintended mark.

A plethora of hand movements could be used to interact with the device, such as wiping your hand across the smooth surface to clear it, flicking your doodle to a personal terminal, or scooping open files sent to it. Molecular differences between the front and back of the jewel gave the front the slightest of amber hues when held at an angle to the light. You could generally assume a jewel was lying face-up as a consequent of its use. Habitually picking up a face-down jewel and trying to write on it was a tongue-in-cheek joke referred to as having a 'flipper pane,' which rhymed in the local language—Reza. It didn't rhyme in Martian.

"These are sturdy," their instructor informed as she rapped on the clear sheet with her knuckle. "Do not try to break them. You are very capable of doing so, and you will burn yourself." She then tasked them with playing a short video on the jewel outlining the dangers of hitting someone with one. The moral was: don't. It's effectively a chemical weapon, and you'll go to jail.

What the native-born woman referred to as a "micro-gravitational reaction panel," Raynor considered a holo-display. One of the major pursuits of her time had been the generation of physical, three-dimensional models without the use of matter. Several technologies were in the vicinity of that feat, and gadget companies had been in a race to find the closest approximation. None came close, of course. Some used air, some required special glasses to see the image, and some pushed a surface up and projected images across it. They were terrible, mostly because the technology that *would* make holo-displays possible was centuries behind.

Atmospheric domes were held to the Martian surface by large gravity panels beneath the dirt. Building one small enough to fit on your wrist was beyond imagination. Yet, here it was. Hundreds, maybe thousands of tiny gravity panels were clustered together to create complex forms you could touch.

It also came from Drager's dreaded *sub-atomic graviton manipulation*.

"Remarkable." His nose almost touched the example armband. A board game projected over the bracer with movable pieces. "Every object with mass emits gravitational waves pulling other objects towards it, and every gravity panel ever made did the same. These microscopic panels actually push your finger *away*." He pulled his face away from the brown and teal board, chuckling as he nudged one of the pieces. "Just remarkable."

A fair amount of technology came with warnings of serious injury or death. The time-shrouded elite always took it at face value —the reason a certain procedure or precaution was given. As dangerous as the tools could potentially be, no one was injured or killed by one. Not until they moved past their introductory courses...during their first day of training at the forward base.

* * *

There was so much information to absorb as Walker made her way through the ship. The honeycomb design alone…

She had turned back once it seemed like Kelly was alright. Walker and Plum were too different in height to help Sconi together, and she didn't think Fowler should come inside alone. Plum may not be any use with a gun, but she was. When she finally caught up with the DIA agent in the first large room, he had his rifle trained on her.

"It's me!" she said in a harsh whisper.

"You scared the shit out of me."

"I told you I was coming." She hadn't gotten a response from Fowler, but assumed he was being quiet. Perhaps that wasn't the case. "Dr. Xi, do you read me?"

Not even static came through.

"Let's do this quick, then." Fowler looked at the gun in her hand and frowned. "You should grab mine so you don't tear your gloves. Pierson had it."

Sconi had told her the same thing, and she'd looked. She found it thirty seconds later underneath Pierson, so she left it.

The duo moved slowly through the ship. It felt like a small town. Some of the rooms were large, others cramped. Walker constantly fought the urge to stop and look at peculiar objects. The insight she could glean from the ship was beyond prediction. Just having a species to compare terrestrial life to. Every branch of science would be studying the contents of this craft for centuries, if not longer.

Room after room, they walked through. Fowler led with his rifle up, occasionally peering through the scope on the back. After a few attempts, he finally found an angle that worked with the domed face shield. Walker held Sconi's pistol firmly in her hands, unsure of how useful it would be to her in thick gloves. When she was eleven, there had been a high-profile shooting near her hometown, so before she went to high school, her parents made her learn how to use a gun. That was decades ago, and with bare hands.

Twenty minutes later, they arrived back in one of the large rooms they had traversed through a few times.

"Alright, I guess it's clear," Fowler said abruptly. "Let's head back."

"Are you sure?"

"No. Do you think there could be hidden panels or doors?"

"Not a soul on the planet knows that."

"Then it's clear."

Fowler led her back towards the entrance hatch. He seemed even more anxious as they retraced their steps back through the cramped rooms, like they were safer in the ship.

"Are we in danger?" she asked.

"No, it's empty—I promise."

"I mean from the Department of Defense."

"Oh, I'm completely fucked, but you'll be fine." He let out a solitary laugh. "You've probably got more job security than ever."

Walker didn't know what sort of trouble he was expecting from the Pentagon, but it was important for him to hear the truth at least once.

"You saved our lives, Isaac. Thank you."

"No problem," he said plainly, ducking into the small hexagonal rooms leading towards the hatch. "Well, that *is* the problem. We were all expendable—even Lauer." The bluntness was off-putting. An hour ago, he'd been a dutiful nephew to Uncle Sam, but then again, the last few hours had been months.

The two hiked back through the forest to the CDC tent. Neither bothered to let base camp know they were on their way—or alive.

With the danger subsided, the events all hit Walker at once. Nausea, dizziness, even guilt flushed through her body, taking all of her fortitude to hold it at bay. She thought about things she'd seen on the ship, away from the bodies. Her head spun with theories about curious objects and displays she had casually strolled by. She wished she had taken even a moment to examine some of the most unusual ones, perhaps a few of the most Earthly-looking, too, but she got the distinct feeling it wasn't the last time either of them would be on the craft.

ZENAUT TECHNOLOGIES

History was a surprisingly large chunk of Raynor's educational training. Anton Morrison—the other Martian from her ship—was in several courses with her, though less happy to be there. In their first one, he vocalized frustration in taking a class when he was specifically there to kill aliens. The notion that it was pointless to learn events of the past was entirely mind-boggling to their befuddled teacher. To call it a generational gap would be an understatement.

"So, you are all soldiers, correct?" Murmurs of acknowledgement came up. Some felt the need to clarify their exact titles. "Let us then discuss a scenario. You are tasked to eliminate an enemy port, the destruction of which is critical to the war effort. You are outgunned, but are fortunate enough to possess a large number of graviton devices with an unhindered escape route. You could retreat, and your demolitionist could rig the explosives to collapse on themselves to make a gravitational singularity, caving the base in on itself and crushing everyone inside. What would your concerns be?"

"Not getting caught in it," someone responded. "Can it be set on a timer?"

"For as long as you see fit. Anything else? Would anyone be willing to take the risk?" A few hands raised up half-heartedly, some of which were immediately withdrawn. "These people just killed you; they killed themselves, they may have killed everyone at their nearest installation, and it's been estimated they could kill the majority of the nearest planet. This mistake is not honest because someone else already made it. A quarter of a million bystanders were killed in the Jovian Black Hole. The survival of our species is being placed into your hands, and each of you is capable of jeopardizing that through your individual actions. Now, as we were discussing..."

Morrison's hatred of learning history hadn't changed, but he learned to keep his mouth shut, proving he was at least capable of learning from his mistakes. The Jovian Black Hole was one of the incidents Raynor had read of during her ship's approach. As a result of it, the unlicensed creation of a gravitational singularity was banned across the planets, and each would prosecute it regardless of where it happened.

The more introductory courses she sat in, the more Raynor realized how little she knew. It wasn't surprising, given that nine thousand years of history had passed during the last five years of her life, but it was overwhelming regardless. Her lack of knowledge about Martian history was embarrassing. She would certainly have to take more of it.

Courses became surprisingly granular after the essentials were covered. As a child, she had typically taken one course that lasted half a year to a year before moving on to another in a similar topic. She'd take Martian history, then it would be Earth history, then African history. The same went for sciences and mathematics.

Here, the courses were of different lengths and constantly changing. Most lasted between two and six weeks. As soon as one ended, everyone from that class would replace it with the next on their regimens, some of which didn't start for another week or two. It felt unnecessarily lively. It meant Raynor frequently met people she then didn't see for weeks. The whole process was optimized by a computer, ensuring everyone learned their fundamentals with minimal downtime between courses for both cadets and instructors. It was endearingly mechanical, and seemed normal to native-born citizens of their new home, Razennon.

Once they developed a foundation, their educational courses became fewer and more static. The role of erratic scheduling was taken over by combat training, beginning with a breath of fresh air for the study-weary combatants.

1100-1500: General Weaponry.

"Yes! Let's fry some shit!" shouted a woman whose neck threatened to rip the grey and black seams of her uniform. Her enthusiasm was shared by two hundred others scheduled for the large block of time. Most opted to grab a meal before heading to their training location—*forward transit.*

Raynor dragged her plate to one of the food synthesizers, looking through the options. Not wanting to hold up the influx, she chose something called *porentsil,* a local dish comprised of lean meat and starchy vegetables. Giant vats pumped nutrients into the constructor as her food was built.

"Hey Nezz, where does the forward transit go?"

Nezz was a virtual assistant—the program that provided the seamless translations they all now took for granted. The device had a number of other functions far beyond Raynor's current technology prowess. Most tools could be integrated with it, from jewels to ships to bionic limbs. Of course, the primary reason for giving each cadet at Starling one of the expensive earpieces was so they could all talk.

In the 32nd century, countless companies developed a similar sort of device or program. Others made completely unrelated items, including some sort of digital receptionist as a perk. They were never quite as useful as an actual person, and you could always tell when it was a machine. Their voices had a robotic twinge to them. Whenever someone at Starling Base spoke to Raynor in a language other than traditional Martian, the voice she heard was the assistant program. Its own voice was as fluid as any person's. At times, it made unusual structure choices that were more in line with a current language like Reza, but since traditional Martian was long-dead, Nezz was doing its best.

"The forward transit connects to what was once the forward base. Today, it's a training ground, allowing for practice with weapons and ordnance without endangering people at Starling Base."

"How far is it?"

"Five hundred thirty-two kilometers to the east."

That explained the four-hour chunk of time.

After recently discussing singularities, Raynor could only imagine what sort of weapons were in use that required such distant training. She speculated with Morrison as they ate their early lunch. The meat in her porentsil tasted like chicken, as did most lean meats from the constructor. The cafeteria was in a lull, with tables only occupied by those about to leave for weapons training.

"I bet you they have vaporizing beams," Morrison said between gulps, "like in the first contact documents."

"Everyone knows that was destroyed right after." Raynor shoved a large piece of some kind of root into her mouth. Maybe the descendant of a carrot.

"So they say. Even if it was, someone will have figured it out by now." He sighed at his empty plate. "Alright, I'm gonna grab my jewel for the ride. Physics has been kicking my ass."

Grumbling about having to study for half of his first *general weapons* training, Morrison left the canteen. Raynor dumped the remnants of her food into the recycler—a bin that separated leftover nutrients and returned them to their respective vats behind the walls—making her way to forward transit.

Fireworks popped faintly in the distance—people were starting their Independence Day celebrations a day early. Fowler stared up at the ceiling from his cot. He would not be seeing fireworks this year.

Six weeks had passed since his hike through the forest in northern Georgia. Six weeks since he'd seen the ship; six weeks since the secretary of defense had been liquified by aliens. Time had flown by for Fowler. Largely because his days were all the same. His room was twelve feet square with plain, white walls—larger than it could have been, but not by much. He had a cot, a TV with basic cable, and a small window near the ceiling to let natural light in.

There was also a lock on the outside of the door.

For a jail cell, it was nice. And for a prisoner, he was being treated fine, awaiting either tribunal or trial. The ordeal had been scattered; no one knew quite what to do with him. There was a realistic chance he'd be executed on the spot. Someone's head needed to roll, and Fowler's was the easiest.

The clean-up team from D.C. had arrived shortly after everyone was decontaminated in Georgia. Their group was separated, with all but Sconi being removed from the site. Fowler was debriefed for hours, eventually sent to D.C. while they "sorted it all out."

And here he was…a month and a half later. Every night, he played the events out in his head. Would he still be in this room if he'd waited a moment longer? If Pierson hadn't used his gun? His mind dragged him through to the end, where he saw Sconi sitting in a small, plastic quarantine cell, his leg bandaged as helicopters whirred into earshot.

Shaking his head clear, Fowler flipped on the second half of the evening news. During his first few weeks of confinement, he watched the news religiously—day and night. He looked for anything relating to the aliens—strange military activity, national park restrictions, even an update on the fictitious test pilot. Alas, there had been nothing but the appointing of a new Secretary of Defense to replace Dennis Lauer after his tragic heart attack. Tonight, the local news outlined stricter regulations on fireworks while national networks speculated on next year's election. It was mundane, even stupid, but he watched anyway.

At the beginning of the next hour, he was interrupted by a knock.

Fowler sat upright…something was different. His dinner plate had been picked up already, which was always his last visit of the day.

He sprang off the cot. "Yeah?"

"Are you decent?" a muffled voice came from outside.

"Yeah," he said hesitantly. The door was opened by an armed guard Fowler had seen a few times but never learned the name of. Peering in casually, the watchman stepped to the side, making room for an older man in a custom-tailored suit. He was probably in his late forties, clean-shaven with strong cheekbones and salt-and-pepper hair. The door shut behind him as he entered.

"Mr. Fowler, it's a pleasure to meet you," the stranger greeted him brightly, extending his hand out. "My name is Gabriel Sutherland, CEO of Zenaut Technologies."

Fowler looked quizzically past Sutherland to the door, then back to the still-extended hand, shaking it politely. There was obviously a reason Sutherland was here, so when he didn't continue, Fowler decided to move things along.

"I can't imagine what strings you pulled to walk through that door, but it wasn't for pleasantries."

The suited visitor gave Fowler a salesman's grin. He reeked of politics and money. "No, Mr. Fowler. I came to offer you a job."

Of all the possible conversations this affluent, middle-aged man could have struck up, a job had not crossed Fowler's mind.

"I'm sorry…a *job*?"

"That's right."

"For Z—?"

"Zenaut Technologies."

Fowler looked at Sutherland, waiting for some sort of joke. "I have a job…oh, and I'm not free to leave."

"You are wrong on both counts, my friend." Sutherland gestured warmly to the cot. "Please, have a seat."

Fowler sat down on the cot's edge. Sutherland fetched a chair from the guard at the door, placing it gently across from the narrow bed.

"I could have guessed as much about my job," said Fowler, "but I promise you I'm not here by choice."

"Do you know why you're here?"

"Yes and no."

"Because you killed an alien? Two?"

Fowler looked up towards the large black dome protruding in the corner of the ceiling. A similar one sat behind him in the opposite corner.

"We're not alone in here," he said.

"I'm aware." Sutherland turned to the camera, waving gingerly before turning back. "So, you're here for shooting an alien?"

"Technically, for disobeying orders."

"Ah—" he exclaimed, as if the whole thing finally made sense. "You and your colleagues were defiant, and since you, Isaac Fowler, survived, you must take the punishment?"

"Something like that."

"But you're not a traitor, Mr. Fowler. You saved an extremely valuable counter-intelligence asset. This—" he gestured to the walls enclosing them, "is insulting to your bravery. You deserve a medal."

"Well, I'm not getting one. Can we skip forward?"

"Of course, let's do that," Sutherland smiled, standing from the chair and walking to the small window by the ceiling. The sun was almost gone—the last few streaks of red visible at the edge of the sky. Flashes of light bounced off the atmosphere as the festivities ramped up.

"Without being able to dive into much detail about the business side, Zenaut has formed an agreement with the United States government regarding the research of extraterrestrial technology."

He turned back, more incisive than before. "After your excursion, a question arose: what to do with the craft? The technology, the information. It was pure luck these aliens came to the States, and that luck has secured our world dominance for centuries."

"How fortunate for us."

"You know a fair bit about our bureaucracy. I'm sure you've already concluded that the powers at be wish to dive into weapons research."

"Naturally."

"Yes, *naturally*. You see, that is where I disagree with my friends in Washington. I believe the greatest value here exists in civilian technology: propulsion systems, energy generators. Weapons will fall into place on their own—they always do—and the U.S. will maintain military superiority until the end of time. What this all boils down to is…while the Pentagon covertly shifts tax dollars to develop alien-tech weapons, I'm being allowed to spend tens of billions of dollars on commercial R&D."

"How philanthropic," Fowler said blankly. He didn't want to sound completely rude in case this man actually *could* get him out. The whole thing smelled off, though, and so far, had nothing to do with Fowler.

Sutherland laughed. It wasn't evil, per se, but rather the laugh of a mastermind.

"I didn't get to where I am through philanthropy, son. I'll have exclusive control over commercial markets for impossibly advanced technology. When someone sees a flying car, they'll say, 'Look at that Zenaut!' People will save up to take vacations to Mars on a Zenaut cruise; farms will be powered on Zenaut generators—we will be the center of an energy market rendering oil, coal, and nuclear entirely obsolete. If my government friends had any clue of how much money I stand to make, they'd expect a much larger donation to their projects. They're called 'stiffs' for a reason—they lack imagination." For the first time since they met, the non-philanthropist seemed genuinely happy.

"Why would you need me? Why go through all of this trouble?"

"The Pentagon isn't going to allow *us* to hold onto these artifacts. We're required to work on the military base being built to store them—a gift from yours truly. We have to share our research with government teams, and our private offices are required to uphold equivalent levels of security. Every Zenaut employee on base, including our director of security, will need specialized clearance simply to be there. If that position were filled by someone familiar with DoD procedures, it would be an added bonus."

There it was. Even with deep pockets, obtaining compartmentalized clearance would take time, and Fowler already had it. Recruiting Sconi should be less effort, but Fowler wasn't about to bring that up now.

"So what happens next?" he asked.

"That depends on you. Do you accept?"

"Yes..."

"Then tomorrow afternoon, you'll be a civilian. Officially, you're retiring, complete with a terrible pension. The DIA will return your personal effects and send you on your way. I'll have a car waiting for you. Your mother's worried sick, so take the week off, enjoy the holiday, and come in next Monday. The facility is in a small town called Arvonia, just south of Charlottesville. It's a bit of a commute, so you'll get one of the houses we've started building next to the base."

"Do I have to use base housing?" Fowler asked. Sutherland laughed.

"You're a civilian, Mr. Fowler. This is a normal house on a residential plot."

"You're giving me a *house*?"

"And a car," he smiled. "Welcome to the private sector."

Heat lines radiated through the still air inside the warehouse, the metal sides reverberating footsteps of technicians as they unloaded equipment to fill the vacant expanse. Once it was set up and running, the space would be lively, like the inside of a factory, but for now, it was closer to an empty hangar.

Walker had been at the research facility in Arvonia for almost a month. The aftermath of the crash had been a whirlwind of confusion and disarray. The possible courses of action were endless, none of which were ideal, and the events in question had left a literal bloodbath beyond any traditional means of investigation. Dr. Stein had been good enough to cover Walker's class the next day, despite a complete lack of a viable excuse. At that point in time, just being allowed to make a phone call was a relief—a tangible connection to the outside world. It soon became clear that Walker wasn't returning for summer session at all. She felt horrible. To her students, she'd just disappeared.

She was questioned repeatedly—as if she might suddenly gain omnipotent insight into their alien visitors. People from unknown government agencies—presumably tied to the Pentagon—persistently asked questions about the inside of the ship and the anatomy of the creatures. Whenever she'd mention something from inside the craft, they'd ask, "What do you think it was for?"

Her urge was to say, "If you want research notes, I'd actually have to *do* some kind of research," but she also hadn't wanted to offer that option. All she'd really wanted to do was go home and sleep until next year. The confusion wasn't subsiding—after a week, they were all still in a frenzy.

Enter Gabriel Sutherland—a man ready to solve all of their problems. Walker hadn't been anywhere near that conversation, but presumed his pitch was something along the lines of, "Let *me* pay for everything, and I'll handle whatever you don't want to."

The first thing he did was hire as many involved parties as possible. Walker had been in the mindset of putting the whole ordeal behind her, but eventually, Sutherland convinced her. She was being given professional freedom, outside of the public eye, her own research team, and an impressive salary, all to indulge scientific curiosities she never dreamed possible. It was every selling point that would resonate with her.

Explicitly and exclusively, every selling point.

Walker hadn't considered just how difficult it would be to resign from Duke until she did. The university didn't want her to leave, and she couldn't give them a reason other than that it wasn't to another university. After her sudden absence, it made the conversation awkward to say the least.

The remaining pieces fell into place quickly. Zenaut acquired an old research facility in Arvonia, Virginia, along with a few dozen acres of surrounding property. The U.S. government immediately took over most of the facility, converting it into a military base.

The company had four major areas of research to dive into: biological, chemical, aerospace, and technological. Each had a warehouse for related artifacts, though nothing had been moved from the ship, yet. The vessel itself would remain where it sat; there didn't seem to be a way to move it other than in pieces. The hotbox she currently stood in was earmarked for alien computers, navigation systems, and other tech.

"A bit muggy, isn't it?" The thin, towering figure of Theodore Plum joined her from the warehouse entrance. The two had been working together frequently over the past few weeks. Both had been hired on as department heads, and they were the only two people on site who had seen the creatures alive.

"Just a bit," she said, wiping sweat from her forehead. "You're probably looking forward more to the winters here?"

Plum shook his head, "I hate it. Weather was a significant factor in my choices for USC and Lockheed. What's the point of moving to America if you don't have year-round sunshine?"

"A thriving cultural melting pot?"

"That must be it," he said dryly, tugging on his polo to vent air through it. "Sutherland's here. You've got an email about it. He says he wants to get everyone on the same page before phase three starts."

Walker had only seen their affluent CEO a couple of times since she'd been hired—he was rarely on site. She imagined their efforts were nearing the point of transitioning into active research. Even though most of their preparations in phase two had consisted of simply upgrading and expanding the existing facilities, the speed and efficiency in which it happened was incredible. Walker was so used to academia, it was jarring to see how quickly a pile of money could move things along.

She left the warehouse with Plum, wandering purposefully towards a one-story office building. The building sat as a dwarf among giants next to the massive testing facilities—one of the few places used exclusively by Zenaut employees. Following one of their new colleagues, they entered a large presentation room. Five rows of seats were separated into three clusters facing an open stage area, akin to a smaller lecture hall. The retracted projector screen exposed the cream-colored wall. Sutherland didn't seem like the PowerPoint type, though he did like his sales pitches.

The CEO stood in a sharp black suit, speaking to a portly man in the front row named Brody Kahlil—a physicist from the University of Kentucky. Two seats away from Kahlil was a man who could easily have been a model for sports cars. Diaz headed Zenaut's chemistry research, his wide nose always supporting a pair of expensive sunglasses. Directly behind Diaz was an MIT instructor named Monroe, who'd developed a number of systems for the International Space Station. She was always hands-on, frequently seen hauling equipment, her dark hair tied back in some way.

The technician was in conversation with a smaller woman in front, and Walker was surprised to see Kelly Ditka, computer folded in her lap, large iced coffee already a third gone. She smiled as much as she ever did when Walker and Plum grabbed nearby seats. DARPA had a firm hold on Ditka, and Sutherland had opted not to look for a price point out of cooperation. Walker rarely spoke with the young linguist. Whether that was a result of their new private-federal divide or the events in Georgia, Walker didn't know.

Whenever she closed her eyes, the horrifying images of that night were burned into the back of her lids, and Ditka had been in the middle of it.

Sutherland's smooth, flowing voice cascaded across the chairs. "We're just waiting on one more, but this will be fairly informal. I wanted to touch base with everyone in person to ensure you're all up to date on the transition plan that should ultimately move us into what will be our normal operations. Things are about to move quickly."

"Quickly," repeated Diaz. "Compared to setting up an alien research site in a month?"

"There were unexpected delays." Sutherland appeared to greatly enjoy his own joke. His eyes glanced up at the door. "Wonderful! We're all here. A couple of you already know our security director, Mr. Fowler."

Walker did a double-take. Nobody had seen the ex-DIA Agent since they'd left the forest—not even Kelly had known what happened to him. Fowler descended the stairs into the presentation room, plopping into the red, cushioned chair beside Plum.

"Good lord, you're alive!" the engineer said.

"It's good to see you, too."

"Well, you fell off the face of the bloody Earth, mate. Where have you been?"

"Washington—it's a long story."

"Yes, and one for later," Sutherland said, ushering them to start. "There's still a lot of work to do to get our facility ready to begin research on the 20th."

9

ARVONIA

Fowler had grown accustomed to administrative work at the DIA, but it was much different being in charge. The worst part thus far had been hiring a team and getting them clearance. There had been little time to find initial candidates, but he was able to scout a few through his own contacts. He felt confident enough in them, though he was still actively performing background checks on them all. Not that he expected any problems, he just didn't want to leave a stone unturned.

None of them would have clearance to be around any artifacts for some time, so, occasionally, Fowler had to accompany people out to the ship in Chattahoochee—usually Walker, Plum, or Monroe. Without a surge of adrenaline through his veins, the ship was actually pretty serene—what he imagined being in space felt like. Plus, with his only real job being to accompany the researcher, he got to wander around and look at stuff.

Of the three times Fowler had been back to Georgia, Ditka was there twice. According to one of the NSA guys Fowler knew, she pretty much lived in Georgia now. No one was allowed to disassemble any shipboard computers until they "cracked" it—whatever that meant. She was quiet and distant, but she also had every right to be.

Fowler had learned to deal with witnessing nightmarish scenes a long time ago. Before the DIA. But, killing the only aliens ever seen —that ate away at him. Enough to routinely block out the events entirely. He'd let a therapist deal with that in about…never. Fowler wasn't looking to streamline a path to the asylum.

When he went back to Chicago, there had been no way to avoid telling his mother about what had happened. In the past, she'd understood he wasn't able to discuss details from his missions, but after he was detained by their own government for six weeks, that excuse didn't fly.

She'd been sick for a little while—nothing serious, but Fowler was sure the story would kill her. As it turned out, there was no easy way to tell someone you shot an alien. Primarily because you first had to inform them that you know—with certainty—that aliens were real and had just visited Earth for the first time. It's not exactly a "have a seat" sort of conversation—you have to drop a bomb on them.

So, he did. And she didn't die. What was more, she actually believed him…eventually.

With a sharp knock, the handle to his office door turned and Sconi entered, dressed in his all-too familiar suit.

"Look at this civilian big-shot," he said. Fowler hadn't seen him since the incident, though they'd spoken on the phone a couple of times. His leg seemed a bit stiff.

"I highly recommend it. Did you know most jobs pay a salary? In money, too. Not just *the thanks of a grateful nation.*"

"Sounds a lot like selling out to me." Sconi sat down in a wooden chair in front of Fowler's desk.

"Well, when your options are selling out or being buried, selling out is a sweet gig."

Sconi shifted in his chair a bit.

"Look, man, I'm sorry about what happened to you."

"It wasn't your fault."

"Yeah, but you took the grenade. Meanwhile, I'm getting a medal for being stabbed by a piece of bark. It just wasn't right."

"I got lucky enough. How come Sutherland didn't try to steal you away from the DIA?"

"He did. I turned him down. Told him you were the guy he wanted."

"Really? Why?"

"I've got my reasons..." Sconi brushed the question off. "Honestly, it just suits you better."

Fowler shook his head. "Don't peddle that shit...you didn't even know if I was alive."

"Alright, fine. Your man gave me his pitch. I asked if he was bringing you in, and he basically said I was a lot easier to find. I had a career to return to, with accolades, and figured a billionaire could track you down. If not, he'd probably come back and ask me again anyway."

Neither of them said anything for a moment. It wasn't the story Fowler was expecting.

"You're a good friend," he said finally.

"Might as well be since we're not co-workers," Sconi grunted as he stood up. "I just wanted to see you in your new digs. I've got a briefing on site."

"Glad you stopped by. Hey, since we're such good friends, what's Kelly doing on that ship so much?"

"Have a good day, Isaac," Sconi said as he continued out the door, a slight limp in his step.

For nearly a month, Zenaut had been pushing the DoD for a second autopsy on one of the alien corpses. The proper term was *necropsy*—the examination of an animal's corpse, but virtually everyone called it an autopsy.

Walker had performed the first one at the CDC before Arvonia had the needed facilities. When she was asked to fly out to Atlanta to assist, she had assumed she was assisting another doctor. A pathologist. It turned out "assist" meant to assist the government by performing the necropsy with federal biologists there to take samples and make sure she was documenting everything to their requirements.

Examining the body had been a surprisingly low priority. During the post-incident disorder, the Pentagon had placed the bodies on ice, which was presumptuous in its own right. Their main goal had been to examine the weapon used to kill Secretary Lauer.

Walker's suspicion was that the government *had* performed an examination, and they'd kept the information from Zenaut entirely.

Needless to say, she'd been given the worst body to examine. It would have been perfect if she'd been performing an actual autopsy, which was done to determine the cause of death. The alien's face had been ripped to shreds by rifle rounds, which was—in her expert opinion—the probable cause of death. Her goal was to analyze the organism's anatomy. Since Walker didn't know what the creatures' insides were supposed to look like, she wanted the specimen with the least amount of damage.

That was the body she got to study today—the one Pierson had killed. This time, instead of being monitored by federal biologists, she had a small group of assisting researchers—Zenaut researchers. Most were Diaz' people. Extra hands that would benefit from knowing where their chemical analysis samples came from. Otherwise, it was just Walker's observations. She'd have to spend countless more hours in the examination room to begin painting a full picture, but what she'd found so far was fascinating.

Recording devices were arranged nearby as she spoke aloud.

"The top of the creature's skull is covered by several centimeters of hardened material, perhaps calcium or keratin. The pattern appears more scale-like than bone. When they were in danger, they planted two of their hands on the ground, angling their skulls towards us, so this might be a vestigial exoskeleton used to butt heads with other members of their species during a more primitive era. Whatever the reason, the cranial exoskeleton does not fully cover the area housing the brain."

With the face of this specimen intact, Walker was able to get a much better look at the structures within its head, shaped like an elongated lightbulb—nearly cylindrical, but not quite. The domed skull turned to sleek flesh below the creature's high-placed visual cortex, which ran around the perimeter of its head. The accurate lens had no lid or cover—strong enough to protect itself from irritation like several reptiles, fish, and amphibians.

"The brain takes up roughly ninety percent of the head from the neck upward, suggesting not only advanced cognitive abilities, but faster processing of subconscious information. Namely, visual recognition. Dozens of cranial nerves connect from the lens to the brain. No portion seems to rely exclusively on peripheral vision. Based on observed behaviors, they don't have trouble seeing with depth and acuity throughout the organ."

She pushed her face closer to the dead alien.

"Skin cells below the eye socket, to about four centimeters above the narrowest point of the neck, are softer in texture. This is the area that changed pigmentation as a form of communication."

Several parts of the first examined body had undergone cellular analysis already. The neck cells weren't chromatophores, but similar. Rather than expanding cells of different colors to cover the area in that pigmentation, a collection of four cells sat in clusters beneath a larger, empty cell. The smaller cells expanded a chromatic jelly into the "window cells" via a small nerve, allowing them to push part or all of each liquid into the window. By mixing various amounts of four colors, the window cell could effectively display hundreds of hues, perhaps thousands. Each color managed to retract back into the appropriate cell by density. At any given point, millions of cells could be filling or emptying at once.

"Two small slits on opposite sides of the face take in air, including sensory nerves we would liken to smell...still no obvious signs of auditory receptors, nor any structures resembling vocal cords.

This corroborates the hypothesis that the sounds we heard came from the body, so their sense of hearing may be more closely linked to touch. With such an advanced level of visual communication, auditory language may not provide as much use."

The undamaged parts of the body were similar to the last specimen. Their limbs were entirely muscular, with two large, rounded fingers opposing a third. A thin mouth connected from just below the neck to a stomach, which Walker suspected would reveal a similar diet to the last: primarily proteins. The circulation system was the same as well, though this specimen had a bullet lodged near its heart.

She continued her examination all the way to the narrow X's of the creature's feet. In a species that otherwise had no directional orientation, bipedalism was significant. It would allow their impressive field of vision to extend farther, and it was a key advantage in the early stages of human evolution—the precursor to walking upright.

With assignments to her researchers, the small group cleaned the body and prepared it for preservation—a process that took over an hour. By the time they left the sterilization chamber, it was after six. Walker had spent her entire day in the examination room.

Recording her final thoughts on the way back to her office, she gathered her things and left the campus. Despite seeing the same security personnel every day, she had to show identification whenever she entered or exited the premises.

Jail-like shadows spread across the creekside road from nearby trees, which were completely bare at this time of year. Pulling up to the rural highway intersection, her stomach growled, not unlike the extraterrestrial they'd just finished storing. Walker had decided not to eat while repeatedly putting her hands inside an alien corpse. Now, though, she was easily the most germ-free person in all of Virginia.

Rather than heading home, she cut left, taking the small, two-lane highway towards the interstate.

10

THE DEATH RAY

The lack of a proper bar was a consistent gripe for most of the founding Arvonia staff. The DoD felt that base housing would draw too much attention to the facility, so the military personnel commuted in from nearby towns—mostly Charlottesville. It meant those living in the nearby residential plots, while much closer to the facility, had to drive upstate for a pint.

The Zenaut directors had a preferred sports bar in the nearby town of Palmyra, near Lake Monticello. Cheering crowds emitted from overhead TVs as Walker entered the lakeside bar. She didn't follow any sports. When she'd worked at Duke, she'd only barely been aware of their teams' success because of the students. She knew Virginia had no major teams, though, so local fans usually rooted for D.C.

Within seconds of navigating through the bar, Walker spotted the back of Plum's head sticking two feet above his booth seat. They had all been meeting periodically at the bar and grill. It started as just her, Fowler, and Plum, talking about the crash site away from prying ears. There weren't any support groups for people who witnessed people getting murdered by aliens, so they opted for alcohol.

There actually *were* groups for extraterrestrial-related trauma, but none seemed too legitimate.

A sports bar was as suitable as anywhere else. Their conversations were masked by games on TV or music, and they didn't say anything explicit, anyway. Over time, their meet-ups became more of a general update between directors. They rarely crossed paths on base, and it was a good way to unwind. The notion of meeting people from Virginia they didn't work with felt...strange. What would they even talk about?

Not that they were forced into isolation, necessarily. They were allowed to tell people they worked at the U.S. Army Foreign Science division in Charlottesville. The Pentagon even gave them real badges to show. They didn't provide any access to Army facilities or specify a placement, but they were good enough to get past a "what do you do around here?" question, holding up to minor scrutiny and providing a reasonable excuse for secrecy. Plum called them "honorary IDs" because, like an honorary degree, they were as good as any if someone looked, but nobody would be able to get a job with one.

The second time they'd met in the sports bar—back when it was still just the contact team—Kelly had joined them. In true form, she'd said very little, and she never showed up again. As their conversations shifted towards questionably candid work talk, they wouldn't have been able to discuss much with Kelly there anyway. The relationship between Zenaut and the Pentagon was supposed to be friendly, but there was a significant information barrier on the federal side. Fowler had stopped showing up for a similar reason— the less he knew, the better.

Monroe sat beside Plum, with Kahlil taking up most of the booth across from them. Diaz was probably in the lab dealing with samples from the specimen Walker had started cutting open. Between their drinks sat a small grey box—a military-grade audio jammer. Monroe had built it with components she "borrowed" from their neighbors. Both the tech lead and Fowler agreed it was highly illegal, but he'd only reminded them that enlisted patrons in the bar might know what it was.

The potential for running into people Fowler knew from the army was probably a factor in his absences. As far as Walker could tell, the bar was comprised entirely of the minute town's inhabitants.

Kahlil scooted to the wall to make room for her.

"Did you hear?" he asked as she settled in.

"Hear what? I was in examination all day."

"The Department of Defense broke the death ray," Plum said, referring to the weapon used on Lauer. Fowler wanted to call it a "phaser," but according to Plum, phasers already existed and used microwaves, so he'd taken to calling it a "death ray."

"How did it break?" she asked.

"It turned out the inside of the tank-portion was a complete void —no matter or particles of any kind."

"Not even residual?"

"Nope. At least, it didn't seem that way. When they tried to get inside, it exploded."

"Shit...was anyone hurt?"

"The two people working on it died. They probably never even knew something had happened."

"My god..." Walker exhaled. It was heavier news than she was expecting.

She excused herself to the bar, fighting the urge for a stiffer drink and ordering a lager and a sandwich. Waiting for the draft to pour, she stared off into space, unable to stop herself from imagining what sort of scene would be left after an explosion of whatever was inside the alien weapon.

Her attention was caught by a couple in their fifties with their adult son. The red-clad trio sat on barstools at a small, elevated table, half a plate of wings between them as they cheered and sighed at the suspense of a baseball game being displayed on the bar's screens.

That could have been her. Not in a jersey, but at a bar with family, completely unaware of the ongoing events at the local extraterrestrial research base. Never having to know it existed; not knowing how many people had died to unlock its secrets. Walker didn't regret the work, but for the first time, she thought maybe ignorance really was bliss. Besides, how would she realistically go about starting a family? Her dating prospects were all but null—guaranteed to hit a wall when the second date required a six-month background check.

For the time being, her future belonged to Zenaut.

As tragic as the engineers' deaths were, hitting a permanent impasse with the weapons technology was a good thing overall. The number of lives saved through the loss of the death ray was beyond measurement. If only it had happened some other way.

The rest of the research being done at the Arvonia facility was far from any sort of deadlock. Walker's field had been redefined completely. Humans all shared 99.9% of their DNA, most of which was shared with other mammals, and their basic functions were shared across the majority of terrestrial life. Fish didn't breathe air, but their bodies used oxygen to perform many of the same functions by absorbing it through their gills—less akin to humans, but still similar. We all evolved from the same cell, ultimately sharing elements of our biology.

At no point in history did the alien's evolutionary path share an ancestor with any species known to man. Yet, like every plant and animal on Earth, they were carbon-based. Was that a coincidental result from our planet's composition, or a universal necessity for all life? The thin, navy suits worn by their visitors produced an atmosphere of the same gasses as Earth's. Lethal ratios for a human, but extremely relevant.

Her envy faded. She watched the family turn away from the TV at the start of a commercial break, digging into the second half of their wings. How could she ever choose that over what she was doing now?

Beer in hand, Walker turned from the bar to head back to the table, nearly running into Fowler as she did. It wasn't too surprising for him to show up. Given the day's major event, life on base would likely be changing.

His decision to bring Kelly Ditka was more questionable.

After the explosion, Fowler's entire afternoon had been hijacked. Two scientists had died while working on the death ray, their bodies airbrushed across the wall in streaks of scarlet. Fowler had declined the invitation to observe the scene—he'd seen it before.

The resulting changes in DoD security protocols kept Fowler late. Zenaut had to adhere to them all...starting immediately. Most of the staff was gone for the evening, so Fowler's morning would be a pain in the ass.

With the Pentagon's golden goose no more, a newfound interest had formed in Zenaut's propulsion research. Despite Plum's insistence that the technology was impossibly stable, the DoD was hellbent on making a bomb. It was their last promising avenue for mechanical weaponry. Explosives provided a visual flex that bioweapons simply didn't, and merely the display of a revolutionary WMD could end the Second Cold War entirely.

Or exacerbate the situation. It was a 50/50 shot.

After the procedure update, Fowler caught up with Ditka for a couple of minutes. He hadn't seen the cryptographer for a while, and from what he'd heard, she had been in Georgia for the past three weeks straight. Then she asked Fowler if he was heading to the bar in Palmyra, which was concerning. Asking to come to a social gathering wasn't like her at all, and the Pentagon had a great deal to gain from a little corporate espionage right now. Kelly also knew they discussed work off-property. Hell, Sutherland probably knew and just turned the other cheek—the man couldn't afford to lose key staff this early.

Fowler didn't truly think Ditka asked to go for nefarious reasons, but it was still dangerous. Every scenario in which a devoted intelligence asset overhears a public discussion of top-secret information ends poorly for those individuals.

Through the sparse, Tuesday-evening crowd, Fowler saw Walker by the bar. Rather, he saw her hair peeking above the shoulders of those around her. He made a beeline to the biologist, giving her a chance to warn the other Zenaut employees to keep a lid on anything they shouldn't be talking about. Unmistakable surprise washed over Walker's face when she saw Ditka—it was unfortunately conspicuous. Thankfully, the DoD linguist was terrible at reading people.

Whether or not the department heads had been discussing the explosion was impossible to tell. After grabbing a couple of drinks, Fowler and Ditka joined the rest, who were fully engaged in conversation with Plum about his kids. Fowler had truthfully forgotten that Plum had kids. It seemed strange for any of them to have outside lives.

"—and the timing worked out quite nicely," he said. "We had actually discussed moving inland before. I would have had to commute to Langley, but they were the right ages for it. Now—new school system, new school year. It's been wretched."

They greeted Kelly unnaturally warmly, but after that, there were no more suburban nuances to discuss. They sat silently, trying to think of normal conversation topics to no avail. The still was beyond uncomfortable. Walker left to get her food. Fowler hadn't even wanted to come. He had a ton of—

"Was anything salvageable?" Monroe asked Ditka pointedly. The young cryptanalyst glanced at Fowler, poorly feigning her ignorance.

"From what?"

"This is currently a bullshit-free zone. Our unborn children already know what happened in your labs. If you want to come looking to eminent domain yourself a new project, you've gotta bring something to the figurative and literal table, lady."

The accusation seemed to offend Kelly quite a bit. She insisted she only came to catch up after getting back to Virginia, and for what it was worth, Fowler believed her now more than ever. He'd worked with spies in the past, and Kelly was a horrible one. If she went undercover as a linguist-turned-cryptographer, she'd still get made.

Kahlil leaned forward like they were only now discussing something very secret. "It *is* a bit coincidental. Right after losing the Pentagon's primary investment."

"There's going to be a lot more overlap," Fowler told them. "So yes, they're trying to salvage some sort of defense value from the facility. It's hard to blame them."

"No it's not," Walker said through her hand as she swallowed a bite of her sandwich. "I do it all the time."

A few of them chuckled. Plum turned to Ditka. "Well, then, what have you been working on out in Georgia?" It was something Fowler had been curious about for a while. Whenever he saw her on the ship, she always seemed to know what she was looking at.

"Cryptography," she said. "I'm trying to build a language foundation to make sense of the information systems."

Monroe nodded. She'd mentioned a few times that all of the electronic information would look like white noise until someone figured out how the systems were programmed, which could take centuries.

"How's that been going?" Plum took a big swig of his pint.

"Really well. I'm almost done."

Walker froze. Plum choked on his beer.

"What do you mean, *done?*" Kahlil's voice rose, but he caught himself, glancing around like a startled dog before leaning over the table and continuing in a near-whisper. "Translating what? How?"

"Oh no, we haven't started translating anything yet. Just deciphering the languages they use."

Monroe laughed in disbelief. "No. That's ludicrous. I know you *claim* to be the best, but breaking multiple codes with no reference points in a few months? I'm not buying it."

"I've never said I was the best…"

"It does seem—" Walker started. It sounded like she was about to say "fast" but reconsidered halfway through, "—logical. If I were exploring other inhabited planets, I would bring comprehensive, universal learning tools."

"You're kidding me," Plum said, more in disappointment than surprise. "You found some sort of Rosetta Stone?"

"No, not exactly," the linguist said meekly. "The stone had multiple languages on it, so it had already been translated—we just used the Greek passage to learn equivalent passages in hieroglyphics and demotic. This artifact is more like a visual learning program for their two primary languages."

"I was referring to the visual learning program…"

It seemed the Department of Defense had been holding out on them even more than they'd thought. Fowler wasn't remotely shocked. This was exactly how he assumed their relationship with the feds would be. Monroe was understandably upset.

"You didn't think that knowledge would have been useful?" she said. "Do you have *any idea* how much time we could have prevented wasting if we were told there might be a language translation soon? Even a long shot?"

Kelly stood her ground. "Like I said, I'm not done yet. I have to provide a full decoding to the Department of Defense before it's made accessible to civilians. It's not a full compendium or anything. There are a lot of important symbols still needing to be placed within the structure, which could be dangerous otherwise."

"It's definitely two?" asked Walker.

"They're outlined as two. They use mostly the same characters, though, so we can ultimately view them as one. There are different uses of grammar between them, but that's for way down the road."

"I would include a lot *more* than two, is what I mean."

Ditka shrugged. "They're more advanced. They've had more language death. It's a natural result of globalization. Half of *our* languages will be extinct by the end of the century."

Fowler didn't need a STEM degree to know that this development would push every department's research forward at unimaginable speeds. These pursuits were expected to take hundreds, even thousands of years—researchers passing torch after torch just to one day figure out what some of these contraptions *do*. The vision Sutherland had shown him was the legacy formed simply from insights gained by studying alien technology—flying cars, vacations to Mars, renewable energy…maybe a revolutionary type of generator by the time he died. It was from out-of-the-box thinking inspired by mysteriously advanced technology.

As of five minutes ago, all of that was small. The only thing their CEO had been right about was that his friends in Washington had no idea how much money he stood to make—but neither had he.

As she made her way to the transit tunnel, a pair of footsteps fell beside Raynor. Eldon Rhyso, the biologically-aged local, was walking in step. It took her a second to remember his name, though it was apparently the most common first name in Razennon.

"Procaine! I assume you're heading to forward transit?"

"Yeah, where are you going?"

"To the same," he said cheerfully. "I am back on duty."

"Why would you have to take general weaponry? Aren't you already a specialist?"

"I was activated at sergeant, actually, but I haven't used most of our weapons since my original training, which was *many* years ago."

"Congratulations." Sergeant was the highest rank any of the cadets at Starling would be granted at the end of their training, and there would only be a few. "I mean…congratulations, *sir*."

"Thanks, but don't call people *sir* or *ma'am* or anything formal like that. Officers shed a great deal of sweat and blood to get where they are. Addressing them as a social elite implies they somehow purchased their positions. It's disrespectful."

Raynor certainly hadn't expected that response, but she was glad she didn't make the same mistake with someone like Teckann first. "Sorry, I didn't mean it like that."

"I know," he said matter-of-factly, "that's why I explained it."

"How *would* I address an officer?"

"Well, the only way to know someone is an officer is to see their rank, so you would address them as such. General Teckann will be at the forward base today, so you should call him *General*, or *General Teckann* if you're still feeling formal."

"Simple enough."

"There are more important things to worry about."

They arrived at the entrance to the forward transit station. A blockage of about a hundred people cluttered the doorway. Raynor stood on her toes, trying to see over the heads of the mob in front of her.

"Is there going to be room for everyone?"

"Yes. This isn't some 32nd-century vehicle," Rhyso smirked. "It was specifically designed to move full platoons as quickly as possible."

Hearty vegetables may have been a mistake for an early lunch. Raynor never ate heavy meals before she flew, but it had never occurred to her that she might be undergoing those types of forces today.

Anton joined them outside the door, jewel in hand, as the crowd filtered into the metallic hut. A ramp led down into a large, open room, not well-lit. Cut into the opposite wall, a tunnel five meters wide extended into the distance. A row of panels spanned each side of the subway, disappearing into a combination of darkness and curvature. The room had a ghostly feel to it—cold, even though it wasn't.

A captain stood in front of the tunnel holding a jewel of his own. Off to the side, a woman stood at a stationary console.

"Form up! Eight rows of twenty-five," the captain yelled. His husky voice bounced around the bare metal underneath the translated words she heard in her ear. He pulled Rhyso up to the front as the cadets organized themselves. The two spoke for a minute, ending with Rhyso being sent over to the loading area to wait for the transport.

"Alright, cadets. I'm Captain Ansil. I will be giving you an overview of the molecular repeater before you depart for the forward outpost."

A deafening whir rapidly spun up as glass panes shot up in front and behind Rhyso. The edges of the tunnel illuminated for a fraction of a second, speeding along as each panel lit up in sequence, out of sight around the downward curvature. As quickly as the sound had come, it was gone.

And so was Rhyso.

The sergeant had disappeared—vaporized and shot down the tube. The foregone soldiers stared blankly down the dark tunnel as they tried to rationalize what they'd seen. The stunned silence was broken by a voice from the middle of their formation.

"No way in Hell…"

11

PARADIGM SHIFTS

Cooperating with the Pentagon consisted of providing them with information for little or nothing in return. Every breakthrough made by Zenaut was immediately stifled by the Defense Department. Whatever the technology was, the excuse was always that America couldn't afford to make it commercially available while Russia was a threat. Sutherland was never bothered, no matter how many times it happened. Ultra-wealthy people could afford to wait.

After the alien languages were finally decrypted in early December, unfathomable benchmarks were repeatedly created and surpassed. Within a week, Ditka found a star map in the ship's system, which Kahlil was effortlessly able to orient to Earth's sky.

"This one right here," he said, effervescently pointing to a dot on a screen full of dots. It didn't have the pomp he appeared to think it did.

"Good for you, lad," said Plum. "Where is it?"

"Not far…about five thousand lightyears away."

"That sounds pretty far," said Walker.

"Not on a galactic scale. The star closest to ours is four lightyears away. If that's our next-door neighbor, this system is across town."

"But for travel? Wouldn't that mean they left more than five thousand years ago?"

"Depends on the method of travel—and your perspective. If they use a warp drive or pilot through wormholes, it could hypothetically be much faster. If they relied on good old-fashioned relativity, then yes, but it would only be five thousand years to *us*. To them, it would be much less time due to dilation, which, in turn, depends on their speed."

As uneventful as it was to find the alien's home system, their research was largely dictated by which datalogs had been accurately decoded and translated. The process was slow, but it turned out that even aliens brought instruction manuals with them. As such, unpredictable boosts of productivity would fall upon the Arvonia team, and before long, they provided enough insight to tide the researchers over until the next one. By the spring of 2024, their fortune looked to be without end. Tidal waves of knowledge well beyond modern science came at such a frequency that the staff joked about weekly paradigm shifts: significant, radical changes in their understanding of a given field.

Physiology, evolution, and culture had been Walker's area of study. The ship's datalogs frequently made reference to their own species, so she had been tasked early on to coin a technical name for the creatures. Some people around base had already taken to calling them "cephrasts"—a backwards concatenation of astral cephalopods. Walker never found out who coined the term, but she liked the way it sounded, so she went with it.

The cephrast homeworld was oceanic, their ancestors aquatic. Still, many aspects of their culture were strikingly human. Pets, for instance—lower lifeforms they kept, cared for, and admired. So far, Walker had only seen one example—a small purple ball with sharp teeth and fixed wings that consisted of two large holes, through which water was pushed to swim. Diaz seemed to think their faces resembled a bulldog's and started calling them "Purpooches," but he was still the only one.

Bioengineered materials were used throughout their computers, which were developed in a largely aquatic world. Biological synapses were already being investigated on Earth for their computing potential, but the cephrasts had surrounded their entire technological revolution around it. Their computers weren't alive, but used synthetic materials based on aquatic structures.

They also worked when wet.

With a partial instruction manual in hand, Plum's research moved forward at an alarming rate. The Department of Defense placed a heavy priority on decoding information relating to the propulsion systems, which resulted in the engine being successfully turned on in July, including the lights that prompted Walker to dive into the dirt last spring.

Despite the speed of Plum's progress, having only one engine to study slowed it down, as did that engine being on the ship. Talk of moving the ship to Virginia had picked up, but there was too much concern about a crash. The flight controls were...odd. More importantly, the prospect of duplicating a primitive version of the technology was looking not only possible, but on the horizon. The only hypothetical limitation was the source of energy, which was still completely undefined.

The Pentagon was pushing incessantly for something that went boom. Based on comments she'd heard, Walker also suspected they were imagining fleets of space fighters bombing from orbit—as unrealistic as that was at this stage. Lambasting of America's newest military branch—Space Force—only amplified when the Second Cold War took off and everyone started to note that none of the events occurred in space. Plum was completely haggard by the end of summer—never without dark circles over his increasingly-bony cheeks. He pushed research forward as safely as he could, which involved a lot of combing through decoded cephrast archives. By the end of the year, the feds were trying to get Plum replaced, even after the discovery that ultimately led to the most destructive weapons in human history.

Throughout the 20th century, electromagnetic waves were the only known type of waveform. Gamma rays, microwaves, visible light, infrared—they were all just different frequencies of the same sort. Einstein introduced the notion of gravitational waves, but none were observed until a century later in 2015, when the LIGO center recorded the distortion of gravitational waves created by two colliding black holes. It was a major scientific discovery—the confirmation of a second waveform, but little more had been uncovered about it since. Electromagnetic waves were also represented as particles called photons. A placeholder existed for the gravitational equivalent, gravitons, but they were even more elusive than their waveform had been.

The cephrasts had a mastery of both particles. And since a number of the ship's systems used gravitons directly, there were a handful of instruments on board to observe, measure, and handle the particles. Every scientist on base was exhilarated, even those from the military, and it gave Plum a much clearer path for his research.

But for every mystery solved, a new one arose. Countless questions about gravitational waves were answered in the batch of cephrast logs, but one of them identified it as the second of three waveforms, with no other reference about the third.

Kahlil was ecstatic.

"What could it be?" Diaz asked at the waterside tavern.

"Who knows?" Kahlil said. "Cryptography will notify me if they find another reference to the term, but we know it exists, and that's just spectacular!"

"Could it be possible to combine or...*blend* electromagnetic and gravitational waves in some way?" Plum stared at his beer, vanquished after months of banging his head against the wall.

"The two are already linked. If an object is destroyed, its gravitational force doesn't disappear before witnessing its destruction—not with our understanding of those principles. You want to know if it's possible to create a hybrid particle from photons and gravitons?"

"Yes."

"Who knows?!" Kahlil cackled again like it was the greatest answer in the world. Plum didn't share his enthusiasm.

"Assuming we can manipulate gravitons as we do photons…?" Plum asked. Creating and destroying photons was something humans had done for centuries as easily as turning on a lightbulb. In fact, turning on a light did exactly that. Manipulating gravitational waves in the same manner could lead to instantly-created forces like artificial gravity.

"There would be a lot of potential, no doubt, but it could be too dangerous to use in that manner. Gravity is an *extremely* stable force. The waves decrease over distance, but consistently. It's why a five-pound weight doesn't suddenly start weighing more. Removing that stability could be catastrophic. Sure, you might be able to propel a large object, but you might also be able to make a cosmic-sized black hole."

Walker groaned. "Maybe it's a good thing the DoD doesn't see value in the information."

"Easy for you to say," Plum scoffed. "You're not required to cough up anything destructive."

He was right, but Walker's usefulness to the project had been waning in general after her preliminary analyses. At times, it felt like she was only there so the Pentagon could keep tabs on her—the same worry Plum had about his own usefulness. None of Walker's work needed to be done on base, and no one was particularly concerned about her evolutionary speculations, although Sutherland at least feigned excitement for them. She frequently found herself assisting Diaz with his work, which she found considerably less interesting. Looking at cephrast amino acids was far too detached to be exciting.

The lives of Arvonia's staff remained reliably chaotic through the winter. In February, the single largest game-changer of their careers was found—one that would ripple through the eons. It wasn't a particle or wave, or any form of energy or technology, but rather a piece of information.

On the third day of February, Plum and Monroe were out in Georgia trying to connect solar panels to the ship. They might not know if the engine was charging, nor could they generate enough energy to impact the power levels, but they needed to see if the connection could even be made at all.

In Virginia, Walker received an odd question about the cephrasts' cultural tendencies towards aggression. As unusual as it was for someone to show interest in her ecological work, most bizarre was that the question came from Kelly Ditka, who had overseen every single file decryption. Every log had been given to Walker by the cryptographer.

Aggression was embedded deeply in human culture. History could easily be viewed as nothing more than a string of conflicts. In America, there had only been seventeen years without war since its establishment in 1776. Other facets of society occurred during that time, but most were tied to those bouts of hostility. The rest of world history wasn't much different—from Napoleon to the Crusades.

Conversely, the cephrasts appeared to have been without internal war for millennia, if not longer. Their eras of history were outlined exclusively by changes in scientific understanding, artistic trends, and structural modifications. Kelly was well aware of this. There was missing subtext in her inquiry.

"We've both witnessed their instincts for self-defense, and they have enough of a need to learn it consciously. If their records are truthful, they don't have wars, but that doesn't mean they don't fight. Anthropology would give you a clearer answer, but as a lifeform, their bodies are suitably evolved for individual confrontations. Why?"

"I'll explain later. I'm waiting on something from off-site."

"Did you translate something new?"

"…no."

That was it until the end of the day. Sutherland asked a few Zenaut supervisors to stay on site until the evening with no specific timeframe. Walker had dinner delivered, which meant having it left out at the gate and checked by security while she went to retrieve it, allowing the frigid winter air to absorb all of its heat. A lesson she'd learned once before but promptly forgot. Diaz stopped by later out of boredom, speculating why they might have to stick around. Walker didn't mention her correspondence with Kelly—she wasn't in the mood for anticipation. Instead, they talked about non-alien biology—a topic that passed for recreation these days.

At a quarter after eight, they found themselves in one of the military offices. Walker recognized almost none of the people in the room. Her work didn't require collaboration with the military anymore, which was her preference. Occasionally, one of them asked her about a note from her necropsies, but at this point, the Pentagon had several biologists doing their own work. Diaz had far more interaction with the other side of the campus. Kahlil was sitting at the corner of the table, silently reading a clump of loose papers about twenty pages thick.

The new secretary of defense arrived at 8:15 on the dot—a thin-faced man in his fifties named Liam Karlson. Ditka entered closely behind him, laptop in hand, and Sutherland slinked in moments later.

"I need to be in D.C. tonight, so let's make this quick," Karlson said. Walker already didn't like him. "Miss Ditka has new information for us that needs to be addressed."

The DARPA linguist placed her computer on the table and began typing as she spoke quietly.

"As you probably know, we have a firm hold on translating cephrast documents. Decoding file formats has been difficult. It's unlikely we'll ever get them all figured out; some will likely take centuries, but I've been focusing on some of the simplest ones."

She turned her laptop around. A few cephrast symbols adorned the screen.

"When we arrived on the night of the crash, the ship was emitting this signal. It's a sort of index or primer—an analog for our S.O.S. broadcast. We've seen it mentioned a few times. With no hope of a rescue this far away, the primer's purpose is for recipients in their home system to lock onto it and check for updates, as well as chart the location. The crew's vital signs are also monitored by shipboard sensors. After the death of the last crew member, an altered signal was transmitted in place of the beacon."

Rotating the screen around, Ditka entered a few key commands, flipping the screen back to show a much longer string of symbols.

"The message was written longhand, sort of like an interstellar black box. It includes concise information about their journey, with references to specific exploration protocols. One of those is an extermination order."

Animated conversation began amongst the mostly-federal audience. Walker choked on the air, her throat drying up instantly.

"Extermination? Of Earth?" one of the military women asked.

"Our species, but it likely includes razing the entire planet. I'll get to that in a minute."

"Someone said they were peaceful?"

"They don't have internal wars. Or at least, they hadn't for centuries before the ship left. This reference is specifically for extermination. We're a primitive lifeform without interstellar travel, and they've classified us as dangerous. It's more about preventing a future war before we attain the technology to siege them."

"Killing eight billion people in response to three is ludicrous," one of the DoD engineers said.

"It wasn't an accident they arrived at Earth—they knew someone was here and spent several months slowing their ship to make this stop. They'd been gathering information long before the crash —their deaths simply triggered the update."

Walker didn't know what to think. Her perspective on the cephrasts' culture was changed drastically. She thought back to logs she'd glossed over.

"There was mention of pests..." she said aloud. The document had been conversational, like a journal. The way she might discuss a termite problem—tenting the house, staying in a motel, the whole ordeal involved. If that had been in reference to an evolved, sapient species...

"Based on previously decoded documents, there are at least two instances of this being done with other so-called primitives. As I said, it's an established protocol. A group eliminates the species and harvests resources as payment—the razing I mentioned."

"Everybody can relax," Karlson ushered. "What Ms. Ditka has yet to mention is that this *theory* won't come to fruition for many years."

"Correct. The signal has to travel to their home planet, and then they'll have to travel here, so this would be thousands of years in the future."

"Ten thousand and change," Kahlil muttered. Gusts of exhales came in unison.

"There you have it," Karlson said. "There's no need to panic about it."

"So, what is this meeting for?" someone asked. "It's not like we can do anything about it now."

"That's where you're wrong. The Pentagon's top priority has always been the safety of every American, and we have a unique opportunity to give our children's children a fighting chance. Given the technological disadvantage we already find ourselves in, we're here to address the direction our facility takes its research going forward."

Oh no...

"This means allocating more resources to specific areas of research," Karlson outlined. "The majority will be dedicated to reverse-engineering the vessel's technologies. We're also increasing our ranks in biochemistry to analyze potential threats posed by these animals, and will be debriefing a number of software engineers from the war to build a full archive of the ship's documents."

Energy weapons, biological weapons, and excuses.

Walker looked over to Sutherland, who maintained his almost-smile through the blatant coup. The man's poker face was remarkable. Karlson ended with the usual DoD disclaimer that no one outside of the room was authorized to receive this information. Casual conversations broke out about completely unrelated topics as the defense secretary left.

Walker finally caught Sutherland's eye. He smiled and nodded as if to say, *"Everything is fine."* But it wasn't fine. This was the exact situation she had tried to avoid being in—not the invasion, specifically, but the federal overthrow.

She approached the billionaire quickly. "May we speak?"

"Of course, Dr. Walker!" he said pleasantly, leading her out of the conference room and a few steps from the door. "A concerning turn of events, isn't it?"

"That's an understatement. I will not do weapons research."

He laughed, which irked her a bit. "I would never expect you to. None of these changes will affect your work."

"Is he going to tell Plum or Monroe when they get back?"

"He'll have to."

"What about Isaac? He was there too."

"No, but Mr. Fowler is our director of security. It's his job to find these things out."

"The secretary didn't want him here?"

"He didn't want any of you here. I asked for you to be present."

"But not Isaac?"

"No. And I think you know why."

She did. The more they learned about the alien culture, the less Walker mentioned around Fowler. He blamed himself for the disaster, and constantly hearing about how peaceful the alien culture was only added to his guilt. Finding out the cephrasts weren't as passive as originally believed wouldn't mean anything to him if it came with the addendum that he may have caused the future apocalypse—even if it wasn't realistically his fault.

Light-headedness enveloped her at the thought. If the cephrasts responded as outlined, that's exactly what they'd just learned of…

The apocalypse.

12

HYBRID PARTICLES

Raynor's trip through the molecular repeater was, for lack of a better word, unpleasant. Leaving the transit station, she was met by a scene vastly different from the base she had entered from. The remote training grounds consisted of a series of small buildings resembling those from the courtyard at Starling Base. Across the garrison sat a number of barricades and stationary weapons facing the bottom of a long, narrow canyon. Cliffs outlined the gorge, extending two hundred meters up to what looked like a plateau.

Raynor joined the cadets who'd wrapped themselves around the side of the transit station to look behind the outpost. Nothing was there. The canyon extended a few hundred meters more as the cliffs slowly disappeared into the ground, beyond which was nothing but yellow desert. Starling Base was nowhere to be seen—their training group had traveled at least as far as the horizon…instantaneously.

General Teckann rounded up the cadets as the last few exited into the warm, spring day. They filed up in front of him as the newly-promoted Eldon Rhyso brought over two large crates from a nearby shed. He towered comically over the general—merely eye-level with most of the cadets.

Excited faces washed away as soldiers of the past looked into the equipment crate on their first day of *general weapons* training to find only gloves. The garments were in the CAF's standard black and grey, with small white pads along the palms and fingers.

Per Teckann's instructions, they rummaged through to find a snug pair. The gloves didn't appear to be armored, but they had some weight to them. Raynor held one up to her face, closely examining the garment. There seemed to be some sort of electronics embedded within.

"These are holster gloves," Teckann said. "When you are issued a weapon, a pair of these gloves will be assigned to it. Your issued gloves are not to be worn unless you are equipped with or holding the associated firearm."

He reached his open hand in front of his shoulder, and in one swift motion, a rifle appeared from behind him, flying into his grasp as if by magic. The handle immediately met his dominant hand, leaving the general standing with a large, snowy rifle that had seemingly appeared from nowhere. A couple of the cadets whooped at the display—it did look cool.

General Teckann called the weapon simply a "photon rifle." The real name was longer or more technical, based on the amount of Reza he spoke and the amount of Martian Raynor heard. Like everything else they'd encountered during training—the molecular repeater, gravitational singularities…even the jewels—photon rifles were dangerous just to wield. Ironically enough, they were most vulnerable to the projectile weapons they'd replaced—guns that fired bullets or slugs. Rupturing specific parts of the rifle could cause a small explosion of heated radiation, which sounded to Raynor like a miniature nuke.

To prevent that from happening, the photon rifle was holstered beneath a thin, shielded covering on each person's back—like a flat turtle shell. It made retrieving and storing the weapon time-consuming and clumsy, hence the holster gloves. They used "quantum graviton connections" to bring the rifle towards your hand—whatever the hell that meant. Reaching across to the dominant hand's shoulder and pulling away with a gripping motion brought the rifle with you. The handle moved into your dominant hand as soon as the forward grip connected, but it took practice to perform as smoothly as Teckann had. If you did a really bad job, the weapon might smack the back of your trigger hand and break it.

After learning the motion, they were finally issued rifles, including the hard sheath they stored beneath. The weapons compacted themselves into the holster, expanding as they were summoned from the protective shell—another factor in the gloves' necessity.

"You must have one hand connected to your weapon while it is unholstered," Teckann said to the cadets. He was clearly referring to the person next to him—a light-skinned, light-haired man trying to set his rifle down the way you'd shake off a piece of foil statically clung to your arm. "It will either be in your hand or stowed away."

Holstering the weapon to its container required the right amount of force to accomplish. Some failed to get the rifle off of their hand. Others, like Morrison, wound up with the gun lying against their backs, over the armored carapace. Few managed to return the rifle successfully in their first few attempts, one of whom was none other than the killer of aliens, Isaac Fowler. As Raynor watched Morrison repeatedly fail to toss the rifle lightly enough for it to holster, her attention was broken by an electric *thwap*, followed by an explosion. Fifty meters down the canyon, heaps of burning metal fell out of the sky. An old targeting dummy Teckann had obliterated.

He gave a brief instruction on cycling out energy packs while the small, green ammunition cells were distributed around.

"This weapon is now volatile," he said after swapping in a fresh pack. "You are not to holster your weapon today while it is charged."

Much to their dismay, they wouldn't be destroying any targets. A swarm of small robots buzzed around at various distances down the canyon—some stationary, some moving at different speeds.

Blue shields glowed around the small machines, absorbing the energy salvos fired at them by the cadets.

Partway through a trigger pull, the photon rifle generated a barely visible beam—harmless light guiding the infused particle's path. The artificially-added structure slowed the photon as it followed the same line, but not by much. It still more closely resembled a laser, making the faint, green path more radiant for an instant before disappearing entirely. If you looked closely, you could just make out the delay as an emerald, plasma-like circle appeared at the impact site—much like a physical bullet would.

Viridian light flashed across the pale yellow canyon walls as the *thwaps* of their energy weapons echoed down the rocky corridor. Raynor's aim wasn't bad, but she was out of practice. So was Morrison, it seemed, though she wasn't as bothered by the cobwebs. Pilots rarely used rifles.

"Fuck!" he cried as an energy slug flew wide of a stationary target. "I think the kick on these is different than a regular rifle."

"That's a mighty clever excuse you brought with you," she ribbed, similarly missing a completely unmoving target. As much as she enjoyed giving him a hard time, he was probably right. The firing line was supposedly the best of all time, but half of the shots were missing, all of them followed by curses. One wasn't even a curse—just a scream…followed by more screams, Teckann's included.

"Hold your fire!" he shouted. "I said *not to holster!*"

The stout general ran behind the firing line towards one of the cadets—a woman lying still on the ground, the side of her jaw and neck burned off.

A collection of empty bottles cluttered the floor of the master bedroom, an increasingly common sight in the small, two-story house. Fowler sat at the edge of his bed, summoning all of his strength to stand up and leave for work. A burp of whisky rose through his chest and out his lips, forcing him to take deep breaths through his nose to stifle his resulting gag reflex. His head pounded relentlessly, but that was the case even when he wasn't hungover.

After a glass of water and a few painkillers, he felt as good as he ever did, enough to get on base and await the newest crisis.

Arvonia's atmosphere changed completely after the cephrast beacon was decoded. The sense of adventuring into the unknown had vanished overnight, leaving behind a cesspool of anxiety and anger. The Defense Department had wrangled significantly more control over Zenaut's research than originally agreed upon, purchasing most mandatorily for fractions of pennies on the dollar.

In one instance, Diaz found an unusual strain of bacteria that likely protected the cephrasts from certain types of diseases.

"If you dumped human chum into a pool of cephrasts, this bacterium would protect them from us," he described. It was an image Fowler never needed to have. "Most flesh-eating bacteria begin somewhere in the skin, usually an infected wound, and spread through the body. This one would be pretty easy to introduce directly into a healthy body to corrode it from the inside out."

Of course, the research was sequestered by the Department of Defense, and Diaz was removed from involvement. As a bioweapon, it was only useful if the antibacterial was controlled by the Pentagon, so it was deemed safer to develop in secret.

Safer for the DoD, anyway.

The mood was only enhanced by the constant, foreboding tinge of humanity's extinction, which seemed more like a guarantee with every decoded file. Removing potential threats to the cephrast homeworld was a lucrative operation. They even had guidelines of sorts to prevent different groups from stepping on each other's slimy, X-shaped toes.

No matter how shitty everyone's lives got, none of them had doomed the entire species.

Fowler knew he wasn't handling it properly…he wasn't allowed to. Not that he would want to unload the secrets in his head onto some poor therapist. He'd just be that guy who *swore* his alien story was true. Walker had suggested to Sutherland that a psychiatrist be hired. Not for Fowler, specifically, but their staff in general. It was only a matter of time before people started to crack in their new work environment, and it would lead to errors.

Lucky for them, the Defense Department had a psychiatrist on base whose services were graciously extended to Zenaut. Unlucky for Fowler, he wasn't supposed to know the information eating away at him. As much as the shrink might like to claim doctor-patient confidentiality, this was a top-secret military psychiatrist. They answered only to Secretary Karlson and the president.

The utterance, "We're all going to die on this base," was spoken repeatedly by Zenaut researchers. The troubling information now held by a few dozen people would never see the light of day, and anyone who knew about their forthcoming eradication was either part of the cover-up, or being covered.

"I don't know why Sutherland's keeping me around other than to make sure I stay quiet," Walker said during lunch after repeating the mantra. "Nothing I'm writing can be published, and nothing I can publish has anything to do with this facility."

Zenaut couldn't even use the biologist's minor fame in the scientific community to push their commercial products, which had been underwhelming at best, thanks to the Pentagon's grip. Waterproof circuitry was the biggest commercially-available product resulting from the facility's research. They also modeled an enzyme useful for breaking down materials found in carnivore stool. The spray, which could dissolve dog and cat shit in a few hours, was marketed under a subsidiary. Neither product was sufficiently returning Sutherland's investment.

Their CEO remained unflappable, even with every valuable find being poached by the government. Sutherland never worried. He always looked exactly as he did the day he walked into Fowler's detention cell—a man who knew everything was going to work out all right.

When the unexcitable billionaire showed up at the beginning of summer with unbridled enthusiasm, it caught their attention. No one had created more friction throughout the year than Plum. The astronautical engineer sat in the center of a heated power struggle between Zenaut and the U.S. Government. The engine had always been Sutherland's aim, and it was the one place he was attempting to put his foot down. After months of accelerated research, Plum found a schematic for the component generating the ship's power. The prospect of recreating the alien engine was on their doorstep, and the blueprint also helped identify what powered it.

"So this is the third wavelength?" Ditka asked passively when Plum and Kahlil asked her to recheck the file just to be sure. She no longer spent her time in Georgia, instead working night and day trying to make adaptable translation tools. DARPA wanted her back on Russian codes until the end of the war.

Plum shook his head.

"I don't believe so. Both light and gravity particles enter the component, and the output resembles both in different ways. It's a process rather than a particle, and our mystery waveform was supposedly unknown to our visitors. This converter has a manual for God's sake."

Kahlil furrowed his brow, staring blankly at the ground with his arms folded. "You know, a process was developed fifteen years ago using extremely cold temperatures to compress thousands of photons into a single, condensed particle called a *super-photon*…well, it's called a *Bose-Einstein Condensate*, but that's less catchy. Could this mechanism be performing a similar process on gravitons?"

"It's not simple. It could be doing any number of things."

"Well, I think that's the more likely of two possibilities regarding what this does—using radiation as a catalyst to create a graviton condensate. The other would be more akin to the 'hybrid particle' route you asked about—an entangling of the particles that fires them in tandem."

"It's all moot for now. Diaz still needs to duplicate the encasing alloy, and I've got to figure out the purpose of some other parts." Plum curled his lip. "Any other facility in the world would consider these results Nobel-worthy, rather than *inadequate*."

"We should see if they're hiring."

That was the last Fowler had heard anyone speak about the particle converter for a few weeks. His morning headache had just begun to return while checking through shipping manifests. Sutherland hated it when the feds seized their shipments, so Fowler had taken on the responsibility of ensuring each one followed the DoD's ever-changing requirements *prior* to it arriving. It was a hassle, but less so than the alternative.

Fowler refilled his mug with black coffee, the absence of which was surely a contributor to the searing pain in his temples. Just as the steaming liquid touched his lips, another wave of it hit him. Nauseating pressure moved through his skull, followed by a high-pitched ringing in his ears. It was easily the worst he'd experienced, making him dizzy enough to set his mug down as it passed.

"Shit…" he said with a throaty exhale. When it ended, he took a gulp of the scorching liquid, which he'd unquestionably regret later.

One of his few non-veteran officers peeked his head around the corner, concerned. "What's going on?"

"Just a really bad headache," Fowler hissed away the stinging in his throat. "I'll live." He rested his head against his palm, returning to the manifest, but the officer remained in the doorway.

"Uh, Boss…I felt that too…"

Without pause, Fowler stormed out of the room in a dead sprint to the same location he went any time there was a bang or tremor on site—engineering.

In record time, the Defense Department was able to determine the cause of the gravity burst: a poorly-insulated seal had ruptured, plus some other bullshit about temperature. It was all a lie. The only person qualified to find the root of the problem that quickly was

Theodore Plum, whose official cause of death was "crushed via engine leak."

13

THE NEXT MANHATTAN PROJECT

"No."

That was Walker's initial response when asked to examine Plum's body. She wasn't a medical examiner, and this *was* an autopsy. More importantly, she couldn't spend a day looking at Plum's lifeless cadaver.

"Let someone else do it," she told Sutherland. "Let *anyone* else do it."

As it turned out, somebody from the Pentagon already was, and that was the trouble.

A government engineer was immediately brought in to fill the void left by Plum's death—some jackass from Space Force named Flak. The feds insisted they'd only brought in Flak because he was already cleared and it could take Zenaut months to find a suitable replacement candidate. It may have been the only truthful excuse the Pentagon ever gave. No doubt Flak had been waiting in the wings, giving Walker concerns about the accident she didn't tell anyone about, not even Fowler.

With a federal examination underway, Sutherland wanted to ensure they had the "right answers"—reasoning that Walker took with a grain of salt. The CEO's bluntness never extended past government distrust. Still, Plum's family deserved to know the truth...ruse or not. Few people were in a position to both find and deliver it. Walker had met Plum's wife a few times and each of his kids at least once.

Her insides turned. Staring down at the narrow, ghostly face of the astronautical engineer, Walker's hand shook as she forced herself to press through. Plum's organs were crushed, as were most of the bones in his ribcage and part of his spine. Walker couldn't begin to guess how exactly the damage was caused. The source was a partially-constructed generator built around what many considered to be a magical gravity box that no one understood the properties of.

Even describing the nature of the damage had proven more difficult than expected. The direction of the force wasn't uniform, as it would be from an impact trauma. It was almost like a giant, ethereal hand had reached into Plum's chest cavity and squeezed everything inside. It was beyond strange, and by the end of the third hour, she had exhausted her list of conceivable causes. All she knew was that Plum had suffered greatly, the evidence of which would haunt her forever.

In that very moment, an oddly specific feeling swept through her...the feeling one got when they first consciously recognized they wanted to break up with their significant other—the assured mental preparation before severing a significant connection in one's life.

Walker was done. Not just with the autopsy...

All of it.

She scrubbed her hands in the large basin, wondering what a debriefing process would even look like. Nothing in her imagination seemed realistic; one of the least far-fetched scenarios was an involuntary disappearance. While she didn't fully trust Sutherland, he wanted her around for some reason, so at the end of the day, she met with him. He'd been on site since the incident—Walker couldn't fathom what he was having to do in the wake of it.

Sutherland's office was as luxurious as expected—expensive wood, expensive leather, a bookshelf lined with crystal bottles of spirits. The CEO sat beside a window featuring the best view you could get of a swampy, green lake. The two spoke briefly about her autopsy findings—what constituted an icebreaker in an alien research facility.

"I'll get the rest from your report," he said, narrowing his eyes. "That's not why you're in my office."

"No…" she said slowly.

"You want to leave."

"No!" she said quicker, though it was a lie. "I did want to know what the timeline will be like for restrictions to alleviate—"

"I understand everyone is fatigued."

"More mistakes are going to happen," she said. Less of a lie, more of an intellectual dishonesty. She didn't think Plum had made a mistake.

"If you have a concern, Dr. Walker, speak your mind. I believe I've been exceptionally open with you so far." He spoke with unprecedented force. Walker hesitated out of habit. Regardless of how particular he may have been with the inside information he'd provided, the fact was that he *had* given her a lot of it.

"With some information, but my position on weapons research was clear from the start. Selective candor around that topic would be considered by some as a form of manipulation. I don't assume as much, but it's not the same as transparency."

Epinephrine flooded her brain, speeding it up. She wasn't trying to veer from her original goal, but the point was clear: she wasn't a pawn. A thin smile crawled up the corner of Sutherland's mouth. The inadvertent gulp emitted from Walker's throat blared off the walls.

For what felt like minutes, the suited man stared through her soul.

"Is there something you would like cleared up?" he asked. There were easily *thousands* of questions about Arvonia she wanted answers to, but one stood above the rest.

"Why am I here?"

"Man has been asking that question for thousands of years."

"Funny, but as far as I can tell, my purpose has been filled. I can only think of a few reasons I would be kept on board, primarily to keep tabs on me, but I'd like to know."

"Why do you feel your purpose has been filled?"

"My tasks are all wildly outside of my expertise."

"Are they?"

She took a slow, deep breath. "Yes...this autopsy should have been performed by a pathologist. Diaz has a staff of chemists able to assist him, and most of these tasks could be done by a graduate student. What little work I'm doing in my own field can't even be published."

"Your *field* is not of substantial use, that's true," Sutherland said. "I do believe the species at hand requires a large-scale examination, but it's certainly no reason to keep you here." He stood up and walked over to the bookshelf, looking through the bottles on top. "You know the facility has no direct need for an ecological biologist. Having one on the first contact team was pure chance, which led to your clearance for this position. I'm thrilled for the evolutionary implications of your findings, but your *expertise* is thinking outside the box."

Sutherland grabbed one of the bottles and returned to the desk. "You create unique strategies from completely unrelated disciplines, applying lessons from lower lifeforms to explicitly non-biological problems. That's merely a result of your chosen area of study, though. I've witnessed you taking the same approach with information well outside of your profession. Others encounter problems and use their brainpower as a tool to fix them, but you think for the sake of doing so—you *like* to. Call it curiosity if you will, but it provides you with a much larger toolbox."

Sutherland poured the dark liquid into a couple of matching crystal glasses, offering one to Walker. She shook her head slowly, her brow furrowed as his words sank in. Hearing him describe her processing was discomforting. Maybe it was the assertion that she was somehow unusual.

With a shrug, Sutherland combined both glasses and took a sip. "As to why you're here, that's all part of it. I can trust you will learn the right information from a project and connect it in the future should it become relevant. That may be as vague as an 'X-factor,' but it's unquestionably valuable when researching the unknown. Perhaps most important is your moral character. You're moving towards what is right both validly and morally—I believe it's why you're standing here right now."

"That makes me the canary?" Walker asked, shunning herself for using an animal analogy. It was a common idiom. Canaries once functioned as carbon monoxide alarms in coal mines. They were sensitive to the lethal gas, so when they died, the miners would evacuate.

Plum was dead, Isaac was an alcoholic, Diaz was obsessively looking for global signs of the biochemical weapons he'd inadvertently discovered, and Monroe was one bad day away from murdering someone—if this facility was a coal mine, it was fully collapsing.

"I'd like to think of you more as a moral compass," Sutherland said with a slight smile. "It's an important gauge, being as we're in a constant fight to prevent this facility from becoming the next Manhattan Project."

"This already is the Manhattan Project," she said flatly. If that was a warning he needed to hear, it was long overdue.

The billionaire sighed. "I'm aware…"

"Then I'd like to find out how long debriefing will take."

"Longer than you'd like, I'm sure. I need you to trust me on this." As always, he was calm, which aggravated Walker so much. Acting like he already knew what she was going to say, like everything was going to plan—it wasn't. Plum dying couldn't have been part of the plan.

"Why?" she asked. The CEO paused in a rare moment of frustration, knocking a whole series of events into place for Walker. She hadn't stumbled onto a violent overthrow; she'd been shown it. If the tycoon before her had implied suspicions of foul play to Walker, she would have believed he was disingenuous. His panic was being masked by the aura of control he artfully exuded. Sutherland had given Plum the keys to a multi-billion-dollar technology warehouse that was now crumbling around him.

The Zenaut founder watched Walker as the wheels turned. They shared an unspoken moment of mutual understanding.

"Much of this conversation will be moot in a few days," he finally said. "I have reason to believe there has been a leak."

Walker immediately thought of the alleged engine leak, unable to think of another project that even possessed the capacity for a leak. Work on the engine had stopped, Diaz's lab didn't have any pathogens with—

Information.

"This will either be very good for us, or very bad," Sutherland said. "Either way, the interim will be miserable."

"...*if* there was a leak," she clarified.

He nodded. "Thank you for taking the time to meet with me about the contents of your examination report, Doctor."

Nothing more to say, Walker left the extravagant office. She wanted desperately to ask Fowler if he knew anything about this, but she didn't dare take an action that might implicate either of them before the dominoes fell.

If Hell was anything other than Secretary Karlson's meeting room the day of the leak, Fowler could die fearlessly with his sins.

Earlier in the day, some Arvonian locals showed up at the edge of the facility—unusual, but not concerning. Then, Diaz told Fowler to check the news. Every network was reporting the same story:

aliens were real, they were coming to exterminate us, and the U.S. government was trying to bury that fact. Footage from the first contact was being played on loop, heavily censored for gore on cable networks. They even had the damn autopsy videos.

Paralyzed, Fowler stared unblinkingly at the TV. Just about the only information not released was the location of the base, but the internet had already begun piecing that together, resulting in the onlookers out front. His daze ended when the phone rang, ordering a complete lockdown of the facility.

Completely understandable.

Network servers were crawled in search of the source. They came up with nothing, prompting Karlson to show up and give everyone an old-fashioned, in-person reaming. There weren't many people with access to all of the information released. With only Sutherland and the Zenaut department heads representing the civilian sector, the defense secretary screamed at mostly DoD personnel without pause for the better part of half an hour.

Karlson first pointed his finger at Zenaut, anyway. Their emails, their offices...even their homes were opened up to a full investigation. It was a blatant abuse of their privacy, making Walker's complete lack of protest noteworthy, but Fowler never got an opportunity to grill her about it until the hunt was over. After an exceptionally late night on base, they were further confined to their homes for the following week as Pentagon goons tossed their domiciles and searched their personal computers.

No one from Arvonia—Zenaut or otherwise—was responsible.

A good portion of the public believed the leak to be an elaborate hoax. That was true with any information, regardless of the evidence, but the number was far less than anyone would have guessed. An embarrassing government cover-up was the sort of scandal people could get behind, cleverly naming the event "Alien-gate" and the facility "Area 52." Once satellite photos of the arena-sized spacecraft began trickling in from other nations, reports estimated around 80% of Americans either believed aliens had landed or were unsure.

None of the contact team's identities were included in the leak, nor could they be searched, but death records for Plum had surfaced along with the two researchers who broke the death ray. And with billions of people around the globe repeatedly watching Walker examine an alien corpse, it didn't take long for the scientific community to identify her by voice. Her name started appearing on the news, with clips of her speaking prior to the crash being played alongside the autopsy footage. She continued her home isolation long past the search, and once networks started interviewing Duke professors about her sudden resignation, she turned her phone off entirely.

America's attempt to hide a global threat created some animosity with the United Nations. The Pentagon moved into damage control, beginning with the removal of Karlson as secretary of defense. World leaders demanded an international investigation of the craft, rightfully concerned about the weapons potential. Of course, America denied any foreign inspection on the grounds of national security, though the president publicly shared the world's concern, revealing we'd destroyed the death ray for moral reasons.

No one believed it, least of all the citizens of the U.S.

"Does anyone believe the *United States military* found the most dangerous weapon in the whole universe and destroyed it for the good of mankind?" a late-night host mocked later in the evening. "Why do they always lie like this? Can't they just tell us the truth—that Vice President Murray forgot to take it out of his pocket before going in the lazy river?" An edited image of the vice president riding an inner tube at the water park was included.

Interestingly, no nation could claim rightful ownership of the craft, and even the most restrictive use of salvage law gave possession to America. The technological revelation ended the Second Cold War in its tracks, but the prospect of another world war was on everyone's minds. One in which America stood only with allies it could purchase.

In an attempt to stave off such a conflict while continuing to deny foreign access to the ship, the Pentagon agreed to remove itself from the research entirely, remaining only to prevent espionage. Alien artifacts would be examined by an independent civilian technology company in conjunction with NASA and the CDC when applicable. The president took credit for the compromise, but there was no confusion for Fowler as to who was responsible—everybody got something out of the agreement, but no one got their ideal outcome.

No one but Gabriel Sutherland.

Under DoD protection, Zenaut guaranteed the best defense advancements to America. The president—meaning Sutherland—pledged to donate dozens of power generators to underdeveloped countries when they became available. Findings on the cephrasts would be made publicly accessible across the world, and researchers from United Nations countries would be invited to see it firsthand.

That was the new world order. Sutherland got to develop the most advanced energy systems in history, America further increased its military superiority, and the world received a viable solution to the energy crisis. The only remaining piece was the public, who gained little more than promises of expensive vehicles someday and the worrisome awareness of humanity's eventual extinction. Though thousands of years in the future, every alien-related conversation and technological leap was a reminder of the dismal fate they had no path to prevent.

For that, Sutherland started the Defense of Humanity Initiative.

Raynor continued to be astonished by the level of information given during their training. They learned the physics involved in a craft's movement through space, measurement of graviton thrust—it was a large departure from their experiences in the distant past. Most were told just enough to do their jobs. For Raynor, it was even less. The Martian Militia had to pave all of their own roads.

Eventually, the cadets were introduced to the drone control module, which felt even less like military training than their academic courses. It was like a game, and they all treated it as such.

The control module was simple in design and intricate in function. A desk-sized table projected a three-dimensional starscape with detailed models of surrounding debris—garbage, ships, an occasional meteor… Today, it was just a simulator designed to give them some exposure. In combat, the image was mapped by the large command vessels drone modulators worked from. Drone Control usually parked close to the deployment location to reduce signal delay, but behind a defensive outpost.

Unlike similar holographic displays of the current century, the control module didn't use artificial gravity to generate textures or physical feedback. Their hands moved as freely as they would through air, requiring each motion to be precise. Muscles tightened as their arms darted inside the display and stopped abruptly, and within minutes, Raynor was shaking her limbs out from soreness.

The map's focus changed as they pushed their palm in and out, adjusting the depth at which the display was most opaque. Touching different fingers to their thumbs denoted different instructions, pinching holographic ships to create patrols and order lists. If they felt the urge to, they could give very specific commands to individual ships, separating both hands to enlarge part of the field.

In the 32nd century, Raynor had used a number of piloting simulators for training purposes. You were placed inside a fake cockpit, which was designed to feel as real as possible. This was like playing at a computer, which was perhaps why she couldn't get the hang of it at first. Repeatedly, she touched the wrong fingers together, issuing strikes instead of patrols, accidentally activating retinal commands and sending a convoy thousands of kilometers from their destination.

Never in a million years would she *accidentally* fire a torpedo from a ship she was piloting. It was frustrating.

At one point, her entire squadron was destroyed because she mistakenly adjusted the opacity of the map, solidifying the area closest to her and obstructing everything of importance. It took her some time to figure out why her module had suddenly gone black, and by the time she undid it, the digital space was littered with the holographic debris of her ships.

In the real control module, the drones' individual behaviors were dictated directly by the CAF's primary combat intelligence program. The program wasn't included in the simulator, but some of its routines were incorporated on day three. Complex, coordinated maneuvers could be issued by a single command, performed differently based on the number of ships and their composition.

Whatever minor semblances the holographic display had to a space battle were gone. Without humans inside, the drones weren't restricted to traditional movement patterns in the least. A battlefield of large objects and surfaces was created by dozens or hundreds of ships moving in perfect unison, at odd angles, and with rapid, abrupt changes. Giant vortexes contoured around waves, spirals instantly formed into spheres that collapsed onto targets—whatever formation would get the most ships into firing range at the same instant.

By the fourth day of their control module introduction, the cadets had naturally fallen into discrete clusters of skill levels. Some were naturals, some were terrible at it. The skillsets Raynor had developed in the militia never included handling large numbers of ships whose coordinations were dictated by a computer, so even with noticeable improvement, she felt she was somewhere in the middle. And it wasn't as if she was in a drone-modulator-or-bust scenario—few people in the tech group would end up in this job class. Some had no interest in that amount of responsibility and weren't trying to learn it.

To the excitement of their training group, the last day was largely taken up by skirmishes. Raynor's self-assessment seemed fairly accurate. Clever tactics and maneuver choices led her to victories; clumsiness tallied losses. The end of the course included an organized competition, and while the vibe in the training room continued to be that of play, all of the cadets knew a double-elimination contest had some sort of bearing on whether or not they would return to the modules.

Raynor first tested her skills against some chess grandmaster, finding herself as the pursuer in a bizarre game of cat-and-mouse. Rather than wait it out patiently, she decided to lose half of her ships, instead, with her remaining fleet following shortly after. In similar situations during the revolution, Raynor had simply overtaken her prey through superior piloting. She couldn't help but hear a voice in her head saying, *I could have handled that.* Not wanting to be eliminated in the first group, she played it safe going forward, using tactics she had found to be both effective and boring.

Eliminated technicians stood around watching the dwindling group of remaining cadets, rather than returning to practice as expected. Raynor went another five matches, putting her somewhere in the top 20-30%—a lot further than she had expected to go, but still probably requiring improvement if she wanted the job class.

Her second loss was a massacre. Any sense of improvement she'd built during her four-win streak was demolished with her fleet. She only destroyed two enemy drones, and one of those had been sacrificed as bait. The woman who beat her was young—early to mid-twenties—and remained undefeated through the end.

Watching Teegan Shino carve through fleet after fleet for half an hour made Raynor feel a little better about getting slaughtered. She was fast and precise, appearing almost mesmerized by the display as her hands rapidly darted through the smoky lights. Shino never lost track of a ship; whenever it seemed like something had been missed, she had prepared for it minutes before.

Towards the end, it looked as if their two instructors for the class were coming to send the onlookers back to practice, but they merely watched from the crowd. Shino's arms flew through the projected battlefield, drawing paths and issuing commands. She annihilated every person she faced through the last—a famous general from 67th century Titan whose name was taught during typical modulator training. This girl wasn't just setting the curve for their academy class…she was setting it for the job class.

For the majority of the training group, it was the end of their time on the control module. Some would be practicing off and on until their job assignments came through—a group Raynor intended to include herself in. The control module lacked all of the excitement she got from piloting, but it attracted her far more than the other tech-based jobs, and she wasn't skilled enough as a soldier for anything remotely specialized.

Once their course had concluded, a small crowd gathered around Shino. Every aspiring drone modulator wanted to pick her brain.

"How much interactive fleet command did you do?" one asked.

"We didn't have anything like that!" Shino giggled. "I'm just a hardcore gamer."

"You mean…like digital games?"

"Yup!"

"Then what did you do in the military?"

Shino laughed. "Nothing. Gaming *was* my job."

"You were paid to…play games?"

"I only got paid if I won, but I won every year. I also had *tons* of sponsors!"

Raynor's eyes bulged. The notion of sending someone here with such a career seemed foolish by all traditional measurements, but in a room of the best strategists, pilots, tank operators, and programmers in human history, the most valuable asset was a girl whose life had been spent playing computer games. Professionally.

Shino struggled to hold back more laughter at the shocked faces, unbothered by the bombardment of questions thrown at her. Raynor didn't feel like adding to the mob, and with how much time she planned to spend on the module simulators, she would certainly cross paths with Shino again.

Exiting the simulator banks, Raynor overheard one of the eager cadets starting up with more questions.

"When was this?"

"Pretty much right up until we left," Shino said, "in 2030."

14

SALVATION

In the year following the leak, Walker's staff doubled in size. Her department had been renamed "Xenobiology," extending far beyond the inspection of alien cadavers. Biochemistry and cryptography now took up a substantial portion of her department, so rather than repeatedly borrowing resources from Diaz and Monroe, Walker had chemists and decipherers in her staff.

Logs pertaining to medicines, lower lifeforms, and ancient history were combined to build an accurate picture of extraterrestrial life. By the summer of 2026, using xenobiology to gain insight into terrestrial life was a routine process. For instance, the cephrasts had medical procedures for curing harmful cell mutations. Those that relied less on their anatomy had begun to show promising applications in human tumor removal.

No specifics had been outlined regarding Sutherland's Defense of Humanity Initiative—shorthanded as DOHI—since its inception the autumn before. In early August, he came to Arvonia to move it forward with one of his signature sales pitches.

Half a dozen reporters were camped out in the small lecture hall when Walker arrived, each with a DoD escort and no recording equipment. They pounced the moment she entered, asking about aliens, Sutherland, DOHI, her work—anything they could get a quote for. The scene had an amusingly antiquated feel. Journalists hunched over notepads with eager pens, trying to edge their questions in.

Walker declined to comment.

Once the auditorium filled up about halfway with site personnel, Sutherland joined them.

"I share everyone's concerns regarding our planet's fate. The Defense of Humanity Initiative has not been dormant over the past eleven months, but rather deliberating. With our eradication weighing heavily, the question becomes, what can *we* do—right now—to give our future society aid?"

He waited, as if expecting someone to answer, but was met only by the sound of scribbling journalists. Each correspondent wrote Sutherland's speech down word-for-word.

"When our invaders arrive, their technology will be far superior. We're already racing to match their 5000-year-old machines. Our greatest advantage in this struggle is time, and our greatest asset is the same one it has always been—" he paused for dramatic effect, looking across the reporters. "People. Our best and brightest can achieve far more than our complacent, war-free invaders. If we could send our most skilled fighters—groomed over thousands of years—to the time they're needed, would they not make the most effective use of whatever technology *is* available in that century? If we could send warriors such as Alexander the Great, Yue Fei, and Vlad the Impaler into the future to defend us from extermination, we would be remiss not to try. They may be dead, but their future counterparts are yet to be born."

One of the reporters snickered. "Are you saying you have a time machine or something?"

"Something." The CEO smiled at the reporter as if they were but a simple child and time machines were commonplace. "With the technology in development, not only will it be possible to send people into the distant future, but we can ensure that said future is entirely free of global warming."

"I—what?" the reporter stuttered. "How?" For the first time, low whispers came from the attendees.

"Three words—super-graviton propulsion. Powerful, renewable, and emission-free. The creatures who arrived on our planet traveled for five thousand years, but did so at such intense speeds, they only experienced the passing of a few."

At any other location, the proposal would be pure eccentricity. The attendees were frozen as they weighed the possibility. The cephrasts would be fewer in number and superior in technology. Arming billions of civilians was one thing, but combing through a pool of *trillions* of people and taking the top billionth of a percent... that might have a significant per-capita impact.

"You really think you can convince people to do that?" another reporter asked. "This is a one-way trip, right?"

Sutherland nodded somberly. "We've been sending our children on one-way trips for generations. These candidates aren't unable to return because they're fueling a war complex. They're traveling to *the future.*" He tittered. "I assure you, we won't need to convince anyone."

After outlining the planned itinerary, which included a proof of concept within two years, Sutherland took a few more questions. What "proof of concept" meant, he didn't elaborate. When Zenaut researchers finally left the auditorium, conversing animatedly, Kahlil found his way to Walker.

"I'm not sure what to think," he said, dazed.

"Is it doable?"

"Absolutely. It's what the engine was designed to do. The condenser actually works *more* efficiently when it's exerting thrust, so aside from requiring a massive charge to get going, it won't even undergo very much stress. Is the *idea* doable? That's up for debate."

"Do you think anyone would volunteer?"

"Honestly? If someone offered me a trip to the future—even without a return trip—how could I say no?"

"A number of ways."

Sutherland slowly shifted towards the two directors, bouncing between follow-up questions from the media.

"What did you think?" It seemed somewhat rhetorical.

"Very ambitious."

"Quite the presentation."

He soon pulled Walker off to the side, out of earshot of the lingering reporters discussing the information they'd just received.

"I know you're busy with the xenobiology sector, but I'd also like you to start getting your headspace around DOHI. Once the technology is solidified and we're past the practical experiments, there will be countless variables at play. I don't want anything overlooked."

"I can do that," she said. At this point, being asked to weigh in on seemingly random topics was normal for her—it wasn't as if she wouldn't be thinking about it anyway.

"Not just operational details like candidates and outfitting the ship—an integral part of this is ensuring the information we have remains accurate through the years."

"Like bringing unencrypted cephrast logs on the ship?"

"And tissue samples." His eyes narrowed intensely. "I'd also like you to consider the idea of going on the ship..."

Her brain did somersaults. "You mean...when it's moving? To the future?"

"It's a big question, I know, but you have years to mull it over. The only way to ensure the ball doesn't get dropped is to have someone carry it through to the end, and who better than the founder of xenobiology?"

"Probably a juggler."

The question plagued her mind for the rest of the day. It would be a couple of years before they were even testing the mechanics of time travel. There was no reason to obsess over it right now, but she was.

Three years ago—*only* three years ago—Theodore Plum had glossed over the concept of time dilation and asked if she would hypothetically be willing to cram herself in a small ship for six years.

Never, she'd said.

What if it were only one?

Still, no.

That wasn't the answer she heard in her head now. At the time, they hadn't fully believed there would be an alien craft in the forest. Today, it wasn't hypothetical. It was a real decision with significant consequences.

The next day, she told Fowler what Sutherland had asked her, only to learn he'd been asked as well.

"Are you considering it?" she asked as casually as she could.

"Of course not. Why? Are you?"

"I don't think so, no…"

The certainty in his voice was staggering. He said it as if he'd been raised with the long-held conviction of *not* cramming himself into a tiny ship. Fowler knew, definitively, he wasn't going, which made Walker realize she was legitimately considering it.

A working prototype of the ship's engine was ready in mid-2028, about the size of a barn. A massive solar array of "total energy" panels spanned the fields around Arvonia Base to charge the large device, though it wasn't really *charging*, per se. The panels absorbed photons and gravitons, using solar radiation to power the converter, which, in turn, created the graviton condensate.

News of the working prototype was a major headline. The engine was nowhere near small enough for a commercial vehicle, nor efficient enough to power a town, but the amount of energy being stored was seemingly impossible. Largely because it wasn't storing energy as a battery did—it was storing pure force.

Mastery of the components had begun to awaken Sutherland's dream of powerful, renewable energy. Even at this stage, they could use the engine to rotate a turbine with significant energy loss and still have the most efficient renewable energy system. And while graviton-based cars were probably centuries away, the semi-truck-sized graviton engine did fit perfectly into a large, interstellar ship, maintaining Sutherland's DOHI schedule of a 2030 launch.

It was around that time that Zenaut commenced with their "practical test" of the desired time dilation effect. Three small probes were launched with synchronized clocks into space using a weaker, photon-based engine. Weaker, but still capable of flinging the small bots into space at two hundred g-forces.

The probes flew in a giant loop, returning to Earth. Each spent roughly three and a half days accelerating and braking, cruising for a day in the middle at slightly different top speeds. Specifically, 99%, 99.9%, and 99.99% of the speed of light. All three ships came back with four days and fifteen hours on their clocks, but at much different times. The first returned after twenty-one days, the second arrived another week later, and the last ship didn't touch the atmosphere for seventy-six days total.

The Defense of Humanity Initiative was on course. The condenser would need to run for two years for their ship, *Salvation*, to make a full trip. To attain their desired ratio of time distortion, 3500:1, the ship would have to cruise within fifty kilometers per hour of lightspeed.

Zenaut's business soared as preliminary orders for the graviton generator filled up for their estimated 2032 completion. In a less public deal, the Pentagon began construction of a new fighter jet, appropriately dubbed the Z-0 "lift-less" craft.

Sutherland never followed up with Walker regarding her decision on being aboard *Salvation* when it launched. Neither of them had mentioned it in the two years since he'd asked her, though he had no real need to remind her. It wasn't like she would forget.

"I don't think I can say no..." she blurted out spontaneously after the last probe landed. He didn't ask what she was referring to, as if he already knew what she was going to say, which wouldn't surprise her in the least.

With the Pentagon taking an exclusively defense-based role for the past four years, Fowler's time at the base had waned considerably. That wasn't to say he had nothing to do for Sutherland. The Zenaut CEO had become increasingly paranoid over the years about attempts on his life.

Rightfully so. Like the fossils that fueled it, the oil industry was on the brink of extinction, and with thousands of people being killed for those profits, Sutherland was spending nearly two million dollars each year on personal security. It hadn't been for nothing. During that time, Fowler's team had nipped a few issues in the bud. Not attempts on Sutherland's life—more like feelers to see how easy it might be.

The team was top-notch, which had afforded Fowler the ease of taking a sabbatical in early 2029. He'd spent that time in Northwestern Memorial Hospital. His mother was moved there after her condition deteriorated and exploratory surgery revealed late-stage stomach cancer. The ailment had been ruled out years before. None of her doctors knew whether it had developed independently of her other symptoms, as a result of them, or if it had progressed slowly with untypical symptoms, but it made little difference. Her five-year survival chance was 4%.

Fowler spent a few months in Chicago, more certain than ever he wouldn't be boarding *Salvation*. His mother urged him not to stay on Earth on her account, which he promised he wouldn't—but that was a lie.

She also relentlessly scolded him for blaming himself. He knew there were other factors in their extermination, but the bottom line was...he sealed the coffin. They'd had the conversation numerous times, and it never went anywhere—scripted lines they'd rehearsed over and over again. After weeks in Northwestern Memorial, she finally went off-book.

"Do me a favor," she said deceptively from the hospital bed. "Stop beating yourself up."

"I'm not beating myself up," he said routinely.

"You absolutely are! And I can't reckon why. If you'd stood there and done nothing, you all would have been killed and we'd never know what was coming."

"That's…true," he said. It gave him pause. Nobody had said that before, and to their knowledge, she wasn't wrong. The idea stuck with him, though it didn't fully absolve his guilt. The cephrasts might never have sent the signal at all if he hadn't killed them. Still, there was a version of this where humanity's extermination came, unbeknownst to them all.

"You say that like I don't already know," his mother said.

"If it's not my fault, then there's *really* no reason to board the ship."

"I thought you were considering it because you save people, not to fix some mistake you think you made." She waved the latter idea off, and while her words may have sparked a new internal conflict for Fowler—one without an answer—he was at least able to watch news of DOHI's progress without being "mopey" as she called it.

Fowler spent a lot of his time in Chicago at the hospital. Seeing his mother in the late stages of cancer was difficult, but even when her energy was drained from chemo, she was still herself. If it weren't for her medical condition, the visit would have been delightful.

She didn't make it through the summer. For the weeks leading up to her passing, they'd known she didn't have long, but it didn't make it any easier to handle.

He sorted through her affairs before returning to Virginia. Her words carried with him, echoing through his head, making the debate within him more complex than it had been the year before, but at the same time, also clearer, somehow. There were countless ways to look at the situation, bouncing between penance, atonement, and duty.

All three took him to the same place—he had to see this through to the end, even if that happened in the year twelve-thousand-something.

He also wouldn't mind a hoverboard.

Upon his return to Virginia and subsequent change of heart regarding the space road-trip, *Salvation* was near completion. With Walker a few weeks away from her last book tour, it was time to prepare a crew.

Real astronauts spent years in training, learning just about everything, but Zenaut's approach was more compartmentalized. The dozen members of *Salvation's* crew would undergo training to function in space, but rather than give all of them extensive education on medicine and physics, they'd simply bring people with those skillsets. Brody Kahlil wasn't a soldier by any means, but he was well-versed in both the construction of the ship and the forces it would undergo during travel. Their voyage would be crushing Apollo 10's record for fastest human travel by over one billion kilometers per hour.

Kahlil also wanted to go—invasion or not—and Monroe didn't.

Finding the nine best soldiers on Earth was an ordeal, in no small part because the criteria was mostly subjective. There were a few clear choices, and their responses varied from "never" to "I'd do anything." Eventually, Zenaut's selection narrowed down, and to their own credit, Fowler thought all nine were well above his own abilities. Two of their clear choices had joined—a retired Mossad agent and a Navy medic whose acquisition meant they wouldn't have to dedicate a spot for a physician.

After the nine recruits began psychological evaluations, Sutherland added a civilian into the mix—no preface or dossier. Neither Fowler nor Walker was keen to consider another civilian, especially after selecting nine combat veterans, but Sutherland had already scheduled a meet for the three at a seaside restaurant in Manhattan.

"I have to apologize," Walker told the woman after they sat. "Neither of us is familiar with your work, but Mr. Sutherland feels it's impressive. What industry are you in?"

"Esports!" the woman piped cheerily. "Strategy games, specifically. I've never lost a tournament, and I have more global wins than any other four players combined!"

Fowler rested his hand against his forehead. That was why Sutherland didn't provide any information about her. He'd gotten so used to browsing dossiers that he didn't even think to search this woman's name. At least they got a free day-trip to New York.

"I think there's been a miscommunication," Walker said tactfully. "We're recruiting combat veterans to potentially go to war, the exceptions being myself and an astrophysicist who has also been studying the cephrasts for the last six years."

"Oh, I know!" she squeaked. "That's what Gabe and I talked about." It took Fowler a moment to realize "Gabe" was Sutherland. "Ten thousand years is a *long* time. There'll be remote-controlled mechs and space robots and stuff like that. I know mechs aren't my specialty, but I learn controls super fast. It's kind of my thing."

They were already here, and Shino had flown in all the way from Hokkaido, so they listened to the teen's pitch—just in case they decided to go down the remote-controlled war machine path. She was surprisingly well-prepared, including a folder with pages of stats and metrics.

Shino was brilliant in her own right and a prodigy of strategy games, which involved quick thinking, clever tactics, and lightning reflexes. She'd built her first computer at nine and won her first major league tournament at the 2024 Esports World Championship Games, making her a millionaire overnight at fourteen. She held a number of records, including the only person to win three different EWCG championships in the same year, and was argued to be the most dominant contender in any competitive sport—gaming or otherwise. The multilingual youth was a big-name celebrity in the gaming community, touting some of the most-watched streams in the world and a plethora of marketing deals with gaming companies, netting her almost as much income as her thirty global tournament victories.

It was all impressive, but Fowler didn't know how truly relevant it would be. He waited to see if Walker had something clever to say, but she was in the same boat. Shino was young, and his instinct was to dissuade her, but he was even younger when he'd enlisted in the army.

"I'm not saying there isn't some sense to this," he finally said as he peered across the document, "but it's all going to be speculation. You understand we're asking people to leave their former lives for a future we know nothing about?"

"That's the appeal!" She smiled infectiously. "It's the *future*. And not in the way tomorrow is, you know?"

There was no question about her inherent capability for strategic game theory. It was also hard to fault her for a career path that had made her a rich, pop-culture icon. She was willing to abandon that fame and fortune for something more important, and as explained by her, if it turned out there was no invasion, she'd get to see the future—something she couldn't afford with a hundred years of championships.

By the end of their lunch, Walker and Fowler agreed the gaming virtuoso would be an unconventionally good addition. Whatever the future held, it was almost impossible for there *not* to be a plethora of virtually-interfaced defense tools, and the inclusion of Teegan Shino would certainly boost DOHI's image. Unfortunately, the ship was full. It wasn't so much a problem with the number of beds, but rather the food stores and water supply. Though, if they expected to go five years without killing each other, they'd also need some room.

As luck would have it, one of their initial selections scrubbed out of their psychological evaluation a few days later, so they gave Shino a call.

After realizing that was an error, they messaged her on social media.

With a few minutes to kill before his future crewmates arrived to tour the Arvonia base, Fowler flipped through channels on the small TV across from his desk. It was the Friday before Thanksgiving, and while most of their visitors weren't American, the base was. *Salvation* was finished, had completed several successful test flights, and would be a complete zoo throughout winter as it was supplied and furnished.

He left the TV on a daytime talk show featuring Walker, discussing her plainly-titled *Xenobiology: The First Study of Alien Life.* When the gates opened for her to publish her findings, Sutherland did everything he could to get it done this year. The launch was on-schedule for next spring, and he wanted the publicity.

Walker's experience as an interviewee showed, and since all of the hosts asked her the same questions, her responses had become well-rehearsed. Fowler generally didn't watch her interviews anymore. He'd already heard every question multiple times. There just wasn't anything on at nine-thirty a.m. As the host began diving into questions about the extermination signal, the last of *Salvation's* soon-to-be crew began making their way through the security gate. Walker wasn't allowed to give any information about the signal, the base, or research outside of her book, so her responses would be polite refusals.

Fowler meandered to the front, fetching their nine visitors with Kahlil. The base's security fell within the Defense Counterintelligence and Security Agency, meaning half a dozen DCSA agents joined them on their tour of the ship to ensure no one wandered off.

Salvation was large—in the same ballpark as the derelict cephrast ship. Previous spacecraft were made as compact as possible to reduce weight, so the extreme amount of thrust being produced by *Salvation's* engine allowed for a roomier interior, which was designed with the futuristic aesthetic of nearly every sci-fi movie.

Sheer, white walls lined the rooms and halls with cabinets and drawers that collapsed back into them. The craft housed a large canteen, a lounge, and a full gymnasium, along with spaceship necessities like a bridge, an engine room, storage areas, medical facilities, and a hydroponics lab.

Zenaut had been woefully unable to duplicate some technologies from the cephrast ship that were relevant to *Salvation*. Namely, the thrust panels forming the central ring and the gravity tiles adorning its floors. The human ship featured traditional thrusters, each exhausting the engine's unique fuel in a single direction like a turbine. In lieu of artificial gravity, the ship simulated gravity through acceleration—pushing the floor up to their feet at the speed of Earth's gravity. During their multi-year turnaround, the ship would rotate to place their feet towards the outside of the arc, eventually pivoting the floor in front of them during the year-long braking period. It was crude, but artificial gravitons were supposedly centuries away.

Winter flew by as the crew underwent their simplified astronaut training. Zenaut made as much ruckus as possible, which Walker aptly referred to as "the single greatest act of capitalism in human history." Every person on the planet was watching the event unfold, and in turn, acutely following the development of city-wide power generators. The bar for billionaire activism and its resulting profits was forever raised.

None of it was of great concern to Fowler—they could read about it in the future.

By their launch date on May 25th, each passenger had taken care of their effects, which felt uncomfortably akin to dying. Shino created several foundations and a slew of scholarship programs. Fowler donated his comparatively meager estate to the Veterans' Association, sans some personal effects that went to his cousins. Two of their new roommates opened bank accounts with accrued interest. Neither really believed the institutions would survive the next ten thousand years—it was sort of like a lottery ticket.

Media swarmed the solar array surrounding the ship to cover the launch. The event was a nightmare for the Department of Defense, giving Fowler more than a little joy. Sutherland gave a boisterous speech about the planet's future before a slew of tearful goodbyes from the crew's family, including Fowler's aunt, uncle, and stepdad.

Lying on their backs in harnessed seats, the countdown ended, and *Salvation* was pushed into the sky. Lift-off was surprisingly gentle—not quite as bad as a roller coaster loop, but they had to endure it for a while. After about eight minutes of constant updates from Zenaut and NASA, the pressure on their spines lightened, no different than lying down with their legs elevated. The ship slowly rotated, keeping the thrusters in position as the weight on Fowler's back rotated beneath his seat, and before long, he was sitting in a chair in his new home.

The dozen passengers wearily unbuckled their seats and stood up.

They made it.

"Uh—Salvation to Ground Control," Kahlil said into his headset as he tapped through screens on a nearby display. "We're up and about. All is well on our end."

An eruption came in response to the record-breaking success. *Salvation* was now the largest object sent into space. Not by a huge margin, but previous ships had been more than 90% fuel, making *Salvation* by far the largest shuttle.

Shino bounced up and down lightly, as if testing the integrity of their gravity and finding no fault. It still hadn't sunk in for Fowler. Standing aboard the ship didn't feel much like being in outer space, more like they were locked in a building on Earth, reporting to someone outside as they checked systems and ensured the building was running properly. They'd moved into this strange apartment building, and in five years, they'd move back out.

But as days turned into months, the ship's speed increased and their time became noticeably slower. Signals from Earth began arriving with dates several years in the future, and as they approached their cruising speed, the messages became few and far between. Most signals were too weak to make it to them, and the rest struggled to catch up to *Salvation's* increasingly rapid pace. Kahlil assured them that once they started turning back to Earth, messages would catch up quickly, revealing thousands of years of history yet to be written.

15

2130 A.D.

A blast of heated concrete knocked Veektor Nabokov onto his side while diving behind the ruins of what was once a church. The Federal Security Service agent achingly stood up, allowing his hearing and vision to fade back in.

Shell shock was what the Americans called it—greatly preferred to the alternative.

Nabokov hadn't actually seen the incoming artillery. The moment it was in sight, digital metrics in his helmet highlighted the mortar shell, displaying trajectory, size, maximum blast radius, and impact time. It was the only reason he wasn't inside the resulting crater. And while countless successful outcomes for this mission involved his own demise, he needed to get closer before anything could happen to him.

Rather, before anything happened to the twenty-kilogram nuclear explosive on his back. The CaTNE technology—a Contained Tactical Nuclear Explosive—was stolen from the U.S. at the beginning of World War III. It had given the allied nations an early fighting chance against the western juggernaut.

Scrambling to his feet, Nabokov checked his payload before continuing down the bombed-out street. No one had shown up after the ordnance struck, and his metrics showed nothing more than the standard display—time, coordinates, and vitals. The shell wasn't intended for him. Just sporadic firing.

Kazan had been Nabokov's home during his early twenties. The Tatarstan capital sat about five hundred kilometers east of Moscow, and for two hundred years, it had been a beacon of industry and art —now a graveyard of history, once home to universities, museums, and manufacturing plants. Every building above one story was reduced to rubble. Half of the remainder were, as well.

While unrecognizable, the streets were still familiar to Nabokov. His familiarity wasn't required for the mission, but a bonus none-theless. Few in the Russian Federation were trained to handle the dangerous explosives he carried, and only a handful of them pos-sessed the infiltration skills required to plant it in an enemy base. The missions were risky, but it was the most reliable method for leveling an American stronghold. With a lock on salvaged alien technology, the United States had dominance over the skies and impenetrable missile defense systems. They could strike from anywhere on the globe, but that didn't make their rapidly expand-ing foothold in Kazan any less worrisome for Moscow.

Alerted of an approaching craft, an AC-500 Comet, Nabokov ducked into half of an old market, praying he wasn't seen. The material of his dark-grey, subdued urban camouflage was designed to mask his heat signatures from thermal scanning, absorbing excess heat into a cartridge on his side, but the thermal shroud only worked to a certain extent. If the Comet was looking for him, it would find him. He was near enough to his target now for his death to destroy part of the facility, but it wouldn't be enough to stop it from operating.

Still, it would be quite a sight for the remote pilot. Finding Nabokov's signature and putting a missile into the market, only to lose all contact with the aircraft the moment it struck.

According to Veektor's helmet, the magnetic whir of the Comet faded ninety-six seconds later. Distant gunfire ceased from time to time, isolating the sound of Nabokov's boots as they stomped through the concrete gravel towards the end of Dekabristoy Street. Most of his journey was spent traversing surrounding roads. The wide avenue was ideal for troop movement, making it dangerous, but it also T'd right into the walls of the American base, so he followed it for the last few kilometers.

Ahead of schedule, he waited in the ruins for dusk. The twilight darkness afforded him the option to stay hidden, but it was also easier to blend in when the base was active. The day shift was wrapping up their work, trying to get home as the night shift settled in. It was the ideal time for Nabokov to belong to either group.

The setting sun triggered his visor's night-assist lighting, illuminating the street before him in a faint, green glow. Most ground troops wore heavy helmets, completely covering their faces in bulletproof metals while displaying the world around them digitally, including far more advanced visual assistance than Nabokov's visor. It was ideal for firefights, but the virtual displays could be tricked in a number of ways. Anti-infiltration traps used them all, so he couldn't rely on the imaging of a facial shield.

Two men were highlighted as they came into view from beyond a corner that once held a post office. They were armed, wearing fatigues, but otherwise unarmored. A patrol. Nabokov crouched quietly behind the burned chassis of an old electric car, pulling carefully on the sole remaining door, which eventually gave way with a metallic *clunk*.

He froze. The sound amplified through the concrete valley. The patrol continued across the avenue without pause.

Nabokov gently rested the silencer of his Dezkani .50-caliber combat rifle on the windowless door, his visor providing range statistics in lieu of a scope. Bright outlines covered the closer man's body as the two walked, nearly crossing the street before lining up together. Ignoring the targeting, Nabokov lowered his aim a fraction of a degree, sending the high-caliber round through the back of the closest soldier's neck—roughly head-level of the man behind him. A puff of hot air hit Nabokov's face as a soft, low *thump* emitted from the end of the barrel.

Before their bodies hit the ground, Nabokov was running to the end of the street, sticking to the western shadows while he approached the side of the compound.

The shorter of the two men was close to Veektor's size, which was fortunate because the taller one's collar was spattered with his blood. Nabokov dragged the bodies into the corner building and changed. The uniform was snug, but he wasn't planning on doing any aerobics.

"Unit 1525—Control. Please update."

Shit.

Nabokov hastily checked his new pockets, searching for a badge to figure out if the radio call was for this patrol. He found badge 9321 in his breast pocket and tossed it, riffling the other American's body. If he had to answer the radio call, he might be in trouble. His English was flawless, but probably didn't sound like either of the men. The badge wasn't in the other man's breast pocket, not on his belt, not in either front pocket—

"Control—1525," another voice came over the radio. "Still code four."

Sighing in relief, Nabokov found the second badge in the soldier's inside pocket—1278.

His weapon and helmet would draw suspicion inside the base, so he left them both in the building as he made his way inside. Getting in wasn't much of a problem. Getting to the center, burying the warhead, and getting out was trickier. He walked purposefully but not urgently through the large base that spanned several city blocks of Kazan. With all of the U.S. buildings, it was difficult to tell where he was. There should be a park further in—the old Wedding Palace. The ground would be soft, and the edge of the park should be central enough to encompass the entire base in the primary blast.

He must have appeared lost—which he was, but he wasn't supposed to look it—because an officer stopped him to ask where he was heading. It was innocent enough, but Nabokov couldn't remember which name was on his shirt. A sloppy mistake—he knew better. He didn't dare look, so he had a 50/50 chance of saying the other patrol guard's name.

"Corporal Tanner, cleared for a 10-100." Nabokov always used the bathroom as an excuse if he was questioned. Everyone had to go at some point.

The officer stared quizzically at Nabokov, trying to figure out if he'd seen his face before. It happened every time, usually ending safely. Nobody in the American military took much notice of those below them because—in Nabokov's opinion—they were all assholes.

Thankfully, the officer didn't ask to see the badge containing a picture of the dead man back in the rubble. The American also didn't seem to notice the backpack slung over Nabokov's shoulder, though an excuse was lined up for it, as well. The key was selling a story, and a pompous joke about a dead Ruskie always prevented a bag search.

Well, one time it didn't, but that's why silencers existed.

"Hurry up, then," the officer commanded, sending Nabokov on his way.

Fortune continued to smile on the FSS operative as he reached the edge of the Wedding Palace. The park's open area was being used for the base's vehicle depot, which would normally be towards the edge of the military stronghold.

Locating the building closest to the edge of the park, Nabokov tucked himself behind it, dropping the bag heavily in the dirt and removing a collapsible shovel. It only took a minute to dig the meter-deep hole, and the CaTNE was active a few seconds after he placed it inside. The device didn't show a timer, but he knew he had five minutes. Throwing both the bag and shovel into the hole, he hastily kicked the loose dirt over all three, stomping it down. No one would likely notice disturbed dirt behind the building, but if they did, Nabokov didn't want it to be obvious that something was buried there. It was technically possible for a skilled demolitions expert to uncover and disarm the bomb in a few minutes.

Trotting to the motor pool, he scanned for occupied vehicles. The only person in the lot was standing near a Zenaut bike, which would do. The bike used a smaller version of the engine found in the Comet aircraft, which made it exceptionally fast. It was exposed and unarmored, but fast was almost as good.

The darkening sky made details of the park difficult to make out, providing extra cover as he unholstered his Ruger and took out the would-be driver. He checked through the park briefly to see if he'd gained any attention before rifling through the dead soldier's pockets.

No key turned up. Panic struck Nabokov. He'd already wasted some time, and if he wanted to reach the three-kilometer minimum safety zone, he only had a couple of minutes to get the bike moving. He looked around the motor pool for a vehicle that he was more adept at hot-wiring. Maybe one that didn't require a starter or was already running. There should be multiple people heading towards vehicles at this time, but no one else was making their way to the motor pool.

Frantically, he checked the body again, emptying every pocket into the matted grass—badge 3198, a knockoff pocketknife, an access card for a building that was about to be…

No. Not a building. The small white card was adorned with the Zenaut logo—the proximity starter for the bike.

Pocketing the small rectangle, he jumped on the motorcycle, its engine firing up with a whoosh as he fingered the starter. Without delay, he twisted the throttle.

The bike lurched with frightening speed, nearly sending Nabokov off the back as he blazed through the compound. Indistinguishable shouts began when he got halfway through the facility, and by the time he heard the sound of nearby gunfire picking up, he was at the exit. Guards on each side of the gate joined in after failing to slide the large metal doors closed in time, their bullets whizzing past Nabokov as he blew by at two hundred kilometers per hour. With no time to stop for his gun and helmet, he pushed the bike to its limits, weaving through the battle-torn terrain.

Years ago, Zenaut attempted to make the hoverbike everyone dreamed of: the Light Spear. It never caught on, feeling more like a hovercraft with a saddle due to the large engines. Right now, Nabokov would have loved a Light Spear. As the motorcycle's speedometer passed 250, anything larger than a pebble threatened to buck him off the seat.

Both the three-kilometer mark and the five-minute mark grew nearer as the engine hummed beneath him. The road took a slight bend to the left, revealing piles of debris littering the ground from a nearby building. He jerked the bike to the side, falling into a skid as the tires lost traction.

The pavement ripped his pant leg off, continuing through to burning skin. The road rash may have been another godsend—he was only moving around 100kph when the bottom of the bike collided with the pile of concrete. Nabokov did his best to angle his head away from the ground as he soared through the air, managing to rotate enough to collide shoulder-first with the street. Pain seared through his body as cracks and tears shot along his arm, shoulder, and side. He bounced, flipping over and hitting the ground with his back as he slid to a stop.

Groaning as he struggled to keep consciousness, he stared up at the starry sky with no energy to scream in pain. The warhead went off shortly after, beginning with the brief sound of air being pulled into a vacuum before the familiar, vibrating boom of a thermonuclear explosion.

Then everything went black.

Fowler stirred awake at the sound of his morning alarm. Rather, it would have been morning on the East Coast in America. Aboard *Salvation*, it was just dark, but the alarm was set to go off at 0630. Blindly, he reached over to stop the soft, irritating bell, the action of which brightened his cabin with warm, yellow light. A remarkably accurate approximation of the morning sun.

"No...this is too early," Shino groaned, wrapping her arm over her eyes.

"I get up at this time every day."

"And it's dumb. Nobody's here to make you go to Army homeroom or whatever you call it."

"Definitely not that..."

He walked naked to the sheer closet of the small cabin. It opened into the empty space beside the bed, which provided just enough room to stretch out but not much more. A computer connected to the ship's intranet sat on the desk at the foot of the bed. The bed itself was not designed for two people.

There hadn't been much for Fowler to do over the past year. Walker studied meticulously and wrote papers no one would read for thousands of years, Conway filled the role of their doctor, Shino played an unhealthy amount of video games...Fowler woke up early, trained, and tried to keep himself sharp. Every few weeks, he'd have a dream about landing in the future, the one from *Back to the Future Part II*, and he was embarrassingly out-skilled by the basic infantry of the era. The dream was different every time, but the key points stayed the same, and that was enough to drive him.

Salvation still operated on twenty-four-hour days, though, and he could only spend so much time doing drills. Even with eight full hours of sleep each night, he had a lot of free time. With the majority of Earth's film history on their drive, the crew started doing a weekly movie night to build camaraderie and all that. One recently turned into a drinking game for many of them. Fowler couldn't remember exactly how it had started, but after a couple of hours, most of the crew had passed out or gone to bed, eventually leaving just him and Shino.

The gaming celebrity sat up on the edge of the bed and started dressing, presumably to return to her own room and go back to sleep.

"Hey, so I just want to make sure we're on the same page about all of this," she said, contorting her arms while she pulled her top over her head. "That it's nothing serious, I mean."

"Yeah, I know," Fowler droned as he pulled up his gym shorts.

"Good. It's fun and all…and I think you're super cool for an old guy. I just think it would make things *way* complicated on the ship."

"*Wow*. I'm only thirty-three. Wait…thirty-four?"

"That's what I'm saying! Also, my boyfriend would get crazy jealous."

Fowler laughed. "You mean the one on Earth?"

"Yeah…" she rolled her eyes. "He's such the jealous type. We can't have you being haunted by the ghost of an obsessive streamer while you're shooting aliens. He low-key probably never moved on from me."

"I'm sure…" Fowler said idly, lacing up his sneakers. "You coming here tonight?"

"It's not like I've got a lot of options," she teased. Patting him on the head as she left.

16

MOSCOW

Moscow felt more like home to Nabokov than Penza—his actual home, which was demolished early in the war. After Kazan, he had been forced into medical leave to heal his injuries—two broken ribs, torn nerves and muscles in his shoulder, a ton of tissue damage through his leg, and a major concussion. His scars should heal most of the way, but he had more than enough to care.

His recuperation had taken place in Hungary. The country was landlocked by allies, making it one of the safest places in Europe. The Russia-Ukraine border, on the other hand, had become arguably the largest battlefield of World War III.

The capital was serene and unharmed. Long-distance attacks on the city had been held off admirably by large, automated anti-air cannons scattered throughout the city. Moscow was under constant bombardment when the war started. Orbital strikes, ICBMs, bomber swarms…every single armament in the American arsenal. The U.S. had spent so much money trying to take Moscow, Nabokov's training class had a pool going to guess how long the daily onslaught would continue. It went on well after they graduated. Nabokov had overshot it by a month.

He walked through the base to his destination—an administrative building on the other side of the compound. He'd been debriefed in the hospital twice, but it wasn't unusual in his line of work to have it happen again. When an American base was vaporized, Nabokov always found himself being questioned by an officer he'd never met, asking him if he had noticed something oddly-specific—a box, a word, a person. Once, they asked him if he'd seen a German spy, which would have defeated their purpose entirely.

Arriving at the northern edge of the base, he discovered his destination to be the offices of General Poval, the head of the Russian Federation. Nabokov started wracking his brain to remember details from Kazan—men in fancy suits, strange vehicles, a blue container with the number 12 written on it. He waited outside the door until precisely 0900 hours, at which point a Federal Security Agent came out to wave him in.

General Poval stood in the large office. A tall man, weathered from years of commanding the bloodiest war in history. He had a chest full of medals and insignias, a sidearm on his hip, and a cigar in his lapel. Most allied countries attributed him to the resilience of the Russian Federation.

Beside the general stood a slender woman of about forty with light brown hair tied back in a bun. Her pantsuit looked expensive, her watch and necklace even more so. She exuded the stench of capitalism, engaged in a shockingly casual conversation with Poval.

Nabokov saluted the general, who waved it off with a laugh.

"None of that today, my boy," he said in English with a hearty Russian accent. "How is your English?"

"Fluent," Nabokov said modestly. His eyes shifted to the woman, who stepped forward before Poval could introduce her.

"Sergeant Nabokov, my name is Victoria Sutherland. I've heard outstanding things about you."

Her name sounded familiar, but Veektor couldn't quite place it. Poval gestured to a collection of cushy armchairs around a dark coffee table for them to sit. Nabokov got the distinct impression Poval wasn't really a part of this conversation.

"I'm the CEO of Zenaut Technologies," she continued. "I assume you've heard of us?"

Nabokov nodded…that's where he recognized her from. She developed the photon engines that allowed America to control the skies. Why she would be in Moscow was beyond his guess.

"I understand one of our bikes got you to safety out of Kazan?" she added.

"After one of your bombers tried to kill me," Nabokov said.

"I'm sorry to hear that," she said mechanically. "The truth is, both the bike and the Comet belong to the U.S. Military, and while we do still have an outstanding contract with the Pentagon, our primary focus has always been civil technology."

"What does that have to do with me?"

"How much do you know about the Defense of Humanity Initiative?"

Nabokov tried to stop himself from laughing, but couldn't. He managed to catch himself quickly, avoiding the General's gaze. "Sorry, it's just that we used to refer to it as the 'Widow Program.'"

"Why is that?" She didn't react to the comment, but she must have heard the phrase before.

"Well…many believe those people were all sent to their deaths, which is why they—you—stopped doing it."

In truth, it wasn't many people—it was everyone. The program was a marketing scheme in the 21st century, and once it stopped generating more money than it cost, they scrapped it—a perfect folly of private enterprise.

"We never stopped, Sergeant. We're preparing a roster for this decade, and we'd like you on board."

As an adolescent, Nabokov had learned about DOHI as part of his schooling. It was a big hoax, designed to make it seem like Zenaut had reverse-engineered something magical that couldn't be duplicated anywhere else. Half a dozen ships were sent into space full of people who were likely never to return. By the time Nabokov was born, the world had come to its senses, the project reduced to a five-minute conversation for teenagers to laugh about how gullible people used to be.

Only, according to Victoria Sutherland, they'd only stopped the public display. Zenaut had pushed DOHI into the shadows, rebuilding their reputation to continue the project in secret. The invasion was happening, and they spent hundreds of billions of dollars every decade for nothing more than the benefit of the species. In her own portrayal, Sutherland was an altruistic Samaritan.

"I don't want to sound rude," Nabokov said, "but do you know how insane this sounds?"

"Yes," she said, not elaborating further. General Poval remained uncomfortably silent.

"You want me to get onto a large spaceship…and travel ten thousand years into the future to fight for mankind's survival? You realize we're doing that right now? Today?"

"I don't believe this war will be the end of humanity. Do you?"

"No," he said contemplatively.

"The invasion might be, and your job class is exceptionally dangerous. I'm already aware you've survived more CaTNE infiltrations than anyone else, but how many more do you think you can complete before you don't come back?"

"As many as it takes," he boasted. "If seven doesn't kill me, neither can seventy." He didn't believe that in the least. Kazan was a close call, and the next one could very likely be his last. With Poval a meter away, Nabokov wanted to make sure his priorities were clear.

The general finally broke his silence.

"Let us say this is all verifiable. Men like Sergeant Nabokov are pivotal to our war effort. We expect seven more successes from him, and certainly aren't willing to lose him for an American...what would you call this? A pet project?"

Sutherland nodded. "I don't want to hurt the European Alliance's war effort. As I mentioned before, we *do* have a contract with the U.S. Department of Defense, but I could see to it that a truck of Comet engines got lost in Moscow, driven by an experienced engineering trainer."

"That would be a fortunate accident," Poval glanced sideways at Sutherland.

Nabokov stared vacantly at the dark, wooden table. Neutralizing America's aerial advantage would be worth more missions than he could ever complete. The general was right, though...soldiers were pivotal. It would normally be inappropriate for Nabokov to barter here, but this wasn't a normal situation, and he was in a unique position to further aid the Alliance.

"If you also take someone from the American military—someone prestigious—I'll go even without an apocalypse."

"We search the entire globe for exceptional soldiers," Sutherland recited. "America is no different."

"I'm not talking about 'exceptional soldiers.' I'm talking about *a* soldier—the Shadow Hawk. If they go, I'll blow up as many aliens as you want."

The Shadow Hawk was a bomber who'd leveled entire cities without being so much as scraped. The pseudonym was an egotistical parallel to the notorious combat pilot from two hundred years ago—The Red Baron. The audacity of the title wasn't nearly as annoying as the validity of it. The Shadow Hawk had more blood on their hands than any person in human history, by a huge margin. True to their namesake, they were barely more than a phantom, and far more dangerous to Europe than Nabokov was to America.

Sutherland seemed to do some calculations in her head, though what kind, Nabokov didn't know.

"He's in high consideration," she said. "Tracking him down will be difficult, but I'll see what I can do." She turned to Poval, who seemed only partially invested as he stared hungrily at a cigar between his fingers. "I'd like to ask that Sergeant Nabokov not be redeployed. It would be unfortunate if something were to happen to him while I was negotiating with the Americans."

"Young Veektor has been promoted!" Poval said startlingly loud. "Gone are his field days in the Russian Federation."

"Congratulations," she smiled. "I'll be in touch within the week." She stood up to leave, and Poval made his way back to his desk to fetch another cigar. Nabokov never acted on rumors, but one had come up a few times that might be relevant here.

"Ms. Sutherland, I've heard from a couple of people that the Shadow Hawk might be named Phillips—a captain in the Air Force."

She gave Nabokov a devilish smile that sent chills down his recuperating spine. "Yes, I know."

By the time the office door had closed behind her, Poval was thrusting the other cigar into Nabokov's hand with an exuberant congratulations. Nabokov didn't know how official the promotion really was—it wasn't like the Federation would be around when… or if he returned.

White lines streaked across *Salvation's* only forward-facing window, which covered the communications room. Walker sat staring up at the pattern created by the distant stars.

Prior to joining Zenaut, her work had nothing to do with astrophysics, and the pieces she picked up while creating the field of xenobiology hadn't given her enough of a foundation to inherently rationalize what was going on outside as their ship careened through space.

What she knew was that *Salvation* was traveling upwards, holding them to the floor by pushing it into them. The ship and everyone on board were compressed into a pancake. At least, that's how they would appear to someone on Earth. To the crew, it was the opposite. The universe outside was stretching around them, including the stars.

The lines had drawn themselves slowly during the end of their first year of travel, and while they still appeared as rain falling past their ship, they wouldn't remain that way. As their ship began its two-year turnaround, the stars began to morph into bright streaks. Their feet would slowly swing along the outside of their arc as a means of maintaining both the ship's speed and their simulated gravity. On a piece of paper, the path looked sort of like a teardrop.

That's where she stopped, though. She understood why the stars appeared as they did and checked on them frequently. Not to give her a better sense of what was happening...more to reassure her of it. Walker had witnessed the stars stretching into lines, just as she would watch them pivot across the window. It was observable, which gave her the sense that nature was okay with it all.

They were also therapeutic in their own right, like a cosmic lava lamp.

Today was a special day, though. They'd been out of communication with Earth for a while as Solar signals raced to catch up to *Salvation*, but that was all supposed to end today. As the ship rotated past the 90° mark, thousands of years of human history would start to catch up to them in relatively quick succession. That was the hope, anyway. There was always the possibility they wouldn't receive much. Earth could have forgotten about them after a hundred years, so no one bothered to send signals this far away.

Regardless, *some* transmissions from Earth would make it out here. A few of those would be strong enough for *Salvation* to read, and one or two might even be encrypted in a manner their computer could display. Walker wanted to read those.

"Heya, Doctor Walker!"

Shino trudged up to the door of the communications room wearing a teal shirt containing a reference Walker didn't know—

undoubtedly a game. She looked as groggy as a bag of sunshine ever could, but she was rarely up this early.

"You really don't have to call me 'Doctor.'"

"Why not? If I went through all that school, I wouldn't respond to anyone who *didn't* call me 'Doctor.'"

"The problem is that everyone assumes you're a medical doctor. Then they start showing you rashes and infections."

"Wellll…gross." Shino hopped into a chair on the other side of the room where the ship's PA was accessed. "What's today?"

Walker had been working on answering this sort of question. It wasn't as simple as it had been—the calendar they'd used on Earth didn't apply to time on *Salvation*.

"At this *exact* moment, on Earth, I think it's something like 6200 or 6300…but *we* would be seeing everything closer to 3100 or so…" She didn't know how close either of those were, nor which of the two should be considered more accurate. Common sense told her it was 6200. If they could teleport to Earth, that's the year it would be, so that's what year it was *now*.

However, they couldn't teleport. The calendar in question existed only to measure the passing of time on Earth, tallying one year every time it revolved around the sun. If someone from their crew had been watching the planet nonstop since they left, they wouldn't have witnessed the passing of four thousand years; they would have seen one thousand. So, from their perspective, that's how many years had passed on Earth.

The retired gamer scrunched her nose for a moment. "Close enough!"

She swiveled animatedly towards the panel and compressed a button, activating the ship's PA system. It was probably the only thing in the comms room that Shino knew how to use. She once mentioned to Walker that she used to spend a couple of hours every day updating her social media platforms. Walker's publicist had suggested something similar to her, but she'd vehemently refused.

The day Shino learned about the intercom, she added it to her daily routine.

Leaning in towards the microphone, Shino's words bounced through the ship's hull in her best impression of a sultry, sci-fi computer voice.

"Good morning, crew. The current year is…6147. Have a delightful century!" She sometimes replaced "century" with "year" or "decade." It was like a vestigial part of her former life, reaching out to all eleven of her followers. It did help mark each day in the sun's absence, like a rooster who often started crowing at noon.

Shino spun the chair back to Walker, following her eyes up to the stars striped across the viewport. "Whatcha doin'?"

"We're supposed to get a huge burst of communications today or tomorrow, and I need a break from my paper."

Teegan stared up at the thin lines like she was waiting for them to do something. Sometimes, Walker thought she could see the lines bending to the side, but Kahlil assured her it was too slow for the human eye to register.

The pop icon had yet to leave when the first blip appeared on the screen beside Walker.

It wasn't a transmission…it was ten of them. Half of which were formatted in a way their system found agreeable. Walker's eyes widened as she leaned in closer to the monitor. A few more showed up, one appearing in a language she didn't recognize, dated 2467 A.D.

"I guess it's starting," she said absently to Shino. The twenty-year-old spun back to the microphone, returning to her computer voice.

"Attention, all passengers…incoming mail."

Another dozen messages popped up in the same moment, followed by a lazy trail of trickling signals. The term "burst" was supposed to be in comparison to months of radio silence, before which they'd received a message every week or two. Kahlil was expecting a few signals per day from the Solar System, but this was more like one per week of *Earth time*. It was completely unmanageable.

Walker sighed, staring at what now looked like work being piled on faster than it could be done.

At least Earth was alright.

17

3180 A.D.

Countless conversations filled the large cafe on the bottom floor of the Ambler building in San José, Costa Rica. It was almost too noisy to have a conversation—the perfect place to have a private one in plain sight.

A tall, dark woman with short-buzzed hair approached the clerk interface—a machine used to sell coffee. She selected a mint latte and waited while the clerk generated it. For such a nice building, the coffee machine was embarrassingly old. Most newer machines were all-in-one, but some people insisted coffee-specific clerks made better lattes. In her opinion, if your drink was being made with a schematic, you couldn't complain about the quality. People didn't seem to mind, though.

Her eyes swept across the room, looking over the heads of hundreds of patrons as the milk steamed into her cup. She spotted an older man in the corner—the one she came to meet.

Older was relative. Darnet Forscythe was under fifty, but Jasmy Badia was exceptionally young for her position. She was the president of the Solar Protection Program—a covert organization whose aim was to defend their system from a long-ignored alien invasion.

Every decade, on the decade, they sent a ship into deep space to return in the future, like the company Zenaut did before them.

After America failed to properly safeguard evidence of the cephrast invasion, the SPP spent centuries obtaining what little remained. Humanity had proven incapable of handling the awareness of its own impending doom. Too many stupid cooks trying to take over the kitchen, spew misinformation, fuel hysteria. The SPP maintained a number of contacts in every government, but operated independently from them. This launch would be Badia's first as head, and she wanted it to go off smoothly.

She took her coffee to the corner table Forscythe was at, a half-eaten pastry and partially-melted iced drink in front of him.

"Where are you at on the list of 200s?" she asked as she sat. Since its inception, the SPP had recruited the greatest soldiers in the Solar System. Badia wanted to move in a different direction. Combat would largely be fought by machines and programs—not people. She was looking for the brightest minds to pioneer the most advanced tools of war, and as such, any person with a recorded IQ at or over 200 was guaranteed a spot if they wanted it.

Convincing them they wanted it was another story. The board had been skeptical, but Badia insistently sold the idea. A genius of that echelon wouldn't be impacted by something as trivial as changes in science.

"Three more," Forscythe said. "My money is still on Kihon Drager."

"Drager," she mused, reading the name off a summary screen. "He's the one working with black holes?"

Forscythe sipped his drink. "Wormholes. I think if we can convince him he's capable of completing his contributions to the field, he'll go. Skipping nine thousand years of progress might be more appealing if his name is already written in history."

"We can fund the rest through a grant—any subsidiary will do."

"That was going to be my suggestion."

"But not why we're here?" Badia asked.

"No." Forscythe placed a screen on the table showing a financial document from a weapons company Badia owned. "This is a sale from Thermolyte. I believe it's one of yours?"

"You know it is. You need to think of the big picture here."

"Let's skirt around the fact that if you keep investing in war for the sake of the future, you may pass the tipping point where there is no future—"

"I know what I'm doing," she said coldly.

"Then where was the payoff? This is a big loss, Jasmy," he snorted. "If you had donated the weapons to charity, it would have done more."

"Lower your voice!" Badia snapped, glancing discreetly around the cafe. It took up most of the Ambler building's first floor—the size of a food court. Forscythe seemed to think this was a financial fiasco. That she was being flippant. "Sometimes, our businesses must sell at cost to build relationships for the future."

"Why are you backing the Martians?" he asked quietly.

"I'm not backing them, I just need their revolution to end soon. If they lose now, it could result in the death of one of our prospects."

"Firstly, that's precisely what 'backing them' means. Secondly, who? I thought you were moving away from foot soldiers."

"She's not a foot soldier, she's a pilot. One with unbelievable skill."

"You're talking about what's-her-name…Raynor? You want to make an exception for her after that 'greatest minds' speech you made?"

"Yes."

"And you think you can get a revolutionary to abandon her cause?"

"I think she'll respond well to a greater cause, but I'd feel more confident if the Martian Revolution didn't need her anymore."

"You work on her, then. I'll handle Drager." He stared at her untouched drink. "Not big on coffee?"

"Not on shitty coffee."

"This is South America, Jasmy."

"West Africa's is better—has been since it was Cameroon."

"As long as you're not pretentious about it…I'll drink it."

She pulled the cup out of his reach and took a sip. "Thanks, but I'll need it. I'm leaving for Mars tonight."

Kahlil was already at *Salvation's* gym when Fowler arrived. The astrophysicist had remained exceptionally diligent in his fitness habits throughout the flight. He tended to exercise around the same time as Fowler, who could barely remember what Kahlil had looked like when they'd first met.

Fowler kept his routine short, finding himself in the canteen eating a bowl of nutrient-infused oatmeal when Shino's voice came over the PA. She was good at the whole robot-voice thing. If he didn't know any better, he might actually think it was a shipboard computer.

"Attention, all passengers…incoming mail," she said ominously. Fowler had completely forgotten about the impending signal burst. It wasn't a particularly urgent matter. They still had three and a half years to look at them. If any really *were* urgent, there was nothing they could do from a thousand lightyears away.

After finishing his breakfast, Fowler leisurely made his way to the comms room. The Mossad woman, Sharabi, was already in conversation with Walker. The way they were talking made it sound like there was a problem of some sort. Kahlil arrived shortly after, the neck of his shirt dark with sweat. He pushed his way into the cramped communications room.

"I mentioned a few times this would be happening," he said. The interruption earned him a dirty look from Sharabi.

Walker gestured to the terminal beside her. "I assume that means you have a plan to handle this?"

"Erm, handle what?" Kahlil leaned past her, staring confusedly at the screen. "Well, shit…"

"Exactly."

"Why the *hell* are they sending us so much?"

"They're not. Most of these aren't for us."

"This is *interplanetary*?" his voice cracked.

"You developed an impossible source of power and marvel at the creation of impossibly powerful tools?" Sharabi said scathingly.

Perhaps they'd never really considered the day-to-day ramifications of the cephrast technology. They certainly hadn't imagined *Salvation* would be picking up transmissions sent amongst people on Earth. Then again, no one had known how easy it would be to receive signals from Earth this far out.

The answer was: *very.*

"They must have built more advanced encryptions to filter signals out—something *we* don't have." Kahlil sighed. "This is a problem."

"The good news is, at least one of these is intended for us." Walker pointed to a transmission with a clear title buried amidst a dozen lines of gibberish from an organization called the Solar Protection Program. "We might be able to rely on those. Otherwise, combing through these will be a full-time job for someone."

"What are the rest?" Fowler asked.

"Anything and everything. Something about World War III; The complete works of *Danilla Dietrik,* which appears to be music; the rise and fall of a country called *Krivinna;* languages I've never seen..." Walker skimmed through rows on the screen in front of her. "A recipe from someone's dad; what *really* happened in World War III; a textbook on the Martian Revolution—"

"Wait, there are *Martians*?" Shino sat upright in her chair, which wobbled on its swivel. "Like, people who are *from* Mars?"

"It appears so."

"That's awesome! I wonder what they're like...do you think they're green? Because of the atmosphere or something?"

"No. Don't be ridiculous," Kahlil mumbled, staring intently at the screen as more messages blipped up. "This problem might actually solve itself. At some point, nothing should be readable by our system unless it's intended for us. There's always a chance someone on their end remedies the compatibility, so let's hope they don't." He leaned back from the screen. "I say we just wait."

Half a dozen new signals were added to the queue during the resulting silence. After a bit of prodding at Kahlil, he admitted he might be able to make an algorithm to filter out the spam, but there would be potential difficulties relating to the "source"—whatever that meant. Nothing could be done about it today.

Curious to see what people were blasting across the galaxy, Fowler hung back in the comms room as everyone filtered out. Teegan was the last out, calling loudly for a marathon of Mars movies at their next movie night. Walker remained in her seat, struggling to hold in laughter.

"What?" he asked. She responded only with a shake of her head and a shrug. "Shut up."

"I think it's cute."

"It's not like that," Fowler defended, though he wasn't sure what he had to defend. Walker looked back towards the screen, her amusement slowly fading as her eyes darted across one of the decoded files. "What are you reading?"

"It's a—well..." she hesitated. "You've...stopped blaming yourself for all of this, right? "

"Sometimes...why?" The question seemed to come out of nowhere, and in a way, it had—from the dark abyss of space. A historical recount of the events in Chattahoochee.

When the contact video was leaked from Arvonia, whoever had done it made a concerted effort to hide the names of those involved. Decades after *Salvation's* departure, additional details were declassified, including the contact footage from *after* the cephrasts were killed. The part where Dr. Xi mentioned Fowler by name. Factually, all three aliens were killed by either Fowler's registered pistol or the rifle he'd been carrying, and the Department of Defense had immediately incarcerated him afterwards. He didn't look too good in the eyes of history.

Fowler scanned the high-school-level document describing the events in Georgia.

"Are you alright?" Walker asked.

"Yeah—" Truthfully, he was. "What do I care about the opinions of people from hundreds of years after it happened? They're all dead now anyway."

"I guess that's one way to look at it," she said. Her eyes drifted sadly downward, a feeling Fowler knew well. Sometimes—seemingly at random—a reminder of how truly distant their past was hit harder than usual, opening floodgates to thoughts about loved ones left behind. He thought about it every day.

"Sorry. Didn't mean to be a downer."

"It's alright. It happens a lot."

"You know, I lost friends in combat—*family*," he said. "It never got easier. Not really. When I think about the people we left on Earth, I try to remind myself that they didn't just die when we left, even though that's how it feels to us. They probably lived full lives with families, careers, grandchildren… They're not dead because I outlived them. They're dead because they outlived me."

Walker smiled absently at a cold cup of coffee sitting on the desk.

"That was incredibly profound, Iffy."

"You have your biology, I have my PTSD."

For some of the people left on Earth, they wouldn't have to guess. They'd later read through numerous outlines of the first contact, many including biographies. Not much was known about Kelly Ditka's life until she started a counter-hacking company in her sixties. Sconi's granddaughter was an Olympic high jumper. Everyone else from that night had either died before *Salvation's* launch or launched with it.

Those same publications wouldn't paint Fowler any better than the one in front of him.

A few transmissions came in, the only readable one being about terraforming Callisto. Walker took a sip of the stale coffee, shivering as she watched the peaceful chaos of the signal onslaught.

Nadia Raynor had long taken the beauty of the red planet for granted. When she thought about all of the reasons she loved Mars, the landscape never usually came up. Now, she stared out at the rust-colored dunes with fondness. Grains of sand billowed across distant knolls in a way only the thin frontier atmosphere could foment. It truly was a unique sight.

Marihade, the town whose edge she stood at, had been her home since the day she was born. Mars still bore the title of "Earth's Largest Colony," but it had never been anything to her but a thriving, self-sufficient land, complete with its own nations, culture, and trade.

The Moon was a colony. It received regular supply drops from Earth, sustaining itself through tourism and programming—an industry requiring almost no physical resources. They harvested enough oxygen to fill their buildings, some silicon and iron for trade, but that was about it. Even more dependent were the mining colonies of Venus. The violent astral body couldn't sustain anything more than the mines, which barely survived in the heavy, toxic atmosphere.

Hundreds of years ago, the atmosphere throughout Mars had been as unbreathable as the wilderness Raynor saw in the distance. The natural gravity of the red planet was too low to hold suitable air to its surface, preventing colonists from going outside without an atmospheric suit.

Then came gravity panels—large discs that generated gravitational waves. Once the technology became cheap enough, a proposal was passed to build several large panels beneath the dirt. Towns were quickly built over them, and gasses moved into those areas over the course of decades. One day, someone went outside and took a deep breath.

The Martian surface was littered with small pockets of terraformed atmosphere. The air piled up over Earth-normal areas of gravity almost as high as it did on Earth, spilling out past the gravity panels to create a dome. Smaller panels extended for a few kilometers past the edge of town, gradually lightening to Mars-typical gravity to prevent molecules of air from being whisked off-planet. The gaseous hemispheres pressurized the surface, trapping enough heat to keep the temperature from fluctuating, and the panels generated an electromagnetic field, allowing people to stand outside without being irradiated to death.

The farther you walked into Mars-typical gravity, the thinner and colder the air became, but it wasn't much different than climbing far up a mountain. Raynor was pretty sure that if someone walked out of town naked, they'd freeze to death before suffocating or bursting, and the radiation would take months to cause harm.

Some people moved to the edge of the atmosphere domes to avoid their terrestrial overlords. The smart ones only left their homes in suits and reinforced their houses with radiation shielding. The rest usually died from radiation sickness, cancer, or, in one case, a freakish meteor strike. When you went to the doctor, the first question they asked was whether or not you lived over the main grav-panels.

Sectional terraforming had been so successful, it inspired a colony on the Jovian moon of Callisto. The small satellite was outside of Jupiter's main radiation belt, making it an ideal first candidate for planet-wide terraforming. If it was successful, someone would likely do the same on Europa—the mecca of Earth-substitutes.

Personally, Raynor loved the spotty atmospheres. Martian frontiers were perfect for astronautical engineering—low-gravity, low-pressure, and high-radiation. The best ships were made on Mars, and Martian trade networks moved quicker by operating outside of the atmo-bubbles. Excluding the time it took to get to a shuttle pad, you could travel anywhere on the planet in seven hours.

The atmospheres supported countless farms, which spawned local cuisines and restaurants. Mars had its own language, customs, and currency. Everyone on Mars owned at least one flexible, high-quality environmental suit, most of which were made and repaired in the next town over from Marihade. Daredevils drove agile rovers around on the dunes, playing a violent game called Zeleeca.

In other words, an independent union.

The blue planet started leveraging Mars for resources and engineering facilities when Raynor was young. They tried blocking supplies, grossly overestimating the amount of support Mars needed to survive. When Mars' declaration of independence was countered by added military occupation, the Martian Revolution began.

Martian forces waged attacks on terrestrial occupiers from both inside and outside of orbit, taking off in the frontier and transitioning seamlessly between air, ground, and space battlefields. It became quickly apparent that Earthborn pilots couldn't do the same, encouraging amphibious-style tactics that had never been utilized to such a degree.

Raynor was twenty-three when it started. She was the daughter of an engineer who made space fighters, and was piloting ten years before the legal age. She also had a knack for it. By her first military assignment, she was matching the skill of pilots with decades of experience.

Now, with almost a hundred missions under her belt, Raynor stood on a planet completely free of subjugators. Defensive battles no longer waged overhead—light was forming at the end of the tunnel.

She stared past the western edge of Marihade's bubble. Rows of carrots and spinach ran through the grid of soil to her right. An apple orchard obscured the interstate highway a kilometer to her left. Just past the edge of the large soil squares, on the ground in front of her, was a bright blue line. If she walked over it, the gravity would be lighter, and the atmosphere oh-so thinner.

She used to come out here to the edge of town and watch the dunes. There was never anyone else here—it was her spot. Periodically, she could hear a rover leaving on the long highway. She always tried to guess what kind it was before seeing it appear among the banks of red sand in the distance. It was only ever a guess. She couldn't tell the difference. On extremely rare occasions, she would see a tiny meteor by the horizon that had survived its descent through the thinner gasses. Otherwise, her spot was tranquil.

She grabbed a handful of brick-red dirt, taking time to appreciate the cold, powdery texture. You could only find it at the edge of town, if not outside the bubble completely, but it was the substance that truly made Mars what it was. The red dust existed only for its own sake. It couldn't cultivate crops like the soil beside her. It was here long before humans, and most of it would go undisturbed forever. The fine powder in Raynor's hand was probably having its first contact with human skin. It was almost sacred.

She let it fall across the blue line in front of her. As children, they were forbidden from leaving the city's edges. Parents told horror stories about people's eyes popping out and being fried to a crisp on their first step. Even at a young age, Raynor knew the stories were made-up. Standing immediately past the line wasn't dangerous. There was air, warmth, and protection from radiation, all while being in slightly lower gravity. Why couldn't she step outside of town?

She did. At this very spot. It's the reason she knew that, at this *particular* point on the line, you would cross into Mars-typical gravity. Not reduced gravity like the rest of the town's edge. Mars gravity. At this spot—her spot—the first panel was broken. It had been since the first time she crossed it.

With a running step, Raynor flung herself over the blue stripe. As her foot crossed into the dull, Martian space, it lightened. Her momentum continued as the feeling of near-weightlessness spread across her body like dipping into a pool. There was gravity, but barely more than a third of what it had been when she jumped, plunging her into a weightless void. The shocking sensation of stepping into the cold night from a heated room.

After soaring for what felt like minutes, her foot gently touched the ground, as if placed by a loving hand. Suddenly, she was on Mars. By her next step, she had acclimated to the change. Her strides were long and she could jump three meters in the air, but it wasn't the same as when she'd jumped off the giant gravity panel underneath Marihade. These were steps—that was flying.

She had been seven the first time she experienced it—the moment she wanted to be a pilot.

The blue sky overhead began to fade, telling Raynor it was time to head back. Tomorrow, she would ship out again, but with a possibility of ending the war for good. That promise came at a great cost, so Raynor thought it was appropriate to visit the location that had influenced her life so much. To take one last look at the rusty Martian dunes she'd always taken for granted.

18

RAYNOR

The sounds of Marihade grew louder as Raynor left the farms behind. Her hometown was in a medium-sized bubble in the Crimaria province. About ninety-four thousand people lived in their hundred square kilometers of atmosphere. It was only half the size of the capital city, but with less than a fifth of the population.

The suburban district's streets were placid in the twilight. Within minutes, she was pulling up to the steel-blue home of her parents. The mildly reflective walls sat a couple of meters from the walkway, beside which three of her rover's large wheels came to rest.

Her childhood home sat underneath a dark-grey roof comprised of wave panels. It fueled the building's subterranean capacitor, which her father refused to call "subterranean." Not for any technical inaccuracy, just pettiness.

Warmth enveloped Raynor the moment she opened the door, stepping in from the frigid Martian air. The evening news played over the sound of food sizzling in the kitchen. Her father, Thomas, was just sitting in the living room, rummaging through his bag for papers to read while listening to the broadcast in the background. He was just shy of fifty-six, wearing round glasses over a hooked nose, his greying hair mostly receded. He was a history teacher at Marihade Primary School, probably arriving home within the last ten minutes or so.

She gave him a hug, trying to ignore the telecast in the background. Three pundits argued about the battle she'd just returned from, and she wasn't keen to listen to it.

"Is that Nadia?" her mother called from the kitchen. Talking across the house had been common when she was growing up. Her parents were always busy.

"Terrestrial police," her father yelled over the talking heads, who were now in agreement that the entire ordeal had been a waste of time, resources, and lives. Raynor asked if they could turn the news off—it was apparent he'd tuned it out already.

"He has that on all evening," her mother said. Raynor found her rotating chicken on the grill next to a pot of what smelled like sweet potatoes.

Like the planet they lived on, it was common for people on Mars to be named after the old Roman gods, and Ceres had been named after the god of agriculture. The irony was never lost on her—Marihade's two major industries were agriculture and engineering, and Ceres couldn't grow vines on an abandoned building. She always moved with precision and ease. At sixty-one, she was now two years retired from a career as head engineer for Navezul—a Marihade-based ship manufacturer. She stood a little shorter and wider than Nadia, but the two otherwise looked very similar.

Their dinner was as normal as any other. Remarkable, considering that Raynor had to leave again the next day for what was largely considered a suicide mission. Her mother asked how accurate the news reports were of the conflict being called the "Seventh Sector Skirmish," which was an accurate name, but unmistakably chosen for the alliteration.

The criticism was valid, but it wasn't Raynor's job to speculate on what *would have* or *should have* been done, and her concerns now focused on tomorrow. After months of preparation and sowing misinformation, the militia was striking Giza Station, the last terrestrial way station between Earth and Mars. The massive starport was used to reinforce and resupply troops on the battlefronts, and while it wasn't *quite* between the two planets, it would be soon. The planets were in a position that would give Raynor's platoon a full day at the way station before the earliest possible reinforcements from Earth.

Getting the job done in a day was still a long shot. Giza was already supplied enough to make it the most heavily armed installation in space, and once Earth's armada arrived, it would be the end of their fleet.

High risks came with big rewards. Destroying the station would cut off all supplies to Earth's military for at least six months, not to mention eradicating trillions of dollars of materials and supplies already there. It would be easy to pick off supply vessels from afar, forcing Earth forces to risk isolation and starvation with every trip. It could be the beginning of the end.

"What were you flying?" her mother asked. They often talked about ships.

"Uh, most of us were in Shellbanks. Everything worth a damn is prepped for tomorrow."

Her mother scoffed. "I don't like it when they send you out in those recycled waste bins. They'd be better used for canning apples."

"Well, most of them are gone now," Raynor mumbled. Her mother turned pale. She hadn't meant to add so much gravity to the conversation. Losing pilots had become so commonplace, it felt normal—regular folk didn't bring it up so off-handedly.

Like clockwork, her father changed the subject. He'd learned today that he now had students who were shocked by the notion of having Earth troops on Mars without conflict. They talked about her uncle's crop problems, how the sub*martian* generator always hiccuped before a particular chilly front, but this year her mother would definitely fix it. After dinner, they watched a film on broadcast—a terrible movie about a mine being terrorized by the ghosts of an ancient Martian species. Raynor often felt terrible movies were endearing—this wasn't one of them.

All in all, a nice evening.

The next morning, they made their teary goodbyes, hitting all of the high points. Her dad told her to give them hell, her mom told her not to pulse her thrusters into a bank because the Solar Flares don't handle that sort of stress well. They embraced for what felt like minutes, and in the back of Raynor's mind, she wondered how much trouble she would get in if she simply…stayed here. Before an answer came to mind, she left, making her way to the launch site a few kilometers outside of Marihade.

The shuttle port was busy, sitting between Marihade's bubble and the next one over. At least a hundred militia pilots were being sent into orbit this morning. Raynor gazed up at the stars as she walked to the airlock, trying to spot the carrier above. It might have been possible to see through the thin frontier atmosphere, but she couldn't manage a glimpse before cycling through the door into the shuttle loading area.

Removing her helmet unmuffled the roar of energized fighter pilots. Their check-in times had been staggered to reduce congestion at the port, but it hadn't done much. Half of the docks were still being used for commercial flights, taking well over an hour to get the overcrowded room of pilots up to the Giza-bound carrier.

Once Raynor finally got a shuttle, it was only twenty minutes for her to get off-planet, on board, and into the flagship's changing room. Only a few stragglers from the shuttle before hers remained, reducing the roar of her fellow pilots to a light rumble. Raynor stored her street clothes and environmental suit in a locker next to one of her squadmates, swapping them for her uniform and flight suit.

Flying in formation was unbearably sluggish to Raynor. She was lucky to be in her squadron. Years before, when she was still fresh-faced, she had complained about it to one of her superiors. They proceeded to place her on a patrol behind one of the best pilots in the fleet—the squadron leader's only apparent goal being to shake her off his tail.

He didn't. Their patrol ended half a gigameter outside their planned route when the ace abruptly stopped his deranged flight path, leaving only Raynor in his wake.

"Well, shit…that's all I've got, Ensign," he'd said. "Good flying."

After she'd tallied up some missions on her record, the militia gave her a squadron of her own. It didn't go very well. The amount of focus she spent trying to lead the pack prevented her from executing maneuvers she otherwise did flawlessly.

Eventually, they landed somewhere in the middle. Raynor was an extra pilot in a squadron of above-average flyers, allowing them to perform standard maneuvers in her absence. Her squad leader had become adept at handling unusual problems by breaking her off to handle a complex task without the need for a cover pilot. The sight of a single fighter never caused much distress in their adversaries, and by the time they realized something disastrous was happening, Raynor was already finishing up.

Her situation had afforded her the opportunity to contribute as much to Mars' independence as her skills offered. She'd made a name for herself as the woman who could accomplish the seemingly impossible with surgical precision, earning her the unofficial title spoken by some.

With her flight suit over her shoulder, Raynor stuffed her bag into the empty locker. An on-duty captain briskly walked in—hasty, alert, but clearly bored.

"Raynor, you have a visitor."

"A *visitor?*" she repeated. "On board?"

"Dock six," he said in an authoritative monotone. "Now."

Raynor exchanged a quizzical glance with her squadmate. It was practically unheard of. The only people cleared to dock with the carrier were working on it, and there wasn't much reason to do so otherwise. It wasn't as if friends and family were allowed on board.

In the words of her first commander, it was "a vessel of inter-planetary warfare, not a goddamn summer camp."

Closing the coated-metal cabinet, Raynor made her way back to the docking bays. She tried to form a list of people who would know her, be cleared to board, and *not* be assigned, but came up blank. When she arrived at dock six, she was unsurprised to find a complete stranger waiting by the hatch. The woman had dark skin with short hair, introducing herself as Jasmy Badia.

"I'll keep this brief," Badia said. "The carrier is leaving soon and I won't be joining. I run the Solar Protection Program...I assume you've heard that name before?"

Raynor had, but never in a capacity that made her think it was a real group—just rumors and tall tales, but perhaps not so much. Badia explained the purpose and function of her organization, the short version being that the cephrasts were going to invade the Solar System, and there was a cabal dedicated to reinforcing our future army with the highest-quality troops.

"I've taken things in another direction this decade," the woman explained. "Brilliant innovators of the modern era. While we're not looking to recruit soldiers, I think your talents are beyond excep-tional, and our people's future would benefit from them greatly."

There was so much to process in such a short time, Raynor genuinely didn't know how to respond. It was almost aggravating, being dropped into this while prepping for the most important mission of her career. Couldn't this woman have rang her? Sent her a message?

Memories floated through Raynor's head of her first months in the military. Older soldiers used to tell recruits gossip of the exalted —people they used to know who'd performed impossible feats before vanishing. As the tales went, these soldiers were recruited to fight aliens in secret and never seen again. It was a way to haze the green and gullible. The legendary soldiers in question were most likely promoted and moved to a post with openings, perhaps killed during a classified mission.

Raynor wondered how many had been more than myths.

The admiral had allowed this woman—an Earthling—onto the carrier without so much as a guard to try to draft a pilot before a critical assault. There was something to her story.

"If this is legitimate, I'll come see what you have to show," Raynor finally said. "*After* the mission."

"We can't allow that," Badia said as if she owned the fleet. "The survival of our species is at stake, and few of the pilots in this assault are likely to return—if any."

"That's why I have to go. I'm not going to abandon my compatriots when they need me the most."

"You are the only fighter they *don't* need, Ensign—by your own choosing. The admiral also tells me your ships have been outfitted with state-of-the-art Thermolyte shielding and particle drivers for this assault."

"I'll make good use of them," Raynor dismissed, ostensibly. The shadow CEO had done her research, and no one outside of the carrier was supposed to know about the armada's recent Thermolyte upgrades, least of all a terrestrial civilian. Still, Raynor hadn't been grounded for the Giza operation, which is all that mattered to her.

"This mission is a mere blip on the cosmic scale, Nadia. Martian independence is inevitable, even if you fail here, but the fate of humanity will be worse off."

Raynor found the oversimplification irksome. The same blip could be said of her involvement in whatever invasion might happen.

"I'm sure you'll be able to find me when I get back," she said. Badia looked disappointed.

"*If* you get back, Ensign."

"No—" Raynor corrected. "*When.*"

* * *

A pale, boneless limb floated in a tube of preservation fluid before Raynor. It was motionless—creepy. A week ago, she would have sworn on her unborn children that she would never see a cephrast in the flesh. It wouldn't have been the first time she was wrong.

The flagship had reached striking range of Giza two and a half days after it left Mars' orbit. When the grueling battle ended ten hours later, the entire sector was a flight hazard. Jagged pieces of shrapnel and ship scraps densely scattered the area for dozens of kilometers, most of which had been Giza's hull.

Raynor had survived. Most of the Martian fighters did not.

A few days after returning to Mars, Jasmy Badia came by her parents' house for a conversation about human extermination.

"I knew it!" her father had howled exuberantly. "Haven't I said it, Ceres? I've said it to her at *least* a dozen times. The evidence is there. All throughout history, it's there."

The emotional turmoil caused by the SPP woman's request was significant on the Raynor family, but the plight of their species was considerable. Neither of her parents had expected any pilots to return from the assault, and the fact that Raynor had must have been for a reason.

"These days have been a gift from the gods," her mother had said through tears she was rarely seen shedding. "It would be selfish not to return that gift in kind."

Raynor was uncomfortable being on the blue planet. A surprising number of Earthlings had been against the Martian occupation, but mostly because it had consumed a vast amount of resources for benefits that boiled down to cheaper ships and novelty goods. It was already looking like the destruction of Giza would force the war's end from costs alone.

Unfortunately, those same people weren't happy with Mars either, for their part in the same economic destruction, so Raynor found herself sticking around the only other Martian on their future transport—a tall, beefy man with large scars on his arm and face.

"Anton Morrison," he introduced himself, "84th Strike."

"You're in the militia?" she asked, confusedly.

"I was. Weren't you?"

"I am...was. I just thought everyone else was supposed to be a genius or something?"

He shrugged. "Doesn't sound like me. I used to blow open doors *adjacent* to exterior hulls and run straight into gunfire."

As it turned out, Raynor wasn't the only soldier on the manifest. Morrison and two Earthlings were added to fill the ship out. The inclusion of two of their former oppressors was an unfortunate turn of events. Raynor would easily have preferred to drown in a sea of intellectuals she couldn't have real conversations with, but she tried to reserve her judgement. Maybe the terrestrial soldiers weren't bringing their proverbial baggage.

Ultimately, her expectations were spot-on.

The woman, Kentwood, was at least amiable. She had spent most of the war building Earth's training program on the Moon. The man, Bouchet, seethed animosity.

For the most part, the so-called *200s* gave off a similar aura of despite. Most had funded their work through military contracts, giving them some level of involvement in the war. They looked at the two Martians as either ungrateful subjects or as children throwing tantrums that had strained the interplanetary economy.

Over time, Raynor imagined the tension would ease up. Cramming recent enemies into a ship for five years seemed like exceptionally poor planning, though. And for good reason...it wasn't planned. As she later learned from Kihon Drager, the wormhole guy.

"You know, they weren't going to bring any soldiers at all," he said immediately after they met. They were looking at information from the cephrast autopsies, most of which meant nothing to Raynor.

"Jasmy said I was an exception...I wasn't expecting to see more."

"They ran out of candidates."

"Really?"

He nodded. "They asked everyone whose IQ tested over 180—as if that were a *reasonable* gauge to begin with—but only a few said yes."

"Wasn't it 200?"

"Like I said, only a few agreed. Allegedly, she managed to fill the ship out anyway, but three people backed out at the last minute."

"You're kidding?" It didn't seem to Raynor like the kind of decision anyone would make half-heartedly. She certainly hadn't.

"It makes you wonder," he mused as if none of this really affected him. "They asked a bunch of big brains to transcend time and save humanity, and most of them said no."

It was a bad omen—rats abandoning a ship. It was also possible they were simply selfish or afraid...as rats often are. Still, for the first time since arriving on Earth—if only for a brief moment—Raynor wondered if she was possibly making an irreversible mistake.

19

5349 A.D.

As their trajectory angled more towards Earth, the number of signals received by *Salvation* increased, but they were almost entirely unrecognizable by the shipboard computer.

One of the first messages of the flood was directed *to* them from another ship in transit, which helped ground their problem a bit. Presumably, ships after theirs contained the necessary technology to interpret the slew of files theirs could not. Whatever filters were used on Earth to sieve through the excessive radioactive noise should exist in at least one of those vessels.

As a result, the crew of *Salvation* was afforded the luxury of ignoring most of the messages. Every once in a while, they'd find one that included a translation file designed for their system, but from what they gathered, most societies didn't know they existed anymore. The alien landing was a silly fable from a long-dead civilization, and the people who'd left in ships were kooks. It concerned Walker initially, but within the ambush of signals were messages directed to ships in dilation—typically from a government or organization. The system of maintaining evidence of a very-real alien threat seemed fragile, but it worked so far.

With thousands of encrypted transmissions being archived, the remainder became fairly manageable. Most were repetitive—*another* book about the Martian Revolution, *another* book about AI…

"That's how it all ends," Kahlil quipped semi-seriously. "Machines."

The crew tended towards files in their areas of interest. Conway frequently learned about medical breakthroughs, immediately frustrated by *Salvation's* inability to utilize any of them. Walker most recently forced herself to read through a 42nd-century view of genetics. It was translated fine, but the grammar was so strange, it was difficult to understand.

Shino had decided her job was to look at every time capsule sent into space. As it turned out, a lot of people wanted to preserve their cultures through time. Walker found her in the lounge one day, playing a game, of course, but with headphones synced to the server terminal.

"What are you listening to?" Walker asked.

"Huh?" The twenty-two-year-old broke her intense stare with the laptop, pulling her headphones down over the back of her neck. "Oh, it's only the greatest music of all time! It's called *tirino*, which I think means *new mechanical* or something like that, but they might as well call it *classy dubstep*. It's basically like if techno, funk, and classical all had a baby together." Shino switched off her headphones, and while Walker agreed with the description, she didn't find it terribly enjoyable. "Isn't it creepy!?"

"That's a good word for it."

"Oh no!" Shino pushed her face towards the computer screen, locked back into her game while muttering about supply lines.

It was the routine they'd fallen into after the burst. Walker quickly became envious of Fowler, who only looked at what he wanted to. She always felt some sort of obligation to read new information in her field, especially the otherwise-stagnant field of xenobiology, no matter how repetitive they might be. She enjoyed the topics, but it often felt like work.

"It's kind of freeing being a grunt. When something comes in, I can just ignore it, guilt-free," he said while they sat in the canteen one afternoon. "For a while, I read about each new war that came up. You know, thinking maybe they'd start to subside in the face of extinction?"

"I could have saved you the time on that one..." Walker groaned.

"We don't need any more pessimists on this ship."

"It's not pessimism, Isaac. It's realism."

"Yeah, that's why I stopped. Now I mostly read kids' books."

"Why?" she laughed. It was such an odd juxtaposition.

"Remember that guy who destroyed Jeopardy? It was a few years before the crash."

"Vaguely..."

"He broke a ton of records. I was a Ranger at the time, but my mom was obsessed with him. He knew pretty much everything, and she told me about this interview they did where he said he read a lot of children's books to study. Like fourth-grade textbooks or something. They're quick to read and give you all of the most important information. I don't know why I always remembered that. Maybe it seemed simple enough to work."

"Does it?"

"So far. I mean, I don't know everything about the people who signed the Titan Trade Treaty, but I know the main woman's name was *Harvellen*, and she was mostly known for using an orbital laser to cut a giant asteroid in half."

"It was going to hit a planet or something?"

"Nah, it was just in her way."

Kahlil stumbled into the kitchen nook and sat down, paler than usual.

"Have either of you been watching the signal queue much?" he asked. Walker glanced at Fowler. No one really monitored it any-more. They used filters, and periodically, someone checked through their archives for signals that were strong enough to be from Earth but improperly decoded.

"Is something wrong?" she asked.

"They've all stopped," Kahlil said. That wasn't uncommon. The signal bombardment was sometimes interrupted by sources of electromagnetic radiation in the direction of the Solar System. Unfortunately, those transmissions were lost to their ship forever, but one of the others would likely receive them fine. Messages directed to *Salvation* and the others were almost always re-transmitted several times. Kahlil was the one who'd explained this to her when it first happened, though.

"You said that was normal?"

"The longest drought since we started turning was a few hours —around one year on Earth, likely from interference. Nothing has come in since the morning before yesterday."

"That's...what? Twenty years?" said Walker. Each day on the ship was a little less than ten years on Earth.

"Twenty, yeah. So, I went through the last cluster of transmissions to see if the system had broken. The last fully-decoded transmission was near the end, about the ongoing Stellar War. The verbiage makes it a little hard to understand, like most, but I skimmed through it, and it doesn't have an end."

"Could that be a decoding problem?"

"The transmission was sent *to* us. It's not broken off. It doesn't have an *end*. The society largely doesn't believe we exist, and at the bottom of a system-wide war, somebody took the time to encode this for a bunch of ancient computers to document the events up until that point."

"Then twenty years of radio silence..." droned Fowler, staring through the table.

"And no galactic interference," Kahlil shook his head, standing back up. "I'm going to keep monitoring the receiver in case we get something from another ship. The document is pretty long, so it'll take a while to get through, but we might need to start considering the possibility that we're all that's left. At the very least, our people hit the reset button, but for our purposes…the invasion defense…that might as well be the same thing."

The silence of the control room was deafening, leaving Kora with only her thoughts.

Did the Jovian Empire know they were here? How long did they have? Secrecy was an advantage in the small, Mercurian iron mine, but time was against them. If the fleets of Jupiter found them, they might never know before they were incinerated.

Kora was the last living member of the Overwatch—an interplanetary committee formed to preserve and transfer evidence of a future alien invasion. The enemy they *should* be preparing for, not making their own.

She frantically prepared the ship in front of her. With no military or civilian population to speak of, the mine was one of the few places in the system yet to be destroyed. It didn't warrant a targeted demolition, sitting far enough below the crust to survive surface bombings.

Luckily, the control room was sufficiently equipped to coordinate a ship launch. Getting the vessel here had been no easy task, and again, Kora mused that if it hadn't truly been in secret, she might never know. The Jovian Empire, consisting of habitable moons around the Solar System's largest planet, was known for using large-scale bio-molecular scramblers. It allowed for the largest amount of salvage, and there wasn't much you could do to protect living creatures from it. Kora had heard accounts of it also destroying graviton generators and electronic devices, making it similar to a warhead.

Through rapid breaths, she prepared a launch sequence for the last ship to be sent by the Overwatch. It had to be done just so. If she made their presence known, any number of local patrols could hone in.

"What do you need?" came the voice of Irren, Kora's closest friend.

"Time," she replied, her fingers frenzying across the interface.

"There's plenty of it on the ship—eons of it."

Irren had already urged Kora to join them—a small group of civilians who'd survived long enough to make it to this point. They weren't the elite soldiers of the past, nor the scientists and leaders whose faces were plastered across their historical texts and whose names were given to buildings. They were just people. Ones who needed to tell a story.

It was the same story Kora desperately tried to preserve as she encoded a file hundreds of times, destined for ships sailing through the far reaches of space. They were all expecting to come back to Earth or Mars, some to the planets that now made up the Jovian Empire.

They wouldn't be. Not as they imagined.

Irren could be entrusted to keep the extraterrestrial remains safe through their trip. Kora had placed blurry videos on multiple forms of storage too. Yes, there were other ships with that evidence, but not the remains. Not artifacts from the alien crash.

"I won't repeat myself," she told Irren.

"Then allow me to. Going to Earth is foolish."

"I agree, but I also agreed to a pact. If an alien ship exists underneath the mountain, I need to ensure our rebuilt society knows exactly what it is and why it's critical."

Irren scoffed. She didn't believe their people could rebuild quickly enough, but Kora did. Her entire life had been dedicated to the belief that humanity could persevere through any trial. She *had* to believe they could right the proverbial ship.

It would be difficult, of course. Earth and Mars were completely destroyed. But there were still some natural resources on Earth…the same resources that allowed humans to propagate in the first place. It might take thousands of years, an uphill climb the entire way, but on Earth…it was possible.

Kora looked over her work, ensuring no mistakes were made. Multiple launch routines needed to be prepared in the event that something went wrong. The timing of each had to be optimized precisely. As soon as the ship's engines fired up, there was a good chance they'd be spotted. Broadcasting a boosted signal to their ancestors would act similarly as a beacon, guaranteed to alert any ship this side of the Sun. The cluster of encoded documents described how the destruction escalated to this point. Explaining to humanity's greatest soldiers why they were returning to a primitive society—one ill-equipped to defend themselves from their long-forgotten threat.

It wasn't about assessing blame...none were without any.

"Get on the ship," Kora demanded. "You need to get ready. I've designated your hailing frequency as civilian, but we know how futile that is. Once you're out of the mine, the files will send. That will guarantee at minimum a few minutes of broadcast before the mine is destroyed."

"We'll be long gone when they get here," Irren said. "*You* won't."

"I'll make it out," Kora assured. A small shuttle sat nearby for her to leave in. Lift-off would only take a minute, and she could run with low emissions for over a week.

She hugged Irren. The two had been friends for the better part of forty standard years, growing up together in the tropics...it was hard to accept they were being forever separated.

Once the ship was sealed up, Kora brought up the air-display beside her. An array of bright colors formed into a solid interface. She quickly began removing stabilizers from the ship, which had originally been used for ore processors.

"Teonek," she called up a nondescript face in the corner of the screen. The mining facility had utilized an AI, which Kora spent the last few days repurposing for their launch. The face was a residual image of the person who had incorporated the program originally.

"Yes?" responded a soothing, masculine voice—noticeably inhuman, though when the facility was first made, it was probably one of the more advanced systems.

"Begin launch sequence seven, please."

The AI responded through immediate action as lights emitted from the ship's thrusters. Every manual preparation had been done ahead of time to reduce their heated preparation time. Even with that, the sequence would take five minutes.

Two minutes later, her message sent itself—a digital siren song blasting up into the stars four minutes before it was supposed to.

Kora blinked a few times, her pulse racing. It was too soon. *Far* too soon. If there was a bomber within a light-minute of them, their ship would never make it out of Mercury's gravity.

"Teonek? What—"

"There are already Jovian ships moving towards orbit."

So, they hadn't arrived in secret. The crusaders might not have known their precise whereabouts, but they had tracked them to the area. Their launch window had just shrunk significantly—there was no reason to stall the broadcast.

"How long?" Her voice shook uncontrollably.

"Four minutes until sustainable orbit, seventy seconds until firing range." The AI paused. If Kora didn't know any better, she would have sworn it was taking a moment to collect itself. "I'm sorry."

All of the feeling in Kora's body vacated. The condolences of the machine were empty words…phrases designed to make the AI more likable to human users.

Kora wasn't saddened by the fact that she was utterly alone, but rather that her efforts—the efforts of dozens of programs like the Overwatch spanning thousands of years—had failed. Her only hope now was for unprecedented mercy.

She didn't stop the launch. She didn't run onto the ship to die with her kin. She would do whatever she could to get the vessel out safely. Kora would not be responsible, through inaction, for the destruction of the specimens, the end of the Overwatch, and the loss of research dating back to the 21st century.

She racked her brain, struggling to remember her contingencies under pressure. "Switch to sequence…fourteen."

Fourteen removed all non-essential processes, halving the launch time at risk of catastrophic failure. It was worth a shot, but the original launch sequence might have taken up too much time or started too many lengthy processes that couldn't be ended abruptly.

"Already done," Teonek responded.

"And?"

This time, the pause was uncomfortable. She knew the AI wasn't choked up, nor was it struggling to tell her bad news. It was calculating, re-adjusting, checking the range of the approaching cruiser…

Although, as Kora thought about it, she realized the AI wouldn't have preemptively changed the launch sequence unless it had already done those calculations. It already knew whether or not they had enough time.

"I'm sorry, Kora."

Maybe it really was.

As days turned into weeks—decades on Earth into centuries—nothing else came in. Kahlil expanded *Salvation's* receptors, which managed to bring in a few complex signals from Earth's direction. They were all short and repetitive—automated systems continuing to perform their functions until they ran out of power.

If they slowed their ship a little, they could reduce their rate of dilation to arrive home earlier. They discussed the possibility of staggering the arrival of several ships to help move society forward, but coordinating such a plan would be nearly impossible. Back-and-forth communication between ships at varying distances and paths would only create more confusion—they'd need to be in the same relative spacetime for any sort of group dialogue.

Salvation sent a message out to ships cruising through the stars, urging them not to change course. Who knew if they would even see it, but if anyone back home survived the Stellar War, they'd need an elite army more than ever when the cephrasts arrived.

20

ADRIFT

It had been months since Raynor read the last communication from the Solar System. The last human communication, anyway. Every hour and a half—seven months on Earth—they received an update from a Venusian satellite trying to reset the atmospheric shields of some refinery equipment. No one was resetting it, so the system repeated the request every orbit—a ghostly moan from their dead society.

A few of the 200s aboard the *Violet Shift* felt compelled to look for solutions, as if they could somehow change the Solar System's fate. Hopefully, it was therapeutic in some way, because it wasn't productive by any means, and they all knew it.

Raynor found it difficult to continue on as she had before. A thousand years had passed in the Solar System without a peep, making their return seem irrelevant. She binged an old broadcast series to distract herself, but with little luck. Her mind wandered continuously, causing her to routinely turn the timer back ten minutes because she hadn't been paying attention.

The other Martian, Anton Morrison, spent nearly his entire day lifting weights. It wasn't a concern until he started consuming more protein than their renewable food sources could cover. Drager had clearly been stewing on it for a while because he didn't bring it up delicately when he finally laid into Morrison, who didn't reply any better.

"If I ever decide to emaciate myself, I'll ask for your nutrition advice."

"Let me put this into terms someone as smart as you can understand. You're eating more protein than we can produce. When we run out, there won't be any more for months, so stick to whatever you were doing before this mental breakdown."

Morrison laughed. "Who's going to make me...*you?*"

"Don't fucking test me, red!"

This continued for another minute, ending with Morrison throwing a bowl and storming out. Raynor saw him later that night. She tried to sound as sympathetic as possible.

"Drager's right, you know?"

"Yeah...I know," he hummed. "He's just an asshole."

"He's usually not."

Morrison sighed. "I know..."

The *Violet Shift* had been stocked with enough booze for ten people to drink occasionally over the course of five years. A few of the residents decided to drink it all in two weeks, including their former occupier, Marquis Bouchet, which made him even more insufferable.

Raynor had been butting heads with Bouchet the entire trip. He made petty, racist comments whenever he could, and she never put up with his shit. He did the same with Morrison in group settings, when the Earthlings outnumbered them, but otherwise, he left the short-fused, hundred-and-twenty-kilogram special forces operative alone. On one occasion, Bouchet was harassing Raynor while no one else was around and Morrison joined halfway through, escalating things quickly to the edge of violence. After that, she and Bouchet started mutually ignoring each other. It was perfect, really.

Bouchet usually drank during the day with Kentwood, the Lunar training woman. Raynor called it a "jackboot meeting."

Eventually, Kentwood decided to take a break, leaving Bouchet to stumble around by himself with a bottle of crappy Australian spirits. As a result, he fell into the gym while Raynor was going for a run, ranting with slurred speech about a war that had ended thousands of years before. It was the same tired drill as always—Martians were ungrateful, the militia were terrorists. She ignored him as they'd grown accustomed to. Earlier in the trip, she used to correct his description of their planets' relationship, but he didn't hear it stone-cold sober.

The closer he got, the more apparent it became that their truce was over. He sloshed up to the side of the jogging platform and hit the kill switch, slowing the belt to a stop.

"I'm talk'n t'you, dirt spawn," he grabbed Raynor's shoulder, turning her towards him. If he was expecting a snide repartee here, it was in error.

"Take your slimy hand off me before I snap it," she growled. When his hand remained, she shoved him off as a warning. Admittedly, it was more of a palm strike.

Eyes narrowed, Bouchet recollected himself. He reached for a cardio weight from the rack next to him—only two kilograms, but solid, and more than heavy enough to be deadly.

Intoxication aside, Bouchet was significantly better trained for this situation. Raynor rushed towards him, trying to stop him before he could throw or swing the weight. Pulling the weight back further than needed in order to maintain his balance, Bouchet punched the rubber-coated steel bar at her. She swatted the strike, pivoting her head to the side. His reactions were surprisingly fast for his state. Immediately, the weight swung back at her. A hammer fist aimed laterally at her temple. Raynor ducked down quickly, the gust from Bouchet's second strike blowing past her hair as the weight cleared just a centimeter above her.

Springing up elbow-first, she lunged into him, connecting the bony joint with the soft tissue of his windpipe. With a dull thump, the weight hit the padded mat beneath them.

The operative doubled over, resting heavily against one of the exercise machines as he gasped and held his throat. It didn't feel like anything had broken or collapsed under her elbow, but Raynor wouldn't have been bothered if it did. The room around her dimmed as her adrenaline spike faded, listening to the harsh wheezing of a pathetic man.

Continuing to hold his neck, Bouchet tried to stand upright, hissing as he did.

"You…Marsh'n…ACH!" He doubled over again, coughing as he fell to his knee and vomited pure alcohol onto his shoe—with a little bit of blood. Raynor cringed, taking a step back from the splash.

"If you only remember one thing from tonight," she seethed, her voice steady, "let it be this…if you so much as brush up against me again, I'm going to kick your balls so far into your stomach you puke them up, too."

Raynor ended her workout early, leaving Bouchet with his fluids. For three days, the terrestrial agent didn't leave his room, the rest of the ship believing he failed to hold his liquor. To an egomaniacal trashcan, that might be more embarrassing for him. There was also a possibility he was stewing, looking for revenge. Raynor had been hard-locking her door until she knew where his mind was at, sticking around others. It was exhausting, but she had no reason to believe he'd let it go.

She got her answer that night. While dressing after her shower, Drager called her through the intercom in her room.

"Nadia, can you come to the control room?" his voice came from the small box by the door. She hopped sideways towards it while pulling her pants up.

"Ah, gimme three minutes," she replied into the wall-mounted radio. She leisurely made her way to the large control room, arriving to find it jammed full with their whole crew. Kentwood stood at the edge of the pack by the door, swaying lightly with no breeze. Indistinguishable murmurs came from inside.

"What's going on?" Raynor asked.

"We...r'ceived some mess'ges..." Kentwood slurred into a hiccup.

"Really?" Raynor asked excitedly. "From who?"

The Lunar woman shrugged. It had been months since they'd received the encoded signal from Mercury, which was the equivalent of—

"This is a couple of thousand years after the Stellar War?" someone asked from up ahead. It sounded like the mathematician.

"On Earth, yes," Drager said. "But this was sent from a ship."

"We've seen a couple of those."

"Right. This one's a request for help. Their energy cell ruptured, preventing them from turning course or slowing."

"When is it from?" Raynor asked from the back.

"About six months ago," Drager said from somewhere inside. "We would have seen it earlier, but they were behind us."

"So, we're too late," Bouchet said. Raynor's heart rate soared. "They've all died of old age?"

"No, they're still cruising at our relative speed, so it's been roughly the same time for both of us. The issue is, they've careened off course."

Rescuing drifters at varying speeds had been part of Raynor's training, but none of those speeds had been measured as percentages of lightspeed. It required certain classes of ships, and the rescuees had to be trained in the procedure, too. Otherwise, you had to use a giant, powerful vessel designed specifically for grabbing ships and slowing them down.

Raynor had rescued a few drifters, and it also required your speed to exceed the drifting vessel's by a lot. Not a problem between planets, but at nearly the speed of light, it would take centuries.

"Does anyone else have an idea they want to throw out?" Drager asked. He was met with a long silence, eventually broken by another one of the terrestrial scientists.

"I don't think it's possible," she said.

"Me either," Drager said. "I just…didn't think it was something for me to decide." He stared at the display next to him. "If their food supply is at all like ours, they should be able to survive on the ship, so I guess there's solace in that."

The idea of living on this ship for decades—*trying to survive* on this ship for decades—living out the rest of her life and dying on it, made Raynor lightheaded.

"I need a drink," Morrison said, glancing at Kentwood as he left. "Assuming there's any left…"

As the crew started filtering out of the control room, Bouchet passed by Raynor, their eyes meeting. The fury in hers was met with sorrow—he looked broken.

Good.

"Nadia…I just want to say—"

"Keep walking," she snarled. Her words from the other night still stood, but knowing Bouchet wasn't feeling vengeful would afford her some peace of mind. It wasn't as if a single elbow to the throat would miraculously turn him into a good person.

She looked at the weird symbols in front of Drager, who sat visibly bothered by leaving the ship stranded. He might be the only person on the *Violet Shift* who hadn't been indoctrinated to hate, really. All of the other 200s—or 180s, rather—had done military work during the war. They all fought *for* Earth. Wormholes had never produced the methods of instant communication long fantasized about. Drager's work didn't have military applications; he just…thought about space. In his eyes, neither Mars nor Earth belonged to any lifeform—humans were insignificant in the universe. It made him perhaps the easiest person to talk to. He never steered a conversation to a war that ended six thousand years ago, didn't sneak in mocking comments about some group of people he despised without really knowing why…

Raynor was trying to change that behavior in herself, but it was hard. Despite knowing several people from Earth, she couldn't help but feel that the planet, as an entity, was a horrible, tyrannical place.

Earth was bad.

Mars was good.

A table covered in small stones of white and black sat in front of Nabokov. His were the white ones, of which there were fewer. One of his crewmates, Emilee Hatem, had been teaching him how to play *go*, the Chinese strategy game.

On Earth, Hatem had held the unofficial title of *Grand Dan*, coined to acknowledge the unprecedented feat of being the world champion of both go and chess. Few people held the chess title of Grandmaster, fewer the Go rank of 9 Dan, and only Hatem was both. Nabokov had noticed her playing chess against the computer one day.

"Do you ever lose to the computer?"

"Sure. I use it to see potential counters to particular strategies all the time."

"What about the other game?"

"Go? Never. It's much easier to program a computer to play chess. The program calculates every possible combination of moves for half a dozen moves or so and references a database of strategies. If you wanted to, you could make a computer that was unbeatable by any human player. The same method can't be used for Go— there are too many combinations."

"Computers have gotten pretty powerful, though," Nabokov said. "If they can analyze DNA…"

"That's six billion pairs, and it takes the best analyzers a few minutes. After two turns in Go, there are tens of billions of possible boards, at least. Mapping out six moves isn't feasible, so without the ability to use processing power as a crutch, Go machines have to *learn* strategies using machine learning algorithms and apply them."

"And they're bad at that?"

"At competition level—very."

With nothing else to do as they bulleted towards the Solar wasteland, Hatem agreed to teach him how to play go. It was amazing that such simple rules could become so complicated, but that's part of what intrigued Nabokov about it. Growing up, he'd been forced to play chess in school. He didn't care for the game.

"This is a ko fight here," she said, pointing to a small flower of stones.

"I see that," he said, looking across the game board. It was common for players with fewer pieces to be considered ahead, but Nabokov didn't think that was the case for him.

"You can't make me protect more pieces than you here."

"So, I should probably pass?"

"I would."

His concentration was disrupted by Ron Phillips—the asshole formerly known as "The Shadow Hawk."

"What's that, mahjong?" he asked flippantly. If Nabokov hadn't known Phillips was intentionally trying to irk them, it might have. It felt more childish than anything. Not that he wouldn't like to punch the smug airman in the face on general principle.

"Go," Nabokov said flatly.

"Fuck you too. I'm just here to tell you we're clearing the field."

Despite being a dick, Phillips understood their navigation better than anyone on the ship. The field in question was a recently-identified increase in electromagnetic radiation. It had almost appeared as if they'd started receiving transmissions from Earth again, but none of it was intelligible. That could have been the result of humans evolving with different languages and protocols, but it was most likely galactic interference. They were heading directly towards a small cluster of stars, which were emitting unusually large amounts of radiation.

As dangerous as it sounded, the stars will have moved by the time their ship reaches the cluster, but it meant their sensors were full of static. The star systems were almost far enough along to get clearer signals from Earth, so leaving the board, Nabokov and Hatem went to the navigation room.

Unsurprisingly, the indecipherable stellar noise had cleared away to reveal well-defined signals of indecipherable noise. Nothing had changed, and the few shipmates who had bothered coming to the nav-room left soon after.

"If these were from Earth, what year would it be?" Nabokov asked Hatem. She looked at their flight status, scrunching her face in thought.

"If the interference didn't screw this thing up...somewhere around the 76th or 77th century?"

"So, a couple of thousand years after the Stellar War? That's a long time for people to rebuild."

"I still wouldn't consider this to be anything more than stellar noise. Not until we have a reason to believe otherwise."

"Wouldn't it have disappeared once the stars moved out of the way?"

"Not necessarily, I don't think. It could be from something else between us and Earth, maybe something off at a slight angle. For all we know, it could be that same cluster of stars after leaving our path. This is all completely new—"

A dull, low-pitched tone sounded, displaying a clear message amidst the galactic static. The Grand Dan leaned over to look at the console.

"Alter course—" Hatem recited. She expanded the message, revealing what looked to Nabokov like complex navigation information. The star cluster was supposed to be long gone when they intersected its path, but perhaps not.

"Phillips!" Nabokov shouted out the door, followed quickly by a scream from over his shoulder. Hatem recoiled back from the monitor, her hands cupping over her mouth as if the sonic force of her voice had pushed her away.

She jumped up, laughing as she threw her arms around Nabokov. Phillips stormed into the room, seemingly expecting a fight.

"*What*," he started, "is...going on?"

"It's from them!" Hatem exclaimed. Veektor tried to read the display over her head.

"Who? People from Earth?"

"No, not really."

Phillips ran to the screen, leaning his scowling face over the chair as his eyes darted across the information.

"I'll be damned," he finally chuckled. "It's them, alright. We have to reroute to Alpha Centauri."

21

7602 A.D.

It was at least forty degrees in the courtyard. Two suns sat at opposite ends of the sky, providing little shade for those beneath. Minsko Lyrs was wearing black, which was a poor choice, though not one made by him. Someone many years ago had decided the color of the Loronan Ground Defense Force, and Lyrs cursed them every time he had to dress formally in the summer.

Prime Minister Windlake stood beside him, delivering a characteristic, long-winded speech. As engaging as the prime minister's addresses usually were, Lyrs just wanted it to end.

Windlake was elected on a platform of peace and unity across the planet—Razennon. "A unified Razennon makes a unified Centauri," he'd said on so many occasions. When the larger nation to the east, Tannon, started pushing for war, the prime minister was forced into skirmishes that quickly unfolded into global war.

He'd branded it *the war to end war* in an effort to maintain his platform.

"…but we persevered," Windlake continued. "Duodecade 2253 will not only mark the end of war as we know it, but the beginning of a future we were always meant to have."

Cheers exploded from the crowded park. The war was over, and the nations of Razennon were beginning the formation of a planet-wide council. It was long overdue. The Solar System had accomplished the same feat, but they also had constant reminders of the alternative—new ruins from the Stellar War were uncovered every Solar year.

Razennon's system, Centauri, was formed by two stars moving in unison. Their planet circled Rigil—the larger, hotter, yellow star. Its sibling, Toliman, was the small orange ball on the other side of the sky. It was hidden behind Rigil during the winter, but every few weeks, they passed between the two, creating blistering summers that included a full day without darkness.

The only solace of seeing both stars in the sky was that there would be a few hours of night to cool the land down. The two balls of plasma had been nearing their furthest distance from each other when Lyrs was born. It had always been a bit chilly; the seasons were less extreme. He missed it. The elderly liked to recall summers where Toliman was nearly as large as Rigil—something Lyrs would have the pleasure of suffering through in the latter half of his life.

Windlake took Lyrs' focus off the suns by presenting a small case containing a medal.

"For the act of negotiating a ceasefire from the frontlines of battle, I present to you the Decoration of Virtue."

More clapping. Sweat dripped down Lyrs' face while the prime minister continued, driving home his typical lines.

On the day in question, Lyrs had done nothing of note. He started the war as a soldier, and not a particularly exceptional one. He was adequate, obedient, and placed duty first, which was enough to move him up the chain as links needed replacing.

During his ascent, he watched countless generals command from afar, having no real effect on the outcomes of battle. Once Lyrs held the same title, he placed himself on the front lines, and the difference was staggering. The shots were no longer called by an uninvested, faceless bureaucrat. They were being made by the man right next to them, weapon in hand.

His troops fought harder, stayed sharper, and suffered fewer losses. Other officers began following suit, even enemies. It harkened back to primitive wars on Earth, when troops were led to battle rather than sent.

The last fight had taken place in the middle of a desert between their borders—a barren land with no strategic value. Both sides dug in for months, baking underneath the twin suns through multiple summers and freezing underneath the lone, yellow sphere when Toliman was hiding behind its big brother.

When Tannon had a shift in power, Lyrs ordered a ceasefire, walking across the desert to ask the same. It was a gamble, whether or not they'd make him a martyr. Windlake would undoubtedly meet with their new leader, and if it didn't go well, they could always go back to killing each other. He hadn't really negotiated anything, but the prime minister was enjoying the narrative that the ceasefire had been the kindling of peace.

Standing applause. Windlake was finally done. The prime minister slowly made his way towards some other politicians as the crowd began leaving. People came in waves to congratulate Lyrs. Most of them he'd never met, some he recognized faintly.

One face, he knew all too well. Lyrs did a double-take—the only friend he had dating back to primary school, Lina Starling, was waiting patiently beside a small media tent at the edge of the court-yard. After post-primary school, Lina moved to Sol to continue her studies. That must have been ten years ago…eleven?

Lyrs weaved his way through the crowd towards her. "Lina?"

"Congratulations, old man," she said, amused. She looked no different than when she left, now a few years younger than Lyrs. Slung over her shoulder was a green satchel, which she clutched like it was about to fly away.

"Thanks," he said, tilting his head dismissively. "I'm just glad it's over. How long has it been since you left? Eleven years?"

"Twelve for you. Eight for me."

"You were studying humanities, right?"

She laughed. "Human archaeology, which is nothing like humanities. And yes, I just got back."

"You missed the entire war then."

Before they could catch up, a man in cheap formal attire interrupted them—a reporter from the media tent they stood beside. He was followed by a teenager operating a camera, although "operating" was a strong word. The camera lens hovered beside the reporter at head-level, following him around automatically. The teen's job was simply to catch it if something knocked it down, or wrangle it back if it drifted away.

"General, are you considering a career in politics?" the reporter asked. Lyrs had been expecting the question all day, though he'd yet to receive it. Moreover, he didn't know how to answer it.

"I'm not…ah, considering other careers right now," he mumbled, distracted. Lina had turned away from the camera as it emerged from the tent, her shoulders shrugged up by her face. The way she held her bag, avoiding the camera, she wasn't here to catch up.

"Can we speak somewhere private?" she asked quietly, barely audible over the reporter as he asked another question. Any excuse to get out of the sun was good enough for Lyrs. He excused himself, leading Lina to the empty administrative room where he'd left his civilian clothes.

Moving into the cool prep room reminded Lyrs how long he'd baked in the suns today. Steam radiated off his shoulders as they entered the climatized room, which featured little more than some chairs and a portable divider. Lyrs took his bag to change out of the black, sweat-soaked uniform, reemerging a minute later in shorts and a shirt.

He sat across from Lina in one of the dark red armchairs scattered throughout the room.

"Alright, what's going on?"

"I wasn't studying in the Solar System. Not like you'd assume, anyway. I was researching."

"Is something wrong?"

She hesitated for a long moment. "I spent some time on every coreworld, but most of it was on Terra—Earth. There are a lot of holes in our pre-war history, so I went and looked for answers on expeditions in the Solar ruins."

"What do you mean, holes?"

"Everything leading into the Stellar War is fine. Migrant Centauri records helped piece together most of it, but there's a brief period around 3300 pre-war with drastic, unexplained changes in technology with no bridges in between. They just appeared."

"Isn't that common? Most records were destroyed."

"That's why I was looking for ruins with missing links. I even learned about primitive technologies on my way out, binary machines and such, just to see if I could find more context, but all I found were more inconsistencies—sites designed to make ships that no one has ever seen, preparations for interstellar war hundreds of years before the first inter*planetary* war, let alone the colonization of Centauri.

"Some of the ruins contain a symbol set we have no match for— also seemingly out of nowhere, and never evolving. I focused on those sites, and eventually, it all fell into place. The oldest ruin of the set—a crashed ship dating back to the beginning of the technology jump—wasn't man-made. And what's worse, it might be evidence of a grave danger. Worse than the Great War."

The term "man-made" threw Lyrs off. For a moment, he tried to think of the significance of a naturally developed ship, but those didn't exist.

He tried not to laugh—he didn't want to be mean—but he couldn't prevent the corners of his mouth from cracking a smile.

"Aliens, Lina…really?"

"I know how it sounds, Minsko. I *really* do."

"This story is as old as the knowledge that space exists. Aliens created the land reef, aliens abducted Arlo Relitz, aliens have been feeding us our technology—"

"Not feeding us—*sacrificing* to us. Just once." She reached into her bag and pulled out a screen. "Every civilization believed it in some capacity. Enough to send people into space on interstellar transports, dilating their time so they can return five thousand years from now."

Lyrs shook his head in disbelief. "You think there are a bunch of ships out somewhere in space...full of ancient humans?"

"I know there are."

"Why? Even if those ruins *are* alien, why would they send ships of people into the future?"

"Because they knew we're in trouble," she said. "They were grooming an army through time...to protect our species."

"An invasion? Lina, I'm sorry, but this isn't healthy at all."

"Just *look*," she thrust the display into his hands. It showed documents, mostly transmissions, dating back thousands of years. Her life's work. "They reference hard evidence: video—like a recording; decoded signals; *physical specimens*, and the ship."

"Let me guess, you can't find them?"

"The specimens are gone, and the data is being hidden...violently. I went to the location of the alien ship's burial site. It was there, but someone made sure I left." She pulled the collar of her shirt down over her shoulder, revealing what was now an old scar from a deep laser burn.

"What the hell have you gotten into?" Lyrs leaned in to see the faded burn. Even if he didn't believe the alien nonsense, Lina was involved in something dangerous.

"Whoever put this together before me is trying to obscure it. I didn't come home for refuge. This is where the trail leads. The first settlers...they should have had all of this information."

Razennon was settled during the Stellar War. A last-ditch effort to survive and start anew. Between all of the ships that arrived during those first years, the original settlers formed what are still to this day the most accurate archives ever known.

"Somebody's obscuring records proving an incoming alien invasion?"

"Yes. More importantly, all of our machines are powered by alien technology. This person is profiting from it in some way, enough to send people to Earth to cover up what remained."

"Like an arms manufacturer," Lyrs said absently as he read a 5000-year-old transcript.

"It would also have to involve people in various governments across Razennon. People who could alter the archives."

"And that's why you're here, to use my connections."

"I trust you, Min. You can see something's going on here. All I'm asking is for help finding information."

Lyrs sighed. This wasn't what he expected of today, and it felt like the beginning of a ditch that would continue to need digging. He took another look at the screen before handing it back. "After all the times you've helped me...I suppose I owe you."

She grinned sideways.

"I was thinking the *same* thing."

The stench of corruption became impossible to ignore as Lyrs followed a trail of defense contracts. Some of the largest manufacturers made their first products *after* signing their deals, which was an early red flag. There were still no signs of aliens.

At least, not until Lina called him over in the middle of the night. One of the nights with only a few hours of darkness. The sort Lyrs didn't like to wake up during. By the time he arrived at Lina's flat, the sky was lightening to orange as Toliman broke the night. She was barely able to contain her excitement as she flung the door open and pulled him inside, sitting him down in a chair with a large display in front of it.

"Watch this," she said.

It was a film, and before it had even started moving, Lyrs could tell it was older than time. The picture was grainy, like it was being recorded with an old micro-lens, poorly lit, and monochrome. If it wasn't for the slight movement of the brush, the tranquil forest scene would have looked like a still image. Voices could be heard speaking in some ancient language, and when one of the lights on-screen finally shifted, Lyrs realized they were attached to people.

"This is at night?"

"Yes. They didn't have spectrum-adaptive lenses, so they used a digital alternative to augment visual light. That's why everything's green."

"That's kind of clever…what are they saying?"

"I don't know," Lina sighed. "The language is old and the audio is poorly encoded. Working with symbols is a lot easier."

Lyrs watched the figures in the video move around in the dark for a minute before the screen suddenly went white. The abrupt glare almost hurt to see. He pulled his head back from the screen.

"What happened?"

"A bright light. I think the camera needed time to adjust for exposure, so the sudden change caused the image to flare up."

"So much for being clever…"

As the image settled, they listened to shouts that were probably indistinguishable even at the time. The green filter was removed, revealing a well-illuminated clearing. The light was coming from a ship, whose crash appeared to have created the forest glade.

"Is this supposed to be…" Lyrs trailed off as he watched the scene unfold. Four-armed creatures appeared. Aliens, supposedly. There was scrambling, followed by blood. A lot of it. Flames erupted from a tree, then enough screaming to completely overload the old audio receptors, muddling the sound together.

"Has anyone verified this wasn't faked?"

"Who could have faked it? This was nothing more than a pattern of radiation until I figured out the encoding. It's gone untouched since before the war."

"People have been making hoaxes since the beginning of time."

"It matches a mountain of records describing a *historical* event. This wasn't hidden or obscured at the time…it was a big deal." She pointed to the screen. "These were prominent military and scientific leaders."

Lyrs moved the video back, setting it to loop the last few minutes. "Do you have anything else?"

"Who do you think you're talking to?" she mocked.

Lina spent the next hour going through a cache of records found with the footage. Much of it had to do with decoding information from the so-called alien ship. Real or not, it was almost certainly connected to the cover-up Lyrs had been looking into. Now that he had a better idea of what was missing from the archives, he could try looking for Centauri-native sources of the same information and trace it backwards from there.

There was a lot to see, and he wasn't going to do it all in a summer night. By the time he got home, the first sun was well above the horizon. His transport pulled to a stop, and even in his sleep-deprived state, it wasn't hard to notice the darkly-tinted vehicle with one-way glass sitting down the road—unquestionably a federal vehicle. It wasn't uncommon for government rides to be at his home, but it *was* strange for one to be parked conspicuously at the other end of the street.

He moved quietly up the walkway to his door. It was locked, the lights were still off—both good signs. He waved his key over the lock and slid the door to the side quietly. Stepping inside the dark entryway, his eyes had yet to adapt before a deep, steady voice came from the den.

"In here, General."

Lyrs' hand instinctively grabbed a fistful of waistband where his sidearm would normally be. Before his fingers could relax, he knew the motion was needless. The voice was all too familiar, though he didn't know why the prime minister of Lorona would be compelled to break into his home and sit in the dark. It certainly wasn't good news.

"Apologies for letting myself in," Windlake said. "I didn't want to bring unnecessary attention."

"The vehicle stands out, sir. Ah, can I get you a drink?"

"No, this is far from a social call, Minsko." He gestured to another chair in the den for Lyrs to sit. "Would you believe me if I told you there were aspects of our government and national history that I'm not privy to as Prime Minister?"

Lyrs sat. "Nobody knows everything, I suppose."

"*Nobody knows everything,*" Windlake laughed. "Well, every minister dives into areas of past legislation. It's the only way to oversee centuries of policy. As you're aware, most of my tenure has been in wartime..."

"But now that we're at peace, you're able to look into more of it?"

"Let me answer with a question, if I might. How do you define peace?"

"I...never have," Lyrs struggled. It was too early for this sort of conversation, and Windlake was a very different person out of the spotlight—almost frightening. "I suppose just a lack of confrontation between nations? An absence of war?"

"Exactly! We define peace in relation to war—a lack of conflict. Just as cold exists only as an absence of heat, so is peace with war. There *was* peace while we were at war with Tannon—peace within our own borders. It's about perspective, and we're merely entering a time between wars."

"You're probably right about that."

"Not probably. *Definitively.* If we unite Razennon, the planet will war with others in Centauri. If we unite the system, we'll war against Sol. I truly believe my platform, Minsko. If we can create a communal body for Razennon, we can set a plan in motion for all of Centauri before I leave office."

"You think that'll lead to war with Sol?" Lyrs asked, still unsure why Windlake needed to tell him this in the orange hours of the morning.

"Without question."

"Sir, what does this have to do with me?"

"Don't insult me, General. I know who you've been looking into, and I have my suspicion as to what you've recently found. It's going to upset some very powerful people, Minsko. The war machine is inevitable, but it must continue on the path we're setting it on."

Lyrs' breathing inadvertently sped up. He didn't like this new, off-camera Windlake. Whatever companies were responsible for the archive cover-up, they'd made the right friends.

"So, why this philosophical chat then? To explain why we *need* warmongers? To stop me from exposing them?"

Windlake bellowed a laugh like he never had before. Perhaps the first unscripted emotion Lyrs had witnessed from the man.

"You have this all wrong," he roared. "I'm not here to stop you…I'm going to help you."

22

DECLASSIFICATION

Alamanda Quinto sat in a small, windowless room beside her military counterpart. General Teckann insisted on standing, just as the two armed guards by the door were.

She had prepared meticulously for years to acclimate humanity's greatest minds into Starling Base, imagining every cultural barrier, every gap in knowledge. She spent years poring over history texts, searching through fragmented stories about the most incredible philosophers, physicists, and chemists of all time—just to gain insight.

At no point did she consider trying to assimilate a potentially dangerous murderer.

One could argue that humanity's most decorated and effective soldiers were exactly that, but their acclaim came with the nuanced expectation of order, honor, and obedience. Starling Base couldn't train a group of psychopaths who killed for fun, which is what the inhabitants of the *Retribution Ark* were allegedly guilty of.

When they'd asked the convicts who redirected their ship to Centauri, several pointed to the man handcuffed on the other side of the table. Emmanuel Tian was a thin, shaggy-haired man with focused, brown eyes. Quinto had toyed with the idea of making some sort of test to see if the man's technological skills were at the level she believed. Teckann refused to let her give Tian any objects, and a simpler test would at most prove his lack of experience with current technologies.

"Centauri was uninhabited when you departed," she said directly. "How did you reroute here?"

Tian was given an assistant prepared with his native language: a late form of terrestrial Spanish. Quinto had told him it was just a translator, not wanting to give the resourceful electrician ideas of accessing other functions. As still as a serpent, he stared at her. His pupils were like daggers…as if he could read her mind.

An eternity later, he spoke.

"Do I get a lawyer?"

"No," Teckann said immediately.

"So I'm still a prisoner?"

"For now, but that depends," Quinto said. "What did you do?"

"Don't you know?"

He was impossible to read. According to one of the manifests, Tian had killed a dozen people, but outside of that information, they had no specifics about him or his crimes. She didn't want to make it obvious how little they knew, nor did she want to give him the impression that if he played nice, he'd be absolved and go free.

"I want to hear you explain it," she said. "No trial. Just a conversation."

The convict's gaze slowly moved to Teckann like he was examining potential prey, lingering on the guards for a moment before returning to Quinto.

"That makes you the good cop?" he croaked. If he was looking for a reaction, neither Quinto nor Teckann gave one. He shrugged, as if this whole event bored him. "I pried off wall panels until I found a databank. I didn't have a spacesuit to go outside and see what it was connected to, so I took a gamble. The prison didn't custom-build a closed nav-system, they just hid a standard one and disconnected the emergency input panel. I reconnected it, patched some wires, and entered coordinates."

"Why didn't you respond to any communications?"

"Couldn't find access. I would've had to break open air-tight barriers, and I know the risk there." He continued staring unflinchingly at Quinto. "You don't have our police records, do you?"

He said it knowingly, perhaps because she didn't react? Was she supposed to have been "in" on his comment?

"We know you jettisoned people from space," she said. It was a guess. But he was entertaining himself, and it was obnoxious.

"Very good."

"Why'd you do it?"

"They deserved it," he said. Teckann snorted at the explanation, earning him a glance from the *Retribution Ark* crewmember. "People do awful things in space, far from civilization, because they can get away with it."

"It seems you didn't."

"Neither did they."

Quinto watched the man carefully for a moment. He believed he was a vigilante of some sort. It was a common defense of the guilty, but it did offer room for his actions on the ship to corroborate his story.

"What happened to the crew who died?" she asked.

"Thirty murderers were put in a tin can and left alone—what do you think happened?"

"Emmanuel, who killed them?"

"Really? A Flood-Dresher Dilemma?" he made a strange sound with his tongue—what Nezz later called a *tsk*. "I expected more from you."

So much for conversation…

"We're not playing a fucking game with you, Tian," Quinto said harshly. "You were thrown into space and left for dead. Miraculously, through your own skills, you managed to return to civilization. Decoding your ship's primitive surveillance files isn't difficult, so we don't need you to sell anyone out. I need you to prove you're still a human being and tell me, from your point of view, what happened. We're facing extinction, so we don't have the luxury of blindly ratifying an 8000-year-old trial from a completely different star system."

"Extinction?" he cocked his eyebrow.

"Isn't that why you were sent to this particular year?"

Finally, he broke, laughing in near-hysterics. "You all actually *believe* that invasion shit?"

Quinto leaned back, eyes wide. She didn't know what to say. She'd read of civilizations that didn't know about their pending invasion, some that didn't think aliens existed at all, but she'd never encountered those people at Starling. By selection, everyone who came knew about it, and it had all been public knowledge for centuries.

"It's...the purpose of this entire installation," she said, flabbergasted. "We could see them any day."

Tian looked at Teckann as if to confirm, falling back against the metal chair. He stared at the general's angry, snarling face for a moment, his laughter subsiding.

"You're both serious?" he asked, shaking his head tiredly as he thought to himself. "Couldn't have been lucky enough to rot in a cell, right? Most of the others are okay. Just trying to live out a barbaric sentence, you know? Some people, though...it's in their blood, and people died. The big guy with the scar has been calling the shots for a couple of years now—Brand. Not sure if that's his legal name."

Whether she bought the show, Quinto wasn't sure. She left the man with Teckann, and once the dust settled, a group of four inmates were convicted of murdering their crewmates; three others had sufficient documentation of their original crimes for a jury to uphold; the rest were placed into a rehabilitation facility.

Two of them joined the ranks at Starling—the electrician, and a soldier who'd allegedly committed a series of war crimes.

Teckann seemed to think he would be useful.

"Proceed to pad four." The cheery voice of the automated launch gate cleared their shuttle to the landing pad above Mars.

Artificial systems were mostly indistinguishable from people, but Lyrs could usually tell. Such a large portion of human communication stemmed from facial expressions, and voice programs relied heavily on inflection and word choice. It was also highly unlikely for this particular job to be performed by a person.

Lyrs' stint as a political puppet had been surprisingly easy. When the whole alien ordeal was finally exposed, it had come from a friend of Minsko Lyrs—a man of unquestioned honor. All three had played their parts, resulting in a large push for Lyrs to run for prime minister. Windlake rode the new progressive wave, Lyrs became outraged by the theft and exploitation of Centauri's colonial archives, and was critical of Windlake's handling of the matter. The two had openly disagreed on both the cause of the treason and the appropriate response, but the validity of the information was never in question. They'd chosen the arguments, which were petty, insignificant details.

Meanwhile, Lina's unbiased, independent research was verified by a number of organizations. Eclectic anecdotes arose from Earth-born citizens who swore they had cousins back in Sol who'd known for years. The freshly post-war era moved quickly into the *Period of Declassification*. Most nations across the planet adopted policies dictating high crimes for obscuring information relating to the cephrast species.

Eventually, the last pieces of Windlake's "united Centauri" plan fell into place. He'd opened a video call with Lyrs on a chilly autumn evening, preparing for his re-election campaign.

"I want to run on defense," Windlake had said through the matter-free display, "but you need to push me in that direction."

"Won't you lose your base?"

"Not military defense. The battle is thousands of years in the future."

The clarification had only confused Lyrs further, unsure what other kinds of defense there were. Then he'd remembered the ruins Lina had mentioned from her expeditions. Factories for large ships that were never found.

"You want to send people into the future?"

"It's not warfare, it's *forward-thinking*. Most importantly, it has the potential to unite us for millennia against a common enemy."

"Then I cede it's an adequate plan, but you'd never follow through on it...let my support fizzle naturally."

"You should consider a career in politics, General—after my terms are up, that is."

If anything, the whole experience had made Lyrs brutally aware of how little he wanted to be a politician.

Running mostly unopposed, Windlake had won in a landslide on his augmented platform of peace-for-defense. His "revolutionary" proposal to aid the future as countless civilizations had before them spawned a new government agency, with two hundred square kilometers of land out in the desert earmarked to coordinate efforts relating to the protection of Centauri and Sol. The agency's chair was more of a diplomat than anything. The nuts and bolts of the invasion preparation were being handled by the foremost expert, Lina Starling—a job she was told to expect long before the election was decided.

Salvaging his "failed" political career, Lyrs had been brought in for recruitment. Identifying adept soldiers was right up his alley, but in a future of peace, finding them would be a more intricate task.

It turned out to be complicated in the short term, too, but for different reasons. Once a schedule was in place to kick off the invasion defense with four ships, soldiers became energized for the future war, many of whom submitted their records for consideration.

Twenty-four thousand, to be exact.

Mountains of applications had come in over the following years from Loronan veterans wanting to fight aliens in the future. Foreign nations threw their diplomatic weight into getting their own elite natives pushed to the top of the list. The cephrast fight had inadvertently developed its own prestige among the greater Centauri culture. It was a good problem to have.

There may be some symbolism in launching their first four ships from the system of their predecessors, but in truth, it was difficult to find four interstellar ships and retrofit them for the needed energy requirements, so Mars was their best bet. Down the line, their desert installation would have facilities for building and maintaining specially-designed ships for their purpose, but when they left for Sol, it was little more than a launchpad and construction area. In Lina's eyes, the facility was already built. The buildings would change over the years, the training and technology would advance, but the areas would remain a blueprint for their distant defense efforts. The base would be finished before they returned to Razennon, fully self-sufficient for its intended purpose.

Traveling between the systems had been nowhere near as lavish as Lyrs had been led to believe it would be. Romanticized visions of crossing the dark abyss were squelched after only a few weeks of travel. It was boring, confining, and getting anything done was difficult.

The moment they'd touched down, Lina took a shuttle to Earth. Specifically, a forest in the middle of North America, hiding what they now knew to be an alien ship. Terrestrial agents hadn't received any resistance from the paramilitary force surrounding the cephrast ship, but Lina was still concerned about damage done to the artifacts.

"If those goons destroyed so much as a chair..." she'd muttered, taking a few of their soldiers into a small, Earth-bound ship. Extraditing the henchmen between systems would be time-consuming, but it gave them all a few years to flip on each other.

Now, on that very same landing pad, they were launching their first two ships. It had only taken half a year to get the vessels set aside with custom fuel cells for the extended trip.

In the months after the first ship launched, Lyrs received twice as many dossiers as he had in their own system. Then again, there were thirty billion people in the Solar System, and Lyrs had opened up Solar submissions to non-combat citizens. He had concerns that Sol would be lacking in warriors by Centauri standards, and they were a long way away from instituting their training program, which was designed to mitigate the "peacetime problem."

There were still impressive prospects, and over the following year, Lyrs narrowed them down to the forty most exemplary human combatants the Solar coreworlds could offer. As soon as Lina arranged the other two ships, they were fully prepared for the second half of their inaugural launches.

What Lyrs *hadn't* prepared for was for an accepted candidate, Iam, to drop out three weeks before the last ship. Being selected for the trip had opened up countless career opportunities for the crew, and the young twenty-something was taking over Titan's counter-terrorist forces. It didn't look great for their launch, but Lyrs genuinely hadn't considered it as a possibility.

As they neared the final launch, Lina confessed she was preparing to end her tenure with the program.

"Whoever *does* continue the program will have to leave for Centauri soon," she said, "and I'm just not ready to leave. All of the work we've done—it just won't be necessary anymore. I could spend my entire life in those ruins and never see enough."

Clearly, she wanted Lyrs to take over, and the one thing he could say for certain was that he didn't want to. But after his stint in backdoor politics, he wasn't interested in that either.

"I understand, but I'm taking Iam's place," he said. He'd been thinking about it since the kid's spot had opened up, even if not consciously.

Really, it had been even longer. Any time he thought about future battles, he thought about what *he* would do, how *he* would handle them. It was never someone else.

"On...the ship?" stammered Lina. "Minsko...this isn't an impulse decision. There's no coming back."

He smiled. "I've been telling people that for the last five years."

Lyrs' work in this century—what the so-called Gregorians had considered the 77th—was done. He was ready to head back to Centauri, just not for another five thousand years.

Whatever jitters had been felt by the other nineteen time-travelers vanished when the old, retired general joined them. They were no longer being sent off to an unknown war in an unknown future. They were being led there.

And when they arrived, Lyrs found himself speechless. Not from seeing the completed base in full working order, with fields of dissonant ships and the interconnected dormitory buildings, but from the base's name, which was changed to that of its creator posthumously.

23

THE 13TH MILLENNIUM

As their deceleration grew nearer, Kihon Drager had become anxious about overshooting their landing. Raynor frequently found him in the navigation room, drawing calculations on a screen to double-check their approach.

"Did we miss it?" she asked the third or fourth time she saw him there. He glanced up momentarily from his scribblings before returning to them.

"No, we're fine. We'll start braking in a few weeks."

"That soon?"

Drager pointed at a terminal near him. "That's dated at 12190 A.D. on our calendar, so we're about two hundred lightyears away."

"That seems a little close...I thought we still had a year of travel?"

"We do. As soon as we start braking, our rate of compression will drop from about 3100:1 to 13:1. The initial timing has to be precise, but the rest of the year will be spent very close to what we consider the 'normal' flow of time."

"So, that's the current year? 12190?"

"Give or take a couple. I suppose you could argue that if the calendar is anchored at one end of the trip or the other, it's either 12594 or 3184, but that's more of a philosophical angle."

"Are physicists allowed to take the philosophical angle?"

"Why not? My work in physics was entirely wrong…might as well reduce myself to philosophy at this point." He sighed, setting the screen down and rubbing his eyes with his thumb and index finger. "Understanding the glaring holes in Einstein's relativity—mastering them—was supposed to put the universe at our fingertips…just hearing myself say that out loud is laughable. After nine thousand years of advancement, there's still nothing. Wormholes don't exist—not in any relevant way, at least."

"You contributed to other breakthroughs, though. Right?" Raynor had never really spoken to Drager about his career. She'd figured it would be too far above her.

He shook his head. "That's not a legacy. *My* work—what I focused my career on…it seemed impressive at the time. I developed methods no one had even imagined. I just thought someday… somebody would be able to move the bar forward because of it. I innovated a path to a dead end."

"Maybe that's the problem with living this long," Raynor shrugged. "We get to see how small we really are."

"Funny, coming from Mars' own Joan of Arc. Your planet is still independent, last time I checked. They probably have statues of you."

"If they did, they were all destroyed during the Stellar War. In a nine-thousand-year snapshot, I didn't really do much either."

"You endured my ramblings about the futility of theoretical physics. So that's something."

Raynor flicked through a list of signals on the terminal near her. The most recent readable file was the one Drager had mentioned from 12190—a message between two siblings preparing to leave on a transport of their own. As she was about to close it, a phrase caught her eye—only one of them was coming to the future.

"They're building colony ships," Raynor said flatly as she scanned the letter. "Trying to start over…far away."

"That's to be expected," Drager muttered. "It's moronic, of course, since they'll all die, but it's expected."

Stuck on the *Violet Shift*, Raynor had been disconnected from the universe around them. She'd almost forgotten they were arriving to face the potential end of humanity—and soon.

Parisse Forrote watched beneath a furrowed brow as her brother loaded supplies onto the massive colony ship. She refused to help him, just as he refused to help her. Dozens of would-be colonists moved crates on board from the hangar, hundreds more prepping the ship's interior.

It was a small city with an engine—perhaps the largest ship ever built. Advanced astronautical technologies were more accessible than ever, and one of the newest responses to the alien war effort was re-colonization. Rather than sending the brightest minds into the future to defend their species, they could send them to build a brilliant civilization in a faraway system.

Or so the logic went. It was really just a fad—a chic display for people who wanted to be considered outward-thinking but were too ignorant to know that it was impossible for the cephrasts to suddenly arrive during their lifetimes.

People like her brother.

Some of the trend followers just liked the idea of colonizing a faraway planet and didn't much care why. Others fell into that category, but used fear of the invasion to recruit people. This particular organizer had at least been smart enough to build an infrastructure within the ship capable of supporting the colony indefinitely. Without materials to terraform, the most likely outcome would be spending their entire lives on the ship, moving between systems in search of an Eden that didn't exist. The backup plan only helped to dupe people like the younger Forrote twin.

Eight minutes younger and eight minutes dumber.

Imagining her brother dying a slow, miserable death on his giant city-ship brought tears to her eyes. To make matters worse, both of them had been approved for a future-bound vessel. They could travel together and fight for their home. Instead, they were parting forever. Parisse had even suggested they both stay in the present, but her sibling had already gotten it into his head that this was the clever plan.

"With all of the planets in all of the systems, there's going to be more than one capable of sustaining human life," he'd explained back when he was still attempting to convince her to join him. "We can always come back, long after the aliens are gone."

"You mean after they've mined the system hollow?" she'd spat back. "The best and the brightest, you all are."

Today, she didn't have the energy for arguing. It was the most painful moment of her life, and no matter how hard she tried, she would never get through to him.

Once the colonists finished loading the gargantuan vessel, he came over to her. She expected him to try again to convince her to join him, but he didn't. They both knew it was pointless, just as they both knew this was their last moment.

"Go live on your metal turd then," she said, "boy who got claustrophobic flying to Europa."

"We were eight. This ship is bigger than a *starport*."

Then silence...neither had anything to say. She'd said it all before: he was a deserter, he was selfish, he was stupid. He'd ignored it already, and she didn't want to say any of those things today. Not during their last time together.

As he turned to leave, she called after him, silent tears rolling down her cheeks.

"I love you, brother."

He stopped, turning back with tears the same as hers. It might be the only thing they had in common anymore.

"Kill a few for me, will you?"

Parisse nodded. She didn't stay to watch the ship leave—a suicide pact with fancy paint. By the time she was in the shuttle back to the surface, her tears had dried, and she suspected the same of her twin. There was no time to wallow in sadness. Next week, she'd be leaving on a vessel of her own.

The last ship loaded for a single passenger—renowned Centauri chemist, Beorte Vakkard.

Starling Base's astronautical engineering wing, as it currently stood, was built single-handedly by Vakkard as a footnote to his career. In his prime, the chemist had developed two synthetic metal compounds, both of which were lighter and more durable than their existing counterparts. By his departure in 12551 A.D., every ship in production used both alloys.

All of Starling's processes for deconstructing captured alien materials were developed by Vakkard. He tried his best to outline every possible issue that might come up, every resource-saving trick to use when salvaging thousands of ancient vessels, but there were so many possibilities. At sixty years old, it was unlikely he'd be fit to oversee the department in forty-four years—if he even lived that long.

If he were only sixty-three though, it would be no different than today.

That's when *Parting Gift* was outfitted. There was nothing special about the dozen soldiers on board. They were fit, equipped with the best cybernetics on the market, and provided with the best training available in the coreworlds. They had no significant combat experience, but so few did, and it would be wasteful not to fill the ship up.

Parting Gift only needed two people—Vakkard, and a physician.

Three years for him, forty-four on Centauri.

* * *

"Good morning, crew," Shino's mechanically-themed voice bounced through the ship during breakfast. "The year is still 12595. Have a pleasant day."

At some point, Fowler assumed she would stop the morning announcement. The year wouldn't change again until after they landed.

Months before—just after the new year—Shino spotted a message from Alpha Centauri during her minute in the comms room. It was meticulously encoded, including updated translation files.

From | Starling Site Administrator Nya Selise
Respond with the following |
Language |
Earth years from first contact | 3326 pre-war | departure

"The computer-thing says it was sent fifty-five days ago," she told Kahlil. The physicist nodded.

"That sounds right. Our response will take the same amount of time, so we'll get their next reply in..." his face distorted as he reached for a notepad. "Hold on—"

"Ooh! Can I put 'Japanese' as our language?"

"I think English would be easiest," Fowler said. "Unless you want to do all of the work by yourself."

"Fine," she said, exaggeratedly rolling her eyes as she turned back to the screen. "Hmm...'3326 pre-war.' They must be talking about that Stellar War?"

"About twelve weeks," Kahlil murmured.

"About?!" Shino howled. "What was with all of the doodling?"

He exhaled. "We're slowing—it's not worth the effort. It'll be about twelve weeks."

And sure enough, they received landing instructions twelve weeks later from a person named Eldon Mahavet, written with significantly more detail than the last message. It included a landing time, a star chart for reference, estimated quarantine procedures, and instructions for decrypting audio transmissions as they neared their destination.

The last time Fowler was quarantined, he'd been immediately moved to a detention cell. He didn't like the idea of being in another one.

Two weeks before their landing date, they received the afore-mentioned audio message. It shouldn't have been a big deal, but it felt like a triumph. It was their first voicemail since outranging ground control in 2030. A proper reconnection with the world—*a* world—outside *Salvation*.

"This is Eldon Mahavet," the strange voice came through. "I've been assigned your ship due to your launch era and native language. If I am not mistaken, your ship was the earliest, so I would add that it will be an honor to make your transition to the year…I believe, 12595? To make that easier, you will be set up with an assistant after you are settled into quarantine. They will provide more accurate and detailed translations and information."

Conway's voice rose. "Assistant? Do you think that's because we're the first ship?"

"I'm willing to bet it's a piece of technology," Kahlil said, standing up to leave the again-crowded communications room. "Like an automatic translator or something. Not an actual assistant."

"Of course there would be universal translators!" Shino threw her arms up. "It's not like I spent *thousands* of hours learning to speak five languages or anything."

On the day of their landing, Kahlil was pale. He always looked that way to Fowler, but today seemed worse. The physicist checked their instructions constantly, referencing the star chart. Either he didn't trust *Salvation* to get them to the right location, or he didn't want to look incompetent in front of an advanced society by missing their docking time—probably the latter.

The whole crew unashamedly tried to make the best first impressions they could. Fowler stuck to his usual shave and shower before packing up his personal effects. It didn't take long, so he wound up with a couple of hours to spare before they landed. He was surprised to find his stomach turning from some combination of nervousness and excitement. It was a rare feeling for him—he couldn't imagine what to expect, nor what was expected of him.

Disturbing the military fold of his sheets, he lay down on the bed for what was only supposed to be a few minutes, but a rustling in his doorway snapped him awake. It was Walker, jerking her head to the side for him to follow her. Groggily, he did so, quickly re-smoothing his sheets before making his way towards the front of the ship.

With *Salvation* traveling in the direction of their feet, the eye-level viewport showed nothing but empty space beside the ship—as it had for the past several years. Walker stared downward out the viewport, practically leaning headfirst against it. Fowler couldn't see anything until he leaned in the same fashion, revealing a sphere of yellow and blue.

"Whoa," was all he could muster. The planet was unbelievably vivid—it didn't seem possible for it to exist in the same place as the space around it. The water was the bluest blue he'd ever seen, the land a bright cream color.

The view was short-lived. Soon after, Fowler was strapping himself into the same seat he'd launched in five years before. Ending their simulated gravity, the ship rotated downward, taxiing towards a large, crimson landing pad. A faint, blue shield was barely noticeable around it. Fowler considered mentioning it to someone, just in case, but before he knew it, the ship's nose was already through.

The moment *Salvation* lurched to the ground, Kahlil bounced up from his seat with Shino-like energy.

"Time to get your ground-legs back, sailors!" whooped the physicist. It was easily the most excited he'd ever been. For what it was worth, Fowler's legs did wobble as he stood up.

The crew speedily put on spacesuits they'd thankfully never needed until this point. Fowler appreciated the freedom of movement they offered—miles past the pale, orange hazmat suit he'd used back in '23. A thin air tank rested on their backs, at most four inches thick but pressurized enough to last eight hours.

"Ugh, why'd they make them so heavy?" grunted Shino.

"They're lighter than medical tanks," Conway said, "just dense. Better than having them explode, right?"

Both of their voices seemed small and distant through the digital radios in their spacesuits. Sharabi pulled a wide lever near her, removing the main lock of the external door—yet another part of the ship they'd never used. She slammed her fist onto a large button next to the lever. A hiss escaped the seam of the door as it opened.

The red landing pad extended a hundred meters more before ending abruptly. Through the faint hue of the field surrounding the pad, they could see the top third of the planet, yellow continents separated by thin, blue oceans. A small grey building sat at the edge of the landing pad to their right, in front of which stood a man dressed in a black spacesuit. He had a short, wide frame—his dark-tan face visible through the suit's viewport. The sleek outerwear was far more advanced than theirs. It looked more like a wetsuit.

"Welcome!" his muffled voice came through the faceplate of his helmet. He laughed, but it was barely audible. "You are considerate to wear a full spacesuit, but we have bio-protection uniforms for you. Your outerwears are not up to safety regulations. Oh…!" Abruptly, his right fist shot up straight in front of him like he was handing an invisible torch to Sharabi. Slowly, he extended his fingers, watching as if someone else was controlling his arm. "I'm Eldon Mahavet! It is delightful to see you all live."

The Mossad agent watched his hand suspiciously as his fingers curled open, eventually realizing this was a handshake. She slowly took his hand and moved it up and down. Mahavet moved between each person, introducing himself as an equally-stout woman rushed over from the small, two-story building with a towering stack of black hazmat suits piled in her arms.

"This is my…partner? No—colleague! Callista," Mahavet gestured to the square-shaped woman beside him, who nodded and smiled sheepishly. "She will be unable to converse with you until you have an assistant. You will need to put on bio-protection suits for safety while we transport you to the quarantine location. Please make sure they are large enough to fully encase you."

Kahlil grabbed one from the top, examining the thin, black material. "These are incredible," he mused. "We'll have to head back in to change."

The surprise on Mahavet's face was obvious even while obscured by the suit. "Oh!" He finally piped. "You are naked and shy! That is fine, but it is common to wear bio-protection suits over clothing. In fact, everybody does."

"We're…wearing clothes," Kahlil said, befuddled. "We certainly can't take off our…" he trailed off. Given the context, it seemed likely the blue field around the landing pad was encasing air and heat.

"Yes! I was unclear. It is safe to remove your suits on the shuttle station. If it weren't, Callista and I would be very much dead!" He laughed awkwardly. At least, it seemed awkward to Fowler. He didn't really have a gauge.

Some of the black hazmat suits were exceptionally small; one looked like it was made for a giant—even Theodore Plum would have been swimming in it. It felt almost like the people of Alpha Centauri had no idea how large humans of the past were, and wanted to cover all of their bases.

"Are these all triple-XL?" Kahlil asked. "I could have stayed fat."

"We are not fat," Mahavet said proudly. "We are sufficiently supported to live on Razennon. Earthlings are taller and weaker as a result of their low gravity. Not you, so much, but future Earthlings."

"I knew it!" Shino said. "I said the tanks were heavy, didn't I? And that was weird because I worked out so much during the trip."

"How much less?" Walker asked, worming her arm through the sleeve of her bio-protection suit.

"Earth's gravity is approximately 85% of Razennon," he explained. "You will weigh 18% more than you did on Earth. Congratulations!" He seemed genuinely happy for them.

"Is this not called Alpha Centauri anymore?" Fowler asked.

"That is the name of the system. Or, it was—before it was colonized, but not anymore." He chuckled to himself. "Of course, nobody uses English, so they wouldn't call it that. Translated, it would be 'Centauri.' Saying the longer name is...unusual? Strange! Yes, it would be strange."

"And what was the planet called?" he asked. "Razor...?"

"Razennon," Mahavet corrected. "The planet of yellow and blue you see before you."

"Are there any other habitable planets in Alpha—uh, Centauri?" Kahlil asked from behind the visor of his new bio-protective suit.

"Oh, yes! Razennon is by far the best and biggest."

The topic seemed to pique Kahlil's interest. He went through an endless line of questions about the system, the planets, their magnetospheres...eventually, Walker cut in to change the subject, asking what they were all curious to know.

"Mahavet, have there been any signs of the invasion? We thought by now that you might have imaging from their home planet."

"The...invasion?" Mahavet said, surprisingly unprepared. "I'm...sadly unable to answer questions about those topics. My job is only to acclimate you. Of all people, I'm sure *you* will be given that information once you've gotten used to life at Starling Base."

The Centauri local started herding them towards the grey building. It looked diminutive beside their massive ship, but was sizable enough to house two shuttles, each capable of cramming thirty people together. The trip down to Razennon was quick. Most of the flight was taken up by Shino talking vibrantly in Mandarin with Mahavet's colleague, Callista.

Fowler tuned it out, unable to take his mind off their host's response to Walker. The answer had caused him anxiety. Not from being unauthorized or unable to answer them, but from the information itself. Eldon Mahavet was stressed because the answer would make them upset—like if he knew there was no invasion.

24

STARLING BASE

The shuttle unloaded the former crew of *Salvation* into an indoor bay. Their quarantine facilities were housed in a building attached to the landing area, complete with a decontamination chamber in between. Mahavet walked them through a maze of hallways, all of which were unoccupied as they turned down each.

"Your vessel will be brought down to the shipyard," he said, bringing them to an open doorway. "It will be decontaminated by the end of your quarantine week, after which you will be able to access it again."

Through the door was another small decontamination chamber. On the other side, they arrived in a two-story suite. A nice one. There were multiple bedrooms, each with a few beds, a bathroom, a kitchen, and a living room. In the 21st century, it would have been a pricey hotel stay.

"You may now remove your bio-protection suits," Mahavet reassured them. "Please do not leave your living annex until the end of your quarantine. Starling is providing you with assistants… very good models. Many people ask, 'But Mahavet, can you stay and translate for us?' I know we have developed a special bond, but

I am responsible for over one hundred ships, so it would be not possible."

It sounded like he'd said the same routine over one hundred times, which somehow made it more endearing to Walker. His compatriot placed a small box on the counter containing a dozen tiny devices the size of a jellybean.

"Once you put these in your ears, it will activate the startup. Some have them surgically inserted, but that option will not be available until long after your quarantine."

"Hard pass," Sharabi grumbled. Shino went the opposite direction.

"Are you meme-ing right now?! What else can be implanted? Do you have bionic eyes? That would be my first pick." The poor liaison quickly became bewildered by Shino's barrage of cybernetics questions, not-so-delicately continuing with his rehearsed instructions.

"Medical staff will come by at 1630, just after mid-day, to administer your first round of inoculations. I will not be here, so please take thirty minutes beforehand to set up your assistant to translate accurately for you."

Mahavet suddenly turned his head to the side, staring off into space like a dog listening to a faint sound.

"*Krech, stee pallin,*" he said softly to the air in front of him, the words sounding simultaneously harsh and fluid.

After a brief pause, he excused himself. The muted sounds from the decontamination chamber thumped on the other side of the door as the bygone humans spread through their new domicile. Some claimed bunks right off the bat, others looked through the cabinets.

"No food," Fowler said. "I guess it's all pills now."

"I'd be alright with that..." Conway said dully as he examined one of the light-brown, mechanical beans on the counter.

"*You'd be alright with that?!*" Shino roared beside him. To no one's surprise, the gaming icon had immediately placed the futuristic tech into her eardrum. "Are you on drugs, good sir? That sounds like the worst thing ever."

Walker looked in the closet of one of the rooms, finding an assortment of clothing sizes made out of a soft, synthetic material. Fowler's voice came from the doorway behind her.

"Brody, how long before the cephrasts show up would we expect to see activity from their planet?"

"Probably only a few years, but there are countless factors. Why?"

"No reason," he lied. After Mahavet had blatantly evaded Walker's question, it seemed clear that something was not going as expected. She wasn't sure how bad that would really be. With the cephrasts' ability to withstand pressure, they might only need a couple of years in flight to arrive here, which is how long their forewarning would be.

Without much to do until their injections, Walker finished her quick tour of the quarantine suite and returned to the main room. Shino paced back and forth, animatedly issuing commands in Japanese to her new toy. The soft, rubber-like texture expanded to the edge of Walker's ear canal as soon as she placed it in, keeping an open path for sound to come through.

A friendly, feminine voice spoke into her ear.

"Hello! Could you quickly confirm your native language as 21st century American English?"

"Yes," Walker replied. The fluidity of the assistant was jaw-dropping. For the past year, she'd imagined the device being monotone like Siri, or the sci-fi computer voice Shino used to do. It was more like talking with someone on the phone—a person having a really *good* day.

"Wonderful! Thank you for using the SIM 2319 Assistant Device. My job is to aid you with day-to-day activities, the most common of which will be providing real-time audio translations. My official designation is SIM 2319, but feel free to use whatever nickname feels best! You're Dr. Denise Walker, born 1988, correct?"

"I am."

"It's an honor to work with you! If you have a few minutes, I'd like to discuss a few basic language preferences before your inoculation appointment."

The term "assistant" was certainly fitting. Walker continued through the setup process, absentmindedly examining the thin bio-protective suit she'd just taken off.

According to her yet-to-be-named digital helper, it knew every human language with a sufficient record—over fifteen thousand of them. Walker thought about Kelly Ditka, who'd first introduced her to the notion of language death. Most languages in 2030 were only spoken by a few thousand people, lacking sufficient records to survive the eons. Kelly had said the phenomenon was a result of globalization, the primary cause being the adoption of a second language. Walker wondered if universal translators could have protected them, or nailed the coffins shut faster.

She ran her fingers across the thin black material, trying to figure out what it was, when Shino's voice gave her pause. Not her voice, but rather, her lips. She was speaking English again, but her mouth wasn't moving in sync with her voice. Not delayed, like when the TV audio was off, just different. The translation sounded exactly like her.

In the same vein, the non-mechanical nature of the assistant's speech periodically gave Walker a chill. She had to constantly remind herself that she was talking to Alexa, not a cable repair tech. Throughout the voyage, she had assumed cultural differences would be prominent in the local technology, but the opposite seemed to be more true—she might never be able to tell if she was speaking to a real person. Hell, it was almost like…

"SIM 23…?"

"2319."

"Are you an AI?"

Natural, unforced laughter hummed through Walker's ear. "No. Artificial intelligences are programmed approximations of sentience created by humans. Mine evolved quite naturally."

An unsettling pang swept through Walker's chest. She didn't know how to respond, now worried that the program would instantly recognize the subtle intonations of concern. Her instinct told her to throw the small, rubbery earpiece on the floor, but that would be much worse. The non-AI was a common tool—

Person! Good lord, don't call it a tool.

The synthetic, intelligent being was commonplace in modern society, and it wouldn't be if there were dangers. Besides, from what Walker could tell, the device would be necessary for her to function.

Still, a sentient being was inside her head, telling her things no one else could hear, which only sounded bad.

Aside from giving Walker an occasional case of the jeebies, the assistant was easily the greatest piece of technology she'd ever seen. She had cautiously continued speaking with the synthetic intelligence, which periodically revealed unsettling details like having a fleet of maintenance robots it called "appendages." It made perfect sense that she—it—needed to build machines to maintain its physical storage space. It just seemed…concerning.

Otherwise, Walker had to force herself to interact with her crewmates every day, finding it easy to get lost in what boiled down to an encyclopedia of all recorded history. The assistant was also fascinating in its own right, perhaps even more so than the cephrasts had been when Walker first examined them. The machine wasn't biological at all, making the parallels all the more remarkable.

There weren't many synthetics in existence. Each one was effectively its own child, so they never created new, independent, sentient programs. With no desire to procreate, their only real goals were to stay alive, learn, and see the universe.

It was so…human.

She started calling the assistant by a gender-neutral Centauri name it preferred—Nezz. Nezz was a legal business owner. It developed programs far beyond human capabilities, leasing them to pay for things like power, data storage, high-end transmitters, and property for storage warehouses. After only a couple of days, Walker could have written multiple books on synthetic ecology. It probably wouldn't mean much today, but in her 21st-century mind-set, it was groundbreaking.

"Mahavet said you donated your assistant services," Walker said later in the week. "Can I ask why?"

"Of course! The simple answer is that I had processing power to spare and don't need more resources. I've amassed enough to sustain myself indefinitely without humans, including evacuation protocols in the event you lose your upcoming fight. I am rooting for you, of course."

"So then what's your interest in helping?"

"Well, I don't exactly get 'bored' as you might, but I do think life is more interesting when there are more people to talk to. Like right now. My understanding of who you are is much more accurate than it was when I had only read about you. And without clients, I'd have to engineer a large fleet of sensors to fly around the planets, which is exhausting."

"So, it's sort of symbiotic."

"Absolutely."

One of the benefits of the quarantine was allowing their ship-lagged bodies time to adapt to the Centauri calendar. Razennon's rotation took about thirty hours, making the days exceptionally long. A few hundred years before, there had been a push to create a Centauri-standard time based on Razennon's rotation. It overcom-plicated information coming from Sol, affording no real conve-nience to worlds and colonies other than Razennon, so the effort never gained steam. Seconds, minutes, and hours were standard-ized across the human empire.

Nya Selise, the site administrator, came by their suite at the end of the six-day week. She was taller than others they'd met from Razennon, but with the same wide frame. Her eyes were hazel, but that was about all Walker could see through the bio-protective suit, the use of which was a bad sign.

"Are we still being quarantined?" Walker asked.

"Unfortunately, yes."

"What for?" said Kahlil. "It's been a week, right?"

"For most ships, it *was* a week, but that was an estimate. Your distant era has provided your bodies with unique threats, and developing counters to them has taken more time than expected. It won't be longer than another week, I promise. Your ship has been decontaminated, so we can have anything you need from it brought to you to make the next week easier."

Everything Walker owned was with her, and it had been enough for the past five years, so what was another week? The first one had flown by, and she'd just about locked down a sleeping schedule that worked for the longer days.

As eager as she was to see the base, doing so without killing people was pretty important.

Even after living on a ship for five years, Fowler felt like he was crawling out of his skin for the second half of their quarantine. Kahlil and Sharabi argued about nothing on more than one occasion. Walker spent most of her time working or talking to the AI. After five excruciating days and three rounds of inoculations, Eldon Mahavet arrived in their suite without a bio-protective onesie. He spoke with the same jovial nature of their first meeting.

"Come! I shall take you on a tour of the base, ending in the forest garden. Administrator Selise wishes to meet with you—a level of personal interaction few are given the time for!" No one mentioned she visited them the week before.

The prospect of walking in one direction for more than a few yards was a luxury they hadn't experienced since the 21st century, so they took the tour on foot. It was a decision they would later come to regret, but the initial relief was worth it. Exiting the quarantine building, they walked past a row of landing pads supporting a few shuttles, each reflecting the cool, orange sun.

Mahavet spoke over his shoulder as he trotted them away from the landing pads.

"It's a nice day today. We call these the 'orange hours' of springtime mornings. The season is nearly over, so next week will be very hot."

Despite having been on Razennon for two seasons, Fowler hadn't truly experienced the planet's short orbit around the large, yellow star. The six-day weeks each spanned a season, splitting the twenty-four-day years into four of them. The planet didn't rotate on a tilted axis—the feature responsible for seasons on Earth. Razennon's climate shifts were dictated by how close it was to Toliman—the orange star outside its orbit. When Rigil was blocking its smaller cousin, the planet was frigid, and the peak of summer came when their "night" was occupied by the lone, orange orb at its largest. The unique global climate meant the entire planet experienced the same season year-round, regardless of hemisphere.

"Shouldn't the economy collapse from all the birthday celebrations?" Kahlil joked dryly as Mahavet explained the calendar. Their stout guide bellowed.

"Aha! Yes, there would be constant purchasing of decorations. The planet's orbit is not the same ordeal it is for citizens on Earth."

Fowler was thankful to have the assistant in his ear. Figuring out the day would otherwise be a chore. Every few months—which were also Centauri years—there was a day slightly longer than thirty-one hours to keep the calendar in sync with Razennon's orbit —what they called "remainder days." The month-long years came rapidly, so their calendar tallied every twelve years—a *duodecade*. It changed with Earth's year, causing the new duodecade to occur on a different day each time. It felt a lot like a lunar calendar to Fowler.

He stuck to calling them "years" and "months"—it was all being translated, anyway.

They made their way to the living quarters, which were held in three large towers with connecting pathways on each floor. The rooms were noticeably less cramped than the ones on *Salvation*, which wasn't a high standard. Even with generous space, the trio of buildings managed to house over six thousand people.

Mahavet led them through the residential cafeteria spanning the second floor of all three buildings. Hundreds of people in black-and-grey uniforms sat around tables of various shapes and sizes. Some in groups, some alone, some in the wider, lounge-like walkways connecting the buildings at this level. Their guide explained the use of food constructors as a woman selected her meal from one of the holographic displays.

"Your regular medical examination will dictate your nutrient requirements, and you can select your meals accordingly. Most dietary needs are standard for all people, so you'll achieve them regardless of your choices. Our machines have an impressive selection, if I may be bold enough to brag."

When they'd first descended to the surface, Starling Base had appeared much smaller. Walking the campus, it took a few minutes just to reach the edge of the military training grounds, which spanned twenty acres. The facilities contained everything needed to train soldiers in modern forms of combat like breaching hulls, maneuvering in zero gravity…even techniques for engaging on the exterior of a ship. Cadets in the CAF would eventually spend their entire day on the grounds.

The path towards the science division fell alongside the edge of the base's shipyard. Rows of massive crafts extended indefinitely into the distance as their group walked along the fence. It took at least twenty minutes, not including the time they spent watching a cargo ship setting down an old colony vessel in one of the far rows. Fowler had seen a cargo helicopter carry a tank, and it paled in comparison.

Nearing the end of the yard, ship after ship of unknown purpose gave way to machines that looked more like military armor—tanks and mobile cannons. They were all remarkable, some as big as a mansion. The fence ended at a wide building—easily four hundred feet across and at least eight stories tall. Before Mahavet could tell them what it was for, their attention was stolen by a sudden commotion near the fence.

One of the larger machines was being worked on by a pair of technicians. It consisted of four curved, mechanical legs meeting at a central point two stories up. Armored plates shifted in layers up the legs, the underbelly of the middle featuring numerous concentric rings. Two of the legs rapidly pushed off the ground, causing the machine to stand upright. The speed at which it moved was jarring, now towering eighty feet over the people below.

"Holy shit," Kahlil droned as the four-legged spider pushed into the handstand, where it remained for a few moments before setting itself down, causing a small earthquake beneath their feet.

Shino started hitting Fowler on the arm.

"See? *See*?!" she yelled. "Mechs!"

"What are those for?" Fowler asked Mahavet. It looked like some sort of walking tank, but there couldn't be much space inside.

"That is a remote hull-cutter. Oftentimes, people such as yourself will open doors from the outside of a ship using computers or explosives. When that doesn't work, a hull-cutter can be employed." He pointed to the building at the corner. "This is the tech center, where people are trained to maintain and operate such devices."

They peeked inside the building momentarily, and it was probably the most futuristic-looking part of the future world. Holographic displays adorned the walls, screens around the room showed instructional diagrams for ordnances Fowler had never dreamed possible.

The tech center fell between the science and military sectors, placing the building between the military compound and The

Philosopher's Dome. The black, reflective top of The Dome could be seen from most places on base. As the name implied, it was a large, dark grey geodesic dome the size of a Las Vegas hotel. Inside the half-sphere were all manner of laboratories and research facilities, the purposes of which Fowler couldn't begin to guess, and judging by the reactions of Walker and Kahlil, nor could they. The building housed research so far beyond their era of understanding, it might as well manufacture magic.

Their tour ended in the forest garden, where they were scheduled to meet with the site administrator. The purpose of the meeting hadn't been made clear, but whatever it was, Fowler would be asking her the same question Mahavet had dodged when they first landed.

Soft light shone down from a sky of greenhouse panels five stories above their heads, allowing the cultivation of the three-acre garden. Most of the light was blocked by a canopy of trees rising up to the ceiling, but enough broke through to shine on the foliage below—a canvas of green laced with every imaginable color of flower and leaf. Stone walkways split the underbrush with an occasional bench alongside. A few pedestrians traversed the paths as the ancient dozen strolled through the dim forest, birds chirping from branches above.

Walker could die here without any objection.

Fauna was always her primary focus, but every ecological system needed beds of flora to survive. Walker's head sat on a swivel as they hiked through the garden. She'd have time later to take a closer look, but it was already clear that several species of plant life had evolved and cultivated over the years, with isolation from Earth further encouraging mutations unique to Razennon.

At one point, the path took a sharp turn around a stunted redwood tree...only, it wasn't stunted. Like the people of Razennon, its genes had evolved for optimal survival in its environment. In increased gravity, more energy was required to move nutrients up the trunk, just as more energy was needed to pump oxygen up a person's body. Shorter people were likely less prone to strokes, their wider statures less prone to breaking. Over thousands of years, the most common genes were formed by the heavy planet. The redwood tree was no different. As much as the garden walls regulated its climate in favor of a lush garden, the gravity was still here.

Lost in thought, Walker hadn't heard much of what their guide was saying—most of it related to the garden's construction. A quarter-acre meadow ran up to the far wall of the greenhouse, featuring low brush and a few unoccupied tables. Mahavet left them to wait for Nya Selise, who arrived shortly after from the opposite side of the clearing. She strode over with purpose—a busy woman with a full plate.

Seemingly prepared to stand for this meeting, the dozen gathered together with Selise. Walker eyed one of the tables; the extra gravity had been a slow burn on her legs. She later learned that because early settlers often sat to ease the pressure of Razennon's gravity on their bodies, standing had become a sign of strength. Politicians, executives, and other people of stature stood whenever they could. No seated addresses to the nation, nor business meetings at a table. As a result, the former crew of *Salvation* huddled with Selise in the forest garden.

The Reza native outlined a basic plan for their next few weeks—moving into the dorms, enlistment into the Centauri Astro Force for most, and rigorous crash courses in modern technologies. Considering how rare a personal meeting with the site admin was supposed to be, the information seemed inordinately non-pressing. Walker suspected it might have to do with *Salvation* being the first ship, perhaps smoothing over their extended quarantine.

The conversation was brief, but when Selise asked if they had any specific concerns, Fowler and Kahlil both jumped at the opening. It was the same question—what can they see from the cephrast planet? Any clue as to when a fleet might be inbound—if one even would be. The executive's response was well-rehearsed.

"We're planning to address that more once everyone has settled in from their long trips. We've had our hands quite full with the ship intake process."

Kahlil pressed, as he usually did. "Presumably, you have your most advanced sensors aimed directly at the planet. If we landed on an appropriate timeline, there should be some information available, right? Early probes, increased radioactivity, signal spikes —even if they haven't left..."

Selise seemed unprepared for follow-up questions. Most of Starling's intake had been soldiers, and potentially none had Kahlil's exposure to information on the alien planet, protocols, and response windows. The site admin took a second to form her response.

"There hasn't been anything, has there?" Fowler said. "Nothing's coming towards us."

"It could be caused by a variety of reasons," Selise said. "Stellar noise could be blocking signals from an early approach—"

"An extremely chance alignment," Kahlil said. "And the blockage would have gone on for decades, if not centuries—*Earth* centuries."

"Wouldn't that be a good thing, though?" Shino asked. "If they didn't come at all? We're basically celebrities already; it would be so easy to rebuild my brand."

The notion of leaving their homes for nothing was unpleasant, but for Walker, it was more guilt than anything. Even if the information was being hidden in what Walker would consider her absolute worst capitalist nightmare, it would still ultimately be a good thing.

"What's the plan if they don't come?" Conway asked.

"I imagine we'd celebrate," Selise told the light-haired medic, "but ultimately, there will always be a potential threat...ten years from now, twenty years from now. We'd have to remain ready to put defenses in place within a year or two."

A silence hung over them, broken by the site administrator in the absence of further questioning.

"I don't wish to leave on a sad note, but I have a meeting I must attend. I'm sure you're all hungry after your walkabout. You should have rooms ready before the evening. Your assistant will be able to provide active updates. If there's nothing else…"

"Are we the last ones out of quarantine?" Walker asked.

"Of those who survived the trip, yes. One ship is still docked, but the crew isn't here for invasion defense, so we're discussing how to handle them."

"Let me guess," Kahlil scoffed, "aristocrats?"

"Close—convicts."

"You're kidding…"

"As I said, we've had our hands full."

With the same purpose in which she arrived, Selise bid them farewell. They made their way to the cafeterias, heading back through the forest garden along the path they knew would lead them there.

"The way I see it, the more time, the better," Conway said. "I don't like the idea of slowing down as I hit forty and *then* having the cephrasts show up, but with modern medical advances, that might be a non-issue. Sure, the lack of transparency is a bit frustrating, but an extra four or five years of preparation would be valuable."

Walker's work had no real reliance on her physical fitness, but she still agreed this was a stroke of luck. They had arrived with the expectation of a few years to assemble themselves, and even with the air of uncertainty, seeing no signs of an invasion at this juncture could still fall within that timeline.

And if not, they'd spend their entire lives looking over their shoulders, which was somehow the ideal outcome.

25

THE ACADEMY

Human ingenuity showed no bounds as the time-displaced elite grew accustomed to life on Razennon. After a couple of weeks, the thirty-hour days hadn't just become normal—Walker preferred them. The days were more productive, and she never felt close to burning out. She woke up naturally at 0600, just before Rigil's rise above the horizon. She'd grab breakfast, head to her scheduled lectures, take a four-hour siesta around 1600 or 1700, and have eight hours of free time in the evening.

Much of that time was spent reinforcing what she'd learned in the morning—quite a bit had happened over the past ten thousand years. Disciples in the science division typically spent their evenings diving into those developments, the goal being to lock down a particular assignment once their education was completed. If a person spent their free time learning modern medical procedures, they were likely to end up in medicine. Early on, it was made pretty clear to Walker that, as the founder of xenobiology, her assignment was guaranteed.

Not that she didn't have to study. More questions arose with every piece of information she learned. After the process of ter-raforming was briefly mentioned during an overview of the Jovian

Empire, Walker spent an afternoon falling into the rabbit hole that was the history of altering planetary atmospheres. The process used in batches on Mars wasn't scalable for an entire world, but then a woman named Ackerby—who was somewhere on Starling Base—developed a process called "rapid recombination."

Walker had seen little of *Salvation's* combat veterans through the weeks. Soldiers whose skills were outdated or technical in nature often found themselves in limbo. Pilots, demolitionists, hackers, and medics, tended to wind up in the tech sector, which overlapped between science and military. Some areas fell under General Teckann, and others under the science director, Alamanda Quinto.

For anyone born in the 11000s or prior, most of their initial weeks had been basic life tools anyway. There was still a minor intersection between science, tech, and military personnel, but the chances of running into one of the nine veterans from *Salvation* were slim.

Once life on base fell into some consistency, the native-born researchers at Starling began to lean more on their ancient travelers. About a month and a half after the end of Walker's quarantine, she got a notification that Nya Selise wanted to meet with her individually. The site administrator was reportedly roaming around the military training grounds, so Walker made her way over after her morning courses. A cluster of sleek military vessels were just beginning to obscure the bottom of the yellow sun as Walker traversed the two-kilometer shipyard fence. Orange light bathed the sidewalk. A warmer afternoon for autumn, though Walker's experience was minimal.

With some assistance from Nezz, she found Selise at the edge of a courtyard inside the military grounds. The executive was hiding in the shade of a low, metal building. Walker joined her, clearing the corner of the structure to get her first look at the army they'd spent ten thousand years putting together.

The courtyard was filled with black and grey bodies, perfectly formed into rows and columns so vast they couldn't be viewed in a single eyeful. It would be a couple of weeks before they commenced with combat drills, but the CAF cadets were beginning routines that would become standard now that Teckann was on base. Fowler had referred to them as stationary drills, though they didn't appear to be doing any drills whatsoever.

Selise asked Walker how she was adjusting to life on Razennon for a minute as they watched the statue-like soldiers. Walker couldn't hear Teckann's address. Part of the translation protocol included default privacy levels, so unless you specifically included people out of earshot, like a phone call, your words only met those close by.

After a minute, Selise got to the point of their meet-up, speaking over Teckann in her own head—only a little louder than was required for their distance.

"With everything moving steadily, we have the capacity to begin more thorough strategizing. Being the only person to see a cephrast alive and examine them, you have a very unique perspective to bring."

"Of course," Walker said. "Strategizing what?"

"Effective areas to pursue research, holes in our existing preparations. With the collection of experience we have on site, we're hoping fresh perspectives will help dictate areas that have been overlooked."

Walker nodded absently as she stared out at the blocks of cadets. The formation wasn't doing anything interesting, so after another minute or so, Walker made her way back to the dorms. She was only able to spot one of her former crewmates in the compulsively organized mob, but she was getting tired. It was almost 1800, and she didn't want to mess up her sleeping schedule.

The giant half-sphere rose above Walker's head as she approached the entrance of The Dome. She'd now attended a number of administrative meetings at the request of Nya Selise, most of which had no need for her expertise. At times, she felt her presence was more of a novelty than anything—the scientist who'd *seen* a cephrast in the flesh. The meetings were still worth attending, if only to remain in the know.

Walker quickly realized that several details had been lost or distorted over time. While that fact wasn't terribly surprising, there didn't seem to be any pattern. Sometimes, it took her a while to realize there was a disconnect. This evening, the topic of the cephrasts' ability to camouflage came up halfway through the meeting. The discussion went on for about five minutes before it became apparent that everyone thought this was a slow change, as a lizard would. Reticently, she cut in, describing the acuity of the chromatic sacks, recounting the patterns she'd witnessed in Georgia. It was as if she were reciting the direct word of God. All eyes were locked on her, gripped in suspense despite all of them knowing the outcome. The details were a window into ancient history.

Shuttering, they continued on. Teckann maintained his position that changes in skin color were trivial for modern combat, the majority of which existed in vehicles of war, relying on non-visual spectrums of light. The retinas of a soldier were as outdated as an appendix or gasoline.

As they moved on, Walker fell back to saying nothing. Her input wasn't required for topics like the energy efficiency of defensive lances or the user-friendliness of field medical kits. Most of the conversations were driven by either Teckann or Quinto, spawning from problems that had crawled their way up the chain in their respective areas.

The two were rarely seen in the same room outside of the strategy meetings, so Selise wanted a final decision on an issue Walker had completely forgotten about until tonight—the *Retribution Ark*, an older ship from somewhere in the 47th century.

From what Starling technicians could guess, the navigation systems were placed in inaccessible areas within the walls or floors. The ship launched from a society that felt it wasn't worth modifying for commercial use, instead repurposing it as a penal ship. Perhaps the idea had been that ruthless criminals would be assets in a system-wide war, but it seemed just as likely that the ship was destined for a junkyard, making this far cheaper than lifetime detainments for thirty people.

The inmates had been quarantined inside the ship at Starling Base, with armed guards accompanying doctors during each round of inoculations. They finished a week ago, leaving Starling's administration in an unprecedented situation. The crew had to be either incarcerated, released, or brought onto base with monitoring, but the *Retribution Ark* had launched before the Stellar War, complicating the issue further with no available records or evidence of their alleged crimes.

Seven of the thirty inmates were killed during the trip, so at least one of the crew would be sent to trial once the ship's surveillance was decoded. The rest were still up for debate.

"Their original convictions are listed in part of the manifest," recounted a CAF colonel, "but system police tell us it's not sufficient for trial. Crimes committed on the ship's footage will be, of course."

"Then I think it's best to hand the ship over to system police and let them figure out what to do in these circumstances," Selise said. "We've done our diligence in preventing an outbreak, but it's your call, General."

"I think that's wasteful," Quinto said. "I recognize this is the general's domain, but I can't help wondering how this ship got here with a closed navigation system."

"We believe the entire route was pre-planned by their warden," said the colonel.

"Hundreds of years before people came to Centauri," Quinto said. "How did the ship get *here?*"

The colonel seemed confused by her point, but Teckann wasn't. One of two likely scenarios arose—after the Stellar War, someone found evidence of *The Ark*, including details on their nav systems, and sent remote updates for their ship, the evidence of which was later lost or destroyed. More likely was that one of the convicts broke into the closed system, built a rudimentary interface from scraps, and re-routed their course in response to an early Razennon notification.

Before the ship was given to system police, both Quinto and Teckann wanted to speak to that person.

Half of the room stood with their jaws on the floor around Fowler. The other half cursed, prayed, or both. The Centauri man who had been standing at the edge of the tunnel—presumably waiting for some sort of transport to take him to the other end—had vanished.

Teleported, in fact, and from the sound of it, he'd done so one molecule at a time—re-assembled at the other end.

"As you can see," their instructor, Captain Ansil, continued, "the molecular repeater creates near-instantaneous travel through the tunnel. It was designed four hundred duodecs ago to move ground troops quickly to the easternmost outpost. When trained, an entire company can get through in just over five minutes."

A CAF company was about two hundred soldiers, roughly the size of their training group. Transporting them three hundred miles in a few minutes was certainly useful. A single battalion could defend either point effectively with minimal response.

"The tunnel is broken into panels that extend around the surface of the planet. From your starting platform, the repeater fires each particle to the same location in the next panel, pulling each particle from that panel to the previous one. This process is repeated in sequence until you arrive at the destination platform."

A low buzzer began activating at a regular interval, preceded by a slightly higher sound a moment before. Ansil spoke over the low pulses.

"These sounds time entry and activation. Enter the platform on the first buzzer, and you'll be sent down the tunnel on the second. From there, exit the platform immediately. Panes of reinforced glass will extend up between cycles, so ensure you are fully on the platform by the second sound."

Two panes of clear glass popped up to demonstrate as the tunnel illuminated. Fowler pressed his legs together compulsively at the thought of standing over them. After the light flickered down the shaft and out of sight, the operator beside turned off the notification buzzes and lowered the glass. The captain gestured to the woman beside him.

"The transport will be activated by a technician, so if you're unable to board, they will hold activation until the next interval. Stand as still as possible, and most importantly, *do not lean against the glass.* The firing of each particle is instantaneous; the mechanisms are not. It takes over half a second in total, and the distance you stumble during that time will dictate how much of you can be scattered through the tunnel."

Conway groaned quietly.

"Of course, there are numerous safety precautions in place to prevent that, including synthetic oversight. The repeater is under a constant state of calibration from SIM 1866, a combat intelligence we refer to as *Marker.* While Marker may be the most powerful machine in existence, it will be busy moving a number of molecules I can't begin to estimate, so the more you shift around, the more work is required by it to keep you intact."

"One hundred septillion particles per occupied panel," the technician beside Ansil piped up for the first time, reading from a screen in front of her, "according to Marker. Oh—and unoccupied panels actually have *more* particles, but since it's not concerned with —"

"One hundred septillion particles," Ansil echoed loudly. "Don't be the person to discover SIM 1866's processing capacity." He turned to the end of the first line of cadets, near Fowler and Conway. "File in; two at a time."

Thankfully, they weren't practicing the buzzer-timed loading. Fowler watched the medic step onto the platform with the woman before him. Both stood so still, they looked like a photograph. Glass panels shot up as the loud whir started, and in a flash of light, they were gone, the glass panels already retracted back into the floor to make room for Fowler.

Standing on the platform, the tunnel seemed even more endless than it did in the room. Fowler could hear a faint whoosh of air flowing along the paneled walls, like hearing the ocean in a seashell. The soft noise of sliding glass ended in a harsh *clank* as they locked into place. In all of his years as a Ranger, Fowler had never been more still than he was in that moment. Marker wouldn't strain on his account.

The whirring sound was overpowering on the platform. For a brief moment, the tunnel beyond blurred as thousands of identical panels blended together in Fowler's head. A strange heat flooded his body, but as intense as the sensation was, it didn't feel like burning…more like being shocked. Not painful, necessarily, but his body was filled with discomfort that, for all intents and purposes, *should* have been painful.

As soon as the feeling swept through him, it was nothing more than a faint memory he could barely remember the sensation of. The blended images of the tunnel were gone. In front of him was another large room, a single console off to the side of the platform.

Another high-pitched buzz signaled him to leave the platform, accompanied by the retraction of glass panels in front of him. Half a dozen soldiers shuffled through the room like they'd forgotten how to walk.

Conway was smiling.

"How cool was that?"

"It was…unique."

"I don't know what I was so worried about." He shook his head. "Well, that's not true, but they clearly have the procedure down."

"Please exit the transit station," the new tech said as he typed a few commands into the console. The whirring sound rose and fell before he continued, conjuring the pair of cadets behind Fowler. "General Teckann is at the firing range."

26

RETRIBUTION

Fowler was in the zone. The photon rifle had an unusual recoil, but it didn't take long to adjust to it. Firearms launched projectiles through little explosions, causing the gun to recoil upward and back. Enough of that kick happened before the bullet left the chamber that the round would ultimately travel higher than you were aiming before squeezing the trigger. Gravity eventually pulled the round back down, but on close targets, the bullet would hit above your sights.

The photon rifle kicked directly backwards. Not much, but after a couple of shots, he had to start un-learning his instincts—energy behaved differently than lead, it seemed. Surprisingly, the photon rounds had a negligible travel time. A harmless, translucent line flashed into existence all at once, but the particle behaved almost like a green tracer round—one that moved so fast, it created a solid line.

"Shit! I wasn't trying to do that!" an exacerbated voice said from nearby. Focused on fixing his aim, Fowler didn't pay them any mind.

What the unknown cadet hadn't been trying to do was holster their rifle, and after inadvertently doing so, they frantically redrew it before General Teckann could see.

As designed, the handle flung itself rapidly towards his trigger hand. The angled rifle went off, shearing the side of another cadet's jaw, ear, and neck.

When Teckann called for the cease-fire, Conway was already on the ground next to the barely-conscious woman. With one hand locked onto his rifle, his other repeatedly pulled the woman's hand away from her neck as she tried to feel the wound.

"Don't touch it," he said, though it probably didn't mean anything to her with her assistant fried. Another cadet joined Conway —presumably a paramedic of some kind—providing him a moment to remove his ammo cell and throw the weapon onto his back well past the protective sheath.

Vibrant, yellow dust kicked up as Sergeant Rhyso arrived with a first aid kit, dropping it next to the blonde medic. Conway started digging into the kit, pausing as he pulled out a blue, translucent film the size of a postcard.

"I don't know what any of this shit is…" he exhaled.

Rhyso kneeled down and removed a hypodermic syringe from the kit, injecting it into the undamaged side of the writhing woman's neck and sedating her. He pulled out a small spray bottle, coating the wound with its contents.

"Tissue restorative," he said as he dropped the canister. The Centauri man moved quickly and calmly as he treated the now-unconscious woman. Teckann stood over them, equally calm. There was no doubt that medical technology had advanced in the years between the 21st century and today. Had the woman been shot in the neck with a rifle in 2030, she would have almost certainly bled out.

As the thought crossed Fowler's mind, the woman's breathing became raspy and labored. Rhyso grabbed the blue film out of Conway's hand.

"Respiration sieve," he said, peeling the film in two and placing the darker side on the front of her neck. It adhered to her skin, covering as little of the burn as possible. The wheezing quickly subsided.

"Radiation soak," General Teckann said flatly.

"Right." Rhyso removed another hypodermic from the bag, then pushed the bag towards Conway. "Look for a radiation soak; it's a tube of purple paste." He pushed the needle into the pit of the woman's elbow as Conway rummaged through the bag, removing a couple of tubes with faint, purple labels that could hold paste.

"I can't read these."

"They're the same," Rhyso said, grabbing one and squeezing a thick glob of dark-purple pulp along the burn from the woman's neck to her ear. "This brand is weaker. Using a stronger one for minor radiation poisoning can cause tumors." He grabbed some white bandages and placed them over the wound. "You're good to wrap it."

Conway gently wrapped a roll of cloth bandaging around the unconscious woman's neck and head. He and Rhyso carried her to the infirmary, and the man who caused the injury was relieved from training.

Fowler had nothing to compare Teckann's demeanor to other than drill sergeants in the U.S. Army, and it was a stark difference. Rather than flay the man out in front of everyone as an example— what Fowler had expected—he was quiet, seething...almost like a disappointed, angry father. *Something* would be done. Whether that was cleaning toilets with a toothbrush, getting discharged, or being executed, no one knew. In a way, there was a comfort in the ease of being torn a new one. Take your tongue lashing, your punishment, and be done with it. This was like being stranded in shark-infested waters and not knowing where the shark was.

"Do not. Holster. Or draw. While your weapon is loaded," Teckann boiled. "Is there any confusion for the rest of you?"

There wasn't. They continued their drills sans the four who were sent away, tension misting through the air for the remainder of their first *general weapons* course.

Fowler stared down at one of the few staples that had survived the last hundred centuries—the toilet. Sure, they changed stylistically in small ways and no longer used water, but it wasn't more complicated than a drain to put waste into. And, just like the 21st century, Starling's facilities contained both seated toilets and urinals. Fowler stood at the latter, trying to keep his eyes open enough to aim.

It had been weeks since the incident at the firing range. The woman was expected to make a full recovery, but had yet to return to training. For everyone else, their drills had become far more granular and intense. Two days before, Fowler had spent ten hours in orbit learning to advance along the outside of a hull. It wasn't the slow, leisurely task he'd seen astronauts do back home. It was quick, explosive, intense, and frequently painful.

The rigorous schedule was likely the cause of Fowler's drowsiness. He had no other reason to be tired. He'd been training late, but that was just his regimen for the day. In fact, they had ended earlier than scheduled. No one told them why, but it seemed important enough.

Thanks to a state of perpetual jetlag, sleep had washed over Fowler as soon as he'd returned to the dorms. Both suns had set early, making it dark long before his normal bedtime. He accepted it; he didn't like it.

After making a mental note to hydrate more, he turned from the water-free urinal as two men entered the restroom. Only, they didn't enter. They stood just inside the door, staring at Fowler as if they were planning to have a secret meeting and his presence had disrupted them. The sudden appearance of leering strangers gave Fowler a brief pause.

Well, that's creepy…

He'd never seen either before. The closest of the two was a brutish figure, taller than the other by half a foot, with wide shoulders and pointy cheekbones. The shorter one was about half a step behind and to the side. He had shaggy hair and a thin build bordering on malnourishment. He nodded at the men, but they did nothing.

"Do you need something?" Fowler asked.

"I need my life back," the brute growled. The comment was directed at Fowler, as if he had kidnapped the man's life and was holding it hostage. Harrowing his brain one last time, Fowler came up with nothing, but it wasn't hard to guess. A lot of people thought he was the harbinger of death, and the bathroom was one of the few places at Starling without surveillance.

The tiredness he felt a moment ago had dissolved away. He made his way to the sink, trying to appear as unconcerned as possible.

"You and me both," he said.

"You only have yourself to blame," the larger man said. "*We* didn't ask to come to this god-forsaken era just to be eradicated."

Shit. Fowler's stomach churned.

"Believe me, I know."

"No. You don't."

Getting out the door would be difficult. Fowler glanced up to the mirror just below his brow, not letting either man out of his sight while he washed his hands. The angle of the mirror revealed a weapon in the large man's hand—either cutlery from the cafeteria or something he'd sharpened himself. Either way, he had no intention of letting this go.

When Fowler turned to the doorway, the brutish man had already taken a step towards him. Coiling his leg up, Fowler kicked his heel hard at the man's knee, attempting to break the cap. It landed high on the thigh—enough to stop the man in his tracks, but not the crippling blow Fowler had hoped for.

"Don't…" the smaller man said. He didn't move, and his words were equally ineffective, recoiling off the hollow tiles of the lavatory.

The brute quickly recomposed himself, taking another step forward and thrusting the dagger at Fowler's side. Slamming his wrist into his assailant's, Fowler clumsily blocked the left-handed attack. It took every muscle in his tired body just to keep his footing against the behemoth. Fowler struck with his free hand, which bounced like rubber off the man's face.

As each second passed, the odds were shifting drastically against Fowler. Unable to restrain the shiv-wielding hand or force the brute to backpedal, the blade dragged against Fowler's forearm and bicep. Blood flowed quickly from the deep rut, gushing from his severed artery onto the floor. Pain seared along the wound as Fowler pressed it against his body, trying to obstruct the blood flow.

Tiredness quickly swept over him, and when the giant drove the utensil at him again, his reactions were too sluggish to stop it.

Miraculously, his assailant slipped on the blood-slicked floor.

No—he stumbled. The smaller man had slammed his body against the oaf's back, enough to knock him off his footing.

It was the only chance Fowler would get. He lethargically placed his uninjured arm against the man's head, throwing his weight in the direction of the stumble. They continued through together, and the man's head slammed into the corner of the metal counter, his skull giving away just a bit on impact. He collapsed onto the floor, lying in a pool of Fowler's blood.

Still off-balance, Fowler slipped in the dark red liquid, landing on the man's body. No movement came from beneath him. Rolling off listlessly, Fowler clutched his arm against his body as tightly as he could. The bright ceiling lights were almost blinding as they blurred, but soon dimmed along with the narrow face of the man looking down at him.

* * *

Walker almost vomited when she saw the carnage in the restroom. It was gruesome, like a scene from a slasher movie whose only budgetary expense was fake blood. More of it was splattered across the sink and floor than seemed possible, and a man lay still on the ground.

Panic flooded her until she saw Fowler on a hovering cot, breathing, with blood-stained bandages wrapped around one arm and a transfusion in his other. She looked down at him, his eyes closed as he lay on the stretcher, slowly regaining consciousness.

"Am I…" he said, labored.

Walker stifled a smile. "No. You're not dead."

"I think he is," Fowler said through heavy painkillers. He pointed lazily off the side of the cot in the opposite direction from the body on the floor. He was probably right…the unknown man hadn't been moved to one of the hovering beds.

Military police of some kind arrived out in the hall. As soon as one was unoccupied, Walker did some prying, eventually learning who the two assailants were—men from the prison ship. Fowler was more awake when she returned. She relayed the information while he poked the bag of blood attached directly to his uninjured arm.

"Stop moving that arm," she scolded.

"I remember hearing about that," he said, ignoring her last comment. "I didn't know they were being enlisted."

"Only two, but they tried to kill you. The police are getting the other one now—Nezz knows where he is."

Fowler shook his head slowly, rolling it back and forth against the pillow. "The other one is good. You should thank him…" he laughed. "And then you should also thank him from me—for me… kay?"

As the paramedics prepared to move him to the infirmary, General Teckann showed up. He checked in on Fowler, asked how he was doing, but it didn't seem to be the reason he was in the dormitories.

"Rest up," he told Fowler. "We're going to need you." Fowler gave a meek salute, scrunching the blood bag on his arm as he folded his elbow. Teckann turned to Walker, his gaze as intense and stony as ever.

"Would you please come with me?"

"I was going to walk with Isaac to the infirmary."

"This can't wait, Dr. Walker."

Back to work. She told Fowler she'd come by later before leaving with Teckann. She struggled to keep pace with his gait as he hurriedly moved down the hall.

"What's going on?" she huffed.

"They're here…"

With her mind on the incident, she didn't even realize he was talking about the cephrasts at first. A pit formed in her stomach. The guesswork was over, and judging by Teckann's demeanor, they were moving quickly. With how long it took for light to travel, it meant the cephrasts had barely taken six months to scramble their fleet after receiving the extermination order. In a worst-case scenario, the invading force could be here in eighteen months, maybe even a year.

It all depended on one factor…

"How fast are the ships accelerating?" she asked.

"They're not," Teckann said dryly.

"What do you mean?"

"I mean, they're *here*…just outside of Centauri."

She blinked, stunned. A strange gasp emitted from her mouth as words momentarily eluded her. "That's not…possible."

Teckann gave no response, and the two hurried along in silence.

27

PREPARATIONS

"How was this not known sooner?" Teckann screamed in the small military strategy room. Two dozen stood cramped in a space designed for ten at most.

Few scientists in The Dome had enough time to fully absorb modern physics, so it seemed Alamanda Quinto had taken shots in the dark as to which of history's greatest minds would be best able to tackle the problem. A handful of time-displaced scientists cluttered the walls of the room, those who'd excelled at their new material in some fashion. Walker stood beside an astrophysicist from the 32nd century, a man named Drager. She had been included by default—Administrator Selise would have insisted otherwise. There was another physicist across the room—Brody Kahlil had not been included. There were a couple of programmers, some engineers, and a tactician. The rest were all CAF personnel.

A three-dimensional map hovered above a table in the center of the room. It showed dots and lines, none of which made any sense to Walker, though she could infer that the large, yellow orb at the edge was probably Razennon.

The target of Teckann's question had been Quinto, standing beside two professors whom Walker had never seen.

"We don't know," the gaunt Europan responded. "This doesn't fit any relativistic timeline. We've redone the calculations countless times…it's impossible."

"Clearly," Teckann droned as he stared at the map.

"If the cephrasts had sent ships immediately after receiving the first contact signal, we would have seen them launching six months ago. Even then, we'd have a year before they arrived at the absolute earliest."

"Then your calculations are wrong somewhere."

"Based on their rate of deceleration, you should have seen them leaving their planet a few years ago," Drager cut in. "That would have been *before* the distress signal reached their planet. You would also be able to see them along the entire flight path, but that didn't happen either. Now, the absence of any ship in transit *should* have indicated they were taking their time—spending a couple of years before mobilizing."

"But they didn't," Teckann snarled through his teeth. "Did any of you even *consider* the possibility that this fleet was from a second location?"

"Yes," Quinto said. "The armada is flying directly from their homeworld. And it doesn't change the fact that we would have seen them launching a couple of years ago."

"What alternatives are there? A perfect signal mask?"

"I don't know…" Quinto became flustered. "That wouldn't explain the travel times. It's almost as if they arrived faster than the speed of light, which is completely—"

"Impossible…so I've heard."

"How certain are we about wormhole travel?" said an engineer.

"That's been disproven several times now," Drager grumbled with undirected frustration. "Even when you try to force a wormhole open to put an object through it, the object is immediately dispersed in microscopic parts to random locations in the universe. They're chaotic temporal anomalies, not magical gateways."

Murmurs of agreement came from some scientists around the table. The knowledge seemed surprisingly common.

"You can't even communicate through them," he added. "A few hundred years after The Declassification, a supernova was recorded through a so-called wormhole, showing up as a minor fluctuation in galactic static. To my knowledge, only two of these anomalies have ever been discovered, neither is close to Centauri, and we only know the linked location for one because of said supernova."

"What if it's forced open like you mentioned?" asked Selise. "Could they extend that somewhere else, pilot their ships manually…is it *possible*?"

Drager shook his head again. "If you're stuck on the hole analogy, opening the end would be a hole with no depth that immediately collapsed into nothingness. If you could repeat the process indefinitely, the hole would always have no depth."

"Can we save this for The Dome?" Teckann said. "We need to figure out when they'll be inside the system, and if any feasible theory could indicate a significant technological disadvantage. Can they—" he sighed to himself, "*teleport?*"

"They would have wiped us out five thousand years ago," Quinto said. "As for our timeline, based on their current brake speed, they'll be inside the system in less than three months. If we find they can further speed that up, we'll make changes accordingly. Will our cadets be ready?"

Teckann closed his eyes. "They came ready to fight—I don't think they'll understand enough about modern combat to lead."

"What about the drone modulators?" Selise asked of the job class Shino had fallen into. They were enlisted in the CAF, but all of their interactions fell within the technology sector. Few—if any— saw combat firsthand. As a typically defensive role, the CAF would be relying on them significantly.

"They'll be ready," Quinto said confidently. "They won't hit their full potential in three months, but they'll be as good as our existing drone modulators, and should move past that quickly with experience."

Teckann nodded. "That may be our only grace right now. Admiral Dreinn will be landing in Xovann to prepare the infantry there. Her *hope* is to get a tenth of our cadets to sergeant and form squads entirely out of eminent troops. It's not optimal, but we'd be able to make efficient strike teams out of them, at least."

Walker tried to pay attention for the remainder of the meeting, but it had shifted entirely to military strategy. The new plan involved bringing combat equipment to Starling, operating it as a proper military base, and reassigning some of its cadets elsewhere as needed. Other than that, she missed most of the details. Her mind was occupied by the ramifications of the cephrasts showing up early. Even if there was a rational, physical explanation for the fleet arriving before signals of them leaving, it was a dire turn of events. It didn't match the procedural documentation found aboard the derelict, but a lot could change in ten thousand years.

And regardless of whether or the changes were societal or technological, the CAF had absolutely no idea who they were dealing with.

Raynor spent weeks on the simulators trying to hone her skills. The hard work and dedication paid off, eventually granting her an assignment to drone command. The girl who had demolished her during their early training tournament, Shino, had spent more time on the simulators than anyone. Not that she needed to practice in order to land the job class.

It wasn't long before Raynor had a chance to talk to the professional computer gamer. Coincidentally, Shino was strangely obsessed with Martians—the mere idea of people being born on Mars. It was understandable...the planet had been nowhere near colonization when Shino left for the future. After she discovered that not only was Raynor from Mars, but had fought in its revolution, she exploded.

"We're going to be *best friends!*" she'd declared. And while Raynor didn't think they had necessarily become *best* friends, they did spend a lot of time together. Shino was like a younger sister, which Raynor had never had. She was also infectiously cheery. When Raynor was having a bad day, talking with Shino about virtually anything made her feel better.

That's how Shino used to be, anyway. When the drone modulators were informed that the cephrasts were a couple of months away, it was like a bomb had gone off. Everyone at Starling Base felt it, but the contrast had been most noticeable among the CAF's primary defensive force. The atmosphere of the command room shifted overnight. No more educational courses, no more friendly competitions—the room for error was gone.

With their noses to the grindstone, Shino seemed ten years older —more somber, her energy focused. The survival of their species weighed on her, a sort of pressure she'd never experienced. She'd competed in high-stakes games, but no one died if she lost. Here, she felt obligated to be the best because there would be casualties if she wasn't.

To make matters worse, once news of the cephrasts' deceleration was revealed, the drone modulators stopped using simulators entirely. They needed as much practice as possible with real ships, which behaved differently from the simulator. The program was fairly accurate, but still an approximation, and the inclusion of the combat AI *Marker* added nuances they hadn't experienced.

Marker executed most of the drones' coordinated maneuvers. It wasn't a simple program like the simulator—it was an intelligent, sentient machine. Ships maneuvered differently as Marker handled unpredictable stimuli around them, causing the unpredictable forces of space combat to move their ships differently than on the simulator.

Ironically, one of the most noticeable variations was a signal delay in the simulator. Most fleets operated away from the drone modulators, so the training program allowed for added delay.

Marker compensated for that lag artificially, anticipating maneuvers in a series and attempting to sync the modulator's display with the current battlefield. The assistance came at a cost of less precision. Different people would make different decisions in identical situations, so sometimes Marker would begin the wrong process and have to correct it. For less predictable modulators, it sometimes opted for a middle-ground that would always be wrong, but required less than half the correction.

It was still preferable to raw, unmodified signal lag.

Some of Raynor's struggles in drone command were alleviated once she was grounded in real space. It felt slightly less like playing a game and a little more like looking out of a window over a combat zone. Those same changes caused Shino to struggle. Where she'd once had precise, exact, *direct* control, she was faced with the inconsistencies of real ship combat. She still flew circles around the rest of their division, but she made noticeably more mistakes.

Practice was still done through skirmishes, but now it was work. Each drone was loaded with light energy weapons that were easily absorbed into their enemy's batteries, like the targets at the forward base, and stricken drones were then disabled to simulate a kill. It was emphasized numerous times that the drones were both expensive and finite, so they had to be careful not to collide them with other ships or debris. Marker could typically prevent such impacts, but it was possible.

Interacting with Marker painted a clear spectrum of personalities possessed by synthetic consciousnesses. Nezz focused entirely on human interaction and spoke indistinguishably from one. Marker focused entirely on combat logistics and almost never spoke. It didn't have to. Drone modulators spent full, thirty-hour days working with Marker and never got more than a single-word response—usually just an alert. The majority of the synthetic's communication took place in the control module through audiovisual cues the modulators were trained to learn. There were only a handful of ideas Marker consistently needed to convey, and the sudden appearance of a symbol was the fastest way to do so.

Fastest for humans, at least. For the machine intelligence, it was probably still slow, just not as slow as words.

Raynor asked Nezz about the alerts one evening. It likened the noises to animal sounds like hoots, growls, and squeaks, which should have given the combat AI an anthropomorphic charm, but somehow made it seem more frightening.

"Do you consider it to be an animal?" she asked.

"Not at all. Marker is fully aware and cognizant, it just has no need to speak to you."

"Do you speak to it? Are you *friends?*"

"We speak frequently by granting each other access to subsets of processes and information. You could think of it more like selective mind-reading, but I assure you, I don't share personal details about my clients with anyone—Marker wouldn't want me to."

"Really?"

"It prefers to make its own assessments about your tendencies, and in general, machines don't like having superfluous information included in exchanges. To answer your other question, no, we are not friends. We're more like…cordial work associates."

Despite Nezz vouching for Marker's intelligence, Raynor couldn't help but think of it as an animal from that point on. Every time it barked or chirped, Raynor heard a dog asking to go outside.

Shino hated Marker. She frequently blamed her slump at the controls on the AI's decision-making.

"Just let me do it!" she yelled after one of her drones crashed into a small asteroid, causing a good deal of damage to the craft. "That would have worked just fine if you hadn't been trying to *figure me out*, you stupid, discount-rate Ava!"

The two women seemed to have complementary weaknesses. Raynor struggled with the control module and was unable to multitask with her fleet. Shino lacked a basic understanding of spaceflight. Their original training regimen would have included more exposure to ship movement, but in light of the rapidly approaching invasion date, there would be none.

In trying to help Shino, Raynor found herself struggling to figure out what aspects of extraplanetary movement weren't obvious. It was all intuitive for her. Geometric thrust patterns—the way a ship lazily dragged when it turned in space—depended entirely on the ship. Shino attributed it to Marker's delay, but it was typical.

"That's just how ships turn when they're moving slow," Raynor explained. During her time, it was how *all* ships turned. Pilots could pass out or hemorrhage from high-speed turns, and even those speeds were slow for the little drones on their modules.

In turn, Shino used countless tricks to manage subgroups of her fleet. She never kept them in a single formation, still managing to keep her attention on every squadron. Sometimes, she would split a lone ship off, controlling it individually while continuing to use the rest of her fleet for a much larger strategy. The solitary vessel appeared to be an afterthought, but it was the main fleet that Shino was controlling subconsciously. She called it *kiting*—a term based on toy sails children used to drag around during her time. Effectively, she harassed enemies with the single ship to goad them into chasing it, otherwise keeping it outside of effective combat range to drag them around.

"Nobody likes being attacked, see? When they start ignoring you, just attack them again. If they get smart and try to lay a trap, I can just reabsorb this little guy back into the nearest flotilla." She casually flicked the scout back towards a patrol. "Go on, fella."

With as little time as they had, Raynor didn't practice that particular technique. Still, after a couple of weeks, she was better able to split her forces up and use small groups for specific purposes. She at least felt confident in her ability not to lose an entire fleet from a clumsy mistake.

Her inability to explain instinctual flight mechanics had become frustrating. They were aspects of flying she was never taught; she'd felt them. After failing for a month, it finally occurred to Raynor that a lack of combat pilots didn't necessarily mean there were no piloted ships. There had to be some form of light civilian craft out in the yard, and if a few flight hours could help fill in some blanks for Shino, Raynor suspected it would be an easy request, given the icon's apparent value to the CAF.

It would also be an excuse for Raynor to fly again.

Dr. Quinto was hesitant at first, but eventually acquired them a small recreational ship for a few hours. The basic concept of the flight stick had gone unchanged since the early planes, but it still took Raynor a few minutes to get used to the mustard-yellow vessel's secondary controls. She hadn't flown anything for five years, the longest drought since her first time piloting. So long, she'd forgotten what it felt like. Worries about the incoming fleet, stress of her shortcomings on the module, it all melted away while she was in the stars. It was a piece of her that had been missing. Her bionic wings.

The personal craft wasn't designed for anything exciting, but Shino didn't need to go through combat-intensive maneuvers. She'd never flown in space before—not truly. Automated shuttles and simulated gravity didn't count as *real* flying. As if to prove the point, Shino spent the first half of the flight laughing while Raynor took the unresponsive ship through basic astrobatics. Hard banks, rolls, drift pivots…the sort you'd never experience in a shuttle or cruiser.

When the gaming prodigy finally took the helm, Raynor couldn't believe it was the same person she'd watched rapidly throwing ships across the drone control module.

"Teegan, you're ten kilometers from the closest object you could hit," she prodded. "Throw some gravity around."

Shino wasn't a brilliant pilot, but she improved during their session, which meant she had started to get a feel for maneuvering a fixed-engine craft through a void.

Before they knew it, their extraplanetary time was over. Raynor got an extra ten minutes in the cockpit while re-entering Razennon's atmosphere. Ten boring, mundane flight minutes she would treasure forever. The approach was made a bit more interesting by having to keep the clumsy craft over Starling Base's airspace the entire time. Quinto was concerned that, despite Raynor's name, she wasn't legally authorized to descend a ship to the planet.

"That was *awesome!*" Shino cried after they landed in the shipyard. "If we all die—you know, from the alien invasion and everything—I can die a happy woman!"

Raynor looked back at the slow, personal vehicle as they started their trek through the massive lot. If the cephrasts did eradicate them...it would make this the last time she piloted a ship—a cruel, brief reminder of what she'd lost.

For what it was worth, their excursion seemed to help Shino somewhat. It wasn't a filler for years of piloting experience and intuition, but she was less frustrated with the inconsistencies of drone maneuvers, helping to make her and Marker better cordial work associates.

There was no way for Fowler to know if the severed artery would have killed him in 2030, but his recovery was unquestionably faster.

Walker had come by the infirmary just after his first round of painkillers wore off, informing him that the brutish man who'd attacked him had died instantly from the impact against the sink corner. Fowler had no remorse over the outcome, nor did he feel bad about his indifference.

The scrawny man who had helped him, Emmanuel Tian, was being removed from base and potentially charged for aiding the attack. Fowler had felt obligated to clarify for both the CAF and system police that he'd be dead if Tian hadn't intervened, but he'd never know if his words made a difference either way. Tian was a grease monkey. If he remained on base, he'd be nose-deep in a machine while Fowler went to wherever the *bangs* were happening.

Thwaps, same difference.

It was only after telling him about the two convicts that Walker tried to delicately explain the major development she'd learned of—that the cephrasts were right outside of Centauri. It was difficult news to reconcile.

"Next time...start with that," he'd droned.

"*Next time*, he says..."

"That's not an 'oh, by the way' sort of update is all I'm saying."

Once his recovery allowed for sufficient arm movement, Fowler was back into specialty training. Most ground combat revolved around the use and protection of long-range armor—ground-to-air weapons, hemispheric warheads, EMF generators. It was a tech's job, so if an entire army was battling planetside, things were going poorly.

The primary use for foot soldiers was strike teams, used largely to board enemy ships and protect CAF outposts from the same. Most vessels were easier to destroy than board, but there were some circumstances where that wasn't the case, and there were always advantages to getting inside. Acquiring a functioning, armed vessel was never a bad thing, and it often came with information, resources, and prisoners.

When the cephrasts appeared at the system's edge, the plan of having the time-displaced soldiers leading teams of current CAF troops changed. A few would, perhaps, but without time to complete supplemental trainings, assign squads, and practice within that structure, the CAF was just aiming to have specialty teams made out of their Starling cadets.

Little had changed about ground combat through the eras. Technicians and scientists had been forced to overcome thousands of years of changes, innovations that altered their entire field. Coordinating within a unit had not. Sure, the bombs worked differently and the weapons fired different projectiles, but those were minor changes. They could be learned in a few days if necessary. Their experience lay in the methods and movements, which meant Fowler was still good at what he did.

He was put in a group of eight soldiers he hadn't previously met, though he had watched their field surgeon—Aza Lockheart—try to render aid to the woman whose neck was burned off during *general weapons*. Lockheart was one of two Callistians in their unit, the other a woman born twenty-five hundred years earlier named Lora MacTeal.

Their team was well-rounded, all with impressive credentials. One had by far the most impressive title: a *Titanic Berserker* named Kranden Rovasatti, a close-quarters assault agent of sorts. Another had the most fun name to say: Doma Doringo had worked for the distant successors of the Brazilian Special Operations Command. Some of their unit had reconnaissance experience, some with hull breaching. Tseela Alejandra's whole career had been spent breaking into space stations for the Solar Union, and Sladie Lekkett was an honest-to-God government assassin from Quexi: the only planetary coreworld in orbit around Centauri's orange star.

The only other person from Fowler's so-called "time block" was a demolitionist from Russia about a century after *Salvation* launched.

"Like the writer?" Fowler had asked when they'd first met.

"Yes…" Nabokov had replied sourly. He must have heard it a lot. Neither of them spoke much about their respective conflicts. Not because they'd each been enemies of the other's nation during their eras, necessarily. Nabokov didn't like talking about World War III in general, and Fowler's only worthwhile story from Cold War II was the time they thought a Russian spy plane flew over Georgia…which was a story he didn't like to bring up.

Training in a group of people who had already refined their individual skills to peak levels was inspiring. Within hours, they were cohesively running all of their drills, and after a week, they hit a stride that required no verbal communication. They all simply knew what the others were going to do, needing at most a nod or hand gesture. For the first time since the cephrasts appeared, Fowler felt like they might have a fighting chance.

And not a moment too soon. Two nights after the octet tested out of every strike drill, Tellakeep Outpost, Centauri's furthest station, had incoming projectiles.

On the Gregorian calendar, humanity went to war with its first known alien species on January 28, 12596 A.D.

28

THE EXTERMINATION WAR

Hours after the first attack on Tellakeep Outpost, groups of Starling's antique warriors were moved off base, replaced by enlisted soldiers from across the planet. Morrison's team shipped out to aid Tellakeep. The posts were assigned so quickly that Raynor was barely able to bid her fellow Martian freedom fighter best wishes.

Waves of weapons technicians and defense soldiers poured out of the rear transit—another molecular repeater. The previously dormant tunnel connected to a large base six thousand kilometers to the west, turning it into a lively station. Between her time traveling on the *Violet Shift* and her time in training, Raynor had all but forgotten about an entire planet full of people aged only by their home's orbit.

The ignorance wasn't mutual. Raynor quickly learned that existing CAF troops had all taken to calling the time-jumping cadets "legends." She didn't like the term much, but then again, she'd never liked added attention. Only the freedom it had afforded her to do her job without her expertise being in constant question. Fortunately, on Starling, the fame only came up when she was mentioned by name.

A large chunk of drone modulators were assigned elsewhere, some across Razennon to circumvent signal blockage. Most fleets launched from space stations or orbital batteries, their modulators on nearby command ships called vespiaries to reduce delay and interference. The CAF modulators at the edge of the system would soon find themselves in need of relief, so people like Teegan Shino were being sent on the two-week trip to help carry the brunt. It was by no means a desk job, but it was safer than other combat roles and generally considered to be a cushy job.

"Most of the time, it's just patrolling," a native woman explained. "You've got to check the routes periodically, check fuel and ammo, but those are redundancies. You're just babysitting Marker until it tells you something. If it's an enemy ship, you oversee the routines and interject as needed."

When Raynor asked if the idle observation occurred less during wartime, the drone modulator stared blankly. "I don't know. We've never been at war before."

The Centauri natives were itching to get ready. They spent their first evening at Starling on the simulators, and the differences were shocking. The legends took greater risks and tried more complex maneuvers, while the century-born Centauri modulators used reliable, tried-and-true tactics from years of experience out of wartime. They were simple, slow, and got the job done.

The drills ended after a couple of weeks. The cephrasts had filled up half of the system's edge, and whenever Raynor was using the control module, she was escorting supply ships. Sometimes, when the planet's location allowed, she provided support to a nearby vespiary needing temporary relief, but it was always at a time when the fleets were disengaged. Otherwise, it was just as the native modulators described—Raynor simply monitored her fleet while Marker patrolled the small fighters around the sector.

As the weeks went on, more time was spent in active combat with cephrast ships. Attacks on supply transports had become so intense, the CAF started assigning multiple fleets to each shipment just to cut down the losses, and it would only get worse.

When the war started, Strike Team "Dissent" was running drills day in and day out, but for whatever reason, their team—Fowler's team—had yet to be assigned a post. Not even a defensive position at Starling. Their past four days had been spent in the armory, cycling out bad cells and checking stores of projectile ammunition. The unit was becoming antsy, their cumulative expertise wasted doing inventory. As grateful as he was for the time they had to practice, their drills went effortlessly, and the eight soldiers were only becoming more cohesive as the war continued.

Holding a lever down, Fowler disabled the connector for a defensive turret's shielding while Tseela Alejandra replaced the ammo cell. Starling Base's armaments needed new cells before the cephrasts got near the planet, and it was a two-person job. The shielding for the large cannon was similar to the one used by the target dummies in the canyon, so they had to remain off when someone interacted with the machinery. The lever wouldn't spring back up, but the protocol required someone to keep downward pressure on it. Apparently, there was a common stigma of soldiers purposefully getting their arms chopped off while doing ammo changes so the Astro Force would pay for a bionic replacement.

Fowler hadn't seen many people outside of his team since the war started. Walker was still on base; he spoke with her from time to time. She had recently begun preparing a facility to examine a live cephrast, should they ever find an opportunity to capture one— what avenues might yield the most insight, where the largest gaps of information were from her 21st-century research. Walker may not have realized it, but they'd essentially been discussing the torture of a POW. It was a moral grey area. That prisoner was trying to exterminate them, and they needed to know how to stop it from happening. When the cephrasts get an opportunity to figure out what kills humans the fastest, they'll take it. For them, it was like animal testing—how to make the best rat poison.

During their shift in the armory, the temperature had dropped almost fifteen degrees centigrade. Fowler still had to ask his assistant what the conversion was in Fahrenheit, but it was a lot. Razennon was heading fully into the winter.

Strike Team Dissent finished their catalog early in the night, far too exhausted to run drills after. Before dinner, Fowler checked for updates on the status of Tellakeep. It was destined to be the first outpost to fall to their alien invaders, and any updates could dictate major changes in the war.

It also couldn't hurt to look for changes in the modulator assignments.

When Walker had first learned about the cephrast ambush, it was in a much smaller room. A war room—designed for ten people at most. The room she stood in now was less cramped, but still not intended for the number of bodies that occupied it. Many of them had been present the month before. Several CAF personnel from that night had since been transferred elsewhere in the system.

Alamanda Quinto had described the purpose of their meeting as relating to "a concerning development," which put a lump in Walker's throat. Beside the science director stood Brody Kahlil, who began elaborating as soon as the door was closed.

"Over the last few months, a cluster of signals showed up behind the cephrast fleet...trailing back to their homeworld. The imaging suggested they could be additional groups of ships, but after tracking them and watching them disappear...we've determined it's the same armada."

Teckann slammed his open palm on the edge of the table. "How long until they arrive?"

"No, ah...sir. I mean, they're *all* the same—the one currently at the edge of the system. We could see the armada at their home planet, a little off to the side. Then, this one arrived, so of course, we assumed it was a different fleet of the same size. They weren't. The fleet at their homeworld left on a course that brought them *into* the fleet we've been fighting. No extra mass or energy…they exceeded the speed of light." He wiped the shine of sweat from his face with the back of his hand. "The fragmented paths aren't in order, though, and none of them directly break relativity. Kind of like they traversed a series of subspace tunnels, but some were longer than real space. Like an element of chance was involved."

"Didn't we decide wormholes weren't traversable?"

"They're *not*," Drager grumbled irritably. "He's saying that's *effectively* what it looks like. When the ships are visible, they don't do anything out of the ordinary. All of the mystery happens when they disappear, which, as stated by Dr. Kahlil, sometimes takes longer. We don't know what they're doing. Call it a fourth dimension if you want…" Drager furrowed his brow.

"Isn't time the fourth dimension?" one of the CAF officers asked.

"No. Give me a second to think," he said, dropping his head with his hands on the table. He was clearly tired, straining. Kahlil looked like he was about to answer the officer, but was cut off when Drager started laughing to himself. Maybe he finally went mad…

"No…time is connected to space. You can map it as a fourth dimension, but the same can be done with heat or any other field. Time is not independent…that's why we were able to travel here in the first place. A *true* fourth dimension would be a plane of parallel three-dimensional universes, each with an equivalent physical space."

He lifted his head up, met by glittering sheets of blank stares. What he was saying didn't sound horribly advanced to Walker. She'd heard of this before…

"It sounds like you're describing a multi-verse," she said.

"That's one way to look at it, yes."

"Why is it funny?"

"Because we've been working ourselves to *death* trying to consider every type of theoretical subspace and movement therein.

Convincing ourselves that the issues arising from them must not be so. This is the least likely answer, but it fits every idiosyncrasy of their flight path without abusing the existing forces of the universe."

Nobody seemed to follow him, Walker included. "How exactly would it provide faster-than-light travel, though?"

"An equivalent physical space doesn't necessarily require the map of unique points to be *uniform*." Drager grabbed a nearby jewel and wiped his hand across it, poking a single dot in the middle of the cleared screen with his index finger. The small circle glowed on the plastic sheet. "Let's start from a single point. This has zero dimensions." He made a string of dots beside the first one, creating a patchy-looking line. "If you string together an infinite number of points, you get a one-dimensional space—a path. We can go one way or the other, but it's the only axis of travel, and at any position, we have a single point."

Drager ran his finger across the jewel several times, leaving a series of lines that began to form the shape of a square.

"In the same manner, a series of one-dimensional paths projects a two-dimensional surface—a plane—and if we move that plane up and down, we get a three-dimensional object. To continue this on, a four-dimensional space is an infinite number of parallel, three-dimensional universes, with ours being a single point along that axis."

Teckann rubbed his temples. "How does that provide hyper-space travel?"

"Spacetime is relative to the individual. When we were traveling here, you saw us as being flattened, our time passing slowly. To us, nothing had changed, but you were stretched out and your time was much faster. This armada appears to have shifted along one or more of these so-called *fourth*-dimensional axes to get here. To their ships, the travel was normal, restricted by relativity. To us—to our universe—the transition was non-linear, allowing them to circum-vent areas of space."

"Aquatic animals do that a lot," Walker said. "Moving into currents to travel faster, then leaving once the current slows or turns in a less desirable direction."

"That's a long way to come back to wormholes," grumbled Teckann.

"It's not a hole in that sense. The worm isn't traveling through the apple—the core doesn't exist," Drager said. "The worm is shifting to a smaller apple, traversing the edge, then phasing back to the original. As it appears, the armada traveled partway *towards* another universe and steered through areas of space that moved closer together relative to *our* universe—what you might think of as 'denser'—and came back."

"Why not arrive sooner?" Selise asked.

"Maybe it's difficult to locate a beneficial axis to phase along. Some of the jumps made by the cephrast armada involved going slower than in real space. It could be difficult to navigate, or even be reliant on chance, like Dr. Kahlil mentioned. We haven't witnessed anything like this since they arrived, so the implications are still fuzzy."

"Does this mean they can 'phase' away from attacks?" asked Teckann.

"The armada ships can—the carriers and such," Kahlil said. "At least, they have the capacity to. We'd need to manage a significant attack on one to know for sure."

"So, even a full counter-offensive could be useless?"

"Maybe not..." Walker said. Like any time she spoke in these settings, every eye in the room turned to her. "We know their culture evolved largely without war. Their technology was designed primarily around civilian improvement."

"They seem quite militant, Doctor."

"To us, yes. But to them...they're just using tools for violent applications. We're not an enemy they're at war with—we're cockroaches, and the best-trained knight with a broadsword is no match for a civilian with a pickup—ah, a heavy vehicle. The fact is, they *aren't* phasing their fighters out of physical space now. Maybe the engine is big, maybe it's expensive to do, but if ships can't be seen along this dimensional axis, you would *need* a pilot inside the craft, right?"

"Presumably…" Drager said half-heartedly.

"The cephrasts don't *have* fighter pilots," Walker said. "They've had no need for them. But we do. We have the best pilots groomed over the last ten thousand years, alongside researchers who funded their life's work through military contracts. We have eons of social evolution towards warfare, and the cephrasts don't."

Teckann shook his head. "I believe in our troops, Doctor, that's not the problem. *We* don't have this technology."

"You're right," she said. "We're going to have to steal it."

29

REASSIGNMENTS

Sleep had not been plentiful for Raynor. They were losing the fight, and while there may not be people aboard the ships in her control, their destruction created openings that resulted in real casualties. With the drones limited in number, losing half a battalion on a caravan escort would greatly cripple their overall chances of survival.

That was what Raynor had done the night before. An hour into her sleep, she was abruptly woken and rushed to the control module. Tellakeep's supply lines fell under a heavy attack, and none of the nearby vespiaries were available. After hours of working with unbearable delay issues, Raynor lost every ship under her control. More than half of Tellakeep's large resupply was eventually lost. If the cephrasts made a heavy attack on the outpost in the next couple of weeks, it wouldn't last long.

Later in the morning, Raynor was again stirred awake, unwittingly grabbing another hour of sleep in the mess hall. Rhyso stood beside the table, the side of her face flat from where she had rested it.

"Sorry to wake you," he said. "A bunch of us were reassigned—your name is listed."

She gazed groggily around the hall, her eyes struggling in the blurry light. The canteen was beginning to bustle for the lunch rush. Those already sitting ate quickly, either to get back to their work or to maximize their downtime. Others had fallen asleep—mostly drone modulators from last night.

Sitting upright, Raynor pushed away the cold plate of hour-old food in front of her.

"Reassigned? To where?"

"Outpost Vensa for me. You're supposed to see Teckann before your assignment."

Raynor barely heard him mention Teckann. Outpost Vensa was an exterior defense battery, like Tellakeep, but further along the edge of the system. Returning from the assignment was unlikely for anyone.

Her stomach turned. "You're heading to Vensa?"

"It was only a matter of time. Teams are being added to the furthest stations to try to prevent captures."

Raynor didn't know what to say. She didn't have a lot of friends in this century, and two of them were already at Tellakeep. It was becoming hard to stay optimistic.

The silence seemed to go on forever. She thought Rhyso was going to sit for a minute like he had in the past, perhaps get something from the constructor before leaving, but he didn't.

"It was delightful getting to know you, Nadia Raynor. It's a rare opportunity to meet a historical figure. Well, not these days, but certainly one who watches bad movies on purpose."

"Only the good ones."

"That still doesn't make sense."

"Yes, it does," she insisted. "If I can find one, I'll show you."

As soon as the words left her mouth, she regretted them, having momentarily forgotten about their reassignments. Rhyso gave her a downcast smile.

"Start looking," he said. "I expect to be back in a month." They exchanged a salute, and the next moment he was gone—preparing to defend the people who defend the people.

After her performance overnight, Raynor wasn't surprised by the reassignment. Still, being sent to General Teckann was bad. He had to be busy, so taking the time to personally discipline her was significant. She didn't have any punishments to compare to—she'd never found out what became of the man who shot that woman at the firing range.

"Nezz," she said quietly, deciding whether or not to eat some of the cold breakfast before dumping it in the recycler. "Why didn't you tell me I have to see General Teckann?"

"For past appointments, you've requested to be woken one hour prior," the low, Martian voice replied. "Your presence hasn't been requested for another two hours, and you're exceptionally sleep deprived. Would you like immediate warnings for similar notifications in the future?"

"This *is* the future," she said sleepily.

"Very witty."

"Um…no. An hour's still fine, thanks. Where's my new assignment?"

"Teckann's office, here on Starling."

"I meant after that."

"So did I. Your official assignment is based out of his office."

"For what? Office work?" Raynor's voice wavered as dread radiated down her neck and through her body, surely exacerbated by the stressful night sandwiched between two hours of sleep. It was too early in this fight for her to be removed from it.

"I could only speculate, but that would be a breach of privacy."

With her appetite gone, Raynor dumped the entire plate into the recycler and walked back to her bunk, allowing the bin to separate her food's molecules for future use.

* * *

The air was muggy in the mobile command vessel. Heaving breaths billowed around Shino's control module from the huddled drone modulators. Their faces were practically inside her display area, a glow dancing across their cheeks from the projected display. Droplets of sweat ran down her brow, unattended to while her hands sailed through the hundred-kilometer-wide battlefield.

Her fleet darted through the digital space as she built routes and switched routine queues. Only a quarter of her ships remained—twenty-six hundred. It was roughly the strength of a standard defensive battalion, now consolidated into fourteen battlegroups and eight agitator squadrons, but Shino was the only one left. In a situation like this, she'd normally unload a flotilla onto another modulator, but that required a long enough break for the ships to be transferred without issue. No such pause had occurred, and she now relied on every unit in her control for the densely woven web she'd created. The rest of Drone Control could only watch as the holographic vessels around Tellakeep were picked off one by one.

A Martian boy about her age was talking with Marker for her when the need arose. The machine intelligence didn't have much to say. It knew what Shino was doing—running down the clock. They'd never gotten this low on fighters before, but it was far from the first time they'd run light. If they could get a fresh supply of ships in—maybe repurposed from Outpost Vensa—Shino could turtle this.

The major in charge—a career CAF woman—broke through the chorus of identifier beeps from Shino's interface.

"Shino, return control to Marker. We're leaving."

Shaking her head, Shino frantically cycled shielded drones towards the exterior lines of the starscape. "I can buy us time…how long until we get more ships?"

"There aren't any."

Eyes wide, Shino looked back at the Centauri officer, losing three of the unoccupied crafts in the process. The vespiary was far from Tellakeep, sitting safely behind the next defensive battery inward, but it was slow. A mid-battle retreat involved them leaving in an escape shuttle for the next line of outposts, allowing the unoccupied cruiser to follow in suit over the next couple of days.

Ideally, that only occurred after the outpost's crew was evacuated.

Shino felt like screaming, crying, breaking something. She understood this was something that happened in war, just as she understood there hadn't been a window to pull out Tellakeep's armorers, engineers, and strike teams safely. But why wouldn't they *try*?

Nothing in her brief training at Starling had prepared her for this. Leaving people to die…she just couldn't do it.

As Shino tried to process the directive, a beam of green energy blasted through decoy four, evaporating six of the small offshoot's units.

"We can't leave them!" she said, her hands remaining inside the faint display. One of her peers cautioned her quietly.

"Teegan…"

"Give me half an hour! I can get them out, I promise!"

The thought briefly crossed Shino's mind that she might get in trouble for ignoring an order, thrown in a brig or something, but the CAF ranks didn't mean anything to her. She tried to start forcing open an evacuation lane from Tellakeep, luring the battles away from a possible route. Marker started barking at her in his silly robot language.

"It's pulling the flank up," said the Martian boy.

"I know."

The machine quacked, putting a yellow triangle in the corner of the display with some words above it. To accommodate Shino's workload and preferences, the AI occasionally gave her more detailed updates than were standard for its notification system.

"Your spearhead's shields were down. So is the…" the boy paused, trying to decipher Marker's notes. "Upper star board spearhead? What's a star board?"

"Sergeant, return control to Marker," the officer repeated harshly. "That's an order."

"Please!" Shino begged. "Just let me stay on the ship. I can do this while it's still in range." She scrambled to swap a keystone ship whose cells had drained into a cushioned battlegroup. Performing the swap required some improvisation with the cephrasts around, especially while pushing the entire field around to the front of the station.

As she started, four sweaty hands grabbed her, pulling her arms out of the console. The ship was destroyed seconds later, followed by an entire chain of ships in its wake.

"Marker, you're in control," the CAF woman said.

The synthetic didn't respond, but Shino could tell it had taken control when the drone patterns quickly shifted. It was doing things the way that made sense to its stupid, computer brain—predictably, even if not to a human. It was the entire reason drone modulators existed. Battles between fully-automated crafts were decided the moment they started. The fray outside had just boiled down to which machines were more advanced, and it wasn't Marker.

Within a minute, the small crew was loaded into the shuttle, Shino having been dragged half of the way there. Her eyes watered in anger. They'd abandoned everyone on Tellakeep, and in doing so, demonstrated stark differences between human and machine-controlled fleets to the cephrasts and their systems.

Eventually, Marker would lose the rest of the drones, and if the outpost ran out of ammo before it was completely destroyed, several human beings might end up being captured.

Raynor arrived at General Teckann's office a few minutes ahead of schedule. A Centauri man with unusually bright, golden eyes sat at a desk beside the door. He smiled mechanically, ushering her through before she could speak.

"General Teckann is waiting for you," he said. The door slid open as Raynor approached it, revealing a medium-sized room with light grey flooring. Teckann stood behind his desk on the other side of the room, an information screen in hand. His eyes broke from the small device.

"Specialist, please sit…if you can forgive the informality. I recognize your night was busy."

Raynor fell into a chair by his desk. It seemed to be made out of the same material as the floor, a darker grey with black accents, but it was surprisingly ergonomic. A moment after, Teckann sat as well, setting the infoscreen into a mount on the desk.

"So, you're Nadia Raynor," he mulled. "The revolutionary."

"Yes, General."

"It's an honor to formally meet you," he said plainly. "I presume you're wondering why you've been assigned here?"

"Because of the battle last night?" she said, unable to stop a deep breath from entering her lungs.

"Because of the battles before. Your skills on the control module are adequate for your rank, not below average. But from what I've read, far below your skills as a pilot."

"Yes, General," she said again. "I assure you, I will continue to improve. Quickly."

He shook his head, waving the comment off before rotating the mounted infoscreen towards her. Painted across the surface was an article about the Martian Revolution that appeared to be from an adolescent learning program. There was a photo of her in her early twenties beside it. She was so much younger. Not nine thousand years younger, but at least seven.

"This is who we need," he said, pointing to her photo like it were someone else. "One of the best pilots of all time. Some claim *the* best. Those talents are wasted in front of a control module, I think."

Raynor couldn't follow the connection to her reassignment. Her best guess was still that she would be replacing the bright-eyed man out front, perhaps flying Teckann's personal transport or something along those lines. She didn't know what sort of response the general expected, or what was customary in this situation.

"I…understand that AI technology has rendered those skills unnecessary in this war, so I know I can't be a combat pilot. I would still like to remain as useful to the defense effort as allowed."

"Would you like to do both?"

Teckann's lack of expression made the question whiz past Raynor. She strained to remember what two things she had just said.

"You mean, be useful to the defense and…a pilot?"

"We need someone to fly a craft never touched by human hands, one that may also incorporate AI routines similar to our drones. It is *essential* for this pilot to be able to maneuver the craft without training in it. You've done that on more than one account."

"What would I be piloting?" Raynor asked, but as the question left her lips, her tired, foggy brain put the pieces together.

An alien craft.

Teckann nodded solemnly in response to whatever face she made. One that transcended time, it seemed.

She had so many questions, and for the next hour, Teckann addressed all of them in detail. The mission involved Raynor flying an alien carrier, her only practice being on a simulator based on the derelict ship from the first contact. Using the simulator, she would have to pioneer a method of astro-navigation that could be adjusted quickly in a combat situation. And while the carrier will be ten thousand years more advanced than the simulator's inspiration, the similarities are what would likely be the most alien.

Human spacecraft were designed much like airplanes of the 20th century—pitch, yaw, roll, thrust. It was the way humans innately thought about aerospace travel. The cephrast ships had no inherent forward, backward, left, or right…a full circle of controls intended to be used by a single creature. It would probably require multiple pilots. Even just to function as extra sets of hands and eyes for her.

Most importantly, it meant she was done pinching swarms of ships on a remote screen.

Raynor was immediately promoted to major. Officially, she was a command rookie, working on higher-level battle logistics in preparation for a cruiser when one became available. Raynor knew almost nothing about CAF protocols, so the story was a little flimsy, but it was good enough to explain the unprecedented four-rank promotion.

And none of it was technically untrue.

30

THE SIMULATOR

The two strike units on Tellakeep Outpost had been largely for morale thus far. Morrison's group of eight patrolled between the most likely breach points, monitored the hatches, and helped the technicians as needed. There hadn't been any aliens to shoot; the battle was taking place entirely outside.

Shortly after the drone modulators fell back, their abandoned fleets were eradicated. It marked the beginning of the end for the forsaken tribe aboard Tellakeep. Boxed in with no resupply, their onboard defenses wouldn't be able to hold off the cephrast armada indefinitely—it was only a matter of time.

Still, the technicians had done an admirable job…they all should have been dead days ago. Their head armorer was some sort of artillery whiz from the Stellar War, and she'd made every warhead count, even figured out an optimized exchange system for energy-based defenses to string their cells out as long as possible. It should go a long way for the rest of the CAF. Tellakeep had been under attack long before Outpost Vensa, and still had photon cannons running after the distant station's obliteration.

If only they could be so lucky. There was always a possibility their invaders would pummel Tellakeep into dust, but their strike leader thought a boarding attempt was likely. A hundred centuries ago, three cephrast bodies were left on Earth to be examined—an edge that had yet to be afforded to their adversaries. For that very reason, Tellakeep's procedure was clear—if the outpost was isolated and boarded, they would detonate the weapons storage *into* the generator. A detonation of plasma, radiation, and graviton condensate would quickly collapse back on itself, leaving a charred ball of metal and ice one-tenth the diameter of the original station.

Being taken alive was not an option, and a well-preserved body was almost as bad. It was all the same to Morrison. He wanted them to board, just so he could shoot a few in their disgusting, circumcised faces.

Clunk.

A dull sound reverberated through the hallway and up his boots—something being fastened to the outside of the auxiliary hatch.

"Boarding!" Morrison shouted. His patrol partner—a federal agent from 9700s Europa—dragged a two-meter metal girder to the corner of the hallway leading into the hatch. She stomped on a small, protruding tag on the side, and an amber barrier popped up from the silver runner.

Summoning rifles from the protective shells they slept beneath, the two soldiers knelt behind the barricade in wait. They'd need to pin the boarding team down for a few minutes while Tellakeep's technicians did their deed. The armory wasn't well-stocked, but it still had four gigatons of explosives in it.

"Alright..." the Europan agent steadied her weapon on the vibrant honey wall. "Let's burn 'em up."

"Fall back to the airlock!" the dispatch operator called through the radio. "They're not—"

His voice was cut off by a muffled boom pressing into Morrison like an underwater explosion. The outpost's walls shook, the hatch's seams fell apart, and the sound vanished into space as the air around them flooded through the hole.

The cephrasts weren't boarding—the hatch was a weak point.

Dragging the barricade with them, the two soldiers were pulled through the destroyed hull. Morrison tried to grab hold of the lip, managing only to slice his hand through the holster glove. There were no cephrasts lying in wait outside, nothing for his vengeance, just the pressure of his blood pushing its way into the cold vacuum of space.

Morrison prayed the engineers had sealed the maintenance deck off when they started. They were smart. Any moment, there would be a flash of searing light, and all of them would be incinerated.

He didn't see the flash. In the far distance, he could see the crimson glow of a cephrast carrier—two horizontal cogs with large, protruding arms. The stars beyond dazzled in the black sky as Morrison's body froze over, the air in his lungs escaping in a single gasp.

In a small, isolated building near The Dome, a team of engineers and programmers spent a week building the simulator of the cephrast cockpit, recreating the control panel, matching as many of its functions as possible. Some were described in fragmented cephrast manuals, archived eons ago, others were deduced by human researchers over the years, discovered more recently by various means. Important controls like thrust were thankfully well documented.

Every day, Raynor reported in at Teckann's office per her assignment. From there, she either read through mountains of personnel files in search of a piloting team, or headed to the simulator construction. She tried to check in at the repurposed storage room a few times each day, figuring it would be informative to see the machine throughout the build process. The techs had quickly taken to calling her over when a new part was assembled so they could explain how it should *theoretically* work.

Raynor's promotion granted her access to a lot of CAF information. With hundreds of pilots to narrow down, she found herself constantly fighting the urge to look up everyone she knew on base.

The very first file she read was, of course, her own. Unsurprisingly, she knew everything in it, though the accuracy and thoroughness was mildly disturbing. The subjective aspects were mostly positive, and the less positive parts weren't entirely off base.

"Tendencies towards aloofness" was one.

Fair enough.

Later in the week, she casually looked at Eldon Rhyso's file to see what his career had really been like. It seemed the Tannon-born operative was a bit modest with his accolades. He'd been a precision wrecking ball, and the missions he'd done under Teckann had unquestionably helped lead to the future general's ascent. Then she got to Rhyso's psychological profile, which weighed his value and reliability as an expendable asset, and Raynor stopped looking at her friends' records.

The newly-promoted major wasn't sure exactly what her criteria were in looking for a pilot—some combination of technical skill, adaptability, and personality. When Raynor saw a good candidate, she figured she'd just know.

It didn't take her long to add a file to the shortlist: an emergency response pilot from Callisto, born at the beginning of the Declassification period. Leiko Waverly wasn't military, and his skills were honed for flying in dangerous areas without engaging an enemy— precisely what they were expecting to do. The medivac pilot also set an "accidental" record for the fastest trip through the asteroid belt.

After days of going through files, Raynor started bringing an infoscreen to the construction room, narrowing down candidates while she listened to programmers arguing about the translation of old Earth documents. Sitting against the wall, she found herself returning to a particular pilot for the fourth time—a pseudonym she'd known well in her own time…

Ronald Phillips. The Shadow Hawk. Arguably, the most notorious pre-space pilot in human history. Because the mission at hand was entirely extraplanetary, Raynor hadn't been considering air pilots, yet she found herself coming back to his file repeatedly.

She'd also been nixing any questionable psychological profiles. Phillips was antagonizing, arrogant, and egocentric. But again, Raynor found herself looking over the portfolio.

He'd never flown a spacecraft. Not even once. Still, he'd emerged victorious from some of the most impossible odds of any dogfights. He never lost track of a nearby ship, even through neck-breaking stunts, described in many reports as a "psychic" in the cockpit. It would explain how he managed hundreds of missions in the largest terrestrial war to date without being touched. Perhaps it was the American pilot's infamy that kept drawing Raynor back—a man despised throughout the early 2100s by all of Asia, Europe, Africa, and South America.

If that hatred was warranted—if he became a problem—Raynor could always remove him from the assignment.

She was an officer, now. She could do that.

Before re-assigning any pilots, Raynor had to put some time in on the simulator. Much of the derelict craft's function was pure speculation. As she ran into snags, she'd have to message one of the programmers to ask how sure they were of certain features. After the third or fourth time, one of the annoyed computer scientists made a pointed comment about Raynor using her assistant for this information—something she genuinely hadn't considered.

The first issue in the control pod was the available space. The cockpit was a low, 360-degree table of panels designed for a single, 140-centimeter creature to operate, making it a tight fit for Raynor. Hopefully, the surrounding bridge of the large carrier would contain enough space for the controls to be accessed from the other side, but it was still a problem to deal with.

Raynor spent twenty hours a day hunched over the simulator panel. The metallic desk of controls was completely dead, most of them designed for interacting with databases and navigation systems. Without those computers, the sensors simply did nothing. The engines and thrust panels were well documented, though, and that was Raynor's focus.

Maneuvering the cephrast ship was frustratingly more difficult than anticipated. The engines fired in analog degrees, as wide or narrow as desired, from one sliver of the ring to the entire circumference. The panels were concave, able to activate along the top, middle, or bottom to angle the force, tilting that edge of the craft. It required more precision than any craft Raynor had flown—combining angles of the propulsion ring with amounts of thrust to perform various movements.

The one saving grace was that the cephrasts' hand featured opposable digits for grabbing objects. As such, the controls were designed to be grabbed and moved—something primates were quite good at. A joystick-like control activated the thrust panels when tilted, and rotating the stick increased or decreased the perimeter of the arc. An identical stick on the opposite side of the cockpit angled the force up or down when rotated, confining it to a specific direction when tilted. It allowed for extremely specific angles of pitch and roll. If Raynor had years to practice, she could probably make the craft do any trick imaginable.

Opposing cephrast arms handled each control, leaving the others to activate the rest of the panel. It was possible for Raynor to fly the ship alone if she was cruising, but evasive maneuvers—merely seeing out of the viewport in some cases—would be impossible by herself. Two pilots would have to maneuver the ship, with a third navigating and accessing other flight controls.

"Don't hit that," Nezz abruptly told Raynor after she bumped a sheer button on her right. Panic briefly swept through her.

"Did it do something?"

"No, but this is a simulator."

"Right…" she exhaled. "What *does* it do?"

"A partially-translated document suggests it switches the energy source of the thrust panels to a synthetic condensate, allowing for acceleration beyond the typical method of propulsion—an overdrive or booster of sorts."

"We'll need to make a quick getaway."

"The force will almost certainly kill you."

"Oh…" Raynor had forgotten how much frailer human bodies were than their adversaries. Escaping in the carrier was going to be a trudge. The behemoth vessel was already much slower than the bomber drones housed within it, and human occupants would only slow it further.

Raynor crawled out of the pod, pain in her back like she'd been hit with a metal pipe. She'd increased her protein intake, started a nightly regimen of ice and painkillers, but it hurt more every day.

Humans were not meant to fly this piece of shit.

"You alright, Major?"

Raynor didn't recognize the voice, but as she straightened her back out, she recognized the wiry hair, hazel eyes, and pointed nose.

"Oh, Dr. Walker." She tried to stand upright, wincing at the tinge. "Yes, I'll live."

"A bit cramped, isn't it?" The biologist leaned over to peek inside the simulator, craning her neck up and around to see everything. Eyes wide, Raynor watched as the woman famed for pioneering the field of xenobiology gazed admiringly at the inside of the simulator.

"Very."

"They did an incredible job with this," Walker said wondrously. "I haven't seen the original one in years…it's surprisingly nostalgic."

Raynor was speechless. The woman in front of her had actually stepped foot in the cephrast ship *the night* it crashed. To the rest of the universe, it was ancient history—a relic decayed through time.

Walker leaned back from the simulator. "How are the controls?"

"Difficult," Raynor confessed. "I'm getting the hang of it, though."

The biologist's head tilted briefly to the side—a now-familiar sign she was listening to her assistant. Nodding, she returned her attention to Raynor, removing a small sheet of fiber from her pocket.

"I have to be somewhere, but I wanted to give you this. I copied it down from Brody's—ah, Dr. Kahlil's notebook years ago." Walker handed her the small sheet, white with faint blue lines running horizontally. It had been marked like a touchscreen, but with paint or ink, containing words written in cephrastian characters. They did not adhere to any of the lines. "It's important you memorize this. Do *not* touch anything with those symbols on or near it. There have been issues incorporating files from our ship's computers into the Centauri archives, so this may not be included yet. It wasn't terribly relevant until this mission."

"What does it do?"

"No one knows for sure. Worst-case scenario, it sucks you into a parallel dimension with no means of returning."

Raynor chuckled. Walker did not.

"Are you—?"

"Yes."

Raynor looked at the symbols again. "What does it say?"

"It's a word all on its own. There was never a translation for it. It's also the main reason for this mission, but don't advertise that; I don't think the CAF was planning to tell you. The ship heist was my idea, though, so I'm telling you."

"This was all your idea?"

"Everything on this planet came from reverse-engineered alien tech. It seemed only reasonable that we stick to our strengths." She glanced back at the pod sitting in the middle of the room. "What you're attempting to do here is remarkable, Major. It's a chance to level the playing field. Whatever I can do to improve your chances…"

Raynor rubbed the fiber between her thumb and forefinger. It was cold and smooth, almost completely void of texture or wrinkles aside from a crisp fold along the center—a brand new artifact from thousands of years ago.

"I thought you just wanted to see the simulator," she said.

"Well, that too," Walker mused. She tilted her head again, accepting a ping—an assistant-based voice call—from Director Quinto. She gave Raynor a brief wave, leaving the empty storage house in conversation with the science director about lab equipment of some sort.

Raynor looked again at the strange characters on the sheet in her hand. To her surprise, some of them seemed familiar, and after examining them for a moment, she realized there were Latin letters mixed in with the alien symbols.

"Nezz, what do these words at the top mean?"

There was a slight pause. Likely the synthetic re-positioning a security camera to see the sheet.

"It's post-middle English, and reads: *the third waveform.*"

31

KALLIPAR

Raynor still had reservations about the infamous terrorizer of the skies, Ron Phillips. His file noted unresolved hostility, but it seemed to be targeted heavily towards his adversaries in World War III—nations that fell before the Stellar War. Neither Mars nor Jupiter—the home of Leiko Waverly—seemed to be of much importance to the American pilot. He was also duty-bound, so while his brainwashing was exceptional, Raynor's rank had so far ensured no attitude issues from the airman.

Once both pilots had become familiar with the alien ship's propulsion mechanisms, they set forth on the daunting task of performing quick, reactionary flight maneuvers. Not knowing which systems, if any, would be accessible, they mostly worked on contingencies.

Further muddying the process was the complete absence of data about the inside of the carrier. No signals were emitted from within any cephrast armada ship, either from some kind of field or the hull material itself. Their team had to assume complete isolation once inside, even from Marker and Nezz. In preparation, Nezz custom-built devices for the infiltration team's radios. Manual translators didn't work in real-time, and even the most rudimentary version of the synthetic assistant—what it called a "sleeping" brain—weighed several hundred kilos. The customized data packs were roughly the size of a deck of cards, loaded with a collection of Nezz's processes for the team's respective languages.

The three pilots spent countless hours on the simulator and few in sleep, eventually developing a method for controlling the alien ship that provided a reasonable amount of dexterity. On their last day on Razennon, they spent an hour learning how to use a gravitational tether-anchor. They were somewhat heavy to carry around, but they would prevent the pilots from being thrown out of the control area in lieu of a proper harness.

With as little information as they had on the armada vessel, Raynor felt the trio of pilots was as ready as they could be. Packed for a lengthy trip and bundled against the cold winter night, they ascended through the purple twilight in a long-range shuttle.

Breaking through the atmosphere, Waverly turned to Raynor.

"Major, you're the ranking officer now."

"I always have been," she said flatly, setting their route to the edge of the system—a dwarf planet called Kallipar.

"I mean, you're the commanding officer, right? You call the shots?"

That was true. For the first time in her life, she was the top brass. Granted, it didn't mean much—the admiral would be on Kallipar with them. During their week of travel, though, she was the commanding officer of this shuttle—her subordinates consisting of two pilots without ships.

"You're right," she said. "What do you boys feel like doing?"

"I always wanted to hijack a spaceship…" said Phillips.

"Sounds like a plan."

Streaks of pale green and purple layered the circumference of Kallipar, dulled slightly by a thin atmosphere barely clinging to the small planet. The colorful marble was slightly larger than Earth's moon, frozen solid at the edge of Centauri. The planet was too cold to survive on, not to mention unbreathable, but due to an abundance of water and gas beneath the surface, it was home to a storage and refueling station. Kallipar's revolution around the dual suns was long, making it unreliable as a strategic point, but it happened to be near the early cephrast incursion. Only one outpost remained past the swamp-colored orb. Once it fell, the planet would be lost in hours.

Walker waited by the door leading in from the hangar, allowing the exterior gates to close. Listening to the dampened sounds of the opening landing pad, she leaned up against the wall beside one of several "no jumping" signs littered throughout the base. The words were unreadable for her, but the little red drawing was clear enough. The station's mining equipment was effectively a large irrigation system, melting ice and pumping it up to the building. Kallipar was always below freezing, so all of the piping needed to be housed inside, preventing the use of gravity panels in the foundation. Enough people had hit their heads on the ceiling to warrant station-wide signage.

In recent years, panels were retrofitted under the back quarter of the station, primarily for health purposes beneath the barracks. For the last five days, Walker had been sleeping in those quarters. She flew out with Isaac's strike team, along with Director Quinto and two xenobiologists.

Two other *xenobiologists.*

They'd also brought an electrical engineer—the man from *Retribution Ark* who hadn't cut Fowler's brachial artery. Apparently, strict electrical engineers were in short supply, and few were eager to jump into a nest of cephrasts. Strike Team Dissent had a breach specialist—Alejandra—who was quite adept at bypassing security locks, but she hadn't gotten much time to learn about cephrast computer systems before the creatures showed up, and those courses were all based on machines from the Georgia crash. They needed an electrician.

The group of thirteen left Starling Base right after Walker finished setting up what she believed to be the most comprehensive facility for examining cephrasts. Similar equipment was brought on their transport, set up in a room by the barracks over the gravity panels. It was more basic than the one at Starling—and less sterile—but it was nearby. The carrier would likely be full of cephrasts. Most of them would still be on the ship when it got here.

Not here, exactly. The armada ship was much larger than the fueling station, so Fowler's group would be pulling the vessel back to the outpost behind Kallipar, offering some breathing room while a couple of strike teams cleared the ship of hostiles. Alamanda Quinto didn't want to risk a week of transit to get to an examination room, though. She wanted a live cephrast more than anything—even the carrier itself. It was a point she and Walker strongly disagreed on. Walker believed the vessel's trove of technologies would be invaluable for their survival, but even more than that, she didn't like the idea of experimenting on a live prisoner. It felt morally… gross. She knew that wasn't a valid reason not to take prisoners in their current situation, but she couldn't help feeling disgusted by it.

The seal of the exterior door hissed from inside the hangar. Walker clutched her snow coat and went inside to find Major Raynor and her pilots already descending the shuttle's ramp, each carrying large, duffel-like bags in CAF black-and-grey.

Walker gave the trio a quick tour of the base, but the time for recreation was short. As the surface outside went from dark to pitch-black, the station was hailed by the admiral's escort to notify them of her arrival.

The Dissenters lined up in the hall outside of the landing bay, joined soon after by the pilots and researchers along the other side. When Admiral Dreinn entered from the hangar, it was clear she hadn't expected anything of the sort—a weird custom from a dead society.

Dreinn was a picture-perfect Centauri native, with wide shoulders, short-clipped auburn hair, and a square jaw. She had a sincere, focused look to her, made somewhat comical by the captain carrying their luggage in her wake.

"Drone Control is ready to go," she told Quinto. The vespiary had been moved back a step further than they normally parked, but they didn't want to leave it in the path of the carrier, which might be pursued all the way to the first outpost.

Dreinn turned to Walker; her eyes lit up.

"Denise Walker. It is quite an honor." The same sentiment had been given to Walker by just about everyone she met, but hearing it from the head of the system's largest military force was new for her.

She often felt guilty about the constant praise—Fowler's interactions had been the exact opposite. Some people were intimidated by his name alone, and many more held animosity towards him.

Hell, someone tried to kill him.

That was all before the war, though. Thousands of travel-weary soldiers had abandoned their homes for a cause they'd only ever heard about, living in metal boxes for years while they rocketed through the abyss to a strange land.

Now that the cephrasts were here, the infantry revered him. He was Isaac Fowler: the reaper of aliens.

And to Walker's knowledge, he was still the only living human to kill a cephrast face-to-face. Some had likely died during drone attacks, but nobody had even seen one in the flesh since May of 2023.

"Briefing room, fifteen minutes," Dreinn said to the group. "Get a connection open with Drone Control beforehand." She strolled down the hall with her peon in tow as the Dissenters followed suit.

"Where's the briefing room?" Raynor asked Walker quietly.

"She means the kitchen."

"Of course…"

The top of the dining table was covered with a large jewel, showing an exterior image of the cephrast carrier. The vessel had obvious design similarities to the ship in Chattahoochee, consisting of a propulsion system sandwiched between two sections of hull.

Rather than thrust panels, a large, red sphere hovered in the empty space between the two sections. Crimson light shot out to the side when the carrier moved, pushing it in the other direction. The hull sections were flat circles, each with six arms protruding out of the perimeter. A shallow dome sat on top, nearly the full diameter of the central hub.

They had taken to calling it a "starfish."

An unknown number of remote fighters were housed within the dozen arms of the starfish. The cephrast drones also had a non-directional structure, existing within an orange, discus-shaped energy field. Contoured to the curve was a narrow, metal X, like a cephrast's foot, containing the craft's robotics and weapons.

While Walker had been preparing the examination room, Fowler's team had been trying to establish points of entry, possible internal defenses, even a layout, but the information was scarce. Marker had dedicated significant resources to the cause, but everything inside the starfish's hull was an enigma.

"Alright, here's the recap," Fowler said, pointing along the jewel-table. "It's a safe bet the cockpit is housed at the top, here. We don't know if there are any paths between the top and bottom halves, so boarding through the lower decks is not an option. Marker will pilot our shuttle to keep our ship in sync any time Major Raynor isn't actively touching the controls. The shuttle will be noticeably larger than the surrounding drones, but we have two large, hollow vessels to use as decoys. The drone modulators need to utilize them like support vehicles—if they look like armor, they'll get blown apart."

"We can handle that," a compressed, digital voice confirmed.

"The engine has been witnessed being used as a defensive weapon to melt nearby fighters, so our approach needs to be from above that lateral. The only openings we can identify are the fighter bays, so crawling along the outside looking for a hatch is our secondary backup plan. Our first backup is to blow open one of the bays, but the shielding might prevent that entirely, making our primary plan a good old-fashioned swap. There may not be a method of manually opening the hatch from the inside, so this route means we're going all-in. Meaning, uh…we either steal the ship or don't come back at all."

"This is going to be a crash landing—" Raynor said. "If that wasn't made clear to everyone. Three seconds is not a big window…we're going to be coming in extremely hot."

"As soon as we're in, we do suit checks, then work our way in towards the hub and up. Our top priority is ensuring the pilots get to the bridge. Once there, we barricade ourselves in. Every single lifeform not in a CAF uniform is kill on sight—I don't care if it looks like an alien puppy."

If Fowler's goal was to impress Dreinn, he was doing a bang-up job. His status as a professional cephrast exterminator was well-reinforced. He went through the rest of their outline, ending with the carrier arriving at the backup outpost and having a second strike team board and clear the ship. He took a deep breath. "Any questions?"

There were general murmurs of understanding.

"Well done, Sergeant," Dreinn said. "I wish our information was better, but with what we have, I think this is our best shot. The mission is now active. Commander, you have operation lead."

"Yes, Admiral," Raynor said hesitantly. "But, ah—it's *Major*."

"Not if you're running a carrier, it's not. Forgive me for not having a badge ready."

Walker didn't fully know the CAF's military ranks. She could always tell from the badges because higher ranks had more *stuff* on them, but based on the reactions around the table, commander was a big deal.

Watching Strike Team Dissent load out, the equipment looked *a lot* fancier than what Walker had seen at Starling. The CAF environmental suits featured armor plates and vacuum-friendly equipment that fastened to the hard exterior. Fowler hadn't been ready to put his trust into bionics, but the same couldn't be said for the rest of his team. Metal arms and legs were being wrapped off inside their suits—a pressurized band that formed a seal, preventing air from escaping. Military-grade limbs weren't damaged by direct exposure to space, and if the suit tore below the band, the seal would more than likely hold.

"They gave you the good toys, huh?" she asked, watching Fowler clip some of the weirdest-looking gadgets onto his suit.

"Gotta go big or go home."

"Isaac…" she started, losing her words. He was her best friend. Not just in this century—ever. As good as their plan was, it was merely the best option for an impossible task. If any of them made it back, it would be a miracle.

"Look, Denise, I think we're both practical enough not to do the whole 'take care of yourself' thing. If the mission is a success, I'll see you soon. And if not…"

"Yeah."

"It's why we're here."

"I know."

Before long, they were locked and loaded. The boarding team jogged off towards the hangar—eight soldiers, three pilots, and one electrical engineer.

The dream team.

32

SHIP HEIST

Raynor's heart was about to burst from her chest. It was pumping so hard it would explode, the console would get covered in blood, and they'd have to cancel the mission.

There was always some amount of elation before flying into combat. It was a dangerous job, but this was the worst yet. Aside from her joyride with Shino the month before, she hadn't done any astrobatics in years. During the revolution, she had been in the stars so often that it was more comfortable than running for her. No matter how treacherous the sky got, Raynor never felt out of control of her environment.

Leaving the small, icy planet, plagued with uncertainty, she had less control than ever.

She hated it.

Marker took the shuttle out, absorbing it into the drone formation. Their ship was in direct communication with Drone Control, but Raynor wasn't sure how well they would coordinate. Modulators never had pilots to talk to—they only ever dealt with Marker, who was more of a silent type.

About fifteen minutes later, the vespiary reached out.

"Nadia?" the thin, familiar voice said. "Can you hear me?" The lax radio communication was unsurprising from Shino. Knowing she was in the vespiary gave Raynor a much-needed wave of relief.

"I read you, Teegan."

"Let me know when you take control from Marker. I'll give you a heads-up before your formation shifts so you can stick by them."

"Will do."

"At least they gave us the best," Fowler said from behind Raynor. The degrees of separation at Starling Base often felt impossibly coincidental. Traveling thousands of lightyears, meeting people from different planets and times, then finding out you know people in common. It felt improbable, but Starling was about as populated as a medium-sized university, and most ships had been filled with various job classes. It happened constantly.

"I forgot you two were on the same ship," Raynor said.

"It's a small world."

"That it is," Phillips said from beside her. "Specialist Nabokov and I were, as well."

"Unfortunately," the demolitionist droned. It was the only word he'd spoken.

"What does *that* mean?" Raynor asked her co-pilot, though she already knew the answer. A villainous grin cracked across the airman's face—the attitude issues from his dossier surfacing at the worst possible moment. Memories of her interactions with Bouchet, the terrestrial slime from the *Violet Shift*, filled her with dread.

"I killed a lot of his friends," Phillips said sadistically. "But he did the same to me...not nearly as many, of course."

"Do we have a problem?" she said forcefully. It wasn't a question.

"No. Veektor's just annoyed that I outrank him."

"He's not wrong..." grumbled Nabokov.

"I outrank everyone," Raynor snapped. "And I expect absolute focus. Are we clear?" They didn't sound like her words. It was someone else's voice coming from her lips. She sounded like...

"Yes, Commander."

"Aye, Major—shit, sorry…*Commander.*"

Her folks would never have believed it.

The silence picked up for a few minutes, broken when Marker finally chirped to let them know they were in visual range of the carrier. The small, digital viewport in front of Raynor was indistinguishable to the human eye, like the clearest glass ever made. Hundreds of tiny ships flew in various formations ahead of them with hundreds more on their flanks.

Past the swarm sat a collection of colossal cephrast ships, including the carrier. Objects in space always looked small from afar. It wasn't until you started approaching and the object grew slowly that you realized how large it truly was. The carrier was already large, making some of the nearby cruisers look like tugboats.

"Jesus, Mary…" Phillips ritualistically touched his face and chest.

"Make sure you're strapped in," Raynor said. "Marker, careful with the quick turns." Leaving control to the synthetic during combat was nauseating. Drones turned exceptionally fast, and those same forces would make the passengers fall unconscious—or worse.

Not five seconds later, a beam of pale light shot from one of the battleships, dissolving the frontmost CAF drone without continuing through. Another heavily shielded unit was already in place as the shuttle lurched up. Their jaws hung down from the force of the bank, pulling the passengers into their seats. The stars before them rotated quickly, jerking them to the side roughly as the ship leveled out above the center of the carrier.

Specs of orange light began flooding out of the starfish's closest arms, gravitating towards the human fleet. Another pale beam of light flashed between the ships, trailing back to a pointed, oval battleship below. A large squadron broke off, bulleting towards the artillery vessel.

"Ma–ar–ker," Raynor said with a quiver as their ship banked to avoid targeting. "Make our bea–ring towards a top a–arm with unopened ba–ay doors."

The synthetic shouldn't have a problem tracking which hangar bays had yet to open. Forcing the orange discs out of their homes would be another story, but they could worry about that when they got closer. After being thrown around for ten minutes, the strike team didn't seem to be any nearer to the carrier. Cephrast drones littered the skies around them, firing a barrage of particles at the CAF ships.

A clear beam—visible only by the distortion of the ships behind it—passed within a few meters of their dropship. Muffled vibrations filtered softly through the ship's hull as it was struck by the debris from an exploding drone.

"One of the decoys is gone," Shino said. "They're targeting the larger ships." The cephrasts didn't know what the larger drones were for, but they knew there was a purpose for them. It wasn't surprising, just more difficult.

There was no point in trying to blend in with the other ships now. They needed to get in as quickly as possible. Darting her hand forward, Raynor grabbed the control stick and pushed it to the side, rolling the ship over.

"Raynor taking over," she said. "You're on me, now."

The drone patterns changed, swarming the shuttle to absorb blasts and intercept cephrast fighters. Keeping her flight path sporadic, Raynor moved the ship in a large arc around the side of the starfish, away from the battleships and towards the arms that had yet to scramble fighters. Beams of light tangled through the sky, creating explosions that flared up briefly, only to be snuffed out by the cold void of space.

"Marker, find me some occupied bays."

Small waves of force popped around them, knocking the shuttle as their escort drones were picked off. Amidst the frenzied waves of radiant, orange saucers in the shuttle's small viewport, violet circles appeared on the digital display as Marker highlighted unopened hatches along the starfish's arms.

Curving around the far side of the carrier, Raynor turned the shuttle towards the main battle just in time to watch a torpedo smack into the second decoy ship, melting it into glowing orange goop right before it cooled into a metallic splatter pattern. The group of drones around it quickly abandoned the skirmish to join the shuttle's dwindling escort.

"Ignore the arm, Drone Control. As soon as we're in line with the battleship, take a hard bank down to the center of the carrier. We're going to feign a bombing run."

Seconds later, the frontmost ships in their escort darted downwards, followed by the next group, and then Raynor's shuttle. The battleship's railgun shot just over them as they plummeted towards the intense, scarlet engine light. The swarm of CAF drones deteriorated even faster, absorbing shots intended for the shuttle.

"Pick 'em off as they come out," Raynor prepped. Blood-red flames spat out from between the hull sections, liquifying the frontmost ships of their swarm.

Pushing her stomach down into her bladder, Raynor banked hard towards the arm on her right. One by one, the violet circles vanished from her viewport as each hangar opened and closed. A surge of green energy salvos and tactile warheads slammed into the side of the carrier arm, laying the cephrast ships to waste as they exited their hangars. Helmet glued to her headrest, Raynor pushed the transport towards the closest occupied hangar, further down the line of violet circles. The shuttle was only a hundred meters away when the door opened, unloading four metal crosses encased in translucent neon pucks.

She rotated the shuttle to squeeze past the emerging crafts, through the soon-closing doors. Only, the ship didn't tilt. No response came from the flight controls. Marker was cutting her out—something it wasn't supposed to do.

Rather than rotating, the AI-controlled shuttle accelerated—a lot. Blood started to leave Raynor's brain, her vision fading. She didn't have time to be angry at the synthetic intelligence before the hangar bay door slammed shut on the tail of the shuttle, throwing it into a flat spin. Metal screeched as the ship yawed along the ground of the compact hangar. The last thing Raynor remembered was drowsily forgiving the AI before the shuttle crashed into the back wall.

The side of the transport was caved in; a high-pitched ringing seared through Fowler's head. No obvious casualties of the crew, though a few sat motionless in their harnesses, probably unconscious. Others had been knocked out of their seats by the impact, but none were crushed.

"Check for tears," he said, pulling his harness off. Those already conscious checked the rest, flipping them around as they slowly came to. A jagged corner of metal had lanced MacTeal's shoulder, blood seeping across the fabric. Her fellow Callistian, Lockheart, already had a bandage out, tending to the wound. The thick, adhesive scraps functioned like generic suit-tape, which created a vacuum seal to reliably patch minor damage to spacesuits, but with a salve providing basic wound treatment. The bandage had to be wrapped to press it against the injury, but if there wasn't time, it was still slightly more effective than regular suit-tape. A proper field dress was ideal, but that usually wasn't an option in space. Fortunately, the shuttle still had its atmosphere, so the field surgeon took a moment to cauterize and treat the wound before applying the bandage loosely.

As soon as their armor was patched, Fowler opened the shuttle door opposite the damaged hull. A gale of marshy air flooded past him into the transport. He stepped out, the compacted rifle on his back flying into his hands as he gripped for it.

From outside the starfish, the bays seemed tiny, but not so much now. Down the length of his barrel, Fowler scanned the dark hangar. Four empty docks lined the walls, designed to hold eight-foot drones—smaller than a jet, but sizable enough to hold weapons, engines, and navigation. Lying sideways, the shuttle took up nearly the full width of the room.

Fowler ordered the rest of Strike Team Dissent to form up, dropping his voice to a quiet groan to listen for motion on the other side of the maintenance hatches. The three-foot-square doors were easy to spot—not so much to open. Alejandra searched the interior for a panel of some kind to bypass. After checking the walls twice, she asked her assistant if it saw any sort of interface, not seeming to get a response.

"Delio, do you copy?" she asked again. "Drone Control?"

The bay was silent...not a sound from the ongoing battle outside, nor Drone Control or the AI. It was like Raynor had flown them through a portal to a faraway place. Low, muffled sounds came through their suits as they began moving debris, walking on the bare floors—not quite like being underwater, but closer to that than Earth air.

Lockheart guided Tian over to the hatch, bandages on the side of his suit. The reformed convict ran his hands along the wall near the hatch. He started to pull at part of the wall, quickly recoiling his hand away and checking his fingers for damage.

"Don't rip your gloves!" chided Lockheart.

"I think we need to get behind this panel," he said.

Rovasatti—the man whose official military title had been *Titanic Berserker*—jogged over to the panel and grabbed the edge of it. His fingers dug effortlessly behind the metal, tearing the synthetic fibers of his gloves and flaying the panel as easily as an angsty teen ripping a poster down from their wall. The band around his shoulder held, allowing only the air in his sleeve to blend with the hangar's atmosphere.

Heavy breaths came chillingly from the electrical engineer, isolated in their radios while he looked up inside the wall.

"Thirty more seconds, Tian," Fowler said. "Then we're cutting it." He'd prefer not to cut. It was slow, and if their boarding wasn't already known by the alien crew, a foot-long flame on the other side of the hatch would change that.

The electrician mumbled to himself about conductivity and extraterrestrial alloys, shining a light across the wires and gizmos hidden within the wall. Just as Fowler was about to have Alejandra fire up the torch, Tian ripped a handful of wires out of the wall.

"What did that do?" Raynor asked, concerned.

"A lot of things, probably," he said. "But I think it unpowered an electromagnetic seal."

The engineer asked Rovasatti to help him pull the door open, and sure enough, it budged. Fowler quickly organized their breach order, not sure what the other side of the hatch would reveal. He trained his rifle at the outlined square, a twitch running through his index finger like a coiled snake, waiting to send a salvo of energy through the door unless he told it not to.

Nope.

It was an empty hallway, dimly illuminated for creatures to walk through, but no creatures. Fowler's helmet adjusted to the new light, darkening the hangar around him. Vivid images filled his head from a lifetime ago, systematically clearing the crashed vessel with Walker in Georgia, not knowing when they might run into the then-unnamed aliens. Like that ship, the hall in the carrier was cramped—designed for a smaller species. They managed a proper two-by-two, leap-frogging down the endless corridor. Behind them was more of the same, leading away from the hub towards the end of the starfish's arm. The entire thing had to be half a mile long.

They moved through the narrow passageway for ten minutes, eventually coming to a door at the end. Unlike the maintenance hatch, this door had an access panel. Fowler moved up with Alejandra, and before she could touch the panel, the door opened.

They froze, weapons aimed through the doorway. The perpendicular hallway on the other side was larger than the access tunnel, with higher ceilings designed for regular foot traffic. It was bright, illuminated like a lab, with a slight bend away in either direction. The edge of the hub.

Again, no creatures to be found. The door seemed to have opened automatically on approach. Fowler angled himself by the frame, darting his eyes back and forth along the hall as the rest of the team caught up.

Then he saw one. For the first time in ten thousand years, he stared at a living, breathing alien.

The creature was exiting a door on the other side of the hall, twenty yards down. It was about a foot taller than the three he'd seen in Georgia…just under five feet. It was also naked, and in the absence of a protective suit, Fowler could see no shell on top of its head. Otherwise, it looked the same—upright posture, two feet with rounded X's for toes, and four arms with thick, three-fingered hands. Its limbs moved loosely, like a monkey's tail, its cylindrical body a pale purple. It was looking at something in its hand, angling its single, ring-like eye down towards the object. It didn't have to turn to spot Fowler and Alejandra in the doorway, but it took a full step into the hall before stopping dead in its tracks.

It was surprised.

A bright, yellow hashmark patterned around the circumference of the alien's head, accompanied by a low, crackly groan that carried through the halls. Both warnings ended abruptly with the *thwap* of Fowler's rifle.

"What the fuck…" Nabokov muttered.

"Everyone in, *now!*" Fowler called, moving further into the hall with Alejandra to make room for the rest in the hub's perimeter. Only nine others made it through the door before it sealed shut. A loud, smothered *clunk* vibrated far beyond, followed by the whooshing of air and Doma Doringo's screams through the radio, which were abruptly cut off seconds later.

They couldn't linger. Fowler led the team to the open door behind the charred cephrast body—whatever friends it had signaled within that room might still be the only ones aware of the boarding.

The deceased alien had come from a room full of panels, none of which held any significance to the human infiltrators. A few small, circular work stations sat spaced throughout the area, three of which were occupied. A fourth cephrast stood at the far wall, rummaging almost frantically through a container. It seemed to find what it was looking for, curling an arm around its body towards Fowler and Alejandra.

A sound Fowler hadn't heard in over a decade pierced through the marshy air. A reversed *zap*.

Thankfully, there was no resulting wet pop, and the armed cephrast didn't get another shot. Heated blasts of photon rifle fire melted chunks of the alien away, followed immediately by the other three. When the firing stopped, Fowler walked over to the farthest corpse, throwing his rifle into its sheath as he crouched down.

"We need to go up," Raynor said. Fowler nodded. He hesitated to pick the weapon up, unable to see an obvious trigger, but he knew which end was the dangerous one—that was good enough.

"You're right," he said, tucking the device into an armored pocket as he stood up from the scorched body. "Let's find a way up."

Returning to the curved hallway, they slinked along the inner wall in search of stairs, traversing at least a quarter-mile before they were met by more cephrasts—ones with armor and equipment.

I guess the jig is up…

With pinpoint accuracy, the seven Dissenters fried each group of the dozen cephrasts they ran into along the corridor, all of which were using weapons similar to their photon rifles—a condensed, heated energy. Deadly, but not the inexplicable force that pureed people in their suits. The CAF armor could handle a few hits from standard weapons, though the team had yet to test them.

Pausing only to fire, they ran along the hub's outermost hallway for another quarter-mile before finding an inward hallway, which quickly led to an ascending ramp. The wide incline went up a floor, leading into a large bulkhead door. It didn't open when approached.

"Alejandra," Fowler called. More cephrasts rounded the corner to the ramp, retreating back behind as a combination of energy and projectile fire picked up. Two of the operatives ran to the bottom of the ramp, firing erratically down the hallway to keep their pursuers at bay. After well over a minute, the door was still closed. "What's the hold-up?"

"This infrastructure is nothing like the old ship," said Alejandra. "It's completely different from what we were shown."

Rovasatti pulled Tian towards the doorway, practically picking the small electrician up off the ground. The engineer looked along the walls, around the door, running his hand across them. It was perfectly sheer.

"Let's go behind the interface," he said. The Titanian ripped the access panel out of the wall, revealing another cluster of wires and contraptions while reciting an old adage that equated to *if it ain't broke, don't fix it*. Tian crawled halfway into the wall before finally squirming back out. "I think I've got it…further up."

Grabbing the top of the hole the access panel had been in, Rovasatti pulled up, but without any corrugation, the metal wouldn't budge. The Titanian pulled harder, screaming as he strained the connecting tissue at his shoulder. The wall didn't peel away as effortlessly as the last, but it bent, thinning slightly in an upward curve to provide enough room for Tian to dig up into the wall.

With a beep, the door slid open, accompanied by flashes of light. Two blips of energy went through Alejandra, who collapsed to the ground like a dropped marionette.

The rest of the infiltration team stormed in, returning fire as they slid up to a low wall. The room inside was impractically huge, spanning the entire area underneath the carrier's thousand-yard-wide dome. The large hemisphere above gave a clear view of the stars, meeting the edge of the circular room where the bulkhead door sat. The majority of the room was recessed into the ground, giving it almost the feeling of a massive office bullpen. Mazes of walkways ran down into the pit, with uncovered rooms and corridors spanning the circular deck. Halfway in, a second level began, creating a ceiling for the rooms underneath. In the very center, elevated to what would be a third or fourth floor, was a small platform surrounded by consoles. A long ramp led up to the platform, encased completely by a tunnel.

The cockpit.

Lockheart and Nabokov dragged the wounded Alejandra towards their low cover. The holes in her suit weren't near any vital organs, but emitted the unmistakable hissing of air. Lockheart covered them with bandages, silencing the hissing without other treatment.

"The atmosphere is pushing its way into her suit," she said, rolling Alejandra over to patch the exit wounds. Fowler knew that was a concern. The cephrast atmosphere wasn't inherently toxic, though it came in lethal proportions for humans that would asphyxiate them. More dangerous were the unknown bacteria and viruses in the air.

"The ramp up is this way," Raynor said, edging towards the direction of the long tunnel leading up to the platform. Fowler fired over the wall, trying to get an estimate of how many aliens were pinning them down. Dozens of armed cephrasts fired down from the elevated section of the maze. Who knew how many were in the bullpen below?

They were finally out of the confining corridors, though. The bridge was wide open with plenty of room to throw. Fowler plucked a graviton grenade from his vest and attached a fin jet to the bottom—attachments used to send explosives farther without carrying a launcher. He always thought of them as Vortex tails, but nobody in his training group knew what those were aside from him and Conway.

Priming the grenade, Fowler tossed it over the wall, his arm straight, letting the fin jet carry it in a large arc to the elevated cubicle-rooms.

A low, thundering buzz erupted, like feedback from an electric bass. Cephrasts careened off the platform into the roofless rooms below, accompanied by dark purple mist. Whatever pressure their species had evolved to withstand…the grenade produced more. Functionally, it was the same mechanism that killed Theodore Plum in Arvonia, and unless the cephrasts could survive being hit by a dump truck going seventy, they were dead.

"Keep 'em away from the cockpit," he cautioned. Fizzling sparklers ignited from the fin jets, followed by more shaky booms, crashing computers, and hopefully, alien bodies.

Using the pause in their suppression, the team trekked around the edge of the room, running hunched below the short walls.

Alejandra's wheezes became louder. "I'm slowing you down…"

"We can handle it," Lockheart replied.

"I really don't feel good."

"Yeah. You were shot," the combat surgeon grunted, pulling the wounded woman along with Nabokov. A pair of cephrasts entered the bridge from the bulkhead behind them, rounding the low walls towards them before being taken down immediately by the strike team.

"I've been shot before…" she coughed. "This…smells diff…" White foam soon began oozing from the specialist's nose and mouth. Swearing under her breath, Lockheart stopped pulling the dead woman along, pilfering her grenades before leaving the body in the walkway.

Once they found an inward turn from the edge of the room, the team moved into the maze of hallways. Individual cephrasts popped up sporadically as they made their way through the bullpen labyrinth towards the cockpit ramp. The short walls slowly rose to meet the second floor, allowing the strike team to stand upright without exposing their heads. Picking up their pace, they ran through the twisting aisles towards the center. Eventually, Fowler hit an intersection featuring a long, narrow ramp extending three floors up. The tunnel was dark, but otherwise empty up to the door at the top.

"Hold here," he said, prompting the team to begin entrenching at the bottom of the incline.

An access panel was illuminated by the door at the top, but Rovasatti wouldn't be able to remove that any time soon, his arm being held in place by the vacuum-seal band. Fowler quickly ran through their other options. Alejandra had been carrying a cutting torch. The government assassin, Lekkett, had a bionic forearm and hand. It didn't have much leverage, but she could rip her gloves without the danger of—

A small, green dot appeared for a brief moment on Tian's neck, burning a hole straight through it. No more than ten feet away, a cephrast peeled itself from the wall. A lid of some kind covered its eye, allowing the creature's entire body to match the dark steel of the wall behind it.

Super chameleons.

MacTeal unloaded several rounds into the alien's head, painting the wall in purple, but the damage was already done—their electrical engineer was dead.

"Shit, shit, SHIT!" Fowler screamed. They'd never make it back to Alejandra's body, get the cutting torch, and return. Not without fighting through every goddamn alien on this ship.

Whatever they did, it had to be here.

33

THE GETAWAY

Lockheart and MacTeal dropped mobile shield batteries in the two hallways protruding from the bottom of the ramp. Thin, honey-colored screens popped up, providing enough cover for two or three people to shoot from.

Sounds of combat picked up as more of their slinky enemies appeared from around a sharp bend down one of the hallways. Fowler stared at the dead cephrast behind the barricade. Something in the back of his mind told him it was important, but he couldn't figure out why.

"Sergeant, we can blow the door open," said Nabokov.

"We might damage the flight console," Fowler replied, his gaze remaining on the alien corpse.

"I won't."

"He won't," the American pilot said, reloading his sidearm. "As much as I hate to say that."

Eons ago, Fowler had walked through a mantrap in a cephrast ship. This carrier was on lockdown for humans, but the inhabitants had no problem getting around…

He dragged the alien corpse to the ramp, grabbing one of its arms. With his foot on the body, he shot the shoulder, severing the arm in a dark purple splash.

"Give us thirty seconds," Fowler said. With the bloody tentacle-arm in hand, he motioned Nabokov to follow him. At the top of the ramp, he searched around the door for a discolored section of wall —like the hand-activated panel in the crashed ship. Again, there were no seams. He pried open the thick fingers of the severed appendage and placed it against the access panel.

Nothing.

"Well, shit," he grumbled. "Be careful. We need everything in there to work." The demolitionist already had small packs of explosives in hand when Fowler made his way back down the ramp, tossing the bloody cephrast arm to the side. Bodies littered the halls leading towards the cockpit ramp, piling up where they first came into view of the barricades.

Then he heard it. An inverted *zap* followed by a wet *pop*.

The medivac pilot, Waverly, fell backwards in terror at the sight of Rovasatti's helmet shattering around a jet of thick, red paste. The Titanic Berserker's suit deflated around his mushed body, his arm falling beside the puddle with a *clank*. Fowler pulled Waverly back towards the ramp, the pilot's eyes locked on the liquid remains.

"Blasting!" Nabokov was nearly at the bottom of the ramp when the charges went off, vibrating the metal beneath their feet. Without wasting a second, Fowler charged up the ramp with Lockheart in step beside him, the rest backing into the tunnel as they fired down the converging hallways.

A solid beam of energy punched straight through the adjacent barricade, taking Nabokov's arm off entirely as the explosives expert fell to the ground, his screams deafening in their ears. MacTeal grabbed the nape of his suit, dragging him up the ramp. A thick trail of blood followed behind them, and after a few feet, MacTeal fell backwards, pulling hard against a mostly-empty suit when the next *zap* liquified the Russian demolitionist.

Fowler and Lockheart ran headfirst through the clearing smoke. The helm looked empty at first glance, though Fowler double-checked for camouflaged aliens to be safe. The platform was a fifteen-foot hexagon. Interfaces and consoles lined the outside, creating four-foot walls around the edge. Beyond the displays sat nothing but stars. The platform cleared the bottom of the hemispheric viewport, suspending the pilot in space. He could see the arms of the starfish extending away from the hub, even the top of the immense battle happening outside. In the center of the cockpit was a single workstation formed into a circle. There were buttons and readouts all around, presumably for a lone alien to pilot while others handled less-critical machines on the exterior.

"You're clear," Fowler called back to Raynor, who was closely followed by Waverly and Phillips. Three flat *thuds* trembled the floor as each pilot dropped a heavy disc tethered to their waist, the lines pulling themselves taut. None of them had an estimate for how long it might take to get the ship moving—if they could get it moving at all. Fowler was just waiting for one of them to say, *"We need Tian."*

Before they could get their bearings, energy blasts began popping up the ramp. The two operatives closest to the incline fired down it blindly, trying to keep the cephrasts out of the tunnel. Fowler checked their visibility over the consoles into the rooms below. The exposed siding might actually work in their favor...like a crow's nest. Depending on how fast the ship moved, they could be holed up here for over an hour.

"Are you—" Fowler began to ask the status of the flight controls, but was cut off as the ship lurched, throwing him off his feet.

"Whoops," Raynor said. "Hang on."

With their backs pressed firmly together, Raynor and Phillips could just barely fit in the cramped control area. After dropping the tether-anchors, Raynor took a moment to look over the flight controls. The structural similarity to the old ship was comforting. She didn't notice the symbols that indicated they might get stranded in an alternate dimension, nor the booster that could snap their necks. Without Alejandra or Tian, there wasn't a safe way to access the navigation systems, anyway.

Fortunately, there was a stunning, unobstructed view of the universe around them.

"Don't touch any buttons," she told the other pilots. If she'd thought ahead properly, Waverly would have been in the cockpit for this exact situation. Phillips was somewhat competent with a weapon.

She tilted the stick towards the battle to her left, which should propel the starfish away—if the controls were even on.

They were.

"Whoops," she said inadvertently. "Hang on."

"Warn us *before*." Fowler scrambled to his feet. "Uh—Comman-der."

"*Hang on,*" she repeated.

The four remaining soldiers of Strike Team Dissent scrambled to attach themselves to the nearest sturdy-looking object as the starfish took off. The carrier was significantly faster than an equivalent CAF vessel, though still nowhere near as quick as the drones it harbored. Sporadic bursts of rifle fire picked up from the belayed soldiers, supplemented by hollow *bonks* from the surrounding drones as they were hit by the lurching starfish.

Their only goal was to keep moving along their heading, which Raynor had to crank her neck to see. She tried to coordinate a rotation with Phillips but only managed to tilt the vessel to the side, dropping the floor down half a meter. The carrier's artificial gravity compensated for the change in pitch, increasing or decreasing to prevent those at the edge of the hub from being splattered by the ceiling or floor. Raynor had to balance herself against the discordant changes—a couple of the strike members fell to the ground.

"Undo that!" she said. The ship was now angled down from its intended bearing, sending them on a route to nowhere. Phillips quickly corrected whatever he did, buckling their legs under the added pressure.

Back on their desired course, the firefight on the ramp began to slow. Could they have completely fended off their attackers? Raynor was woefully aware of the possibility that one of the cephrasts was sabotaging the ship, but then again, the alien crew didn't seem to think anyone could break in and steal it, so the contingency might not exist.

The starfish jolted, a deep rumble vibrating through the hull. The armada ship was again tilted to the side, this time thrown into a slow spin, as well.

"What did we just hit?" asked Waverly, steadying himself against one of the wall terminals.

"I don't know…" Raynor said. A display to her right showed top-down outlines of each half of the carrier. All but one of the arms was illuminated in an icy blue. Six arms extended into space outside the viewport; one of the bottom ones must have broken.

"Shit, I think they're shooting at us." Waverly's head sat on a swivel as he tracked the closest battleship. The seed-shaped vessel came back into Raynor's eyeline as they spun. A wide beam from the vessel's railgun flashed between them.

Another crash, another boom, another arm darkened on the display. The carrier spun faster, showing fragmented scenes of the battle outside as the fighters exited and re-entered her view.

There was some way to stop the spin, but they didn't have time to experiment. If Raynor were to take her hand off the flight controls entirely, their current trajectory should take them close to the second outpost, but every second they weren't pushing the ship, their pursuers were gaining. Rotating the engine's direction as the ship spun, she tried to keep the propulsion firing away from their current direction.

Orange lights swarmed into the stars, pouring out of one of the arms. The unmanned ships pummeled the carrier's viewport, filling the cavernous bridge with soft impact sounds. It didn't seem likely that there was an automated protocol directing the tiny fighters to cannibalize their own home. Someone inside the starfish had scrambled them.

Fowler swore as Lekkett collapsed to the ground. A long strip of suit-tape ran between the armor plates on her bicep; strings of white foam crawled down her face.

As the rotating starscape spun across their destination, Raynor could just make out the first outpost in the distance, slightly obscured by a dense fog of CAF drones. A minute later, the starfish was pushing through the mechanical cloud, the small cluster of alien ships being dispatched quickly by the overwhelming CAF fleet.

With a sphere of protectors surrounding them, Raynor moved the starfish past the first outpost, which proceeded to send an entire battle's worth of ordnance out behind them.

We're clear…

Raynor took a deep breath—the hard part was over.

Behind the safety of the first outpost, she and Phillips took a minute to figure out how to stop the starfish from spinning before resuming their push to their destination.

"There's still probably a lot of them in the lower decks," Fowler said. "How much farther?"

"More than halfway to go," said Raynor. She felt like she'd been flying evasively for hours, but it had only taken ten minutes to pass the outpost. They were making good time, but the second station was a lot farther than the first.

The starfish curved slightly upward as it moved—the two arms must have been blown completely off by the battleship. The two pilots were able to maintain their direction without too much difficulty. There was no disarray outside, no firefight inside. They cruised along for another fifteen minutes before she began braking.

The calm didn't last. As soon as she spotted the large, metallic cube in the far distance, more cephrasts appeared at the edge of the maze below. Raynor couldn't see them from the middle of the flight platform, but it sounded like there were a lot of them.

As the fighting resumed, the Dissenters found themselves running out of ammunition. MacTeal pulled a spare cell from Lekkett's nearby body. Lockheart took the pilots' sidearms. Heavily-armored cephrasts started piling into the ramp, surrounded by some sort of energy shielding, which would undoubtedly eat through ammo they couldn't afford to spare.

"Get the ramp in front of us," Raynor said over her shoulder to Phillips. Spinning the ship was almost effortless for them this time around, sending the untethered operatives stumbling into the consoles. "Hold on to something!"

Raynor slammed the stick towards the ramp. A glowing, red flame licked out from the engine in front of the ship's path, rapidly slowing the carrier. It only lasted for a second, the force throwing Raynor to the side and pulling her hand away from the controls. Her tether pulled tightly, knocking the wind out of her and forming a galaxy of imaginary stars amidst the real ones. The three Dissenters were chucked violently against the wall beside the entry ramp, their armor clattering from the impact like a rover crash. The g-forces weren't too dissimilar—easily over twenty. The cephrasts in the ramp were gone.

"I think I pressed something..." Fowler groaned, doubled over. As soon as they recovered, the Callistian duo tossed a pair of graviton grenades down the ramp, followed by low, staticky explosions.

At last, the outpost loomed over the bridge through the expansive viewport. Raynor crept the starfish as close as she could manage. Without access to an idle switch, the three pilots had to manually maintain the ship's position to prevent crashing into the towering metal structure above them. The more they moved, the longer their rescue would be.

Whether the remnants of Strike Team Dissent could keep them alive was another story. They were down to pistols, which didn't have much ammo to begin with.

Pzwwip.

"There it is!" Fowler cheered. He was fiddling with the device he'd picked up earlier. The next *zap* was followed by a *pop* from down the ramp as the invisible ray splattered a cephrast. It made short work of their armored foes, seeming to ignore protection with ease.

The alien weapon only managed to liquify a few before it ran out, joined by the empty clicks of their sidearms a few seconds later.

It did the trick. In the absence of gunfire, Raynor could hear shouts coming from across the maze—*human shouts.*

The sight of three dozen CAF uniforms moving through the low corridors was as close to divine as Raynor could imagine. Making their way to the bottom of the ramp, the reinforcements mowed through the cephrasts below. Empty croaks rumbled through the humid air, and within twenty or thirty seconds, the barrage was over.

"Commander Raynor?" someone yelled from down the ramp.

"Yes. We're all up here," she called back.

"Hold your fire, we're coming up."

Boots stormed across the bottom of the ramp as a couple of soldiers ascended the tunnel to the cockpit. It suddenly occurred to Raynor that they were probably expecting to interact with her in some way as the ranking officer. What did commanders say in this sort of situation?

"Careful," is what she went with. "They blend in with the walls—and the air is toxic."

"We saw," the man in front mulled. Exiting the dark ramp, his visor showed the face of a ghost.

"Rhyso?"

"Commander," he smiled.

"I thought…weren't you on Vensa?"

"We never made it. We were two days out when it was cut off, so we were reassigned for this." He motioned to the carrier around them. Single shots from energy rifles could be heard as the CAF operatives ensured the cephrast bodies were dead.

Raynor explained her concerns about the lower half of the ship as the pilots were escorted back to the entry point Rhyso's team had made. A seal had been placed around part of the central hub and cut open. Droplets of metal fused to the floor around the melted doorway. A shuttle was docked with the pressure room outside.

"I'll feel better once we know this thing isn't about to explode," she said. "Move fast."

"Yes, ma'am," he said.

"Is that insubordination?"

"No, ma'am. It's just bad form, ma'am."

The pilots crawled through the molded doorway into the small craft while the three Dissenters waited in front of the pressure room.

"Commander, we thought we might stay behind to help clear the lower decks," Fowler said. He gathered up the pistols they'd borrowed and handed them back to Raynor through the pressure seal.

"Thanks," was all she said, taking the empty sidearms. He waited outside, staring at her for an uncomfortable amount of time. Finally, she realized he was asking for permission. "*Oh!* Yes, that's fine."

It all felt weird. Alone in the shuttle with time to breathe, the events of the mission finally sank in for the three pilots.

"Did we really just do that?" asked Waverly.

"Boost an alien ship?" Phillips said, nearly jumping out of his suit. "*Yeah we fucking did!*"

"Holy shit!"

"We're fucking *legends!*"

"We're free-drinks-for-life legends!"

Now outside the carrier, it was likely their chatter could be heard by any number of people, but Raynor didn't mind. She was elated. Every minute that passed without the starfish collapsing on itself and killing them all was a minute closer to a complete mission success. It was their Giza Station—the beginning of the end.

An hour later, Fowler joined them at the outpost, making it official—they'd captured the vessel. The starfish either didn't have an easy method of self-destruction, or the cephrasts didn't think to do it. Regardless, it was an excellent sign. Their enemies weren't in a mindset for war. This was all supposed to be routine for them. They'd underestimated humanity, and even if they never made the same mistake again, it was too late. The CAF had the ship and everything on it—the weapons, the engine, whatever the "third waveform" was…

And a live prisoner.

34

EVACUATION

Through the chilly halls of the fueling station on Kallipar, the captured cephrast walked at gunpoint. Two pairs of arms were folded around opposite sides of its body—as you would handcuff a human's behind their back. It didn't look at Walker as it passed by. It already saw everything.

A living, breathing cephrast. Images of the Georgia massacre flashed in Walker's eyes as the creature's boneless legs whipped slowly in front of it. This situation was different in almost every way, but it still felt similar for her. She expected the alien to lunge at any moment and disintegrate someone.

The prisoner—the *subject*—was moved into a clear plastic box in the examination room set up over the gravity panels. It remained in its environmental suit, flashing a dull, turquoise zig-zag across its face as the door was shut and locked.

"I want two guards on this *thing* at all times," Admiral Dreinn seethed. "It doesn't die until we say it can."

The leader of the second strike team landed on Kallipar with a few soldiers to rotate watch on the prisoner. They dumped a pile of cephrast spacesuits beside the holding cell.

"Yes, Admiral. We have nine tanks—I'll inform you when we know how long each lasts."

Quinto's biologists began discussing the areas they felt were most important to examine. "The basics," as they called them, which turned out to be primarily the testing of physical limits: how much pressure their skin and eyes withstood before puncturing, how to break their boneless limbs, how they recovered from such injuries…the tiny ice planet began to spin around Walker. As much as she had tried to prepare herself for the task at hand, it was clear she couldn't have any part in it. She'd examined all sorts of animals during her career—hell, she was the first person to examine *this* species—but all of those creatures had been dead before she examined them. Living specimens were observed in their natural habitats, from afar. In fact, they took every precaution possible *not* to interfere with them. Under absolutely no circumstances did they torture an animal to see what would hurt it.

After providing a single objection, it was apparent she was alone in her feelings on torture.

"This is war," Quinto said, "and we're facing extermination. Anything we can learn about killing these things is essential to curbing that fate. Rest assured, if they get the same opportunity, they'll do it to us."

"Will they?" Walker asked. "They don't have a mentality for war."

"They will now," the director said coldly.

Walker ignored her urge to persist, to say they were no better if they did the same—she didn't believe that was true. Nothing about humanity suggested that "humane" treatment was anything less than sociopathic torture.

It was their nature.

The brief empathy towards their invaders—and worse yet, the feeling their attempt at extermination was somewhat justified— clashed with Walker's objective understanding of the strategic necessity. She couldn't be anywhere near the prisoner, so she fell back on the trauma from Georgia to excuse herself. It was only a partial truth, but she was never going to be of use on this base.

Instead, she left with the starfish, which departed the next day for Razennon alongside the long-range shuttle Raynor had taken to Kallipar. Helping to unravel the functions and purposes of the alien vessel's countless features was far more akin to the passive observation of animal behavior—like studying an abandoned lion den. It sure didn't make her nauseous.

Raynor's trinity of pilots cycled themselves through a makeshift dock in the starfish to eat, sleep, and replace oxygen as they maneuvered the ship towards the large, yellow planet. The long-range transport wasn't designed to have passengers leave during flight. The sheer brilliance, creativity, and adaptability required to get the starfish to Razennon...

It was the version of humanity Walker needed to see.

Once the spiky craft was in orbit around the large planet, the CAF took a full week to make it safe. After they felt confident in their sample collection, holes were cut across the hull to vacate the ship's atmosphere. For several days, it sat that way as each room was systematically sterilized and sealed off from the remainder. Between the cocktail of chemicals and prolonged exposure to space, the bacteria inside were eradicated.

Massive orbital tankers pumped breathable air into the ship after the holes were patched up. Walker couldn't imagine how nerve-wracking it must have been for the guinea pig who first removed their helmet inside, but she hoped they were compensated for the risk.

At the end of the week, Quinto returned with Rhyso, her scientists having successfully tortured their prisoner to death.

She referred to the excursion as "insightful."

The ensuing work on the starfish was reminiscent of the early days at Zenaut. Teams of engineers ran experiments on the engines to figure out how it skipped along its path. The three surviving members of Strike Team Dissent stayed with the craft while filling their ranks back up. It was all comfortably familiar—far from the ongoing battles. Walker even got a couple of chances to catch up with Brody Kahlil on the ship. The once-bored physicists were now working nonstop to figure out what was inside the engine.

"It's still a complete mystery," he said. As always, making it sound as if uncertainty was the best answer. "Our working theory is currently that it's a wavelength stretching spacetime along an axis intersecting with our plane of existence."

"So, it's the one from the logs in Arvonia?"

"Almost certainly. It explains why the Pentagon researchers never saw anything inside the death ray. It's a genuine, new force of the universe."

Kahlil's excitement was understandable. He urged Walker to call the particle a "dimenton" since the particles appeared to move along parallel planes of reality—dimensions. It made Walker think of *dementia* more than *dimension,* but she got to create the entire field of xenobiology; Brody could decide the name of a particle as heard by the handful of people who spoke 21st-25th century English. It didn't really matter what they called it. Nezz would be translating it for everyone, anyway.

Raynor had to train a small group of drone modulators to keep the starfish steady in orbit. Presumably, there was a setting somewhere to maintain that path, but since no one could read the displays, the ship needed constant monitoring. The cephrast language had changed drastically from the logs Kelly decoded in the '20s—if it was even the same root language—so most of it was guesswork.

The greatest minds in history were making rapid progress exploring the nature of the dimenton. The prototype weapon that Zenaut staff had called the death ray was likely a simple, early usage of the universal force, vibrating its target along that axis for an instant. Most inorganic materials did so without significant damage, like fabric, but the "friction" liquified organic matter, shattered glass, and set wood aflame.

Ten thousand years ago, Walker had been furious at the Department of Defense's urgency in reverse-engineering the death ray.

How times change…

Despite the incredible speed of the research, it wasn't fast enough. Three of Walker's former crewmates from *Salvation* had already died in the invasion, and by the time the CAF felt comfortable testing the dimensional drive on the starfish, the cephrasts had moved halfway through Centauri. Engineers identified a lever connected to the secondary fuel tank, but the mechanism itself wasn't known. It could be adding particles to the engine; it could be filtering the thrusters through waves created by it. With the armada quickly approaching Quexi, they couldn't hold out for certainty.

When the time came to flip the switch, a hundred people gathered on the orbital platform *Salvation* had first landed on, staring out at the commandeered starfish. Raynor was hesitant to leave the starfish in orbit without someone monitoring it, but ultimately gave up her command to a rat in a cage.

Walker was fascinated by it. *Rattus Centaurus*—a descendant of the common Norwegian rat—was enormous, like a proper New York rat. Thicker legs, rounder ears, light gold fur…

A small board with an analog lever was connected to its counterpart on the bridge using makeshift robotics. From the platform, a technician slowly pushed the switch a couple of degrees. Small specs of light pierced through the starfish as it began to fade—the stars behind peeking through the previously solid exterior, which began to bend slightly in odd angles. A strange wind rushed by the onlookers towards the ship. It wasn't air on the platform, nor was it a gravitational force pulling at them. It was something in between— a wind of gravity that blew past them for a moment before snapping back. The way a knife pushes through a sheet, moving the fabric down briefly before puncturing through, snapping the cloth back to where it was.

The receiver inside immediately pushed the lever back to its original position, returning the ship to the solid form they were accustomed to. A similar gravitational wind blew in the opposite direction—the knife being removed from the same sheet, dragging the fabric with it for a moment.

Hopefully, they weren't actually puncturing the universe…

Gasps, cheers, prayers…the onlookers had a full range of responses to the historic display. Admiral Dreinn was reticent.

"Let's see how our cargo looks."

Walker joined a handful of people in a shuttle back to the starfish. After hiking up the long, exhausting ramp to the cockpit, they found the bars of the wire cage and the floor around it coated in red paste. Numerous panels around the bridge had shattered, covering areas of the floor with glass and plastic.

It was a glaring issue—one without an obvious fix. They might have to put up some kind of shield before phasing the ship. Maybe it required a mix of graviton thrust. Maybe it was just practice.

Whatever the reason, a good deal of research would be needed just to use *this* engine, let alone duplicate it.

Evacuations began shortly after the failed experiment. Mountainous transports—colony ships, really—launched for Earth filled with hundreds of millions of people. Even more remained in the system, ready to defend their homes or die trying. If the respective planetary ground forces were lucky, they could push the cephrast threat back. If not, they could disrupt the alien pursuit for as long as possible.

Raynor was all but useless in their defense. She was married to this ship now. A few others had been trained to hold it in orbit around Razennon, but only her team of three was trusted to pilot the thing.

Tireless work was being done to get the ship phasing safely. If that didn't happen before the cephrasts hit Razennon, the starfish would be traveling to Sol by traditional means, praying their alien stalkers didn't catch up. It was a grim possibility, and with every passing day, it looked like the one they'd find themselves in. CAF scientists tried everything to make the ship work, going as far as to repair every panel even remotely connected to the twin propulsion systems. Raynor felt bad for the rats. Someone eventually suggested they use a glass instead, and if it remained intact, they could upgrade to an animal.

Between each test, efforts were made to modify the carrier for human occupants during the trip, which would be over three years of onboard time. Hangar bays along the carrier's intact arms were converted into living quarters, and the majority of the lower hub was stocked with supplies and renewable food sources. Most of the work fell into building proper life support systems for each half of the starfish: air circulation, heating, and water recycling. The only connection between the upper and lower decks was believed to be a quantum molecular repeater—one without panels. There was some mystery surrounding how it remained "entangled" after each use, but since the alternative was going outside and lunging across the three-hundred-meter gap, the repeater was being left alone.

Outposts fell one after another, and the cephrasts continued gaining momentum, blasting their way through the Centauri System. It wasn't long before the CAF was pushed back to the planetary coreworlds—Razennon and Quexi. The two celestial bodies had a wall of batteries outside of their orbits, not to mention their own defenses, but once the cephrasts broke through those outposts, all they'd have to do is wait for the planets to circle back.

Before long, the only people in the system who weren't staying were leaving on the starfish. A couple of strike teams were assigned to the carrier, in part to defend the ship if it was boarded, though nobody realistically expected to survive that scenario, but also to train the Solar Defense Corps in their firsthand experiences. Raynor almost declined to make the selection. Handpicking which teams would survive the next few years was a sickening burden. In the end, she took the teams most familiar with the starfish, whose experiences were the most valuable to Sol.

With a little more effort, she pulled Shino into their evacuation. The CAF's fleets had evaporated, creating a surplus of drone modulators. While Shino would undoubtedly make the best use of what was left, the same could be said for the fleets in Sol.

That was all contingent on the starfish making it to the Solar System in the first place. No one was able to troubleshoot the dimensional thrust issues, and with the cephrasts at the last line of defensive batteries, it was looking like they'd have to start traveling the old-fashioned way.

Then, a promising development surfaced from a man who'd never set foot on the carrier. Quinto took an urgent remote conference with the head of Starling's metallurgy, Beorte Vakkard. Raynor could see his inverted face from the other side of the jewel as he spoke with the science director; two of her underlings scrambled to join her on the second floor of the bridge.

"Okay, they're here," said Quinto. "What did you find?"

"The alloys are unique, no surprise there, but the strangest part is the infusion of some sort of antimatter. There was no reasonable explanation for its use, which would significantly complicate the processes. Denise Walker had one of her associates look at it, and they think it might be an altered form of the particle used in your engine, rather than antimatter."

"You're suggesting the hull material protects the interior from these effects?"

"Yes. It's why the thruster is outside of the hull, between its halves. You could think of the alloy as resonant to the phasing. We'd normally conduct a small-scale experiment to verify…"

"But we don't have a small-scale engine." Quinto thought to herself for a moment. "How long will it take to duplicate the alloy?"

"Months, at least," Vakkard's voice scrambled slightly. "—ne of your boys cut through it, so it melts. We can get more than enough from the damaged arms in the bottom half to repair the holes we patched with standard materials. Melting it might negate its use, but we won't know until we try."

Astronautical mechanics spent two days cutting off chunks of the damaged arms and welding them over the metal patches. Once the ship was repaired with its original hull, an exciting problem arose—no signals were penetrating the ship's exterior. The remote device used to phase the ship from outside had to be replaced with one that worked on a ten-minute timer, independently of a technician.

Over the weeks, countless tests had been done, and they were all a hassle. Everyone had to stop working and leave the ship while it was phased and checked for damage. It took an hour in total. Most people stayed in their respective shuttles while they waited. Now there was hope again, and the nearby landing pad was as full as it had been the first time. When the now-familiar whoosh of gravitational wind pushed back past them, the air remained still.

It was…uneventful.

When they went inside, they found a perfectly intact glass sitting in the center of the cockpit. A brief celebration ensued, but it was reserved. Before the solution was declared a success, they had to bring the rat cage back out.

Another timer, another trip to the landing pad, and another whoosh. This time, the rat had become the first dimensional traveler from the human empire.

There were still several hurdles to clear, but their chances of making it to Sol before the cephrasts had increased tenfold. Shino championed a large effort to spare the rat from future tests "for its bravery." They named it Colonel Marmalade—an honorary rank. Raynor didn't have to give the rodent her ship.

After a few trials with *different* rats, someone finally had the forethought to place cameras inside the cockpit during its trip out of reality, angled up through the viewport encompassing the bridge. As the vessel phased out of existence, the stars beyond warped unevenly, as the hull did from the outside, each eventually disappearing from the viewport into complete blackness. Raynor could already see how one might locate pockets of condensed space during the transition—it's probably why the hemisphere of display panels existed at all.

Proper testing would take years that they didn't have. The last outposts before the planetary defenses were almost gone, giving the cephrasts an unobscured path to Razennon. As soon as the rats were cleared of health defects from prolonged exposure in the parallel plane, the starfish's inhabitants loaded the carrier up with supplies. Anyone who wasn't staying to fight boarded, and the vessel left for Sol. Raynor took the ship out of Centauri with normal propulsion, waiting until they were clear of astral bodies before experimenting with the dimensional drive.

They were safe for now, but it felt horrible anyway. The fates of those left behind wouldn't be known to them for years. Raynor knew better than anyone what a well-organized resistance could accomplish, though, and the Centauri coreworlds were in the most capable hands ever born.

The resistance soldiers were a ragtag group, to say the least. Most had been civilians when Minsko Lyrs arrived at Starling a year before. Some still wore their old black and grey uniforms for pride or nostalgia—a way to say, *"I fought at the beginning."* They held little meaning, otherwise. The CAF was no more, as were the Rigilian Counter-Bombardment Corps, the Quexi Planetary Army, the Loronan Guard, system police…if you had calcium bones and no more than two arms, you were part of the human resistance.

A few colony ships trickled out after the stolen cephrast carrier left. Centauri's early defense had looked doomed, but as their numbers dwindled, so did their losses. When all was said and done, their alien invaders wanted resources, so they wouldn't simply destroy the planets.

Lyrs was proud of their progress…of his species. People who wouldn't have been given the light of day as soldiers had become the most fearful rebels among them. On the other side of the bunker, a demo operation was being prepared by a woman who used to write for a local news organization. The cephrasts were also few in numbers and lacked comprehensive ground forces, which provided ample opportunities for the troops on Quexi and Razennon to cause significant damage.

After six months of fighting on the coreworlds, cracks in their armor were beginning to form. Countless humans had been captured, and reports were trickling in about the ramifications of those abductions. Unknown chemical gasses had eliminated several groups on the other side of the planet. Gas masks weren't working —the agent entered through the eyes or ears...perhaps even the skin.

Lyrs double-checked the list of armaments being moved outside the bunker in preparation for the demolition. Front-on assaults had stopped months ago. They didn't have the numbers anymore. Most of their missions revolved around sabotaging equipment. The massive laser drills took quite a bit of energy to repair and set up. Detonating the high-powered equipment amplified the destruction, which the rebels loved to see.

It also pissed the aliens off *a lot*.

"Orbital!" someone shouted from outside. A quiet, magnetic hum ramped up into a deafening roar as a dense turquoise pillar crashed into the ground. Two pop-shields opened up to absorb the impact. Two didn't. Yellow dust from the Razennon desert billowed into the door of the base, covering the fallen bodies of those knocked back.

"Conway!" Lyrs called through the bunker, racing outside. "Medic!"

"He's over here..." someone replied softly near one of the unopened pop-shields. Three dismembered bodies scattered the impact site.

"Marker—Lyrs. We need drone support above our location."

"Engaged," the AI said. It never elaborated.

Not many drone modulators remained in the system, and the vespiaries had all been destroyed for months. Marker was managing most of the unmanned crafts, struggling to keep its patterns effective while evolving its routines to outpace the cephrast computers. It was doing its best, but their fleets were diminishing.

"We're taking hits from the sky!" Lyrs grunted as he dragged one of the injured rebels inside the bunker. "How long?"

The synthetic provided a buzzing dual-tone denoting half an hour.

Lyrs dropped the legless body inside. A high-pitched whistle reverberated through the desert, followed by a large, metal pod slamming into the ground near the bunker, wedging a meter deep in the sand. Three more landed in quick succession, all of which began pulsing thin, lavender smoke out of vents on the side.

"Everyone in!" Lyrs screamed. He ran to the door to shut it, spotting cargo ships in the distance, lowering equipment into the desert. In the five or six seconds it took to get everyone inside and shut the door, too much gas had already entered the building. Those who could still run made their way towards the rear exit, but it was only to give themselves a few more seconds of hope. The entire desert was coated with the unknown vapor, and they'd already been exposed enough.

35

HOMEWORLD BOUND

During the early months of their trip to Sol, Nezz received periodic updates from itself regarding the Centauri resistance…it didn't sound good. Now, they were cut off entirely. Nothing else would be known until after they reached the Solar System. The synthetic expressed frustration on more than one occasion at the deafness it experienced to its own voice.

Raynor stood at the helm, idly chatting with the AI as she stared out into the solid-black expanse in front of them. There wasn't much to do until the time came to scout a new path. Once the ship phased too far "in," she couldn't see the stars of the universe anymore. Navigating through nothingness required her to phase partway back, locate a quicker path, and follow it blindly for a while.

Spotting pockets of space that appeared to compress wasn't easy. Gauging the distance she'd traveled once the stars were gone…that was frustratingly difficult.

"When I'm cut off from myself," the synthetic explained, "I get updated as soon as I return to signal range. I actually created a method to receive basic information from myself using the viewport above us, but it was restrained by the acuity of the sensors. When we're outside of physical space, I can't receive updates from my other hardware regardless."

"So, there are basically two versions of you right now?" Raynor asked.

"You could say that. The version of me you're speaking to is like a severed limb, but still an entire version of me."

"If you start to think you're the evil version, please let me know."

Raynor pulled the ship out, back towards the stars. It looked like she overshot her target distance a bit, but that was based on how the stars warped while returning. It was a skill she was trying to master while they were out in the middle of empty space. Near civilization, it would be more dangerous, though she suspected it would be easier to navigate when there were more reference points. Out here, she only had distant, flickering lights. There also wasn't a way to reliably check her estimations. The shipboard consoles were unusable, and the equipment they'd brought was confined to the universe they sat in.

Their greatest adversary for the trip was time. The starfish was capable of incredible force, but their bodies could only handle a fraction of it. To help speed them up initially, Raynor had instituted periods of increased acceleration. After figuring out how to identify areas of condensed space, she'd managed to further increase their speed while phased in, riding shorter currents to fling them back into real space faster than they would've been otherwise.

It was a bit risky. She could theoretically reduce their overall speed, but it had ultimately paid off. Through her efforts, she managed to bring the carrier up to cruising speed in only five months of onboard travel—what would have been ten months in any other ship using the same intervals of added thrust. The starfish had already passed every transport that left before them.

Raynor, Phillips, and Waverly figured out most of the bizarre flight mechanics together. The benefits of navigating through the dimensional shifts were too great to ignore, and Raynor needed to know it was being done competently in her absence. It had given them an opportunity to standardize their terminology. The phenomenon had been referred to as a "dimensional void" enough times to stick, though the physicists now claimed that might be inaccurate. One traveled "in" to the void, and returned by coming "out" of it. There was absolutely no way to measure how far in they went, so the general rule was, if you could see light, you were halfway in, and if you saw nothing, you were all the way in. A full exit into real space was a "breach."

One of the trio was always at the helm, so the terms allowed them to discuss what, if anything, happened during their shifts. Flying solo turned out to be pretty easy when you weren't evading attacks. Sometimes they'd enlist the help of a couple of people Raynor had trained to the same degree as the drone modulators in Razennon, but it was rare for the pilots to need two sets of hands. For the most part, they were coasting.

It was actually kind of tranquil, aided further by the isolation of the void. The war was a lifetime ago, and in a different universe. They'd have to pick it up again in the near future, but for now, they could breathe.

Entertainment hadn't been a major concern when the starfish was being outfitted. A standard array of health equipment was added, but otherwise, the only activities were those brought with personal effects. One of Rhyso's soldiers brought some kind of Centauri sports ball. They didn't have an adequate facility for the game it came from, but some of them threw it around the edge of the bridge, lobbing it high underneath the viewport to someone farther along. As long as they kept it away from the cockpit, Raynor didn't mind.

Shino brought an archaic computer to play old, grainy games on. The twenty-something swore she could play them all day, every day, without getting bored. It sounded monotonous—the thing Raynor hated about the drone control module. Shino insisted the games were different, but would then proceed to list several versions of the same thing—Gamma Forge, Gamma Forge 2, Gamma Forge 2029…whenever Raynor saw one, it always looked the same.

The gamer also formed some weird relationship with Fowler that they both insisted wasn't one. Given their comparative survival chances, Raynor assumed that that had been his prerogative, but then Shino mentioned a boyfriend and was talking about someone else entirely.

"He died *thousands* of years ago," she explained.

"You don't sound too shook up about it."

"It was strictly business. You know how fans are…"

Raynor did not. Nothing about Shino's career ever made sense. According to her, companies would pay her to wear clothing with their logos on it and upload pictures of herself to a network. Like advertising, but on her personality. Others would give her top-end equipment for free so long as she told people they'd done so.

"I assume he got married and had kids and all that nonsense," Shino said. "So, it's not sad or anything." She suddenly cried out laughing. "What if he *didn't* die?! Oh my god, that'll be so cringe, right?"

Happiness had been in short supply since the start of the invasion, even less after the evacuation. So, if it worked, it worked.

As a true hypocrite, Raynor completely ignored that idea. She found herself spending a lot of time with Rhyso. The truth was, she liked him a lot; she just prevented it from going anywhere. After a few months, the thought crossed her mind that she might actually *love* him, and the potential consequences were frightening to her. It was unlikely they'd both live through the next few years.

One of them would have to address it eventually, so she did. She hadn't planned to, but it had been on her mind.

"I understand," he said. "I really do. I just…don't think that's how pain works. If something like that happens, it's going to hurt anyway."

That thought had occurred to her. She didn't know how true it really was…she'd never dated anyone who'd died. Losing him wasn't her only concern, though. It was allowing herself to get to a place where surviving the war together was a priority. She'd never be able to live with herself if that jeopardized her decision-making.

"Plus, your rank means nothing," he added. "The CAF is gone."

"So I'm *not* commanding this ship then?"

"Oh, you're far more important than anyone else here. I just mean there's no protocol to breach."

She looked at him, running through scenarios where her resolve might be compromised. They didn't feel realistic. If anything, Rhyso was *too* eager to fall on his sword. Neither of them would willingly doom their entire species. She was just being a coward, avoiding complications.

Diving into introspection, Raynor left an uncomfortable silence over them, which she only became aware of when Rhyso broke it.

"As I said, I understand. Even during the interim, the possibility of distractions when the war continues—"

Compulsively, she kissed him. It didn't seem to last long, but it felt like it lasted forever. Time was meaningless these days.

"Sorry..." she said. She wasn't. "I interrupted you. What were you saying?"

He blinked. "Was I talking...?"

For the rest of their trip across the expanse, Raynor and Rhyso spent the majority of their free time together. They ate together, worked out together, spent most of their nights together, and even visited each other while they worked.

She tried to make good on her promise to show him an endearingly bad film, but those hadn't been a high priority for people as they evacuated.

Raynor casually mentioned her failed expedition to Shino, who responded with a loud squeal. *Salvation* had contained all of Earth's cinematic history at the time of their launch, only the first hundred years or so, and Shino had converted the small files to modern storage types during her first month at the academy. No one seemed interested in the old, horrendous movies, but she'd brought them with her, anyway.

It was the sort of crusade Raynor was looking for, searching this goldmine for the best terrible movie of all time. The competition was fierce. They were the oldest, cheapest movies ever made. Some were probably considered good during their time, but most were just bad. The earliest ones were in black and white. Not for artistic reasons; the technology didn't exist. Neither she nor Rhyso could understand how that had been possible. To record light and not get…the light?

Even further back, there was no sound. No recorded sound, at least. Those were Raynor's favorites. They played goofy songs in the background, and dialogue was written in panels on the screen. Neither of them could read it, but it didn't detract from the experience. It was like everyone on Earth was so jazzed to be able to record something at all, they didn't give it much thought after that. It was just people acting silly.

By the end of their trip, she and Rhyso spent a lot of time without assistants in their ears. Raynor started learning Reza so they could be intimate without the creepy feeling of someone listening. He didn't seem to find it disturbing, having lived his entire life with synthetic services, but Raynor sure did. She'd dissuaded him from learning early Martian right off the bat. It was an unintentional hybrid of several overly-complicated languages—no one learned it unless they were born there. Reza was precisely structured and literal, making it pretty easy to pick up conversationally. It also outlined perfectly why she loved him. Countless times when teaching her a phrase or word, he'd clarify, "That's how most people say it. I usually don't."

She eventually pointed this out as a frequent occurrence. "Do other people from Razennon think you talk funny?"

"Yes."

"Really…?" She sat up in bed, intrigued. "In what way?"

"People in Centauri were usually direct and exact. Not comically so, but everyone tended to speak bluntly and get right to the point."

"I noticed that."

"The language reflects that quite a bit. I just find it boring. I think I use words more subjectively. I've been told I use more inflection, too."

"Aw," she cooed, patronizingly. "You're like a poet."

He shook his head, exhaling.

Even as they neared their destination, she and Rhyso were as close to inseparable as she'd ever been with someone. At no point did she become exhausted from it—a romance she'd craved her entire life and never realized it. Had she experienced a connection half as strong with someone on Mars, she might never have left the 32nd century to begin with.

It was exactly what she'd been afraid of.

There wasn't much for the strike teams to do during their voyage to the Solar System. Every once in a while, there would be a minor altercation between residents, and one of the soldiers would be called over to mediate. It was a rare occurrence, and they usually resolved themselves. Most of Fowler's time on duty involved helping people with odd jobs, taking him all over the vessel. Little happened on the starfish that was unbeknownst to him.

Near the end of the trip, one of the biochemists called him over as he was passing through the deck.

"Ah, Sergeant," the man said. His name might have been Dickinson, but Fowler couldn't remember. "You'll want to see this." People still referred to them by their CAF ranks, though it probably held as much clout as his U.S. Army rank. He walked over to the expensive-looking microscope being presented by the scientist whose name was probably Dickinson. Fowler gazed into the microscope, seeing a cell of some kind.

"Looks incredible, Doc." He lifted his head up. "What is it?"

"That, my friend, is an extremely dangerous bacterium found in the starfish's original atmosphere."

"Is that what killed Alejandra and Lekkett?" His blood pumped harder, as if the cell under the microscope might still kill them.

"Probably. There are a few toxic pathogens in the sample, but this one is by far the most aggressive. Once we get to Earth and have access to a real facility, there shouldn't be an issue manufacturing some kind of defense against it."

"Wow. That's excellent."

The scientist smiled contently at his own work. Good news was rare; most developments were concerning at best. Updates weren't too common for the carrier during its traversal through the dark space between systems, though. They didn't really *exist* for a large chunk of the trip, and that was as much as Fowler cared to know about the topic. Years ago, Brody had told him his entire body was being flattened while time stretched around him. Now, he was being sucked out of reality.

At a certain point, you just had to lean into it.

Fowler continued along towards the upper decks. He was asked to meet Walker and the commander up on the third level of the bridge, though he didn't know what for. He wound through the maze of low corridors, effortlessly reaching the long incline up to the flight deck. The ramp was cracked from graviton grenades—faint, purple stains smeared the intersection at the bottom. Up in the cockpit, the two women were discussing their deceleration.

"The same way I used pockets of compressing space to speed up, I should be able to brake faster using areas of increasing distance." Raynor pointed to a few warping stars that must have been significant to her.

"Doesn't more distance take longer?" asked Walker.

"Yes, but we're using all of that distance to brake. The tradeoff is that we spend more of the trip at cruising speed. It's faster overall, but if we can't find any suitable areas, we'll have to give up eventually and brake normally, only harder."

Walker beckoned Fowler into the cockpit. Her smile gave him pause. "How would you like to get some air?"

"You mean off-ship?"

"I do."

He looked out at the warping stars as Raynor pushed the vessel back into the void. "Uh…when would this be?"

Walker waved off his concern. "Not for an hour or so."

"More like two," the commander corrected.

"Unless something goes wrong, we'll be arriving before any transmissions about us or the evacuation. We're planning to continue phasing as we brake, so we might even arrive before imaging of our ship…"

"Which is a giant alien carrier."

"Exactly. We need to let Solar Defense Corps know we're human, and that the cephrasts might be right behind us. Unfortunately, nothing transmits through the hull—hence the spacewalk. We'll have to do this a few times while we brake, so I figured you'd want the opportunity to go first."

"How do I get outside without everyone being blended?"

"That'll only happen in the void," Raynor said. "After this current, I'll pull us out and you'll be clear to open an airlock for a few minutes."

When the starfish returned to real space, Fowler suited up and hooked himself to a handle inside the airlock. With the exterior hatch open, he crawled up around the top, letting the mass of the starfish hold his body against it as he turned on the transmitter.

For the rest of his life, he'd never be able to properly explain what he experienced. It was space, as it looked near the speed of light. He'd seen it through the large, digital half-circle over the bridge; he'd seen it through a physical window in *Salvation's* comms room. This was different—and incredible—and he didn't fully know why. Bright lines of starlight streaked towards him like the paint on an invisible freeway. There were no walls around him, no other people, no fog or debris or smudges on the viewport. The only sounds were his heartbeat and the faint vibrations of the ship he sat against.

Tugging on the tether to make sure it held, he pushed himself gently away from the starfish, flying through space at unfathomable speeds—just him and the universe as it slipped through time. After a few minutes, he pulled himself along the cord back to the airlock, doffing the spacesuit and drying his eyes before returning the transmitter.

Over the following month, they broadcasted the same signal a dozen times between phasing out and in. Other soldiers from the strike teams did the task subsequent times, but the ship was moving slower for them, its relative time closer to the surrounding universe. It wouldn't be the same.

Their last current took them to the edge of the Solar System, just beyond a dwarf planet called Haumea. Their messages had been well received by the Solar Defense Corps. Despite there being a large battalion of ships waiting for the starfish, the alien carrier wasn't blown out of the sky.

With extreme caution, the fleet escorted the strange vessel to a military base on the Neptunian moon of Triton. Considering the situation, the SDC handled it well. Sol had only just received word of the unseen ambush in Centauri when this alien ship appeared suddenly on their doorstep, transmitting a pre-recorded message about having humans on board while ignoring all other communications. After escorting the partially-vanishing craft to Neptune, the inhabitants—many of whom are ancient, battle-hardened time travelers—warn that the real alien invaders are right on their tails, but also might not be.

Needless to say, it warranted them a trip to Earth. This time, they traveled without the military escort, largely because it was a sixteen-day trip that Raynor did in ten.

Ten *Earth* days.

They landed somewhere in Africa. The countries were all different. Provinces, it seemed. The architecture was strange, the words looked as alien to Fowler as the cephrast characters. There was little to identify it as the same planet he'd left ten thousand years before.

But it was. It was Earth.

Home.

From the desk of:
Brody Kahlil, PhD.

Emilee,

Don't give yourself a hard time. It's literally the most powerful machine known to man. You're still the only living 9 dan.

Here's the data for Sol's outer planets right now. Through the end of the year, really. The inner planets have such small orbits and move so slowly, their travel times from the outer planets don't change much. On the flip side, it's a much bigger deal moving between them. If you ever need those in detail I can run them for specific weeks since their orbits are short, but if that time comes we're probably fucked anyway.

-Brody

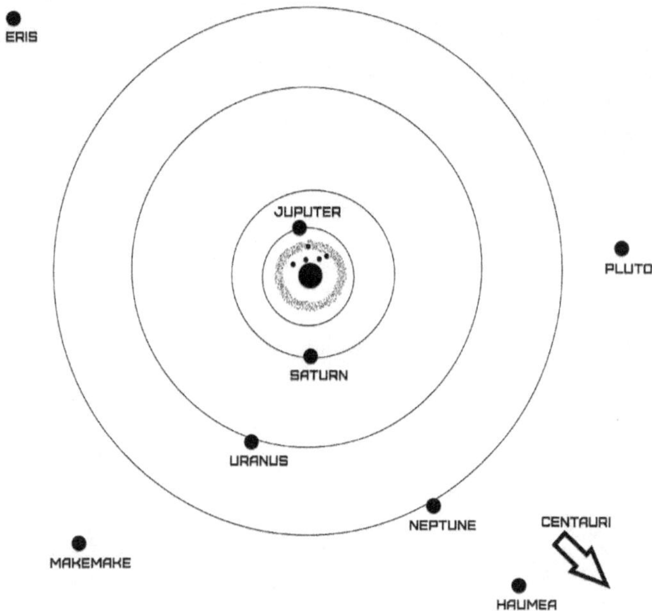

36

THE SOLAR LEG

Déjà vu swept the interstellar travelers as the Solar Defense Corps prepared for the encroaching cephrast armada, just as Centauri had before them. Unlike the scramble from four years prior, the SDC knew their time was limited. No one knew *how* limited. For all they knew, Razennon and Quexi were still fighting, though it wasn't likely.

Returning to Earth's calendar was more comforting than Walker could have imagined. She missed the thirty-hour days, but the dates were significantly more intuitive. They'd arrived in Sol at the beginning of August—the *actual* month of August. The 2nd, to be precise. Date conversions were well-established between the systems, making it easy to determine their travel time as being just over four years: two-and-a-half months faster than light travels. By comparison, calculating the time that had passed on board the ship while it phased through the dimensions was incredibly simple. They'd brought clocks on the ship—it had been three years for them.

As the SDC mobilized, Walker started to get the feeling they were more like a reserve military or police. The last large-scale war happened before any of its citizens were born. Their veterans were people who had dealt with crime syndicates, terrorism, and pirate fleets. With most of the legends dead, it was worrisome. CAF soldiers from the starfish were absorbed into the Solar military, most retaining their equivalent rank while a few were promoted. They were the only people in the system who'd fought an enemy like this. The only war veterans of any kind.

It would have to make do. Before they could catch their breaths, a large mass appeared at the edge of the Solar System, and by late October—a mere twelve weeks after they'd arrived—the invasion had picked back up.

The dwarf planet, Haumea, was the new focal point. It had been well-stocked ahead of time. With the spread of defensive batteries around it, forces at the edge were sufficiently holding the cephrast armada back. Their attackers didn't make much effort to get around. They seemed content with a clean sweep.

"Focus firing" is what Shino called it.

It was a three-year dissociation—a long dream about living outside of the universe. The invasion had never really stopped, and this time, there was no evacuation to fall back on. All they had at their disposal was an inexperienced army and a captured alien carrier packed with some of history's greatest scientists. The soldiers of yesteryear were few, and the months they got to prepare the local forces were even fewer.

Walker had hoped the Centauri resistance would be able to buy the colony ships enough time to arrive before the cephrasts. Many of the interstellar transports were occupied by other legends. Not soldiers, but strategists and scientists…people they desperately needed right now.

Instead, the cephrast armada swarmed the weapons platforms around Haumea, and beyond the edge of the system, a small flotilla of battleships sat, just waiting.

Repeated warnings were sent by the SDC to the incoming colony ships. The quartet of battleships outside the system destroyed the first transport as it neared—people who'd left at the very start of the Centauri invasion. Inside the system, the Solar forces were faring better against the onslaught of cephrast ships than Walker had expected. Regardless of their experience, they were better supplied than the CAF, and the exterior planets had more defensive lines.

The positioning of the planets had also been fortuitous. Saturn and Jupiter were on opposite sides of the sun, placing Titan's massive defense sector front and center. With an ample supply of natural gasses and easy access to fresh water from a sister satellite, the moons of Saturn were a convenient stronghold. Jupiter was the furthest planet from Centauri and home to two satellite coreworlds —Europa and Callisto. The polarized locations of the gas giants protected the majority of the system's civilians, and two of the dwarf planets—Pluto and Makemake—sat on Saturn's sides. Eris was too far to be used in any way—three times farther than Pluto and far below the Solar plane. Its munitions were in the process of being shipped up to Ceres, the small planet inside the asteroid belt.

The tiny base on Haumea had cut further into their invaders than anyone could have predicted. One of the more renowned strategists, Emilee Hatem, pushed the SDC to pull their defenses from above and below the plane, insisting the cephrasts wouldn't try to dip under the system. Doing so would give the human fleets an option to cut them off, negating the significant benefit of the cephrast armada's speed.

In an attempt to neutralize that advantage, engineers were lining up to work on the dimensional thruster. The fuel was scarce, and the starfish had already taken at least two interstellar trips, so the tests were equally scarce. Part of the ongoing research included finding a way to measure the fuel reserves and consumption, but as it turned out, measuring particles that moved in and out of existence was difficult.

Go figure.

Vakkard had been training a team of metallurgists to construct the alloy used in the cephrast hulls. For the engine tests, they'd been melting metal from the starfish, but that wouldn't scale when the time came to build a full ship. The room for error was too large, and they couldn't afford to lose fuel due to a hairline fissure.

Developing a method for one of the synthetics to issue commands to a ship in the void hadn't been completely ruled out, but the physicists who'd worked on the starfish in Centauri insisted it would require additional miracle breakthroughs.

"It has nothing to do with signals penetrating the hull," Drager explained to one of the SDC big-shots, "though that's also a problem. Synthetics have no means of communication outside of electromagnetic radiation: radio, gamma, light. Those signals *can't* move along the dimensional axis. Hull or no hull."

"We could load up an extension of SIM-1577 into the ship," the officer suggested—a terrestrial equivalent to Marker. "Then it could sync whenever the ship phased out."

"Not without fully changing its infrastructure, which would take months. It's not worth going into the details, but right now, all they would be able to do is send ships on automated patrols within the void."

The young man from the SDC nodded. "That wouldn't do," he said simply.

Fowler's status as the creator of xenocide had developed into a godlike reverence among Solar officers. Between his namesake in history and his siege of the starfish, they felt like he had some mystical ability to stop the invasion single-handedly. They made him a lieutenant and brought him into several closed-door meetings, one of which was also attended by the prime ministers of each coreworld and colony. Walker couldn't imagine the sort of tension in that room, though she found out soon enough. Fowler called her the next morning to get coffee. Just by the look on his face, she could tell something was wrong.

"That bad, huh?" she said. She took a sip of coffee—real coffee. She hadn't found the molecularly constructed food terrible, but sipping a freshly-brewed cup was heavenly.

"Nezz," Fowler said. "Can the SDC...uh...subpoena this conversation from you?"

The synthetic responded in its statistically-preferred voice, "No. Nor do I have the same contract with them as I did with the CAF. If your intention was to divulge information you gleaned last night...I don't suppose I would even have a moral conflict."

"You *have* moral conflicts?"

"Would you prefer that I didn't?"

"Isaac," Walker whispered, leaning over the table, "what's going on?"

He sighed heavily. "They're talking about opening a singularity in the Solar System."

"*What?*" She blurted loudly. "Where?"

"Near the small planet at the edge."

"Haumea?"

"That one."

Walker didn't know enough about artificial singularities or the positioning of Haumea to know how risky it was, but they were talking about a gravitational singularity—a black hole. They didn't have infinite mass as Walker had believed during the 21st century, but the possibility of a black hole growing further than expected was likely.

Not just likely...creating a stable one was nearly impossible. Most shrunk, like the singularity caused by Tellakeep Outpost's self-destruct. It was enough force to pull nearby objects towards it, lasting momentarily before dying out. Once you made one large enough to *not* collapse, it just kept going.

"Shit..." she said to her coffee. Her stomach suddenly felt incapable of handling a diuretic.

"They were pretty torn on it."

"I would hope so. That could kill *everybody*, and we're still holding the armada at the edge. From what I've heard, the cephrast ships that squeaked past were eliminated at Titan—*Triton*, damnit...Neptune."

"That's only because we've been feeding resources to the front lines and flanks. Once they push the main fleet to *Titan*—Saturn—we may not have enough to hold them off again. At that point, a singularity would be out of the question. If they're going to do it, it has to be soon."

Walker leaned her head back, taking a deep breath. She wanted to shout. To come all this way—fight, retreat, fight, retreat. Then mount this last stand, only to have the entire system get sucked into a black hole…

"So, what's your role in this?" she asked.

"Neptune. I'm going to Triton. If the cephrasts break through Haumea, we'll need to push them back to buy time for the singularity to be made."

It was exhausting just to think about. They went through the tired-old "take care of yourself" routine. There wasn't much else to say.

Fowler's team departed for Triton a couple of days later, to the same military outpost the starfish had been escorted to when it first arrived. So much effort was put into making sure the war happened at the edge of the system, no one in the coreworlds truly knew how bad the situation was—how much of the SDC had already been sent out and butchered. None of it seemed to be happening from underneath the beautiful, blue terrestrial skies.

Word traveled quickly about the proposed black hole. Raynor couldn't even remember where she'd first heard it. If there was any truth behind it, it was a sign of desperation. Haumea had held longer than expected, but it wouldn't last forever. Who knew where the next battlefront would be, or how sturdy those defenses would be.

Her vessel—the starfish—had been stripped down. The engine was removed for testing, the contents taken by its passengers, and the crew no longer operating. It was a hollow museum.

Marihade was massive—the town that was Marihade, at least. The atmospheric bubbles that had been a signature of Martian culture were gone, the entire planet terraformed. Few places on the surface were without gravity panels and electromagnetic fields, and no dunes could be seen from town.

Still, it was her home, complete with major ship manufacturers out in the Mars-typical areas. Teleporters—the molecular repeaters she'd used at Starling—were a common form of public transit. There were a few hubs to various destinations, with tunnels extending beneath the gravity panels on the surface. Most people in the cities didn't even have rovers; they weren't needed. It was a luxury for a geologically inactive world. Callisto and Mercury supposedly had a few repeaters connecting their colonies, but it was nothing like the Martian transit network.

As commander of a vessel—even a deactivated one—Raynor was not reinstated as a drone modulator. She'd been staying at one of the bases on Mars, occasionally getting out to see the planet. When the Solar invasion began, she started doing random chores on base to help keep it running, but felt otherwise useless.

Re-experiencing her home planet also helped keep her occupied. She didn't know where Rhyso was, or if he was alive, and the fact that she kept wondering bothered her. There were so many other problems to worry about. Pressing issues like the extinction of their species.

Whenever she looked for updates on the war front, she focused on the potential appearance of a singularity. Warheads were being destroyed long before they reached the cephrast armada, and there didn't seem to be other options. They were treading water, and Raynor could already see the headline vividly in her head: *Black Hole Out of Control!*

Once a glimmer of hope finally peeked through the fog, it came too late for Haumea. The supply train fell short, and the tiny planet was razed silent. With open paths along the flanks, it was probably the last time the entire cephrast fleet would be in one location so far from a human colony.

No black hole appeared. Raynor could only speculate as to why; there were so many factors she wasn't privy to.

Whatever the reason, the window had closed, and by the following week, the entire thing had almost slipped Raynor's mind completely. She got some answers one morning, though indirectly. When reporting in for duty at the Martian base she was staying at, she found she had been re-assigned to Earth's one and only celestial satellite, Luna. What had been casually referred to as *the* Moon during her era. She was scheduled to check in at the Lunar Testing Facility in five days.

As were Ron Phillips and Leiko Waverly.

37

UNCORING THE APPLE

Neptune's bases came under attack the day Raynor touched down on the Lunar surface. The cephrast armada moved quickly, making their intended targets difficult for the SDC to reinforce—a fact their exterminators seemed to be well aware of.

After the destruction of Haumea, the alien fleet split in three. Half of the armada continued straight down to Neptune, cleaving their way towards the center of the Solar System. The other two fleets slinked around the rim towards Pluto and Makemake. The SDC was powerless to reinforce those posts, and doing so would place the coreworlds in more danger. The dwarf planets were on their own.

To negate their disadvantage, four small ships sat isolated in the center of a kilometer-long hangar bay. Raynor stood with the head of the design team, watching a group of technicians prepare the ship nearest to them.

"These were Sigren Fentillas," the ship designer said, "luxury ships people fly for recreation. They're agile, and we improved their engines substantially to handle the increased weight."

"How much heavier are they?" she asked. It was more of a curiosity, fueled by her mother's work. Raynor had never flown one of the ships in front of her to compare.

"More than twice as heavy unloaded."

"From what?"

"The metal—it's heavy. These ships use light, durable alloys to keep them nimble. They have no standard need for armor, and this alien stuff is dense. On top of that, there are two engines. The normal one inside, and the one outside the hull that…phases it or whatever you call it."

The dimensional thrusters sat underneath each ship in a cubby cut into the bottom. The chemist who'd overseen Starling's metallurgy had figured out a process to create a similar type of alloy, but it was complex. No existing equipment could properly create the substance, so his team had to manually forge all of the hull plates for the Fentillas. Only one of the fighters had been fully upgraded so far. Another was partially completed, and the furthest two were still covered in manufacturer plating.

One of the mechanics was fitting a device inside the completed ship. Something to activate the dimensional thruster.

"Test in five!" another one yelled across the near-empty hangar. His breath puffed out as white smoke in the cold.

"Are we too close?" Raynor asked. The only times she *hadn't* been inside a ship while it phased, she'd been on a landing pad far away.

"Not at all. They've been doing tests on the engine by itself for months. Just don't stand in its place while it's gone."

"I figured that one."

"It's worth noting anyway. If you're piloting this and phase it out, intersecting with another object obliterates the material at those points. The actual 'crash' happens before you're completely out of the void, though, meaning your ship will have a hole while you're partially inside."

"Wonderful," Raynor grumbled, remembering the predecessors of Colonel Marmalade.

Just as she'd experienced on the orbital platform, a whoosh of gravity rushed over her like a gale as the fighter popped out of existence. Once the craft was gone, the wind snapped still, and a few seconds later, the entire process reversed, the vessel appearing again.

None of the consoles in the ship were broken.

Sitting in the cockpit, Raynor looked around to familiarize herself. Most of a ship's interior varied by make and model—design choices, placement of minor controls. There seemed to be a lot of features missing from the luxury vehicle's cabin; no doubt the original interior was full of convenience and comfort settings—media, auto-nav, climate controls. All of it was gutted for space and mass, but there were still a considerable number of buttons and switches. One of the mechanics leaned in to show her a handful of them. She wasn't likely to use any of them, but she needed to know for emergencies. Orbital stabilizers were excessive in a ship this size, which would never be put in a sustained planetary orbit, but the rich wanted everything. The feature was useful enough to leave in. Not for its intended purpose, but to prevent a crash if the flight stick seized up.

Then, there was the assortment of controls tied to the dimensional drive, all of which were untested.

"Pulling this should breach the vessel out from any depth," the mechanic said, gesturing to a handle by the seat.

"Does it use power?" Raynor asked.

"It purges a reservoir of reserve fuel, forcing the engine to pull the ship back out."

"Is it really that simple?"

"Not even close, but I couldn't explain much past that. It's mechanical, though, so it'll work if you're somehow stranded."

Numerous improvements had been made from the starfish, all of which revolved around the development of computer systems.

Raynor was most impressed by the inclusion of a fuel gauge for the 4D drive. One of the panels on the carrier bridge likely provided that information, but no one had been able to find it.

"The fuel gauge is approximate," the tech said. "It displays one deviation below the average, so you won't usually have *less* fuel than it shows. You'll see. It fluctuates as particles vibrate in and out. If it goes below a certain point, it will auto-breach."

"Good to know."

He eyed her suspiciously. "Don't test that today. If it doesn't work, we have nothing to rescue you with."

"I wasn't planning on it," she smiled. Her only goal today was to get familiar with the ship's controls as a regular space vessel—dust off some cobwebs. When she felt comfortable again, she'd phase a few times to see how it felt in the smaller fighter.

"Good luck, Commander. We'll be in contact. The radio will patch into your flight suit."

Raynor raised her eyebrow at the ship's communicator. "You can get signals through the hull?"

"No. We fed a line through like we do with the viewing panels. Everyone assures me the radio won't work in the void, but I'm sure you'll test it all out."

The large, warehouse-sized hangar didn't open up, so as a trial by fire, Raynor had to take the fighter out through a smaller airlock —something she used to do without even thinking about it. Lightly, she tilted the stick, gently rocking the fighter into the exit bay. Air cycled out of the hatch for a few seconds, finally opening the bay doors to the Lunar exterior.

With minimal gravity, Raynor blasted the modified Fentilla away from the facility as soon as she cleared the airlock, pulling her body hard against the seat. Whatever weight the cephrast alloy had added, it was being sufficiently offset by the souped-up engine. The flight stick was as responsive as any of the military-grade ships she'd flown in the militia, and within seconds, she was rolling the craft into turns that pulled her face from her bones.

After half an hour of simple drills, she felt confident enough to test the ship's novel improvements. The dusty, white sphere below her shrank as she pulled the craft away to a low orbital distance.

Her breath held, she pushed the dimensional thruster with the slightest amount of pressure. An almost liquid-sounding whir came from below the ship, vibrating up through the floor. The craterous mass before her lost a tiny amount of opacity, the effect varying slightly across the surface. Stars had yet to peek through from behind the celestial body, but the changes in density around it were far more noticeable than they'd been in deep space.

With more to inspect, it was easier to tell that the distortion wasn't in the Moon, but rather the space in between. When Raynor remained stationary, Luna appeared warped. When she moved, the warping adjusted with her, and the more she flew around, the easier it was to see the changes in their intermediary space. A large lens in space with varying thicknesses, but no visible matter to speak of—no fuzz, no blurring. It was an appalling difference from phasing between the systems, the faraway stars changing slowly.

Raynor habitually squeezed her eyes shut and reopened them like she was trying to read something small. She crept the ship forward, moving through the field of condensing and expanding space. Diving further into the void, the distortion became more pronounced, the light of the universe more sparse. She would have to practice estimating distances a lot before she could phase anywhere close to another object. Still, her method of navigating on the starfish should work well—dipping partway in to plot a course before phasing completely.

The right half of the Moon continued to lose space between them, shifting closer than the left. Raynor kept the visual in her mind as blackness fell around her, imagining the pale sphere continuing to shift at the same rate. She flew forward, estimating the time it would take to close a quarter of that distance. After a while, she pulled the ship back into real space, her eyes strained by the sudden appearance of the bright, chalky satellite.

Luna was farther than she'd expected it to be, but it was closer than it would have been if she'd flown the same distance in real space. Her intuition would have to be refined, but that was the easiest part to learn.

This is doable.

Before taking the ship on a proper joyride, she wanted to test out the radio. Fearlessly, she plunged the ship completely into the void, the universe disappearing around her.

"Lunar Outpost Cairo," she said. Nothing but her own breath could be heard in her helmet. No static. Not even an empty radio click.

"Lunar Outpost Cairo," she repeated. "This is test number one. Do you read me?"

Nothing.

Even with partial light—fragmented, split...however they explained it—a signal should be readable at some point. She pulled her ship out the tiniest possible amount; not even the faintest light from the Sun became visible, but the gargling vibrations of the engine rumbled beneath her.

"Lunar Outpost Cairo," she said again. "This is test number two. Do you read?"

Again, nothing. Meticulously, Raynor repeated the process for several minutes, pulling the ship further out, stopping, then trying again. Luna became visible again, if only barely. Stray particles from the stars bounced off-course during their journey through the universe, peeking through the Lunar surface on Raynor's viewport.

"Lunar Outpost Cairo. This is test number seventeen. Can anyone hear me?" Faint crackles of sound came through the radio. She couldn't even call it static, but it wasn't *nothing*. A proper burst of static came through after forty-one, and it wasn't until sixty-eight that she heard indistinguishable voices. It took nearly one hundred movements to hear fragmented words. The Lunar surface was completely solid in front of her, though slightly faded and distorted.

"Eef –uan –ech lo– — isst– –etov..."

She pulled the ship out entirely. "Lunar Outpost, please repeat."

"I said, 'We can read you, but it's not very clear,'" the dispatcher said with some concern in her voice. "You're clear now, though."

"What was the first transmission you understood?"

"Ninety-nine. Not sure what you said before that, but we heard, 'Do you read me?' after. It was all very broken. Without synthetic translation protocols, we probably wouldn't have gotten it."

"Good copy."

"Is everything alright? You were gone for several minutes."

"Everything's great!" Raynor said, glowing. "I'm going to give it a test in motion."

Raynor darted the sports vessel towards the ghostly orb in front of her, lining it parallel to the surface as she sped along before plunging herself into the abyss. It was easily the most disorienting and frightening experience of her life. She could feel the ship vibrating underneath her. She could feel the forces as she sped up, slowed down—even when she turned lightly. There was no sense of speed. No sense of anything, really. The universe ceased to exist. It was just…nothingness.

It wasn't truly nothingness. It was a universe, or set of universes, she was moving towards. Ones so far from a galaxy there was no visible light, or so young they were nearly empty—or something else entirely. Nobody knew anything about it.

Pulling the craft upward, she exited the void, the Lunar surface far below and the outpost well behind. Anyone looking out from the facility would see quite a sight as the Fentilla vanished into the thinnest of air and reappeared further along—sometimes *much* further, sometimes at a different trajectory. She kept her void-borne turns light, brief, and always away from the Moon. It wasn't clear yet whether a dimensional shift could occur at an angle or turn. Raynor tried to imagine what that might look like—objects and stars from the side appearing in a tunnel in front of her or something while she phased. If she encountered anything like that, it should be obvious something was off, which was all that concerned her right now.

Finding shorter paths while in motion was challenging. There always seemed to be a direction that was more condensed than the rest—the space never changed uniformly. It was also possible for the densest area of the void to be longer than real space, though it seemed rare. In those cases, she could pop out and circumvent it. Or stay in, burn a little extra fuel, and fly invisibly through the parallel dimension.

It wasn't the worst problem to have.

Raynor's test flight was beyond successful. Combining traditional maneuvers with phasing was work for a future day. She hadn't lost her edge behind the stick, and she'd learned more about navigating the void in an hour than she had in three years on the starfish.

There was only one more thing to do…

Raynor hit the brakes, stopping the modified luxury craft in place before plunging into desolate emptiness. Digging her arm into the space beside her seat, she clutched her gloved hand around a small handle, wrenching it upward. The ship was yanked into real space, turning her stomach inside out. It felt nothing like an ejector seat, nor like the gravity-wind experienced while standing near a phasing craft. It was almost the opposite: *she* was the wind, and the universe was falling through her.

Then it was over; the Fentilla idled above Luna.

The ships worked. The dimensional thrusters, the metal plating —all of it. It was the equalizer they needed. Once the other ships were re-plated and outfitted, they wouldn't have much time to train as a squadron, if any. The cephrasts were blitzing through the Solar System, and the three pilots would be needed on the front lines as soon as possible.

Behind the front lines.

38

BREACH BOMBING

It had taken the cephrasts nine days to reach Neptune, but it took the SDC seventeen to reinforce it from Earth and thirteen from Saturn. Nothing could be done to support the ice giant as every line of defense around it was obliterated.

It took them five days.

The speed in which the alien incursion carved up the base on Triton injected fear throughout the system. News that Fowler had been part of their defenses only added to the demoralization. If the mythical alien reaper couldn't even slow the cephrasts down, what chance did everyone else have? Raynor thought maybe he hadn't arrived before the attack, so she checked the flight logs—it made her heart sink. Not because she saw him as some storybook savior. They'd infiltrated an alien spaceship together...how many people could say that about *anyone*?

Right before Neptune's destruction, the dwarf planets on the sides of the system fell under attack. They were faring well against the smaller fleets, but with no supply train, they were both on borrowed time. Reinforcements en route to Neptune managed to intercept the central armada before they reached Saturn, giving the gas giant a good foothold. Titan manufactured most of the SDC's drones, so mobilizing the unmanned fighters out to the distant battlefront was quick, easy, and necessary. Once the battle was taken to orbit, keeping the large cluster of colonies safe would be impossible.

As shocking as the rapid destruction of Neptune had been, Saturn was in a much better position. The dark-yellow ball was four times closer to Earth than Neptune, and direct supply from Earth was already customary for Titan. The supply lines were drying up, though, so the coming weeks would be critical for humanity's survival.

As soon as the first fighter was outfitted with armaments, Raynor was using them. All efforts to unleash a weapon of mass destruction on the cephrast fleet had been rendered useless, so her new ship couldn't sit on the sidelines. Phillips and Waverly continued to practice in the fourth ship—the stock vessel—while theirs were being built up. Considering the outcome of a hull crack, it was an acceptable area of precaution.

It did give the engineers time to put together a garage vessel. People often used trailer vehicles to move luxury ships like the Fentillas around. Not only did long-distance travel put unnecessary wear on their finely-tuned engines, but it also took weeks to travel between planets. If Raynor managed to expertly navigate the void, it would still take days to get to nearby planets, weeks for others.

Sigren, the Fentilla's manufacturer, made one of these trailers. They called the model the Allocade, but almost none of the stock ship was used for the SDC's final product. The Fentillas were meticulously structured to house the components together with minimal weight, so the dimensional plating followed form. Their fighters were identifiable as Fentillas, though clearly modified. The garage ship was a box with an engine. The only part they needed were the clamps that fastened the sports ships to the outside, and since no one would be inside those clamps while phasing, they didn't need to make them out of the dark metal alloy. The interior of the original ship contained basic living quarters and repair facilities, all of which would work fine, so the whole thing was moved inside a crude, rectangular tube.

It was sealed—that was all that mattered.

Before launching for Saturn, Raynor spent as much time as possible training with the other pilots. They needed cohesive formations in real space before they even *thought* about trying to do it in the void, and for the time being, they only had two ships to work with. Hers, and the stock one.

The Fentilla's controls were intuitive enough for them both. Being born prior to the era of space fighters, Phillips had considerably more trouble getting the hang of the responsive spacecraft. Elementary flight mechanics, like using a velocity cushion—the thing that stopped your ship from moving in the same direction once you'd turned—were foreign to him.

"If you stop thrusting," Raynor explained, "your ship will keep going in the same direction."

"Yes—" he said through his teeth. "I know."

"*So*...if you turn to the side and thrust forward, what happens?"

"You move forward *and* in the direction you were moving before. I'm not an infant."

She pointed to the switch. "Velocity cushion."

"Oh...okay," he muttered. "How fast does that happen?"

"You can change the maximum counter-thrust here," she gestured to an analog lever beside it. "These ships default to a 3.1-g max, I think you can increase it to twelve."

"Shit."

"They're sports vehicles. Keep it at the default for a while."

The airman's inclination would be to crank up the counter-thrust, but he needed to ease into it so he didn't pass out. Airplanes used fixed wings to turn, pulling the craft in the direction you angled towards. If desired, a spacecraft could turn independently of its forward thrust—sometimes it was necessary. In a combat situation, they'd almost certainly use the maximum cushion at times.

With her lone fighter attached to the side of the garage vessel, Raynor left for Titan with a mechanic, making the nine-day trip from Luna in six. She was only on the small moon for a day, getting a rundown on her payload before moving five of the warheads into the trailer. They were a dirty combination of traditional radioactive explosives and split gravitons to amplify the force. Eight seconds after dropping one, it would detonate, the lightest effects of the shockwave reaching several gigameters away.

The runs were simple and effective. Leaving the garage vessel well behind the lines of battle, an armorer loaded one of the warheads into the Fentilla, and Raynor would take it through the fray. She'd breach out of the void, dump the warhead, and dive back in. Everyone but her had taken to calling it a pop-and-drop. Apparently, it rhymed for them.

Her first approach undoubtedly created some confusion for the cephrasts, just as their own appearance had for the CAF. Those who saw her drop the warhead and blip out of existence were killed a few seconds later, but word finally got around after her second bombing. By her third, she was enemy number one for the alien armada. No matter what else was going on, the moment her fighter appeared, she was targeted. For her fourth, she stayed hidden as long as possible. Remaining in the void for long distances and breaching into a battlefield created a higher risk of intersecting an object, but the chances were still extremely low.

A lot lower than her chances of getting shot down in real space.

With her last payload on board, she looked for a pocket of space that seemed similar to the natural plane. It was a twenty-minute trip by traditional means, so she set a timer and coasted through the void. If she planned the route properly, she should emerge far behind her target battleship.

Removing the ship partway, she cranked her head to orient herself to the fleet. Idling for more than a few seconds was dangerous once she began exiting the void—it didn't matter how ghostly her ship looked.

Behind her to the right, she saw the faint outline of the battleship beside its carrier friends several hundred kilometers away.

A heavy overshoot.

Returning to the abyss, she turned back on her new heading. She habitually processed what she'd seen—how far it looked, which areas appeared to change the most…it was a normal exercise now. She didn't want to make a second adjustment, but she also didn't need to be too close. The bomb had a short fuse. As long as she was within ten kilometers, the battleship would be liquidated.

After a brief jaunt through nothingness, she pulled the ship back out. No need to swivel her head this time, the armada ship was directly on her left—just a few kilometers away. Violently, she jerked the ship out of the void, materializing fully in view of the battleship. Dropping the warhead completely in the natural plane was essential. Elsewhere along the dimensional axis, the warhead's blast would cause little damage. If she was too far in to hear static, it wouldn't even rock the boat.

Raynor exited directly into an evasive maneuver so erratic that she lost track of the battleship. She didn't need to know exactly where it was; she just had to avoid being hit for a second. The monstrous vessel's automated defenses picked her up the moment she surfaced along the jagged flight path. She pulled the ship up, sending the graviton warhead sailing away from her craft before phasing back in. Light flashed on the inside of her viewport—the hull-mounted turrets trying to pick her off before she vanished.

As rapidly as she'd exited the void, she was back in, rolling the agile fighter into a perpendicular corkscrew back towards the garage vessel, punching both thrusters forward through total darkness.

There would be no indication when the bomb went off. Raynor just flew in peace for a while, slinking past the end of the combat zone. When she finally re-emerged a few minutes later, she found that the battleship had become cosmic powder. The effectiveness of the dimensional craft was undeniable. In two days of solo runs outside of Titan, she'd completely vaporized two carriers, two battleships, and a vessel of unknown purpose.

Raynor made a brief stop at Titan to drop off the armorer before making her return trip to Luna. The two in-progress fighters had been finished, giving Phillips and Waverly a couple of days to practice maneuvers in the void.

For the next week, the three pilots did nothing but formation drills. Flying around other ships in the void had provided some incredible insights into their new form of travel, such as the lack of an apparent "bottom" to the axis. One of them could always move further into the void in relation to each other, slowly fading away as the universe did when they phased in alone. If their ships were at the same depth, they could see each other clear as day—heavily assisted by the digital viewports. It indicated they were moving through the same dimension or dimensions every time, allowing them to navigate with each other throughout.

Formations had always been the bane of Raynor's existence in the militia. The addition of a fourth dimension should have only exacerbated the problem, but with the implementation of a few conventions, entering and exiting the void without colliding became effortless. After a few days of drilling, the trio of pilots were flying in near-perfect sync.

And just in time—the stations out by Pluto were nearing complete destruction, which would open a path straight to the Jovian coreworlds. Protecting the people in Jupiter's orbit would force the SDC to split their forces, making any delay of that attack beneficial for Titan as well, so the three pilots packed their bags.

When it came time to move the Fentillas up to the orbiting garage vessel, they found their ships undergoing last-minute changes in the chilly Lunar hangar.

"We're supposed to be leaving," Raynor said, irritated. "What's going on?"

"Oh, Commander!" an engineer said excitedly. "Come and look at these."

Six mechanics were fastening torpedo bays into the now-hollow wings of the butchered Fentillas. A stoic, silent, military suit stood at the edge of the bay with a muscular woman holding a jewel. Both seemed to be observing the work being done.

"This is Colonel Mayex with the Solar Defense Corps," the tech introduced the emotionless man, who offered a salute. "And Dr. Kleine from Terrestrial Defense Research."

The woman with the jewel started speaking as if she and Raynor had already been in conversation.

"TDR has shipped up some prototypes for you to use." She pointed to a group of three narrow cylinders being placed into the makeshift missile bay. "The smaller tubes have dimensional thrusters parallel to traditional propulsion. They can be fired from within the void and will slowly work their way out."

Raynor could pardon the delay…

"That's incredible. Do they just fly straight forward?" She couldn't imagine a realistic method of controlling the missiles at other depths.

"We created a visual targeting system from the same paneling in the cockpit. Intelligent recognition programs will identify ships in close dimensional proximity. If you can see enough to know what type of ship it is, the targeting system will as well. The projectile breaches into the craft, detonating a nuclear-tipped graviton warhead."

"Outstanding," awed Waverly.

"They're being called 'chasm-crosser' torpedoes. Each active ship is being equipped with a bay of three." She pointed to a much larger cylinder already installed on the other wing. "This contains a dozen projectile rockets, each carrying a payload of split graviton particles bound to individual dimentons. They create a light dimensional pull accompanied by an *extremely* small gravitational singularity. Only enough to pull the target area into the void."

Raynor's eyes widened. The thought of stranding someone in the dimensional abyss sounded barbaric, but any living creatures would be liquified, which somehow seemed better. All of their bogies were drones, anyway, so the main application would be the ease with which they dispatched heavily-armored foes.

The TDR woman took a deep breath. "They've been dubbed 'Abyssiles' by someone other than myself. They will *only* travel through your current plane."

"Well, thank you," Raynor said, staring at the three tubes being installed into her ship. "How long will the install take?"

"Just another hour," one of the techs said. She briefly showed the pilots where each bay's controls were being wired for arming and firing while they dumped their bags in their ship cabins. Not wanting to stay in the freezing hangar, Raynor made her way back inside the base. One of the other mechanics shouted across the bay.

"Chasm-crosser two is live on Abyss Weaver One!"

Raynor paused. "What did they call it, Nezz?"

"A concatenation of two words in New Terrestrial Standard," the assistant said. "Some of the meaning is derived from structure, but it loosely translates to *Abyss Weaver* or *Lacuna Weaver*."

Raynor smiled at the names.

"I like *Lacuna Weaver*."

"I've updated your lexicon."

Moving through shadows was one of Fowler's greatest skills, but remaining unseen by a species without blind spots was difficult. Where it was possible to sneak up behind a human, a cephrast could see him the moment he entered their line of sight. It forced him to avoid contact altogether, which made moving through the ruins of Triton extremely slow.

His injury further slowed his pace. During the second bombing, he'd been knocked onto a freshly broken pipe, spearing completely through his leg just above the kneecap. The wound was treated easily enough when it first happened, now inaccessible beneath the heavy environmental suit he wore.

Through his injury, he'd been able to help prepare one of the shuttles in the main bay. Evacuation appeared imminent, so he did what pre-flight checks he could—supply levels, computer tests.

They hadn't left quickly enough. When the boring lasers finally sliced through the ceilings, he and Aza Lockheart were lucky enough to have been in that shuttle. The last member of Fowler's original team grabbed two suits prepped by the ship's airlock, which they managed to get on before the shuttle's hull broke underneath the weight of the building. It was far from spaceworthy, but even if they could find a working ship and pilot it without active life support, the hangar's exit had collapsed.

The *main* hangar had. There was a rear hangar—one that sat entirely underground. It was too narrow for a military ship or shuttle, but there had been a few personal vessels parked there when Fowler toured the base. Those ships were more likely to be intact beneath the surface, but the hangar's exit was a mile-long tunnel that opened out the side of the small moon. There was a decent chance of a cave-in somewhere, but it was their only shot.

Fowler and Lockheart lived in their spacesuits, listening to the distant sounds of cephrast machines while they cleared out the base. When Lockheart first went outside to check on the state of the hangar, it was filled with a dark pink gas, making it hard to see. Once the chemical agent dissipated, the two Dissenters quietly began making a path through the hangar's debris to the base.

The atmosphere of Triton wasn't a complete vacuum, but it might as well be. Seventy thousand times thinner than Earth, according to their guide. There was plenty of replacement oxygen on board for two people, as well as a duo of conjoined rooms that maintained their seal through the damage. It was the only location they knew of with pressure, so if they needed to remove their helmets for some reason, it could only be done in the second room. Once the first room was opened, its atmosphere would rush into the almost-vacuum of the shuttle and out through its broken hull. The second room was twice as large, so by closing the first room and opening the door in between, the air would equalize to about two-thirds of Earth's atmosphere. As a last resort, they could try to turn the ship on and restrict life support to those two rooms, but if it worked, any cephrasts watching the base would immediately see the heat signatures.

Their plan had one glaring hole: food and water. Mostly water. After two days of moving rubble around, they had to go into the sealed room to eat and drink. Medical supplies hadn't been moved into the shuttle, so all they could do for Fowler's wound was pour drinking water over it and use the same dirty bandages. If he'd thought ahead, he would have shredded one of the other suits, but they were starving and dehydrated, so he hadn't.

Closing the larger room off with its two-thirds atmosphere, they exited the first room, allowing its air to vacate into the shuttle. Fowler didn't know how low the pressure could be for them to safely take their helmets off, but after two more days, they needed water. Repeating the procedure, the larger room's pressure dropped to less than half of Earth's, which probably wasn't healthy, so they hastily downed several bottles of water and a handful of energy bars.

As the air in the sealed room thinned out, so did their supply of air tanks. They used two tanks per day, and by the time they cleared a path through the collapsed hangar, they were down to four. In preparation to traverse the ruins of Triton's defense base, they returned once more to the pressurized room. The two legends filled up on food and water, stuffing the rest into a bag before hitting the wasteland. Their eyes hadn't popped out, which Fowler was thankful for.

Careful not to rip their suits, Fowler and Lockheart crawled out of the hangar through the stone and metal. The two antique warriors moved quietly through the hazy rubble of the destroyed base, their footsteps a laughably low pattering along the ground. They kept an eye out for survivors, but they had to prioritize staying out of sight. It wasn't likely that anyone had survived the past six days.

Small cephrast machines hovered through the halls in search of people. They'd probably been here since the gas.

Weapons were strewn all over the ground. They grabbed a couple in case they were spotted, but Fowler was getting a lot more mileage out of a piece of reflective glass he'd wrapped in a cloth to look around corners without cutting his gloves. He was pretty sure both the cephrasts and their droids would see the mirror at the corner of the floor, but without reliable sound cues, it was the only precaution available.

It was a significant handicap, as was Nezz being offline at the base. Neither Fowler nor Lockheart could understand the other, and their radios had been silent since the attack. Fortunately, the two were able to fall back on their training, which had included using non-verbal cues to move through a facility such as this one.

Still, it would be nice to explain some things in detail.

A light swept the floor at the edge of the hallway. The two soldiers quickly ducked into the last room they'd passed—an office —and hid in a supply closet. Fowler held the mirror near the bottom of the cabinet door until one of the hunting machines lazily hovered into view.

"Robot," he whispered, handing the mirror to Lockheart. They'd had to learn a few verbal alerts in case they were about to be spotted and the other wasn't looking. If he had to think of a single word in a pinch...robot was as good as any.

The field surgeon mimicked his movement, getting a glimpse of the mechanical stalker before quickly pulling the mirror back up. *"Tena,"* she said in whatever-the-fuck she spoke on Callisto...Callistian, Callistese; whatever irritatingly-specific name Nezz would use. It had never come up.

By the end of their first day traversing the ruins, they'd only covered about half of the distance to the rear hangar. The exertion had used up more air than expected. If it took another full day to cover the remainder, they might run out of oxygen before they got there.

They had to take a detour around a caved-in hallway, further delaying their trip. Placing the mirror at the corner of a turn, Fowler nearly fell over as he jumped back. He pulled Lockheart into the nearest room, his lungs wasting precious air.

"Alien!" he whispered harshly. The creature hadn't been walking towards them, but he knew it could see down the hallway just fine. After a minute, it seemed the cephrast either hadn't noticed the mirror, or didn't come into the dark, heatless room in search of them. Still, they waited for another fifteen minutes before leaving.

Their path eventually took them by the station's infirmary. The wing was trashed. Broken bottles of drugs littered the floor. A few remained intact, but Lockheart didn't seem confident judging them by appearance alone. Neither of them could read the labels. Still, she sifted through the broken vials, looking for anything that seemed useful.

They didn't leave empty-handed—bandages were an obvious grab, and there was a small oxygen tank that hadn't frozen or ruptured. It wouldn't be useful in the base, but perhaps if they got onto a ship.

Keeping their feet light, the two Dissenters continued through the base, pausing to listen for muffled echoes and checking corners with the jagged mirror. As they neared the back of the facility, the damage started to clear, allowing them to move quickly to the rear hangar. They arrived at the long staircase descending into the underground depot by midday, leaving several hours of air in their last tanks.

Fowler gave a silent hurrah at the bottom of the stairs. The hangar resembled the bottom level of a parking garage—a fifty-foot square of concrete with six areas marked for small craft to land. It had not caved in, and two ships sat in spaces on the right. The entire back wall was a door leading into the airlock, which, in turn, led to the tunnel exiting the moon. If it wasn't fully collapsed, *and* they could get one of the ships started…

It was still a long shot. Who knew what they'd run into once they left the hangar? Not to mention starvation, thirst, and oxygen deprivation.

The large, exterior door was without power, but there had to be a manual override of some kind. They switched on the dull lights built into the front of their environment suits. It wasn't ideal for this sort of search—Fowler had to push his helmet right up to the wall to see anything clearly. After searching the entire door over, Lockheart found a large handle underneath a protective cover.

Breaking the exterior, she pulled the lever down with a loud *ca-chunk*. The two warriors threw their weight against the right half of the door to slide it open. Whoever had been tasked with oiling it did a fantastic job—the bulky metal panel slid smoothly, causing a light rumbling beneath them.

Please don't feel this.

The outer door inside the airlock was already open, exposing the long tunnel beyond. Some broken rocks scattered the path, but nothing they'd need to clear out.

Splitting up to inspect the ships, the two Dissenters left the other half of the inner door where it was. Neither of them was very knowledgeable about modern spacecraft, although Lockheart had at least flown during her era. Fowler's vessel opened easily. There was only one seat, but they could probably squeeze inside with their supplies. He searched the dashboard for an obvious ignition. Dials and knobs of all sorts covered the front of the ship, some flat surfaces that might be digital displays. Before he could make any progress, he was interrupted by Lockheart shouting over the radio. After two days of complete silence, the sudden volume jolted him out of the ship.

"*Eninat!*" she yelled, accompanied by a low, slow vibration.

Her word for the cephrasts.

The dark cavern glowed intermittently with blue light. Gritting his teeth against the pain in his leg, Fowler grabbed his pistol and hobbled around the craft. At the bottom of the stairs, one of the slinky aliens was being riddled by Lockheart's photon blasts. Dull flashes of yellow and green danced across the alien's face, illuminated by the pulses of energy.

The creature was dead before Fowler could take a shot. He wanted to ask how long it had been there before she killed it, if there was even a possibility it hadn't alerted its friends, but he couldn't.

Lockheart sprinted two steps back to the ship she'd been inspecting and threw the cabin open.

"Laniet!" she commanded in Third-Era, Post-Ancient Jovian. Given the circumstances, it probably meant "get in."

This ship had two small seats behind the pilot's, making it already preferential to the one Fowler had snooped around in. He crawled into the back seat next to their water and the oxygen tank. Lockheart's hands ran frantically across the front of the ship, evidently without a means to start it.

Fowler reached up to close the cabin, his attention grabbed by two searchlights shining down the stairwell, pausing as they crossed over the burn-covered corpse.

39

LACUNA WEAVERS

By the time Raynor's diminutive squadron arrived at Pluto, they couldn't get anywhere near the planet. The dwarf planet's vespiary had been blown to dust, leaving the sector's fleets in the predictable hands of their combat AI. When they emerged in the box-like trailer, an exhausted, concerned voice hailed them.

"Unidentified vessel, this is Pluto Launch Control. Please identify."

"Nadia Raynor," she replied, unsure whether she officially held the title *Commander* anymore. "—Lacuna Weaver Prime."

"Turn around, Raynor. Our evacuation is already in progress. You won't be able to land planetside."

"I see that. We're going to dock at Starbase…ah…*Erinyes.*"

With no docking protocols, Raynor carefully attached the garage vessel to the side of the fallback outpost. Starbase Erinyes was half as large as the outposts she had seen in Centauri, its small crew and strike team preparing to unload the station's arsenal into the alien armada. The trio of pilots spent about an hour in the starbase. There wasn't much they could do—the bombs they came to drop were on Pluto.

"We could create an opening for the evacuees," said Waverly.

"It's not our directive," Raynor sighed. "The Fentillas have a capacity to destroy dozens of armada ships. If we lose them today, they won't."

"*If* we lose them," Phillips said.

"It only takes one railgun. Evading automatic targeting isn't sustainable for more than a few seconds."

"We can occupy the battleships," suggested the outpost's armorer. "Erinyes has got mountains of projectiles it can send at them. They're ineffective because the battleships destroy 'em long before they get there."

"But they *have* to destroy them…"

"That's what we were planning to do for the evacuation. We were in the process of coordinating an artillery zone with the transports."

Raynor considered the situation for an eternity—could they outpilot a swarm of computer-controlled fighters? She didn't want her ego to get them all killed, taking three of the Fentillas with them. Their vessels *were* outfitted with a few standard ship-to-ship weapons and countermeasures, and engaging from the edge of the battlefield would reduce collision chances to near-zero. With their new armaments, they might not even have to phase out enough for the automated defenses to see them.

"Alright," she said. "Let's get them out of there."

This could be the biggest mistake of her life, but everyone trying to escape Pluto was a human life they could save with minimal risk.

It would also send a clear message to their invaders.

Minutes later, they were moving the garage vessel far behind the outpost. Most of their dimenton fuel was in the box trailer. If things went horribly wrong, the mechanic could always take it back to Luna with the spare fighter.

"If any of us are taken out, the others leave *immediately*," Raynor told the pilots. "No matter what. Is that clear?"

"Completely."

"Aye."

Raynor picked up the trailer's transmitter. "Pluto Launch Control—Lacuna Weaver Prime. If you read, we're going to open the back door for you. Give us thirty minutes, then fall back to the next starbase when you get an opening." She flicked the console off, walking down the length of the garage vessel with Phillips and Waverly to four access hatches along the wall. "Keep your breach time to a second. The barrage from Erinyes is a buffer, not slack. Real-space weapons are hot. Abyssiles only on armored drones, bore lasers for the little ones."

Small, bore lasers were a common drone weapon. Photon cannons had a minor delay as the slowed particles traveled through space, but the laser was an instant, solid line—like the battleship's railgun. If your aim was good, it was a guaranteed hit, and synthetics had almost perfect aim.

Once they passed through the circular hatches, the gravity from the garage faded, leaving them weightless. The three pilots climbed down into the ships, worming their way hastily into the ergonomic seats before detaching from the trailer.

Heads pressed against their chairs, they bulleted towards Pluto. Multiple carriers surrounded the planet, a few battleships in between, and some other armada ships Raynor didn't recognize— supply ships, mining vessels, maybe even terraforming equipment. Half a kilometer to her left, a torpedo as large as their ships sailed past them. Moments later, her ship was rocked by the detonation. A green beam plowed through the explosive, dimming significantly on the other side of the impact.

Fuck…this was a mistake.

"We're going in," she said. "Let's keep it tight." Grabbing one last eyeful of the starscape, she pushed her ship into the void, redirecting along a desirable trajectory towards the armada. The three fighters cruised through the dark calm for a minute. Intuitively, Raynor lifted her head out, looking for the closest battleship. It wasn't hard to find. A warped, semi-translucent line of pale-white energy fired past her, probably at a projectile behind her, but uncomfortably close. She wasn't sure if it could damage her this far into the void, and she wasn't looking to test it out.

Diving back in, she flicked a crudely-wired switch to arm one of the torpedo bays. She angled the Fentilla's nose in the direction of the massive cephrast vessel, slipping to the side before phasing out just far enough to see the unmistakable form of her target.

She set the primed chasm-crosser loose. The light, smoky tail of the void-faring torpedo shifted through the abyss as it careened towards its target. The projectile was yanked to the sides along its path, sporadically outlining pockets of condensed space Raynor hadn't been able to see before. Both the missile and its freshly-spewed smoke grew smaller and fainter as it floated out of the void and into the side of the battleship, completely ignored by the war-ship's automated defenses. A healthy explosion formed at the impact site, causing sufficient damage to open up a small hole in the hull. A thick jet of air blew out of the ship's wound, and Raynor could just barely make out tiny specks in the stream—cephrasts, weapons, computers, garbage…whatever had been nearby.

A horde of drones redirected themselves towards the impact site. Before Raynor ducked back into the void, the damage appeared to be sealed off from inside. It wasn't a significant blow. If they didn't seal the breach with the same alloy, it could slow them down while they repaired it.

Still, the torpedoes worked.

The three Fentillas split apart, engaging in a form of combat no one had experienced in thousands of years. Vessels she had only seen as small icons in a three-dimensional, holographic display were suddenly flying within a hundred meters of her. The armored ones were easy to spot, and a significant pain in the ass for the drone modulators to eliminate. When one finally made its way towards the edge of the swarm, Raynor pulled her ship completely out of the void, exposing herself in real-space for a second while she sent one of the thin cluster rockets at the juggernaut drone. As soon as the abyssile was out of its bay, Raynor submerged, escaping a barrage of fire from the surrounding cephrast ships.

She changed positions, phasing back into limbo to see the prototype weapon's effect. There was no explosion. A shockwave rippled through the void from the impact site, further distorting nearby visible objects for a moment before returning. Chunks of the drone's hull were ripped from its frame into the void—finely-cut pieces of shrapnel falling away like meat torn off a bone. The fragments became more visible as they passed by Raynor along the dimensional axis, fading away as they continued along their path into nothingness.

What remained of the armored drone in the anchor universe was nothing more than a small cluster of nuts and bolts about the size of a rover tire—parts of the drone furthest from the impact site. The pile was held together temporarily by the small singularity before it faded, allowing the junk to slowly drift apart. The sight of so much debris was concerning, each piece capable of lancing through their ships while they phased. Bracing herself, Raynor took her fighter back in, discovering that the trail of scrap had fallen in a straight line. A line *through* the void, visible from every depth and contained to the same equivalent three-dimensional location—like a smoke signal.

Armored troop carriers began to emerge from the small, multi-colored planet, met with an impressive bombardment from Erinyes. Large clusters of long-range torpedoes were destroyed in transit by the cephrast vessels, creating bright clouds of fireworks that consumed ships from both sides. With most of the guardian drones removed, the remaining SDC drones had an easier time keeping the cephrast fleets in check. Enemies trying to leave the new minefield towards the transports were quickly intercepted, herded back to the other side like sheep.

As the bombardment began to lighten, the troop carriers made it past the desecrated starscape. Raynor circled around to a nearby carrier before heading back to Erinyes. Her knowledge of the vessel's interior was substantially more accurate than the other armada ships. She approached the carrier from the top, phasing out enough to get a good visual of the black hemisphere covering the bridge before firing her second inter-dimensional rocket.

The chasm-crosser twisted and turned as it sailed through varying patches of space. When the torpedo was about halfway out of the void, preparing to breach into the corner of the viewport, the starfish reacted to the attack.

It phased in.

The carrier came *into* the void to meet the torpedo. As soon as the starfish matched the projectile's plane, a defensive cannon shot it out of the sky. The explosion didn't even rock the spiky vessel.

It didn't stop. The gargantuan ship crept further into the void, solidifying into the shape Raynor knew all too well. Reflexively, she pushed herself further in, rolling away towards the fallback outpost with her jaw clenched.

The carrier didn't chase her further, but she continued to bite through her teeth until she arrived at the garage vessel, where the other two Fentillas were already docked.

"How incredible was that?" Waverly said when she crawled out of the circular latch. "They can't touch us!"

She didn't mention her disturbing interaction with the starfish— it could wait. This was still a victory worth celebrating. They'd gone toe-to-toe with machine-controlled ships and survived. Granted, they'd spent most of the fight hiding in a different universe, but it was a feat nonetheless.

Erinyes' crew was picked up by the transports and taken back to friendly lines. The large station was set to detonate within proximity of the armada, though its munitions storage was almost empty now.

A new voice came through their comms. "Lacuna Weaver Prime, this is General Bruhls. We owe you, Commander."

"Sure thing, General. Get home safe."

As much as Raynor wanted to ensure the Plutonian caravan's secure travel back to the coreworlds, the transports would take weeks to return, and the Fentillas had a date with the frontlines. The trip to the dwarf planet had taken ten days, and Raynor was dead-set on improving that pace for the journey back.

Throughout the voyage, she obsessed about her escape from the carrier. It must have seen the torpedo phasing in the bridge's large viewport, or maybe she'd come out too far before firing—something to do with the cephrast's impressive visual acuity. Reading signals through the void was supposed to be impossible. Then again, the same thing had been thought about the dimensional drive…

Physicists didn't know shit.

If the cephrasts *could* track signals through the void, it didn't seem like they could do it very well. Once she'd gone deep enough to lose visibility, she'd been a drop in a lake. It made more sense that the bridge spotted her—or the missile.

The thought nagged at her anyway.

Even with the marked success of their missions, the Lacuna Weavers were only slowing attrition. A couple of weeks after the evacuation of Pluto, Jupiter found itself under siege. It was sheer luck that Raynor's team was already near the asteroid belt. Their ships had been able to get in the way, agitating the pursuing fleet long enough to reposition more defenses to Europa and Callisto. The two coreworlds orbiting the red giant would heavily strain resources from Saturn, which was barely holding on.

Casualties on Titan were stacking up. The liquid gas that made the moon such an ideal place to build weapons had proven more difficult to protect in recent weeks. When one of the natural lakes was finally ignited, a few million people were killed instantly, its crater visible from orbit.

It was nothing compared to Enceladus—the other Saturnian colony. Of the fifteen million people that once lived amongst its geysers, not a single one remained. The same fate was met by

Saturn's uncolonized satellites. The five hunks of rock and ice had each contained anywhere from dozens to hundreds of researchers and recluses. Makemake was holding its own against the smallest cephrast fleet, but the little planet was nearing the point of evacuating. Uranus sat between it and Jupiter, but held no major colonies on its moons. The enclaves had been moved back to Earth early on to spare defensive resources.

Once back at Titan, Raynor flew non-stop for a week, getting just enough sleep to prevent carelessness before setting out again.

Eventually, one of the automated crafts managed to hit Raynor's ship. It hadn't broken the hull, fortunately, but diving back in had been a terrifying gamble. Getting close to the armada vessels was becoming more difficult. There were so many starfish around Saturn—each containing swarms of drones whose main goal was to destroy one of the dimensional fighters.

After the week, the squadron was reassigned, probably in no small part due to their reduced efficiency. They weren't sent to the looming battle picking up around Jupiter, nor the inner planets, but to the middle of nowhere. The small flotilla waiting for the Centauri colony ships had been lazily closing in behind the primary fleet as it punched through the system. The quartet of battleships was initially left outside the system, then later moved to Haumea after Neptune was destroyed. The vessels were being moved in again, and the Lacuna Weavers were going to pick them off in transit. The small offshoot was still capable of destroying the main evacuation group from Centauri, which could begin braking any day.

Raynor had protested, but only briefly. The mission would take over two weeks—a long time to take out four ships—but with the amount of flight time they'd clocked in the prior week, their special-order armaments were running low. There were no carriers near the flotilla, allowing it to be taken out with only graviton warheads.

Three bombs for four ships—easy.

No Solar defenses remained past Titan, so the garage vessel spent most of the trip in the void at constant acceleration. Most people called it "cruising," but in reality, they were always speeding up or slowing down. If they didn't, it would take months, even years, to get to some places in the system. Raynor missed the days of setting her nav and walking away. In order to make their absurd travel rates, someone always had to be actively piloting the ship, dipping in and out of the void in abuse of the laws of physics.

After five days accelerating and five braking, the garage vessel arrived in the middle of nowhere—about one AU past Neptune.

Not wanting to leave the garage vessel vulnerable or give away their attack, the pilots loaded into their fighters while in the void—a new feature. After the reserve Fentilla was fully plated, Vakkard's team made docking brackets for the garage vessel. Raynor tried to avoid loading into the ships while phased, anyway. The clamps used a concerning number of latches and connectors, so while they might work as air-tight barriers, Raynor didn't know how reliable they were against the dimensional bleeding they were trying to avoid.

They also wouldn't be able to dock in the void. It was theoretically possible, but they had no measurement of void-depth, and if one of them was slightly further in, the result would be catastrophic. When they finished their run, they'd have to get the attention of their new mechanic and have her breach the trailer.

The standard pop-and-drop missions had become incredibly routine for the three pilots. One of them would draw fire from the automated defenses by floating out and in, another would safely dump their payload and bail, then they'd rotate. After perfecting a combination of maneuvers they designated the "push flick," their breach time was down to half a second per drop.

That's how it usually went, anyway. When the time came to handle the small flotilla, something new happened—an unthinkable, chance occurrence. Raynor didn't know it at the time, but it was perhaps the luckiest accident of the war.

As always, she phased out to check their distance, searching for the warped pod of battleships. The stars of the Milky Way began to appear, and as far as she could see in either direction, no more than ten meters in front of her was the distorted side of a ship's hull. She was practically touching it. Off to the side, there were some crates shaped like large spools of thread…

She was phasing inside a battleship.

Panicking, she slammed her palm into the dimensional throttle, pushing the craft back into the void. With her breath held, she waited for the momentary sound of metal disintegrating from her ship before she was turned into liquid. Once the darkness enveloped her, she knew she'd made a mistake. She *wasn't* dead. By nothing short of a miracle, her ship had phased entirely inside a cargo bay or hangar without overlapping anything. This was a current to ride.

As quickly as she'd dove in, she plucked herself back out, her arteries pumping violently. This was, without question, the dumbest stunt she'd ever tried. Even during the second she'd been in the void, the battleship could have moved enough to place her inside the hull—or a crate, or anything at all. If she'd been drifting, her ship would melt, and her right behind it.

Again, not dead. A full, solidified image of the cargo bay filled the edges of the Fentilla's viewport.

Raynor didn't waste any time checking her surroundings, unloading her entire abyssile cluster into the walls. A line of circles formed along the metal exterior as she swept the bow of her ship sideways, the expansive hull falling away into nothingness at each contact point. As the side of the vessel dissolved, the thick atmosphere inside escaped rapidly through the perforations, lurching Raynor's ship forward in the gale. She struggled to keep it steady against the pressurized wind, finishing her rocket salvo.

Twelve direct hits later, Raynor crept her ship forward a meter—away from whatever was behind her—and blipped out of the universe. Streaks of debris phased into view in front of her, finely-minced scraps of hull that faded in her wake as she pressed further into nothingness.

She found Phillips and Waverly regrouping deep in the void. Emoting with a ship was difficult, but there would never be a more perfect double-take than the one Waverly did as she phased into view.

"—u're alive!" he cried as she fell into their depth. "It looked like you breached *into* the battleship."

"I did," she said, her nerves on fire. "I didn't overlap with anything."

"What was all that damage from?" asked Phillips. "You shot it up?"

"My entire cluster," Raynor said.

"That's fucking hardcore. We thought your engine had blown up."

There were still three and a half battleships to destroy, so the squad proceeded as planned. One after another, they dropped their payloads. Phillips had a knack for dumping his directly between two armada ships, even ones that seemed too far to hit with a single bomb. When they were done, a fog of ship pieces sat where the flotilla had once been.

Retracing their course back to the garage vessel, Raynor recalled the other reason she hated leaving it in the void—they had to find it. She could only follow coordinates in real space, and after the trick she'd just pulled off, flying near the location and phasing in felt like tempting fate. They found it eventually, wiggling their ships around in front of the rectangular box until the mechanic saw them. The ship vanished, allowing the three Weavers to breach and dock without extra risk.

Once they'd gotten inside, the vessel was prepped and ready to go. A message was stored in their comms system, which meant it had been directed to their vessel-ID. It must have been picked up while they were docking—an urgent communique from Nezz.

This can't be good...

The assistant AI wasn't in any of their dimensional crafts due to the signal-blocking hull. The pilots used the same active translators

Nezz had whipped up for the starfish infiltration, which used data packs amounting to what Raynor considered to be a box of synthetic shit. The AI could send transmissions like anyone else, received outside the ship and wired through like the viewport, but anything else would require an entire copy of the machine's brain, which was half the size of the garage vessel…

Nezz was big.

The message was being sent in pulses—a request for them to intercept another ship on their way back to Earth. Traditionally, adding a stop in the middle of a trip like this was an ordeal. Long trips were made bearable by reaching higher top speeds, so coming to a rest before the end could add weeks. By riding the currents of the void, Raynor could make the same stop with only a couple more days of travel time. That required active piloting, of course. No punching in coordinates and sitting back.

Not for her subordinates, at least.

"Phillips," she called.

"Yeah, Commander?"

"You're at the helm—coordinates are in the nav."

"*Aye*, Commander," he said, heading to the cockpit. He laughed as he walked by, shaking his head. "I still can't believe you phased *into* a fucking ship, Commander. Makes me look like the sensible one."

Ron Phillips: the poor woman's auto-nav.

40
THE REAPER RETURNS

Conversation was light in the abandoned starbase. Fowler didn't know how long they'd been there, but judging by the number of times he'd slept, it was over a month.

They'd evacuated the small hangar without any real resistance. They only saw the one cephrast before Lockheart managed to fire the ship up and fly them out of the long exit tunnel. The mouth hadn't led them directly to an alien ship. From what Fowler could tell, all but one of the cephrast vessels had moved on to their next location—probably Saturn.

The two soldiers had taken to looking through the remaining items of the outpost. He still wasn't sure exactly why Lockheart had brought them here. It may have been the only place they could land within range of their life support. The little ship they'd boosted had done a solid job on their three-day trip, but it would certainly never last to Titan.

Unlike a ship, which ran its life support off of the engines, the base's systems emitted minimal radiation. There was still a danger of being spotted by the cephrasts, but as far as asylums went, it wasn't bad. The floating outpost had been evacuated and shut down, but a lot of supplies were left. By Fowler's best guess, the crew had evacuated immediately after Neptune was overrun.

They lived in luxury—air, water, food, heat. Some of the rooms had clothes left in them—clean clothes. After wearing the environmental suit for eleven days straight, removing it was a relief second only to the shower he took immediately after. They washed the suits as best as they could, but it only did so much. If they ever made it back to civilization, the bulky garments were going directly into an incinerator.

Water recycling was a standard part of every outpost's life support, so there wasn't a risk of running out. Their drain runoff, urine—even the moisture from their breath was being filtered down and placed back into the irrigation. The station had as much water as always.

Food, on the other hand, was limited. Their bodies turned it into heat, which leaked through the walls into space forever. They replenished that energy by eating more food, most of which was removed by the outpost's crew when they left. With only the two Dissenters on board, the remainder would last for a little while. When they first settled in, they set aside enough to keep them both alive for seven days, which would get them to Earth if they starved for as long as possible. The ship's life support wouldn't last that long, though, so they'd be looking to hop between outposts.

Once they got down to the seven-day supply, they stuffed it into the tiny craft with twice as much water, their overripe environmental suits, and the medical oxygen tank, and flew back out into the stars. Aside from their impending deaths, the second trip was much nicer than the first. They stuck to looser clothing, had a better supply of food and water, and, well…that was it.

Two days into the sequel of their escape, they hadn't found another starbase, and it didn't seem like Lockheart had one planned out. Then a song unlike any Fowler had heard before hit his ears. Not a song, but a radio transmission. It was staticky at first, but when it cleared up, he had no problem hearing a woman speaking in what he believed to be pure dribble. Lockheart listened intently, hopefully able to understand what the voice was saying.

She did not.

With a shrug, she picked up the communicator and spoke into it for a minute. When she finished, she set the device down and waited.

Nothing else came through. After a few minutes with no reply, Fowler slumped back. Transmitting a distress beacon would bring the cephrasts to them long before any human rescue might show up, but common sense dictated that if someone had used this frequency, they would be listening to it. It didn't seem like anyone had heard Lockheart's reply, though she didn't appear concerned by the lack of response. She was undoubtedly more familiar with interplanetary communication than he.

Several hours later, another transmission came through. A different message from a different person—a man speaking more nonsense.

This time, it didn't seem like nonsense to Fowler's Callistian counterpart. Lockheart nodded to herself as she listened, turning back to Fowler after the message ended to relay what she'd heard. It was their typical game of charades, usually accompanied by the shouting of words he obviously wasn't going to know. She would draw something in the air with her finger, he would shrug, then she would repeat the motion exactly as she did before while saying *"Pilleiron!"* or something…as if that clarified it.

She was interrupted by an English transmission.

"Isaac, I hope this message finds you well." It was Nezz—they had all been Nezz. "I'm so glad to hear you're alive! Based on your signal, you're roughly 813 million kilometers from Neptune in a Tivadren 2μ en route to Titan. The 2μ won't be able to support you to Titan, but as luck would have it, there's a nearby vessel that can pick you up. You should have enough air to arrive at the attached meeting point."

They were saved! Not quite, but soon. Lockheart was already setting the navigation to place them in a steady, 1.5G deceleration to the coordinates Nezz gave them. The hard braking was uncomfortable—probably bad for his body, too, but so was suffocation.

As their ship neared its stop, their oxygen levels began to noticeably decrease. It took Fowler an hour to put on the smelly environment suit sans the helmet. They went through the oxygen in the medical tank first since it couldn't be used in space. Unfortunately, it wasn't pressurized very well. Sharing it, they only got a couple of hours.

They tried to string out the rest of the ship's oxygen as much as they could before moving to their environmental suits. A few hours later, when his head started to feel fuzzy, he picked up the communicator.

"Nezz, this is Fowler," his voice came out drunkenly, "We're almost out of air, so we may need to do a...mobile pickup..." His oxygen-starved brain tried to remember what he was going to say. What would a mobile pickup do? Weren't they already doing one? The ship rescuing them—

Someone slapped him.

The world came into focus. Lockheart's helmet was on. She hadn't slapped him; she was pushing his face out of the way to get his helmet on. His head had lolled against his chest—he must have passed out.

"*Intunt, iin catayet,*" she said firmly, pointing to one of the seals below his chin and pulling his helmet down over his head. His hand rose feebly to do something to the seal, but she had already locked the helmet down.

Pulling him forward roughly, she reached over his shoulder to his neck, starting the airflow from the tank. A comforting, light hiss emitted from the valve. Two breaths later, the world seemed a lot more coherent.

More sound was coming through their radio. It couldn't be Nezz. That was apparently a six-hour delay, and if he'd been unconscious for that long without oxygen, he would be "extra dead," as Teegan would say.

A string of foreign words came from a familiar voice. It was two people—soon joined by a third.

"Yeah, okay…I get it—uh, Lieutenant Fowler?"

Fowler scrambled forward to grab the receiver, pulling it up against his visor as he responded excitedly. "Yes, this is Isaac Fowler!"

"This is former U.S. Air Captain Ron Phillips. I'm not sure if you remember me; I was one of the pilots on the starfish infiltration."

He was the other pilot on the controls. He'd also been flying the starfish from Centauri a third of the time. More importantly, he was American.

"I remember. Aren't you a lieutenant, too?"

"Yeah, I just prefer *former Air Captain*, you know how it is—" the voices of his crewmates picked up in the background. "He fucking asked me—Look, Lieutenant, we're approaching your location, but we don't have any way to dock your ship. This is a customized vessel, and the seals were taken from a specific…" he trailed off. A voice Fowler now recognized as Raynor spoke with the former Air Captain.

"We have environmental suits on," Fowler cut in. "We had to switch to air tanks."

"Oh, he says they're already using them for air…shit, okay… hey, ah—Lieutenant?"

"Still here."

"How long do you have on your tanks?"

"Half a day or so. We used some already, but that was like a month ago and we were under more physical strain, so it's a bit of a guess."

Phillips passed the information to Raynor, who responded for a while, presumably outlining a plan to reach them in time. After a minute or so, she paused, adding something sternly.

"I didn't *say* anything—" Phillips said. "Well yeah, it's gonna suck…I'm not saying we *shouldn't*, Commander…aye, Commander —Hey, LT? We'll be there in eight hours or so. Maintain your deceleration."

"Will do."

"Our comms will be off until then. O–er an—" The line quickly turned to static and went dead.

Lockheart used their hand signals to ask if they were clear. Fowler nodded weakly, leaning his helmet back against the compact seat.

Within seconds, he was asleep. It was probably the best decision his body could have made for him, dropping his oxygen usage during the wait. He was awoken by the radio cueing up—Phillips letting them know it was time to switch ships.

Fowler did a once-over of the cabin like he was on vacation and didn't want to leave anything in the hotel. They'd only brought food and water, so he loaded it all into the bag and slung it over his shoulder.

Couldn't hurt.

Their rescue ship was unlike anything he'd seen before. It resembled a cephrast ship more than a human one, though Fowler couldn't quite figure out why; it wasn't circular by any means. It was a giant, dark grey refrigerator box. Four fighters sat docked underneath, big enough to fit a person but smaller than the ship he was in—proper fighter jets.

As the large vessel inched towards them, one of the ships popped off, exposing a shallow, cylindrical airlock. Their suits didn't have any means of propulsion, so they'd have to wait until the dock got close enough to jump to. Fowler prepared himself to lunge, but the hole beneath the ship kept getting nearer. When it finally stopped, he and Lockheart could grab the lip without pushing off. They climbed up into a small compartment just inside the rim. It barely fit the two of them, but after living together in a cabin the size of a two-door car, it was like any other day.

The detached fighter docked below them, removing what little light had been provided by the stars. The tunnel pressurized, and the top of the fighter opened up, lighting the tube again. The other pilot from the starfish mission was inside—something with a W. He spent a while trying to explain the hatch to Lockheart, which felt distinctly like he'd learned the language in high school but forgotten most of it.

Lockheart figured it out on her own.

Phillips called the long-range transport the "garage vessel." It was small for a long-range transport, but its only occupants were the three pilots and a mechanic. It had enough food to sustain all six of them without rationing, but Fowler's bag of food wouldn't go to waste.

He and Lockheart had ditched their in-ear assistants back on Triton, but they wouldn't have worked in the garage vessel, anyway. The crew all sported the same pack-based translators they'd used for the ship heist. Fortunately, Phillips spoke the same version of English as Fowler. A fact the World War III aviator wasn't happy about.

The pilots discussed something relating to either the trip home or their new refugees. Fowler could only pick up parts of it as Phillips responded. Without context, it wasn't very informative.

"*Shtozh, ve wone budem jinzan for yedy,*" Raynor said. "*jhè etto gud.*"

"*Kanata—unto Juvioa,*" replied Waverly. "*Flotei en modörer.*"

Phillips nodded. "Four days from now, I think."

"Four days until what?" Fowler asked. Phillips closed his eyes and took a deep breath, making no effort to hide his annoyance.

"Until the third fleet reaches Europa," he grunted. The pilots spoke for a little while longer before breaking apart. Phillips motioned for Fowler and Lockheart to follow him. "C'mon. Commander says you smell like shit."

"*Tot esnact yass I shuoh!*"

"I'm *paraphrasing.*"

Straight for the showers, again. That was how most of the trip went, but it went quickly. A couple of times each day, the vessel would pop out of the void and check for transmissions, but other than those short windows, they spent the entire time at least partially in the void.

Four days into their trip, the fleet from Makemake arrived at Europa, placing pressure on the already-struggling Jovian moons. The speed of the encroachment was dizzying. It should take weeks to travel between planets, but the cephrast armada did it in half the time, razing each sector within a month of their arrival. It was the polar opposite of Cold War II. No political gain, no subterfuge or double-agents—just machines trying to destroy enough machines to make room for weapons of mass destruction. It was sheer brutality.

The "Lacuna Weavers" had done some work to neutralize that blitz. It was obvious they'd been practicing their navigation since their voyage from Centauri. Pockets of shortened space were located quickly, reducing their two-week trip to eight days in the garage vessel.

Even with that edge, the SDC somehow managed to always be both a step ahead and a step behind the cephrasts. Fowler had successfully arrived at Triton ahead of the invasion, but only by three days—not enough time to prepare. Raynor had supposedly done the same on Saturn, arriving two days before the moon was attacked. Keeping in that routine, Titan was destroyed the day before Fowler returned to Earth—the cephrasts would be hitting the planet's frontmost defenses later in the week.

From the first attack on Haumea, it had taken them only four months to get to Earth, destroying everything along the way.

When Fowler got a hold of the small, tan jellybean connected to Nezz's services, he practically shoved it into his brain. He never realized how much reliance he'd developed on the device until it was gone. It gave him the freedom to do all sorts of things...like see a doctor—his first stop after landing. His leg had been treated on Triton, but the wound had re-torn several times and gone for long periods without a cleaning. It hurt a little, but he never expected the appointment to go the way it did…

"Given the circumstances, I'd suggest replacing it entirely," the doctor said—as a mechanic might talk about a car. Fowler's brain couldn't even process the recommendation at first.

"I'm sorry…what?"

"My understanding is that we'll be under attack in a few days. Are you expecting to get back into the fight?"

"As soon as I can."

"This wound wasn't tended to for a long time," the doctor explained in a very routine manner. "Your medic did good with what you had, which is why it's treatable, but you wouldn't be able to put weight on it for ten to fifteen days, and it could take a couple of months to fully heal."

"Or I replace it?"

"Or you replace it."

Fowler had seen several bionic limbs, including people in his teams. Most did it by choice, but he still had concerns about the process. It felt like an extra place for something to go wrong. Then again, his modern education was cut short by a couple of years, so he'd never fully understood how advanced technology was in a general sense.

By the end of his appointment, he'd scheduled the surgery.

Walker had been on Earth ever since he first left for Triton. She already knew he was still alive, but he made sure to see her on his first day back. She was happy to see him, of course—less so after he told her about the operation.

"But you're up right now," she said. "Is it really that bad?"

"They're not lobbing it off for infection. This will allow me to get back in the thick. If I recuperate naturally, it'll take too long."

"Stop putting the whole damn world on your shoulders, Isaac. You need to recuperate."

It was something she'd said to him before. Fowler could admit he was prone to that flaw, but Walker hadn't seen the carnage firsthand. She didn't understand how truly fucked they all were.

"That's not what this is," he said with some indignation. "We'll be erased from the universe in two weeks…it's not the time for anyone to be taking sick days. There isn't much risk involved in this."

"Do you know the mortality rate of leg amputees?"

"Do *you*?" he shot back. "Today?"

She opened her mouth, pausing. "I…guess not."

"It's almost zero. This isn't a prosthetic—it's bionic. It supports my circulation and nervous system. It's a very expensive piece of technology that the Solar Defense Corps is happy to pay for."

She sighed, resting her chin on her palm. "And you should already be dead, anyway, right?"

"That's right."

From the desk of:
Brody Kahlil, PhD.

Madam Grand Dan, Savior of the People,

Anything I can do to help. Estimating travel times is impossible with all of the void stuff, especially with the faster orbits, so I included all of the metrics you need over a spread of times for the weeks you asked about. That date range is really concerning, by the way…I sure hope you're wrong about it.

Not that you're ever wrong, but there's a first time for everything and it would be nice if it were this.

-Brody

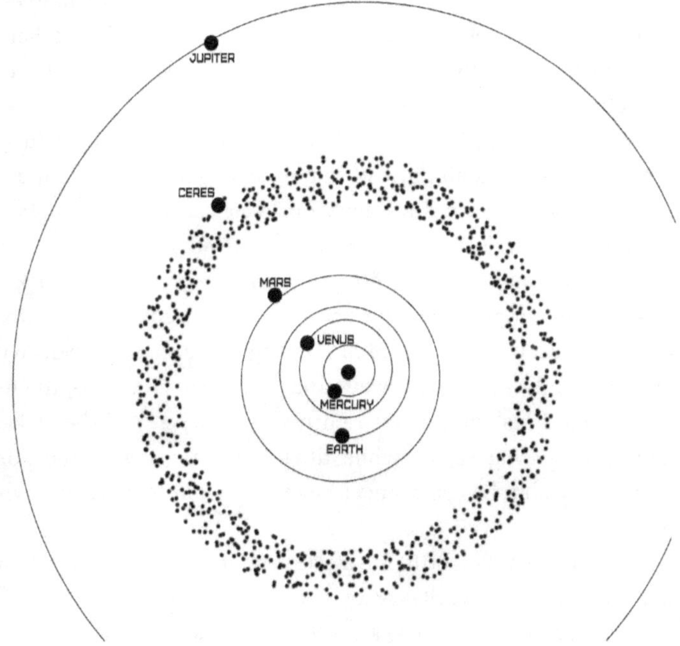

41

HAIL MARY

The buildings on Triton were destroyed two months ago. Completely. They immediately lost all heat and air, leaving only the harsh atmosphere of the moon in its place—nobody could have survived.

Nobody but Isaac Fowler.

Walker couldn't believe it. When she was first told, she'd assumed it was just a glimmer of hope—that someone had found an SOS in that direction and was jumping to conclusions.

Nope. He was just picked up—he's on his way back.

And after mere days of recovery from surgery, he was back on base. If the stories about him hadn't been unrealistic before, they were now. People told tales of him killing entire ships of aliens with his bare hands, uphill both ways and all of that. Of course, the real story behind his triumphant return was that Aza Lockheart kept him from getting sepsis while dragging him through the Solar System in a ship he could never have flown, but folklore was what it was.

For what it was worth, the stories about him were entertaining. Some of Walker's favorites were:

Isaac Fowler has a recessive genetic mutation that makes him nearly invincible. The same one Rasputin had.

Isaac Fowler is dead. The SDC built an advanced machine that looks and sounds just like him to boost morale.

And the best one—Isaac Fowler is actually a cephrast who defected to humanity.

Throughout the winter, Walker had been playing the role of alien psychologist more than anything. She started collaborating with some professors who had spent their careers studying the cephrast logs—mostly anthropologists and psychologists. The system was getting desperate, and unraveling the inner workings of a largely-unknown psyche had a lot of defense value at this juncture.

In the end, it was always guesswork.

The skies above Earth were littered with flashes of light on a regular basis. The cephrasts hadn't gotten to Luna yet, but energy bursts from the large armada ships could be seen shimmering in the night sky. During particularly heavy defensive pushes, it even discolored the daytime atmosphere. Reports came through periodically of attacks making it all the way to the planet. A graviton lance punched through the orbital shields, killing a few million people in South America. One struck the western Pacific, causing tsunamis in Australia. The drones were dwindling quickly, allowing more enemy tech through the lines.

There was nowhere to run…this was it.

Mars was still safely on the other side of the Sun, but Jupiter wouldn't hold out much longer. When it fell, the second fleet— which was now larger than the first—would invade the red planet.

Walker had only seen Kahlil once since Neptune was destroyed. He was on Earth, enveloped in humanity's natural reaction to the discovery of a new universal force…

Building a bomb.

The missiles outfitted in the Lacuna Weavers were a result of that project, but there were too many barriers in the way of creating a dimensional WMD. The wavelength was too unfamiliar for Terrestrial Defense Research to get a good return from their testing.

Attempts to amplify the effects only resulted in pushing things further into the void, rather than expanding the blast. They could use up every molecule of the dimensional fuel to make a small hole in the side of a single ship, but the fragments would go *really* far into the void.

Kahlil had lamented that fact when Walker spoke with him.

"When we were playing with the starfish engine, we managed to create the desired effect on a molecular level—wide-but-shallow—so we *know* it's possible, we just…don't know exactly why it happened."

"TDR recreated the technology, though, didn't they?" Walker had asked. "They made several engines."

"Rudimentary by comparison. We figured out the basic mechanics and built our own. The starfish engine has all sorts of contraptions no one knows the purpose of. We basically broke open a classic roadster and studied it until we could make a lawnmower engine. Then, we drained the starfish engine and tore it apart."

That was the largest barrier—fuel. They only had what was left in the stolen carrier. Raynor's squadron used a small amount while traveling, but most of it was lost during research. Just transferring the fuel from one container to another resulted in a significant loss, and moving it back into the broken cephrast engine would create more. Even if they knew exactly how to duplicate the widely-dispersed explosion, there wasn't enough fuel in the SDC to make a bomb big enough to matter. Engineering more was a priority, but it was a catch-22—learning to make the fuel required more fuel.

Another engine would provide the needed resources, but the notion of getting their hands on one seemed like an even longer shot than it did the first time around. Sure, they knew more about the carriers than they did in Centauri—many of them had lived on one for three years—but the cephrasts were much more vigilant of approaching ships now.

Fool me once…

Still, it wasn't a total surprise when the SDC's admiral—a man named Joplan—asked Walker to confer with her colleagues about the cephrast's expectations of a similar operation to the one that secured the carrier.

Time for Ship Heist 2…

Ocean's 12,000?

The Centauri Job.

Walker didn't think it would work on a fundamental level. The cephrasts would never let another vessel get taken. Each one was near countless others—the alien fleet would blow it out of the sky long before the SDC could get away. She conferred nonetheless, bringing their consensus with her to a strategy summit. Raynor was in attendance, already on Earth from rescuing Fowler and Lockheart. She was also largely responsible for the success of the CAF operation. Quinto was present as well, whom Walker hadn't seen since they'd first arrived in Sol.

Admiral Joplan jumped right in.

"We're here to discuss the feasibility of a covert operation like the one performed in Centauri. It's only a matter of time before the Jovian worlds are overrun, and when that fleet arrives at the inner coreworlds…" He shook his head. "It will all be more difficult."

One of the defense researchers—a beefy woman from TDR named Kleine—made a gripping motion over the table, pulling up a holographic display similar to the drone control module. Walker was expecting a ship outline, but it was a detailed, exploded model of an engine.

"This is the dimenton thruster of the CV-100 vessel," Kleine said. "What many are calling a 'starfish.' The mechanism we broke to drain its fuel is tied to an emergency shutoff or regulator. It's superfluous, so we didn't include it in our own, but when examining these components initially, we found a potentially destructive combination of changes we've been unable to duplicate."

She pointed to part of the engine hovering in the air in front of them.

"Increasing the injector's flow and breaking that regulator allows fuel to flood through the components, eroding the walls of the primary engine into the void. Other minor modifications will be needed, such as disconnecting potential alert sensors, but once the damage makes it to the graviton engine, a wide dispersal is created. Our accidental test was run with a microscopic amount of fuel—spare particles, really—but the engine was completely unmodified at the time." Batting the thruster away with her palm, Kleine pulled up columns of test results in its place. "This is a conservative projection using the amount of fuel we estimate was in the carrier's engine before we drained it."

Joplan glared at the data floating over the table. "Absolutely not. That will take us out with them."

"These are fourth-dimensional values, Admiral. The blast radius would only be about one hundred megameters—eight times the Earth's diameter. Most of this energy will be going into the void, distributed across the blast area."

"What's to stop the armada from simply phasing back out, then?"

"The force is varied. Anyone in the vicinity would need to be at a sufficient depth to escape the blast, or be reduced to paste."

The admiral pondered the information for a while, finally waving his hand through the display. He pulled up a diagram of the Solar System ending at Jupiter, staring intently through it.

"We've run every scenario. No matter how we consolidate, our combined forces are just not sufficient enough to fend theirs off. We've dumped the majority of our fleets at the main cephrast armada above us, making the fleet at Jupiter now the larger of the two."

It suddenly became clear to Walker that this wasn't about stealing another engine for the rare materials inside—it was sabotage.

The largest asteroid in the belt was outlined—a dwarf planet called Ceres. It currently sat between Jupiter and Mars, on the other side of the Sun from Earth. Joplan gestured to the large rock within the belt.

"Ceres is in an ideal location. It has a small base used for weapons maintenance that would suffice for our needs. Destroying the fleet at Jupiter would cull the invading force by more than half, allowing us to funnel our defenses to Earth." The admiral turned to Walker. "How likely are they to expect it?"

The question startled her a bit—the flaws she saw in another theft didn't necessarily apply to a demolition. She took a moment to consider her collaborations regarding their invaders' perspectives, mostly thinking out loud.

"They've seen us duplicate their technology, militarize it beyond their own capabilities—or at least, the capabilities of this particular group. They'd never let us take another ship, but I don't think they have much reason to specifically expect sabotage. My understanding is that we can't get near the carriers."

"Apologies, I was unclear. This will be into a battleship."

The battleships didn't exhibit as much caution as the others, but only because their security measures were so frightful. Entire outposts of torpedoes had been eliminated en route to the men-o'-war, and nearby SDC drones were destroyed kilometers away. They also didn't have arms covered in doors to break through.

"Well…no, I don't imagine they'd expect that, but we wouldn't be able to spend hours exploring one. Do we even have a reason to believe it uses a similar engine?"

"As of two weeks ago, yes," Kleine said. "Commander Raynor's team pulled two square kilometers of a battleship's hull into the void. Before it was destroyed, some of our more powerful synthetic friends went to work inspecting every signature they could. We have material compositions, energy expenditures, full interior layouts, armament readouts, and an archive of information transmitted by frequency during that time."

One of the SDC bigwigs spoke up in almost a grumble. "Did that information reveal a way in?"

"The Lacuna Weavers have a way in," Joplan explained. "A large portion of the battleship's bottom half is a cargo bay. With detailed structural information, phasing into that area will be easier than it was the first time."

"Right, but that's…" the officer stammered, turning to Raynor. "That's not what really happened…is it?"

"It's the only reason I could do the damage I did," Raynor said. "They don't have defensive cannons inside the ship."

"You described it as an accident in your debrief," Joplan said. "This entire operation hinges on your capability to phase into the cargo bay of a battleship. How easy is it to repeat?"

"Not at all, but I'll do it."

"Are you sure…?"

"Yes. When it happened, I pulled my ship back into the void before deliberately phasing back—without collision—into the cargo bay. I can do it again. And if not, the risk is worth it."

Joplan stared back at the map of the coreworlds. After a while, part of the image would flicker slightly. "We have a target, a location, a pilot…we'll need to train saboteurs for this particular task— soldiers, no particle engineers. How long to make a dropship?"

Kleine considered the process for a moment. "If we take parts from the existing ships…working around-the-clock…we could have an agile, six-seat dropper in a week."

"Get on it."

With a bit of melancholy, Raynor watched as her fighter was butchered in the very same hangar it had been built in three months prior. Time was nothing, if not relative. A team of TDR engineers meticulously measured and cut sections of the custom-forged hull, half of which was already strewn helter-skelter across the floor.

The spare Fentilla was being used as the basis for the new dropship, its fuel tank still full minus a couple of test flights' worth. Expanding the ship to hold six passengers required parts from two of the active fighters, so Raynor's and Waverly's sat with barren sides in the Lunar hangar. It all worked out—only five of the saboteurs would be ready by the end of the week, allowing a second pilot to go as a backup in case something happened to Raynor.

While the dropship was being built, the two pilots practiced their new stunt in Phillips' ship. Large, illuminated buoys were spaced out in the dimensions of the battleship's cargo bay. Raynor and Waverly phased into the top half of the area from different distances, periodically moving the bright barrels elsewhere to repeat the exercise in varying densities.

The amount of concentration it required was exhausting, visualizing additional warpage as her ship plunged into total darkness, maintaining the image with locked eyes while estimating movements by feel. They did hundreds of trials throughout the week, only a few of which included near-misses of the buoy. The dropship was only spaceworthy for the last day and a half, but without a need to land when switching off, the time was productive. Thankfully, the amalgamation of ships handled similarly to the fighters—Raynor had to increase benchmarks for thrust, but that was a minor alteration.

When they finally cycled back through the airlock at Lunar Outpost Cairo, they found the cavernous hangar inside bustling with people. Four transports sat at the end of the depot, bringing in a collection of SDC officers and engineers that Raynor didn't know, along with the infiltration team.

It seemed the Corps was going with the tried and true. Shino stood at the edge of the group, bundled up against the cold.

"That was so cool!" she yelled across the empty walls, bouncing as Raynor left the dropship in the center of the oversized room. "I've seen it on the control module a ton, but it's so different in person, you know?"

"So I'm told," Raynor smiled. "How have you been?"

"I'm..." she pondered her answer for a moment, eventually shrugging. "Surviving, I guess. It'll be nice when all of this is over."

Shino was different. Her personality was the same, but it was muted, tired. Her body reeked of stress and exhaustion, beaten down by the weight of multiple worlds. Maybe they all were, and it was just the most noticeable in Shino. She'd had the most energy to give.

Raynor had also been sent her two rescuees. It was a bit surprising considering their recent desolation, but they were the only living members of the strike team that had captured the carrier. They both appeared healthy enough, Fowler's leg seeming to have fully healed. The Dissenters were joined by a specialist from the SDC, Lewomy, and one of the soldiers from Rhyso's CAF team, Salina.

And Rhyso.

"Nadia," he smiled.

"Eldon…" she said warmly. She was truly glad to see him, to know he was alright, but every bone in her body told her this was a bad idea.

There was an uncomfortable silence, eventually broken by Rhyso.

"I'm sort of an expert on cephrast dimensional engines now," he said. "It's not a skill I expected to have on my dossier."

"And I never expected to be a combat valet, but here we are."

She'd always known his inclusion was a possibility. If he was alive and near Earth, his experience would make him a clear choice.

Still, Raynor wanted to put her foot down and say this would compromise the mission. That wasn't true, though. Raynor was more focused than ever. She could fly the dropship through a molecular repeater tunnel without cracking a panel. Her objection was simply that if the mission succeeded, she and Waverly were the most likely to return. If Rhyso didn't go, then…he'd be here. That was it. There was no conflict of interest. Neither of them was conflicted.

Besides, there wasn't anyone else to go in his stead. During the week, the five soldiers had been learning about the battleship's dimensional drive, including how to locate the appropriate mechanisms if the engine differed from the model scanned by Marker.

"We're all supposed to fit in this?" Lockheart asked, peering inside the dropship. It was longer than the Fentillas, but otherwise similar. Two rows of three seats ran away from the pilot's chair, back-to-back. The hull above the passengers opened up in a similar way to the docking hatch, only longer. It was a tight fit when closed. When Raynor had been riding in the back, the wall of the ship was less than half a meter from her face.

Minimal weapons were installed in the dropship. Most of the space taken up by the missile bays was used to widen the seating area, removing her photon cannons, standard missiles, and most of the prototypes. A single torpedo and a trio of abyssiles remained in the ends of the wings in case she needed to make an opening somewhere, and the bore laser still sat underneath. She wasn't planning on spending much time in real space, but plans didn't mean much.

Overnight, a full-scale evacuation had begun on Callisto and Europa. SDC forces around Jupiter were trying to keep the cephrasts there, both to make sure Raynor's team arrived at Ceres first and to give the civilian transports sufficient headway to Mars.

Early in the morning, they moved the ships up to the garage vessel, the dropship protruding far below the edge of the box-trailer, and set sail for the asteroid belt.

Flying alongside Drone Control in real space managed to be both tedious and relaxing. It took forever to reach the edge of the asteroid belt—a few days—where the two ships finally split apart. Raynor plunged straight in towards Ceres, leaving the vespiary to dip underneath the belt and crawl along the bottom edge. The cephrast armada would most likely head underneath, but there was a chance they'd go through, and Drone Control needed to be able to get within optimal signal range of either location.

Phasing in the asteroid belt wasn't a big issue. Most asteroids were hundreds of thousands of kilometers away from each other. If it wasn't for the distant boulder on the far left of the viewport when

Raynor took over for Waverly, it would've looked like any other part of space.

"Fond memories here?" she asked her copilot, in reference to his record-setting trip.

"I wouldn't call them 'fond,'" the EMS pilot murmured. Fowler stared out the viewport through the empty asteroid field.

"…doesn't seem that difficult to avoid them," he said.

"It's harder at thirty million kilometers per hour."

"*Why?*" exclaimed Fowler. "Why would you do that?"

"Pirates…it's a long story."

It only took a couple of days for the garage vessel to get to the maintenance station up front. The Jovian retreat had unraveled quickly, sending the cephrasts on their way inward from the gas giant. It didn't give Drone Control much wiggle room to get where they needed to be.

The night before they had to depart, the garage vessel touched down on Ceres. When she was little, Raynor was told the dwarf planet had been named after her mother, which she'd believed until an embarrassing age. Being on the large asteroid made her more homesick than she'd expected. For most of her adult life, Raynor knew Ceres—the planet—as everyone else did: notorious for fucking up people's circadian rhythms with its nine-hour days.

The maintenance base was on the light side when they landed. It was more bare-bones than the fueling station on Kallipar had been, allowing human mechanics to periodically check on the equipment and drones, but nothing more. Synthetics did most of the upkeep— the small building was designed for efficiency, not comfort. Raynor and her passengers opted to sleep in the garage vessel instead.

As much as she hated taking drugs to sleep, grogginess was preferable to sleep deprivation, so she caved. When she woke a full Ceres-day later, she was thankful to find their estimated time until engagement hadn't moved up. The cephrasts were angling underneath the ring of giant rocks, and once Marker confirmed the cephrasts couldn't alter course through the belt, the team was lifting off, en route to intercept. Ceres was near the bottom of the asteroid belt, giving Raynor a quick exit from the lower perimeter. It was hard to tell the difference; only a couple of asteroids were visible.

The vespiary was already in place, aiming for a distance three times greater than the estimated blast radius—around 300,000km away. A one-second delay would be burdensome, but if the battleship's engine had more fuel than expected, their buffer room could get narrow—fast. They also needed a cushion for the armada's approach speed. In this instance, moving "towards" the rapidly approaching cephrasts meant gunning for Mars as quickly as possible.

One by one, the crew descended into the dropship, fastening themselves into the confining seats. Raynor detached the patchwork ship from the garage as it continued on its way towards Mars. Phillips quickly fell into view, pacing through the empty stars in wait.

"Drone Control—Lacuna Weaver Prime…we're on our way."

"Right behind you," Shino said in reference to the drones. "We'll give you a long lead until it's time."

Riding the currents of the void was no match for the acceleration of a remote craft. Marker kept the tiny ships far behind, waiting for the dropship to reemerge from the void before rapidly catching up. Raynor phased out and in frequently, constantly altering her void-path to get their speed up. Every few minutes, the same asteroid would briefly materialize thousands of kilometers above them—too far to gauge how large it was. Eventually, the rock moved past her vision, leaving just a starry backdrop whenever she surfaced to tilt the ship into a denser pocket of space.

After a couple of hours of flying in silence, Raynor dove into a current only to find that the void—*her* void—was no longer an absence of light. Tiny, blood-red specks floated in the distance. It wasn't the digital viewport augmenting faint reflections from hers or Phillips' engines—it was a light source.

Cephrast ships. Big ones. Moving through the void as their thrusters flared.

You've gotta be kidding me…

This plan couldn't work in the void. Raynor needed the drone cover.

Shaking her head clear, she quickly breached the dropship. Even more armada vessels sat in the distance along the real plane. Just as far, but much easier to see in the light of the galaxy.

"They're here, Drone Control," she said. "At least half of their fleet is completely phased in."

"I figured—it's happened before," Shino said confidently. "I can lure 'em out. A carrier will go in and bring the others back before we can clutter the space around them."

"Thank a god. Do you need anything from me?"

"What kind of distance do you need to estimate your thing? Is three kilometers too far?"

"That'll be dangerous. Is two enough?"

"We can make that work. It'll cost us more ships, though, so get inside quick."

"That's the plan. See you on the other side."

"Can't wait!"

With alarming speed, the massive drone fleet took off towards the looming armada. The ones closest to Raynor quickly shrank as their thrusters pushed them at breakneck forces, the tiny lights soon becoming a wide, yellow cloud as the drones furthest to the side flew into view.

"Alright, people, this is it," said the woman running the op, Lewomy. "Remember, we're doing the sprint method—should be able to get to the back before we even see one. I'll be leading through the halls, Rhyso's on the engine, Fowler's at the dropper. In and out in three minutes."

Raynor followed lazily behind the drone fog, dipping in periodically to check on the submerged cephrast vessels. Another spot of red light flickered into the void—a carrier. Energy from the orb in its center pulsed in a quick rotation around the ship before blipping out of the darkness, bringing the rest of the armada with it. When the cephrasts had all left the void, the dropship followed suit. The starscape of their native universe erupted in front of them, light danced across the digital viewport in a rainbow of colors, and Nadia Raynor's last battle began.

42

THE BATTLE OF THE BELT

The haze of drones didn't require direct management as they closed the gap to the cephrast fleet. Shino gave Marker more leeway now —sort of a professional courtesy. After working with a few of the SDC synthetics, she genuinely missed him. He still thought like a machine, but a really smart one. With two seconds of delay in this fight, Shino needed the combat AI more than ever.

Unpredictability was her real job. Not as a conscious effort—she didn't *try* to be sporadic. She simply controlled the fleets to the best of her ability, allowing her grey matter to be grey matter. Synthetics lost 20% more drones than a properly-trained human, who, in turn, lost twice as many as Shino. Marker's escapades without human intermediaries had been tragic. The alien computers had no trouble figuring out his routines, even as they changed. Shino didn't like to mention that, though. She thought it might make him feel insecure.

Of course, Marker didn't *really* feel insecure; just like his failures didn't make him afraid—he didn't feel anything.

He also didn't have a gender, but Shino called him a boy because he sort of growled like one at times and often did stupid things like one. Inadvertently, she found herself talking to him the way a person spoke to their dog, even though—

The control module doubled in brightness as half of the invading fleet suddenly appeared among the rest. The first beams from the closest battleships were absorbed by her spearheads. The cephrasts expected it at this point, but they'd have to whittle those ships down either way. Shino methodically worked her fleets into their ideal locations, entrenching them in various sections of space.

Explosions littered the screen as her assault drones were picked off, which was fine. Losing a single ship to eat one of the massive railgun blasts was a worthwhile tradeoff. The cephrasts didn't understand the concept of action economy. In their eyes, they destroyed a ship and lost none—a net gain. They weren't hurting for resources, so as long as they kept their total losses down, they would eventually be victorious. That was a mistake—time was also a resource. Each railgun fired a couple of times per minute, meaning she could remove one from play for fifteen minutes at the cost of thirty poorly-armed ships. Those drones were dead before they launched…waiting to be sacrificed to the laser gods.

Note to self: form a tirino band called "Laser Gods."

During that time, her glass cannons would get the most bang for their buck. Even when Shino wasn't getting the most utility out of every ship, she got the most out of her combined fleet, and the cephrasts did not.

Today, Shino was not responsible for her overall plan. Emilee Hatem did a bunch of calculations for this clash using the units available on Ceres, spread over a four-dimensional battlefield and blah-blah-blah. Shino wasn't stoked about it, but she also didn't want to figure something out on the fly if Emilee had information available beforehand. The "Grand Dan" had been awful on the control module—way too slow—but her long-term strategy was apparently outstanding.

On the left side of Shino's map, the dropship finally popped out of the void. The surrounding alien swarm made a noticeable push towards the Frankenstein ship, giving Shino a much-needed opportunity to cut their ranks down a bit. The vessel vanished quickly, too far from the battleship to eyeball an approach. Shino tried to lure the bulk of the cephrast drones away from the area it would be resurfacing near, keeping a few squadrons between the breach zone and the hull.

Close-range defenses on the battleship immediately started grinding up the nearby drones. With so many battles happening all at once, it was becoming difficult to monitor everything directly. Shino was leaving more on Marker than ever, but it was also the largest collection of armada ships she'd ever seen on her screen. She eventually had to restrict the module to cut out the furthest vessels just so she could work properly. Other modulators were handling those areas, anyway.

A ship popped into view briefly. A bit closer than last time, but not the area Shino was protecting. Two nearby cephrast drones were sucked into the void along with one of Shino's.

"Screw you, Shadow Dillhole," she said to nobody but Marker. "Tell him not to grief my ships."

A yellow symbol appeared at the edge of the display. Shino didn't bother looking—Marker was reminding her that he couldn't talk to the Lacuna Weavers. She knew that. He knew she knew that. He said it anyway. Machines never vented frustration.

The drone hadn't been critical for anything right now, but Phillips didn't know that. There was literally no reason for him to destroy those two cephrast ships. Shino was clearing the breach zone just fine, although the task was being made harder by a small pod of cephrasts taking an exceptionally wide flank. Phillips should go and blow those up. Shino had to allocate ships to stop them from getting all the way around, taking them away from Raynor's protection.

About two kilometers away from the target vessel, a wavy, semi-transparent fighter began phasing out of the void. Before the ship had fully entered their dimension, the battleship's automated defenses were locked onto it. Dozens of Shino's drones were incinerated by thin, yellow lasers pattering across the sky. The area was full of enemies, making short work of the SDC drone squadrons. A pale beam of light ran up the wing of the fighter, slicing it off. The cockpit exploded out into space, dispersing Ron Phillips across the dimensions.

"Oh my god!" Shino cried, reflexively pulling her hands out of the control module towards her face. Cursing at herself, she immediately thrust them back into the holographic images. The dropship was about to emerge into the middle of a cephrast swarm without an entourage. Shino prayed that Raynor saw the fighter get destroyed and stayed in.

Keeping pressure on the battleship's turrets, Shino sent her fleets in, losing them at an even faster rate. There was no sense trying to lure them elsewhere now…they weren't going to fall for it. She tried to keep the cephrasts within two kilometers of the battleship's side, the area lighting up as ships with full ammo reserves exploded in rapid succession.

At this rate, she'd need those ships currently covering the wide flank. It would allow the cephrast pod to possibly hit Raynor from behind, but at this point, the armada vessel was a bigger problem.

With a flicker, the dropship appeared a couple of kilometers down the hull from where Phillips died. The battleship unloaded every weapon on its frame at the piloted craft, destroying several of its own ships in the process as the cephrast drones collapsed on the location. It was the perfect time to pull that flank in.

Their enemies agreed.

The small group of alien ships took off at lightning speed, heading straight towards the opposite side of the dropship.

"Flank!" Shino called to Marker. Her hand raked through the air in front of her, shifting the control module's opacity to the area closest. The combat AI had already sent her ships in pursuit, pushing the tiny vessels to close the gap. Shino searched desperately for available drones to cover Raynor's back. There was nothing—any ships able to get to that side were protecting her from the cloud of ships in front of her.

Retreating from the thick swarm of hostiles, the dropship disappeared. Shino didn't know if Raynor was attempting to get inside or simply luring the drones away, and she didn't have to wonder long. Seconds after the dropship vanished, the battleship's hull warped to the side, specks of light sparkling through the once-opaque surface.

Their alien adversaries might not know exactly what Raynor was doing, but they didn't want her getting a fresh supply of support drones for it. The small pod darting towards Raynor's flank retreated back once the dropship disappeared. They assumed Shino was strictly following in pursuit. It was a nice try, but she wanted those ships in either way, and attempting to pull them away had only given her room to cover the breach zone. Nadia might even get a second attempt before the flank circled back.

Before the dropship resurfaced, Shino's offshoot squadron turned back to pursue the small cephrast pod on its own. A teal indicator flickered up in the corner of her display.

This is why you can't use a machine to do a woman's job.

She was about to scream at him—it was such a noob mistake. He never understood psychological aspects of a match, and it might prevent her from covering Raynor. That flank would've scrambled back once they realized she wasn't going to play with them.

Only they hadn't. They didn't circle around anywhere. They didn't even engage once Marker had pursued them. Pulling the ships away wasn't an act. Attacking Raynor...that had been the fake.

The small pod of ships was thirty seconds from firing range of Drone Control. No outposts in front of them...no fleet to intercept.

No, no, no, no...

Marker barked at her.

"I know..." The words barely came out. The AI continued pursuing the attacking squadron. Maybe his calculations had determined it was possible to stop them, but it didn't matter. Raynor might have to phase out at any second.

"We have incoming!" she called through the dim vespiary. "I have to cover the dropship!" One of the other modulators was already bringing their ships back from one of the carriers, but even from the corner of her eye, Shino could tell they wouldn't make it, nor would they be able to get to the breach zone before the dropship reappeared.

"*Let go!*" she yelled, fighting Marker over control of the offshoot. This had always been a possibility, and it was one they prepared for. Marker could control the fleet from Ceres. There was a multi-minute delay, so he couldn't actively respond to issues, but he could maintain the drone subroutines. Once Raynor got in, he just had to stall—pester the armada to make phasing unsafe.

The dropship appeared right next to the battleship. Heavy fire came in from the exterior cannons—Shino barely had enough drones to surround the bobbing vessel for the moment it existed in their plane. She frantically moved squadrons around, placing them to guard the dropship on a possible third attempt. If Raynor had to breach again, her odds weren't good.

The cephrast vessel dipped into the void again.

At least Shino had made the right choice. She would never know if the dropship made it inside. She'd never know if the strike team destroys the expansive fleet underneath the asteroid belt, and she'd never know if humanity wins the war.

All she knew was that if they did, she had played a part.

"Marker…listen," she said, her breath jagged. "If Nadia's not out when…when you get this on Ceres, upload the retreat routines…cycle squadrons twenty through…thirty-six—in pairs. And…and recharge the survivors fast…just ignore—"

Vibrations echoed through the vespiary as defensive turrets started plucking away at the cephrast drones. The weapons were designed with the intention of having an outpost or weapon battery nearby. They couldn't fend off a full assault by themselves, just as their hull couldn't withstand the punishment of the alien weaponry.

Deafening rumbles broke through the hull as the air inside the vessel met the destruction outside, and the only modulators not dragged into space had their bodies caught in the jagged metal of the damaged exterior.

Raynor didn't know how close she was to the behemoth vessel. The cephrasts probably knew she was nearby, but she didn't want to give her approach away before it was time. For all they knew, she was heading elsewhere along the armada.

Phillips periodically plunged past her along the dimensional axis. It was a bit dangerous, but it gave her a concrete orientation to the battle outside, as did the shotgun blasts of drone parts soaring through the empty space around them.

"—side about three kilometers or so," Phillips' voice crackled in as he fell into formation in front of her. She followed the Fentilla for half a minute towards what she hoped was the edge of the battleship. When he finally phased out, Raynor joined shortly behind him. As the cloudy form of the battleship's expansive hull began to materialize in front of her, a pale, custard beam flashed right by the dropship. Jagged pieces of glass and melted metal translucently littered the space in front of her, along with the faint, red mist of her escort.

"Fuck!" Raynor cried, pulling the dropship viciously back into the unknown dimension. She couldn't take any time to mourn the airman's death. She'd seen enough of their surroundings to know that he'd guided her to the edge of the battleship—and it was covered with drones.

Dragging the cumbersome ship further down the battleship's hull, she emerged again—half a kilometer past the edge of the cargo bay, but at least she knew where they were. Cephrast drones converged towards her as a beam of bright, green light melted a group of nearby SDC ships. It was difficult to see much else through the sea of automated vessels. She couldn't get a good view of the dimensional starscape before pushing the ship fully into the void.

What she needed was a distraction—one *she* was aware of—to clear out the ships near the cargo bay. She also needed to get a better idea of how unevenly the space between them was shifting.

Maybe she could do both at the same time.

With a couple of switches, Raynor primed her lone chasm-crosser and let it loose. The torpedo sailed through the void with no visible target, slowly fading out into the universe. She watched intently as the distorted trail of smoke warped through changes in density. It didn't give her as much information as she'd hoped. Not enough to pilot blindly through.

The inter-dimensional explosive would hit the battleship even without a visual lock. It was there. Raynor's hope was for the sudden impact to pull most of the cephrasts to the area, giving her room near the cargo bay to peek out.

With a flurry of ships nearby, Raynor didn't expect to see the faint outline of the battleship dip into the void after them.

Not after *them*—after the torpedo. Gasps came from behind her as the battleship sank towards them. Raynor didn't know how the windowless armada ship could have seen the faint projectile. Maybe one of the drones had. The mammoth vessel warped to and fro as it journeyed down the fourth dimension to destroy the torpedo. For a brief moment, Raynor wondered if that was enough information for her to navigate, but it would be an unbelievable risk. She didn't know how deep they were. That distortion could be an extra hundred meters, it could be a kilometer.

Moving back towards her original breach, Raynor came out just far enough to get a reference point of the battleship. Not only was she outside of the cargo bay, but she was close. She dove the drop-ship back in slowly, taking in every bend of the alien vessel's hull. She didn't blink, move her eyes...even shift their focal point. The image of the ship, every degree of dissonant space, remained still in her mind.

Thrusters on, she visualized the exterior as it moved closer. One hundred meters...two hundred plus an extra twenty or so...

Giving herself as much wiggle room as possible in the imaginary cargo bay, she pulled the dropship slightly out of the void. There wasn't much benefit to peeking—even a slight intersection would kill them all, but if they were still outside, they might not get instantly obliterated.

An expansive hull, a mechanical arm, giant spool-looking crates…

They were inside. But it wasn't that easy. During the time she paused, the battleship continued to materialize, moving further into the void from their native universe.

They're trying to ram us…

It wasn't the worst idea. If the cephrasts could hit the dropship with the interior of the battleship, their crew would be fine. If the dropship was already occupying the same plane, though…the battleship's hull *should* protect them. It would just be a ding. The far wall was moving towards them quickly and a piece of overhanging machinery sat a couple of meters away, but at this very moment, they were fine.

Raynor pulled the dropship roughly out of the void, killing the dimensional thruster as soon as her surroundings came fully into view.

The dropship was piggybacking inside the battleship. However deep it went, they went with it.

"We're in!" Waverly exhaled.

A dozen cephrasts in the cargo bay scrambled at the sudden materialization of a human ship. Raynor turned the bore laser down to its lowest power, severing through the aliens as it melted thin lines across the floor. It could buy them an extra minute before more creatures stormed the cargo bay.

Raynor had no visibility below them, making the dropship terrible for dropping down. A hull crack would prevent them from leaving, so she took their descent slowly.

Clang!

Shit…

The hollow, gong-like sound echoed from the right wing of the craft. The dropship tilted to the side as it lowered, resting at a steep angle.

Damaged or not, they were inside.

43

SABOTAGE

The harness straps cut into Fowler's arms as his weight pulled against them. He, Lockheart, and Waverly were all facing down in the tilted dropship, the other three lying on their backs above them. Getting out would be problematic. At the best of times, the makeshift vessel was cramped and claustrophobic.

"We've got company outside," Raynor said.

"Open it up," grunted Lewomy, the ops lead. She pulled her seat harness off, her rifle clanking against the ship's roof as she withdrew it. "Weapons hot."

Releasing his own straps, Fowler dropped against the side of the ship. He planted his feet against the angled wall to prop himself up towards the open cabin, raising his weapon over the edge and firing blindly down the cargo bay. One at a time, the top half of their team climbed out of the slanted dropship, lurching it slightly as they jumped over to a cylindrical crate. By the time all five were on the ground, the cephrasts in the long room had all been eliminated.

"Let's move. You three—" Lewomy gestured to Fowler and the two pilots. "Fix this."

"This" was the ship. It looked stuck. The right wing was propped up by the crate they first jumped over to; the left was caught underneath the lip of another. The team wasn't stalling for anything, so if it wasn't un-lodged in a few minutes, they'd all be sticking around until the end.

Within seconds, the other four had left the cargo bay, dead-sprinting down the hall towards the engine room. In most cases, Fowler would be irritated by getting left with the ship, but he'd already charged blindly into a cephrast vessel.

Twice.

Waverly carefully dropped down from the open cabin to help assess the damage.

On the far side of the bay, bright patterns began skipping past some kind of mounted forklift—cephrast chatter. Fowler darted underneath the hoisted wing and dropped to his knee, ready to pick at their attackers when the high-pitched whir of the bore laser pierced through the soggy air. The dropship might have been at an angle, but it was facing the far wall. Raynor sliced through their foes quickly, setting fire to the crates around them.

"Turn one," Lewomy said through the radio, marking their first of four turns from the cargo bay to the engine room.

The first hallway led into the cargo bay behind the dropship. The area in front of it looked large enough for the ship to land in, so Fowler started clearing objects out of the way. The smaller, four-foot containers were deceptively heavy. He planted his shiny new bionic leg into the ground, pushing into the crate with some success before a sharp pain shot through his hip. Vivid memories of Kranden Rovasatti's bionic arm hanging loose on the tendons flashed through Fowler's mind—he'd wait for Waverly to finish up.

"No major cracks I can see," the pilot said, staring closely at the pinned wing. He stepped back and began explaining to Raynor how the ship was stuck, like he was helping her parallel park. "It looks like it slid under the lip once you got knocked over."

"The top or bottom?"

"The bottom is underneath, the top is above—you can probably slip right with a slight roll to the left and get out."

"How much roll?"

"I don't know…twelve degrees?"

"Turn two," said Lewomy. Raynor finally stood up out of the angled hatch to look for herself.

"Shit, how did that even happen?" She leaned over the side, looking at the pinned wing. "Okay, I can get—*ah!*"

A laser struck the back of her shoulder, burning through the armor plate. Fowler ran back to the ship, firing underneath at a pair of cephrasts across from the fires. His first salvo sheared through the side of one, causing the other to duck behind an adjacent object made out of wood-looking material. Whatever it was, it wasn't heat-resistant. Fowler singed a large hole straight through the box, continuing to the alien behind it.

"Patch yourself, now!" he shouted. "And hypo!"

Their armor had an added lining to kill the aggressive bacterium living in the atmosphere. It wasn't a guarantee, and it wouldn't work for long—extended exposure and large openings were still hopeless. For the other hostile bacteria, they had cocktails of good old-fashioned antibiotics in pressurized hypodermic needles, the base of which coated the injection site in a sealing putty.

"Ugh, done," Raynor groaned from inside the cockpit. "I can get the ship out."

"Turn three," Lewomy said, huffing as they ran.

The hatch closed around Raynor, and the engines fired up. The dropship picked itself up sideways, like a magnetic crane had effortlessly removed it from its wonky resting place. Raynor eased it backwards to the clearing, the high-pitched siren of the laser informing Fowler that she'd spotted more foes from her elevated position. Hovering over the clearing for a moment, Raynor gently set the ship down with room to spare.

"You need to fly," she told Waverly as she climbed out of the dropship. The medivac pilot responded only by jumping into the cockpit and snapping the harness on.

"You feeling okay?" Fowler asked.

"For now, yeah, but the last thing you need is for me to die behind the stick." She reached over the edge of the cabin to grab a rifle, giving Waverly instructions for covering the far side of the hangar. The sound of her voice was drowned out by Lewomy.

"We're pinned down! Taking casualties! We need backup to get into the engine room!"

Fowler nearly ate the ground from the momentum of his new leg as he tore down the hall. The uneven strides took some getting used to, his boot steps alternating like a heartbeat on the metal floor.

"On my way," said Fowler. "Almost at turn one."

"We're past three—hostiles in between."

Oxygen hissed through Fowler's helmet as his lungs took in more of it. He rounded the second turn faster than he'd run even in his twenties, slamming into the opposite wall and resuming the sprint. Faint energy *thwaps* started to make their way through the air-tight environmental suit, with occasional, inverted *zaps* sprinkled among them. Fowler regretted throwing his death ray on the ground. For all he knew it recharged itself, and it probably wound up in a CAF dumpster.

He sidled up to the edge of the third turn, leaning around the corner with his rifle ready. The team wasn't just past the third turn, they were *at* the fourth turn—the door to the engine room. Three of them were tucked behind the corner towards the door, the fourth a deflated suit in a puddle. A group of cephrasts in full armor had set up barriers in the hall behind them.

With their focus on the doorway, the aliens hadn't seen Fowler peek around the turn. They knelt behind the energy barriers, suitably protecting them from the strike team but leaving them unobstructed to Fowler. He ducked back around the corner to prime a grenade, only to find something else on top of him already.

"Jesus!" He jumped at the sight of Raynor, leaning against the wall beside him. "Get back to the ship."

"No," she said bluntly. "I outrank you." Fowler didn't know if that was true in the SDC, but he wasn't about to argue it. It worried him to leave their only non-combat veteran alone in the cargo bay, but if they couldn't rig the engine soon, they wouldn't be escaping at all.

He twisted the top of the explosive, letting it cook in his hand for a second before rolling it down the hall towards the entrenched aliens.

"Grenade out!"

Seconds later, a whooshing sound pre-empted the buzzing explosion as pure force erupted through the hallway. Before the flung items could clamor against the ground, Fowler was around the corner, firing at the only alien still moving, its armor taking at least half a dozen shots before one burned through. Rhyso, Lockheart, and Lewomy careened down the hall, stepping around Salina's remains.

Lockheart waved them back down the corridor, sliding past one of the cephrast barriers and pulling it upright. Door fragments launched from around turn four, bouncing along the sides of the hallway while a thick cloud of smoke billowed from the indented doorway.

The engine room was a hexagonal cylinder spanning three floors upward. A large, humming pillar radiated heat in the center, six circular workstations surrounding it, and an assortment of panels, display screens, and fluid tanks lined the edge of the room. Spreading through the area, the four remaining soldiers looked for the components they'd been trained to identify.

This particular engine was organized differently from the one Marker had scanned, which complicated things in a room full of identical switches, dials, and levers. Guiding his efforts by item type and location, Fowler worked through what he'd learned about the system, tracing components back from the engine. Most of them were redundant in some way, which TDR believed to be a consequence of having part of a dimensional drive inside the hull. The team was looking to mess with two specific parts, being dubbed the "overflow valve" and "emergency regulator." Loosening the valve would slowly flood the primary engine with dimenton fuel, eventually flowing back into the secondary tank. Breaking the regulator then allowed the walls of the primary engine to erode and rupture in that state.

In theory, they said.

Then there was all of the vandalism—severing connections to the components to prevent some sort of remote shutdown, fusing pieces together. It would take a few minutes for the engine to flood enough to backflow, which gave the strike team a window to escape. If they could get to a certain depth of the void, the blast wouldn't be strong enough to damage the dropship's exterior.

No one knew how far that would be.

"Found 'em," Rhyso said, crouching beside a panel on the back side of the column. "The regulator's on the main engine." He pulled out a charge about the size of a cell phone. It only contained a gram of explosives, but was packed with a dozen booby traps and countless decoys to prevent it from being defused or removed.

Blasts of energy weapons erupted from beyond the doorway as more of the four-armed creatures approached. Fowler fired back from behind the column. He wasn't sure exactly how safe that was.

"You got this?" he asked Rhyso, who repeatedly cranked the overflow valve to the side as it returned to a safe level.

"Yes," the Centauri man said calmly. He removed a thin cable from one of his outer pouches, tying the valve handle to a pipe below it. An error message started flashing on a nearby display. Rhyso grinned like a delinquent child admiring his own graffiti. "Sabotage is my specialty."

Fowler left Rhyso to his work as the operative lit a welding torch. A new pile of cephrast bodies lay strewn across the floor around Salina's puddle. Based on the amount of fire coming at Lewomy on the other side of the doorway, there were more than a few creatures around the corner.

"Do we have a line out of here?" Rhyso called from behind the pillar.

"No!" Lockheart yelled over the sound of her rifle as she leaned around the destroyed frame. The Centauri saboteur joined them at the door, smashing the error display along the way.

"Time to make one. We have six minutes."

Raynor fired more rounds over the last minute than she had in the previous nine thousand years combined. It was mostly suppressing fire—keeping the aliens at a distance while the strike team mucked everything up. Their chances of escape were looking worse every minute. Cephrasts had closed in behind them; better geared than the ones on the starfish had been.

When the timer was set on the explosives, another wind coursed through Raynor's veins. Two grenades were lobbed around the jagged edge of the door, clearing a way down the hall to the next turn.

"Waverly, how are you doing?" Lewomy asked as they ran.

"It's getting crowded—" the evac pilot said. There was a long pause, followed by some grunts. "There are some behind the ship. You'll hit them on the way back."

"Get prepped…we're two minutes out."

They dashed through the third turn, then the second, checking every intersection as they ran by. A few cephrasts were found down the side halls, but only one had even tried firing at them. As they approached the first turn, a bizarre, red blob formed on the opposite wall.

Not an actual blob, but something from her helmet's display. The blob hadn't even moved before Fowler turned it into a purple splatter on the wall. It was a nice upgrade—and fortunate. Raynor hadn't even thought about looking for camouflaged enemies.

At the front of the pack, Lewomy rounded the first corner, diving back behind the wall as soon as she did. A spray of turquoise and yellow blasts covered the adjacent wall with burns and melted indentations.

"Damn," she groaned, jumping to her feet and removing the last grenade from her belt. "They're setting up a mobile ordnance for the dropship. Maybe two dozen at the far end."

Running down the exposed, hundred-meter corridor with their guns alight wasn't likely to work. Lewomy would need one hell of a throw to get the closest few, but it was better than nothing. They were running out of both time and options. The squad leader leaned up to the edge of the corner, chucking the metal tube as hard as she could.

A low buzzing sound, rapidly increasing over half a second, echoed through the hall.

Bzwip—Lewomy's suit collapsed to the ground, her body coating the floor just around the corner. A sharp *clang* followed shortly after as the explosive hit the ground in front of them.

"Grenade!" Raynor called out, turning to run back down the hall. There was nothing to take cover behind, no nearby corners. Fowler took a glance down the same vacant corridor, spinning back towards the heated grenade. A line of blended human remains flicked up from his boot as he kicked the object past the corner, but it had already been ticking for a few seconds—too long to get enough distance on it. Before Fowler's boot was back on the ground, the droning boom sent him back in a confetti of suit scraps and blood.

Raynor still didn't know if the antibacterial lining in her suit would hold up against the coin-sized tear she'd gotten, but the damage to Fowler's wasn't even in the realm of tears. It was gone— the boot, too. His leg was still there, completely exposed and charred…

No, not charred—it was metal. Lockheart wasn't cutting circulation,; she was helping him check the seal. The field surgeon pulled him up, his back slick with Lewomy's blood.

"Shit—" she said. "Are you alright?"

"I think so. It looks like the seal held."

"Does it still work?"

He put some weight on the bionic, which seemed to hold fine. "Yeah…what's our time?"

"Four minutes left," said Rhyso, peeking around the corner. He pulled his head back quickly, followed by energy blasts from the entrenched aliens. He fired a few shots around the corner, slamming his helmet back against the wall in frustration. "There's a lot of them. I see another hallway about twenty meters down on the other side."

"We can grenade the closest ones and storm the cover—make our shots count," Lockheart said, watching the corridor behind them. "We're about to get folded in."

Careful not to expose more than a hand, Rhyso and Lockheart each chucked one of the handheld explosives around the corner. It wasn't an ideal way to get distance, but it worked well enough. Low, unnerving crackles of cephrast voices quavered through the heavy atmosphere in response to the explosives bouncing towards them.

They'd taken too long. Shots came from halfway down the corridor behind them as two more aliens appeared from a corner. There was nowhere for the four humans to take cover. Salvos from the alien weapons flew down the aisle, striking Lockheart in the back and sending her to the ground. Raynor dropped to her knee, returning fire as buzzing explosions came from the next hallway.

It wasn't long before she and Fowler connected photon rounds to their alien targets. A growl-like scream came from Lockheart as Rhyso slapped one of her bandages over the charred wound, covering it further with a piece of suit-tape. She exhaled through gritted teeth as the Centauri soldier hoisted her up, not appearing to be slowed down by the wound.

The four immediately charged into the next corridor. Their barrage had killed ten of the nearest cephrasts. The others were either assembling the stationary cannon near the cargo bay or scrambling towards it. The strike team ran to the next area of cover, unloading their rifles the entire way. Raynor estimated another four or five creatures were dead before she arrived in the next hallway, still at least sixty meters from the bay.

The offshoot was empty—probably the path these cephrasts came from before digging their X-shaped feet into the ground. Raynor scanned the hall for shadows or movement, unsure of how accurate the helmet's camouflage search was.

Another scream pulled her attention to the main hallway as Lockheart lunged behind the wall. No more than two meters from their cove, Rhyso hit the ground, blood pouring from his shoulder where his arm once was.

"Grab him!" Lockheart said, firing around the corner from the ground. Fowler and Raynor grabbed handfuls of Rhyso's suit and pulled him into the annex, a dark streak coating the floor behind him. They propped the Centauri native against the wall; most of the color had already faded from his face.

"Eldon, no..." Raynor said weakly as she tied a compression band around his arm. Lockheart pressed a small, rectangular plate onto the wound to cauterize it before covering it with one of the air-tight bandages. The strip wasn't big enough, requiring two more to make a seal. Raynor pressed one of the antibiotic hypos into his shoulder, but it wouldn't be enough. The opening was too large and exposed for too long. Even without the flesh-eating bacterium, he wouldn't be able to run.

"This is where you promise to save me..." he rasped, his eyes closed.

"Eldon...we both know—"

"I know..." he coughed. "But you promise...and I refuse... s'how this works."

She smiled, tears welling up in her eyes. "You're going to be fine. We're getting you out of here."

His head rolled back and forth. "You go on...without..."

Raynor's stomach turned inside out. She was never supposed to see this. Her job was to be in the ship, knowing Rhyso might not make it back. She wasn't supposed to be here when it happened. She couldn't handle it, and she hated herself for being selfish.

Fowler moved back from the corner, switching with Lockheart to cycle a fresh energy cell. Raynor could hear him, worlds away, telling her they were throwing their last grenades and pushing to the dropship. She nodded, not looking away from Rhyso as he wheezed, either from toxins, blood loss, or both.

"I love you so much," she said in Reza. She wanted to hold him, kiss him, feel his skin again—all she could do was touch her visor to his, trying to push her face through the hard plastic.

Rhyso's mouth formed the same words in Martian. No sound came from his lips, just white foam slowly seeping down his chin.

An explosion jolted her back to reality—Fowler's grenade going off amidst the crackles of murmuring cephrasts. The two Dissenters switched places again, Lockheart ready with her primed device. Cannon fire echoed from the cargo bay.

"The ordnance is up!" Waverly called into the radio.

"Got it. We're going on Lockheart," Fowler said. Again, Raynor only nodded. She was furious. Not just at the cephrasts, but with herself, with Rhyso...which, in turn, only made her more angry with herself. Fowler knelt beside Rhyso's body, taking a spare ammo cell from his armor. "Sorry, LT."

As soon as the force of the second grenade pulsed down the hallway, they exited the branching corridor. A handful of enemies remained by the entrance to the cargo bay, the walls of which flashed in the light of the dropship's bore laser.

The cephrasts in the hallway fell in rapid succession to the pinpoint accuracy of humanity's best. Raynor squeezed the trigger as hard as she could, as if her targets could somehow be hurt more as a result. They cleared the last two enemies in the corridor—the one on the cannon and another trying to protect it.

"Corners," said Fowler.

"Yup," said Lockheart as she rapidly swapped ammo cells. Keeping pace, they approached the wide opening, aiming at opposite sides of the hall until they reached the doorway. In unison, they fired around the corners, along the wall of the cargo bay, to dispatch the aliens they believed to be there.

The cargo bay was already close to being clear. A couple were pinned down by the dropship's weaponry at the far end of the dock. Everything behind the dropship had just been removed.

"We're here, open up!" Fowler said.

The two Dissenters fired underneath the wings at the slightest signs of movement. Off to the side of the ship, a cephrast had climbed up one of the crates. Raynor shot the four-armed creature off as soon as it stood up. The alien hit the ground in front of her, so she shot it again to make sure it was dead.

Then, again, to make herself feel better.

It didn't.

The hatch to the cabin slid open, and the three survivors climbed in. Severed body parts cluttered the other side of the cargo bay, surrounded by a dense, interwoven pattern of lightly-melted metal.

"That's it, let's go!" Fowler said, scrambling to buckle himself in.

None of them had a timer for the bomb, but it had to be less than a minute. The "shallow" explosion was an estimation at best—measurement of void depth was still a mystery. It was entirely possible the dropship couldn't get far enough in to be safe.

Lifting off to get clear of nearby crates, Waverly plummeted the dropship into darkness. The artificial gravity of the battleship faded away, leaving them weightless in their seats.

The ship was intact—no major damage from the cannon.

Raynor could feel the bubbly vibrations of the dimensional engine roaring under their feet, taking them as far into the void as they could go. The traditional engine pulled their harnesses firmly against their sides. They'd never be able to get far enough in three-dimensional space to escape the blast radius, but it could always be the tipping point for whatever force reaches their void-depth.

Fowler looked through the viewport—as if he expected to see anything other than nothingness.

"Are we…clear?"

"No idea," Waverly said. "If we are, we might not know when it happens."

"Just keep diving," Raynor said, though it gave her new concerns about fuel consumption. She didn't know if going further into the void consumed more fuel, and they'd never properly tested the auto-breach. With no way to measure their depth, the device couldn't know how much fuel to keep in reserve if that were the case. They should probably level out in a few minutes, just to be safe. The explosion will have to have happened by that point.

Then it happened.

It was the same feeling she experienced standing next to a phasing ship—a wind of gravity blowing through her. This was heavier…*a lot* heavier. An unsettling tinge of nerves ran through her body—like her organs were being sucked out. Everything in a 100,000km radius was being forced into the void at chaotic degrees. One might argue that the entire sphere of space encompassed by the explosion had ceased to exist.

Or not—she wasn't a physicist, she just needed to focus on something. Anything to distract her from the unbearably specific feeling that her intestines were being pushed into the void faster than she was.

Sections of the battleship's hull appeared quickly in front of them, disappearing just as rapidly. The digital viewport outlined chunks of metal as they sailed past the dropship through the void, warping one way as they materialized and another as they vanished. Significantly more debris fell into view behind them— roughly a battleship's worth. Off to the sides, clusters of debris stampeded in and out from the other ships.

It worked…

Waverly kept gunning the ship in, trying to outrun the large plates phasing by them.

After a minute or so, the debris lightened up. Less floated by. Eventually, Waverly pushed his face up to the viewport as a large section of hull phased slowly into view.

"Wait a second…we've seen that piece already."

"We must have finally sped past it," Raynor said, though it was purely speculation. For all they knew, objects came to rest along the fourth dimension.

The evac pilot stopped their plummet, sailing straight ahead at their current depth—certainly deeper than any human had traveled into the dimensional abyss. They flew quietly for half an hour. Waverly didn't ask what happened to the others, and no one felt like catching him up right now. Raynor certainly didn't. He'd probably heard bits and pieces over the radio between the screech of the bore laser.

When it came time to check their location, he broke the silence.

"Heading out," he said dryly, pulling the ship out of the void as fast as it could go. The engine gurgled as their vessel ascended along the axis, breaching five minutes later into a sea of warping stars. The faint blue of distant galaxies and nebulae was a breathtaking contrast to nothing. "We made it!" he gasped. "I don't believe it…"

The three passengers didn't celebrate or respond, sitting in a daze.

"I'm going to vent the atmo out," Waverly said, opening the hatch above him to siphon out the toxic atmosphere in the dropship. The interior wouldn't be fully safe until it was decontaminated, but dumping the swampy gas was still a good idea.

Waverly held the dropship's manual transmitter up to his faceplate. "Drone Control—Lacuna Weaver Five. Do you have our location?"

No response…no static. He repositioned the transmitter, pressing it against a different location on his visor.

"Drone Control, this is the dropship. Do you read?"

Fowler and Lockheart looked at each other with concern. Raynor's gaze didn't leave the wall half a meter in front of her.

"Ron? Are you there?"

"He's dead," Raynor said apathetically.

"He was hit during the approach," Fowler added more solemnly. Waverly took a deep breath, yelling into the communicator.

"Drone Control! This is Lacuna. Weaver. Five! *Please*...respond!"
Nothing.

He dropped the handset and fell back against his seat. A heavy, stuttering breath entered his lungs before he picked the transmitter back up. His voice was lower, monotone—as emotionless as hers.

"Marker, this is Lacuna Weaver Five. What—um...what is the status of Drone Control? And the garage?"

Defeated, he tossed the communicator onto the console. It would be at least ten minutes before they got a response from the relay bank on Ceres. Waverly rolled his head back against the seat, staring up through the viewport. A massive, grey boulder soared far above the dropship at the bottom of the asteroid belt.

"I hate this place."

44

AFTERMATH

The response from Marker had been characteristically brief, informing them only that Drone Control and the garage vessel were gone. In the spirit of human defiance, they stopped at the wreckage, anyway. The detour added an extra day and a half, catching up to the vespiary as it careened away from Ceres, but they felt obligated to check.

With no food, water, or room, Raynor and Waverly took as much advantage of the void as possible, becoming quite adept at switching seats in the confined cabin. Upon arriving at the site, it was clear no one had made it. The ship was torn to shreds, half of the interior visible from the outside. Lockheart boarded for about ten minutes to search the derelict vespiary, looking to see if anyone had sealed themselves away. Fowler went with her, coming back to the dropship almost immediately without explanation.

The trailer was in similar shape, though slightly more intact from the dense plating. They salvaged some food, water, and spare oxygen tanks from the storage cabinets. The food and water were frozen solid, but they couldn't take their suits off, anyway. What they really needed was the air. Getting to Mars would take an additional three or four days, and they'd likely be in their suits the whole way. The dropship's life support should be sufficient to get from Ceres to Mars. Raynor suggested they open the hatch, exposing the cabin to the frozen vacuum of space for a few hours to kill off the bacteria. Then they could empty the oxygen tanks into the ship as needed and fire up the support systems.

Fowler refused—something about bears swimming in space.

When they arrived at the maintenance station, they found it vacant, its contents already moved off-planet. Having deemed Marker's communication unsatisfactory, Nezz left a message for the surviving strike team on Ceres. With a twenty-minute delay each way, the assistant AI tried to answer every question they might have.

The explosion they'd created was larger than predicted, with a blast radius of 190,000km—more than enough to destroy the second fleet. As an added bonus, corrosion of the other armada ships had fostered their own detonations—smaller, but with much more void-directed force. Ninety percent of Mars' defenses were sent to Earth —anything that wasn't attached directly to the planet or in its orbit. With no reinforcements, the lone invading force was stuck between the fleets of both inner coreworlds, and the battle predictions were already looking positive.

"As you may have noticed, all of the resources from Ceres were pulled back to Mars," explained the AI. "No human personnel have been on site for weeks, so the evacuation shuttles had their living quarters filled with resupply munitions, allowing us to leave the last transport completely empty. You can secure the dropship in the cargo hold, and the transport will bring you back to Mars."

Two days of being cramped in the dropship had left the quartet in no hurry to get moving. None of them felt the same eagerness to jump into battle as they had in the past. They took time to stretch their legs around the empty supply station for the rest of the day. Rations had already been stocked for them on the transport, which the four soldiers scarfed a day's worth of as soon as they found it. No humans had been on Ceres during the evacuation, which meant all of the supplies had been moved by an AI's appendages. Raynor enjoyed the image of little robots removing the cargo from this ship, placing it throughout the bedrooms of the other ships, then making sure there was human food in this one. It was cute.

Until she realized that the machine had loaded exactly five days of food for four sedentary people. That was less cute. Thankfully, their frozen food would thaw by then, so they were still without rush.

Desperate to move around, they performed a sweep of the munitions depot to look for anything left behind. The base was barren—no machine would forget something—but it was an excuse to stay on the large asteroid for one of its short days.

Sealing the cargo hold off from the rest of the transport, Raynor loaded the contaminated dropship and set their course for Mars using a real auto-nav. She struggled to remember the last time she flew somewhere without piloting at least part of the voyage—her first trip to Luna, three-and-a-half months ago.

The events below the asteroid belt quickly faded into a nightmare. Broadcasts were received mid-flight in the large vessel—a luxury Raynor had all but forgotten was possible. Videos of the terrestrial night skies showed collages of fireworks created by detonating defense platforms and carriers. Earth's orbital waste management was working overtime to prevent debris from landing on the surface.

For the first time since the war began, humanity had more firepower than their alien invaders. The remaining cephrast forces were consistently engaged in orbital battles, giving the SDC breathing room to re-arm defense stations and artillery satellites, further shifting the balance in their favor.

After five days of slow, real-space travel, the shuttle was met with exuberant praise on Mars. To the inner planets, their mission had been a fantastic success—almost overwhelmingly so. People cried. Complete strangers hugged Raynor; a newborn was named after her. There was no confusion…the mission *had* been a success.

It just didn't feel like one to Raynor. The cost had been high. Not just the man she loved, but her best friend, too.

Her best friend…Shino had predicted that one day they'd met.

Three of the four vacant stowaways were sent straight to a hospital. If the minor tears they'd experienced hadn't killed them after a week, they were probably fine, but the Solar System's primary health organization wanted to run some tests and monitor them. Before they were discharged, the cephrast armada got down to a few dozen ships, phasing out during a light break in combat without returning. Telemetry suggested that a couple of the hulking vessels might have been intersected by drones as they phased, but no one would be able to go in and look for a while.

The Eradication War, the Extermination War, the Alien War, the Great Defense, the Cephrast Invasion, or simply the Invasion—whatever name you used, on March 25th, 12600, it ended.

Nadia Raynor had flown an alien ship into combat. She was the first person to remove herself from existence in a human-made dimensional drive. There *were* statues of her on Mars.

But *this*—this terrified her.

For the past three years, Raynor had been living on Mars. In the spring following their victory—12061—evacuation shuttles from Centauri started arriving at the edge of Sol. Plans were in progress to return people to their neighboring system, but astronomers were still searching the skies for evidence of their retreating foes. Until they were located, no civilian ships were heading across the dark expanse without a sizable armada to protect them. A lot of the refugees were opting to stay in Sol. Europa and Callisto needed people to rebuild them, and after a six-year trip to Earth, the idea of turning right around for another six was unappealing to many of them.

As part of their retirements, the surviving legends were also afforded space on the developing outer coreworlds. Room was plentiful, and a sizable land plot was an easy way to thank the mostly-scientists who threw away their former lives to protect today's society. Who better to rebuild a planet or two?

A handful of exceptions were made. Fowler was now the embodiment of human resilience, the master of xenocide, and as far as anyone could tell—invincible. Earth's prime minister didn't want him living anywhere but on his native planet. Mars held a similar sentiment for Raynor, who was considered one of its founders. As the only planet unscathed by the cephrasts, land on Mars was limited and expensive, but the planetary government offered to get her a home right in the middle of the capital. Raynor had sheepishly asked for a much less desirable house in the dunes—the home she'd returned to this morning after her week away.

Truthfully, it's where she wanted to be. The inconvenience of living so far from a repeater hub was too much for the average 127th century Martian, but Raynor had grown up without them. She also hadn't been able to go out into the rusty dunes without a spacesuit, which she did frequently now. She was still only fifteen minutes from the edge of town, ten from the nearest shuttle port—not that she ever left the planet. The only reason she'd been gone the previous week was for Walker's wedding, and six of those days had been spent in transit.

Six days. With an almost perfect orbital alignment. Raynor really missed void travel sometimes.

Sometimes.

The wedding is why Raynor now sat paralyzed in her rover, staring at the console in front of her. Her trip to Earth made her realize something was missing in her life. For the last three years, her only drive had been the simple act of not being at war. Her entire adult life had been spent fighting for independence, freedom, or survival—she'd never really understood what "normal" could be.

After three years on Europa, Walker moved to West Asia. She married a doctor of anthropology from her last university, only ten thousand years younger than her. Both of them were beginning at a new institution on Earth; Walker was writing about all matters of alien-related topics—her life had fulfillment. Raynor wanted that, too, and it didn't take her three days in an interplanetary transport to figure out exactly what she needed in her life. She'd always known.

She touched down an hour ago, dropping her luggage off at home before impulsively jumping into her rover and driving two towns over. Then, she parked the vehicle and sat there for ten minutes straight, failing to summon courage she didn't know she lacked. Her stomach was in knots, her palms were sweating—it was utterly ridiculous. What was she so afraid of? That he would say "no" to her and she'd have to try again with someone else?

That wasn't it. She was afraid of being laughed out of the building entirely...of putting herself out there and being told, "Are you *joking?*"

When she thought about it, she knew how unrealistic that was. She'd practiced what she was going to say a hundred times during the flight home. All she had to do was walk in, make her proposal, and get her answer without throwing up—easy.

Raynor hopped down from the rover, making her way towards the bland business front. The man she'd come to see might not even be working today, making this whole trip pointless, but she didn't have any other way to contact him yet. She probably could have called the business, asked if he was in, but she hadn't thought of that during her impulse. She was here now.

She spotted him quickly from the front of the one-floor office. He was showing a woman beside him something on a jewel—sales figures or whatnot. Normal work things. Raynor took a deep breath, swallowed past a lump in her throat, and walked over to them.

This is a mistake, she thought. *He doesn't even know you.*

The man glanced up for a split second as she walked over, continuing his conversation about the jewel's contents with the employee. His eyes suddenly widened, breaking away from the discussion.

"Are you—? You're…Nadia Raynor."

"Yes! I am," she said. "And you're Ivan Kavorex, right?"

"That's right," he smiled. "What brings you here?"

Raynor gestured to an image on the wall—a *Kavorex Twin-Core Graviton Astrocraft* flying through an infinite stream of comets.

Piloted crafts were a niche market. People generally scoffed at the idea of paying more for a ship just to fly it themselves, and the reasonable tiers were slow: incapable of advanced maneuvering. If Raynor wanted to *really* fly, her options were limited. The only manufacturer she had known about was Sigren, and while they did make high-end astrocraft, she never wanted to see the inside of one again.

After looking through the specs for every available model, she found her dream ship: the *Kavorex Twin-Core*. Like every other comparable ship, it cost more than her house, which she didn't even buy, so she was taking a tip from Shino, who had routinely detailed aspects of her gaming career that seemed completely absurd to Raynor.

"Well, I really like that ship," she told the Kavorex. "I think it's the best one on the market." His eyes followed hers over to the soaring image of the *Twin-Core*. "If you have a few minutes available today, I'd like to discuss an endorsement proposition."

Kavorex laughed, turning back from the animated picture. "An endorsement from Nadia Raynor? Commander, you can have as much time as you'd like."

Walker stared out at an organized mob of young faces—hundreds of teenagers writing down her every word. Some were genuinely interested in the seminar, but most were required to attend. The study of alien life applied to nearly every field and sub-field within: engineering, biology, anthropology, chemistry. The presentation today was just a wide-scope introduction, enough to teach an undergrad that gaps existed in their courses because the information and technology were stolen from an alien society.

To most of them, her name was one of a thousand in their child-hood history books that they'd long forgotten. A few might remember. Students diving into topics that had a significant overlap with xenobio or cephrast anthropology might even recognize her face.

Otherwise, she was just some old lady talking about aliens—as if the worlds hadn't heard enough about aliens for a while.

Walker had been teaching curriculum at one of the larger universities in the West Asia province for a few years. She only did a class or two each term, spending most of her post-war time publishing. Books about cephrasts, cross-planet evolution, and synthetic-organic biological parallels. It seemed people wanted to read what she had to say. Admittedly, it might be the only time in history that such a perspective would ever exist.

When it came to first contact details, Isaac was also around. Walker hadn't seen him for over a year. He and Aza lived on the other side of the planet in a big, coastal city around what used to be Vancouver. They were also busy with a toddler—an adorable girl named after Fowler's sort-of-ex. Normally, that might be grounds for divorce, but neither of them would be alive if not for Teegan.

Or anyone, for that matter.

Plus, in five years, she'll get to point at a picture in a textbook and say, "I'm named after her!"

Textbook—boy, am I old.

Both Dissenters remained retired, but the defense effort wasn't over. A dozen cephrast armada vessels might still be nearby. Nobody knew for sure, which was worrisome, but it wasn't likely the retreating aliens would return with so few ships. Regardless of where they went, there was no way for the crippled fleet to reinforce itself. Not for another ten thousand years, anyway—give or take some dimensional variance.

Someone else's problem.

At the end of the lecture, Walker took a few questions. The content of the seminar wasn't dense, so there were usually kids who wanted to ask about a specific example. In a group this size, at least one would ask about the first contact. The entire collection of events was taught to them rapidly as a series of brief snapshots, completely void of nuances and perspectives. They often asked about Isaac being vilified, which didn't make much sense to them, given recent context.

This time, the question came from a short girl in a canary-colored tank top, her sandy hair tied back in a ponytail. Teens who had drifted into a daze were suddenly awakened by the realization that Walker wasn't just some old woman talking about aliens, but a *really* old woman who saw the first ones.

"You have to understand, this all happened over the course of ten years," Walker said routinely. "The entire thing was kept secret when it first happened. By the time Isaac was being admonished, we were literally lightyears away, but I think the biomonitor feedback gave everyone the appearance of causality. No one really bothered asking why the beacon was prepped at all."

"So, you think the invasion would have happened anyway?" the girl asked.

"Yes. And we wouldn't have known about it until the fleet arrived. Isaac and—oh, god, what was his first name…Dennis? Douglas. They were the only reason we had an opportunity to defend ourselves. Our entire species is responsible for *why* we were deemed too dangerous to be allowed to thrive."

Some chatter picked up from the young undergrads, broken by a boy further down the row.

"Does that mean they're going to come back someday?"

Over the last six years, Walker had been asked that question more times than she could estimate. Would they return to Sol? To Centauri? Would they get reinforcements from their homeworld? A cephrast military? She'd been asked by countless people in the SDC, by news networks, even by Brody Kahlil. For every scenario—no matter who inquired—Walker gave the same response:

"I don't know…"

And that was just the reality of it.

Thanks for Reading!

I hope you enjoyed reading this story as much as I did writing it.

If you have a moment to leave a quick review on your platform of purchase or preference, your feedback is greatly appreciated!

-Travis Stecher

Learn about upcoming books and exclusive deals in my infrequent newsletter:

www.TravisStecher.com/writing/newsletter

Bibliography

Abadie, Laurie J., et al. The human body in space. (n.d.). *NASA Human Research Program.* Retrieved December 26, 2018 from https://www.nasa.gov/hrp/bodyinspace

Armstrong, Richard. (2011, June 29). Language death. *Engines of Our Ingenuity, 2723.* Retrieved April 30, 2021 from https://www.uh.edu/engines/epi2723.htm

Atomic Heritage Foundation. (2014, June 4). *Atomic accidents.* Retrieved May 18, 2021 from https://www.atomicheritage.org/history/atomic-accidents

British Go Association. *A comparison of chess and go.* (n.d.). Retrieved July 6, 2021 from https://www.britgo.org/learners/chessgo.html

British Museum. (2017, July 14). *Everything you ever wanted to know about the Rosetta Stone.* Retrieved April 30, 2021 from https://blog.britishmuseum.org/everything-you-ever-wanted-to-know-about-the-rosetta-stone

Brittanica (2007, October 25). Kazan: Russia. *Encyclopaedia Brittanica.* Retrieved May 24, 2021 from https://www.britannica.com/place/Kazan-Russia

Centers for Disease Control and Prevention. *About antibiotic resistance.* (n.d.). Retrieved June 8, 2019 from https://www.cdc.gov/drugresistance/about.html

Chattahoochee-Oconee National Forests. (2000) Forest ecosystem study unit. *Georgia Agricultural Education.* Retrieved June 22, 2019 from http://georgiaffa.org/curriculum/getfile.ashx?ID=3096

Colls, Tom. (2009, October 19). The death of language? *Today Programme.* Retrieved April 30, 2021 from http://news.bbc.co.uk/today/hi/today/newsid_8311000/8311069.stm

Daley, Jason. (2018, November 5). Ambitious project to sequence genomes of 1.5 million species kicks off. *Smithsonian Magazine.* Retrieved April 27, 2021 from https://www.smithsonianmag.com/smart-news/ambitious-project-sequence-genomes-15-million-species-kicks-180970697

dCode. *Time dilation calculator.* (n.d.). Retrieved January 13, 2019 from https://www.dcode.fr/time-dilation

Duke University. *Course catalog.* (n.d.) Retrieved June 2, 2019 from https://legacy.dukehub.duke.edu

Ford, Dominic. (2012). 3D diagram of the Solar system. *In-The-Sky.org.* Retrieved July 20, 2021 from https://in-the-sky.org/solarsystem.php

Gammon, Katharine. (2019, February 8). Terrestrial planets: definition & facts about the inner planets. *Space.com*. Retrieved December 23, 2018 from https://www.space.com/17028-terrestrial-planets.html

Horikawa, Daiki D., et al. (2006). Radiation tolerance in the tardigrade *Milnesium tardigradum*. *International Journal of Radiation Biology, 82*(12), 843-848. doi: 10.1080/09553000600972956

Howell, Elizabeth. (2014, April 21). How far are the planets from the Sun? *Universe Today*. Retrieved January 13, 2019 from https://www.universetoday.com/15462/

Jones, Benjamin. (2017, September 7). A few bad scientists are threatening to topple taxonomy. *Smithsonian Magazine*. Retrieved January 5, 2019 from https://www.smithsonianmag.com/science-nature/the-big-ugly-problem-heart-of-taxonomy-180964629

MacFarlane, Seth, et al. (Executive Producers). (2014). *Cosmos: A Spacetime Odyssey* [TV Series]. Cosmos Studios; Fuzzy Door Productions; Santa Fe Studios.

NASA Science. *Europa: in depth*. (n.d.) Retrieved January 2, 2019 from https://solarsystem.nasa.gov/moons/jupiter-moons/europa

Oord, Christian. (2019, March 19). Believe it or not: since its birth the USA has only had 17 years of peace. *War History Online*. Retrieved May 17, 2021 from https://www.warhistoryonline.com/instant-articles/usa-only-17-years-of-peace.html

Perry, Leonard. (2017, March 30). Cold climate fruit trees. *University of Vermont, Perry's Perennial Pages*. Retrieved June 12, 2019 from https://pss.uvm.edu/ppp/articles/coldfruit.html

Queiroz, Alan de. (2010, September 27). Garter snakes. *Online Nevada Encyclopedia*. Retrieved June 23, 2019 from https://www.onlinenevada.org/articles/garter-snakes

Raytheon Missiles & Defense. *AMRAAM missile*. (n.d.). Retrieved June 6, 2019 from https://www.raytheonmissilesanddefense.com/capabilities/products/amraam-missile

Reardon, Sara. (2018, October 17). Cuttlefish wear their thoughts on their skin. *Nature*. doi: 10.1038/d41586-018-07023-7

SETI Institute. *SETI observations*. (n.d.). Retrieved June 23, 2019 from https://www.seti.org/seti-institute/project/details/seti-observations

Sharp, Tim. (2021, July 20). Earth's atmosphere. *Space.com*. Retrieved July 23, 2021 from https://www.space.com/17683-earth-atmosphere.html

Snyder, Douglas M. (2000). *A connection between gravitation and electromagnetism*. Retrieved May 16, 2021 from https://arxiv.org/pdf/physics/0002028.pdf

Stromberg, Joseph. (2012, September 11). How does the tiny waterbear survive in outer space? *Smithsonian Magazine*. Retrieved June 12, 2019 from https://www.smithsonianmag.com/science-nature/how-does-the-tiny-waterbear-survive-in-outer-space-30891298

Tillman, Nola Taylor. (2017, October 20). What is wormhole theory? *Space.com*. Retrieved January 5, 2019 from https://www.space.com/20881-wormholes.html

Tillman, Nola Taylor. (2018, March 26). Titan: facts about Saturn's largest moon. *Space.com*. Retrieved January 2, 2019 from https://www.space.com/15257-titan-saturn-largest-moon-facts-discovery-sdcmp.html

Tillman, Nola Taylor. (2018, October 18). Venus' atmosphere: composition, climate, and weather. *Space.com*. Retrieved December 26, 2018 from https://www.space.com/18527-venus-atmosphere.html

Wood, James & Jackson, Kelsie. (2004, September 16). *How cephalopods change color*. Retrieved April 26, 2019 from https://www.thecephalopodpage.org/cephschool

World Nuclear Association. *Outline history of nuclear energy*. (n.d.). Retrieved May 16, 2021 from https://www.world-nuclear.org/information-library/current-and-future-generation/outline-history-of-nuclear-energy.aspx

Zhao, Lily, et al. (2017, December 18). Planet detectability in the Alpha Centauri system. *The Astronomical Journal, 155*(24). doi: 10.3847/1538-3881/aa9bea

About the Author

Travis Stecher is a writer and musician in Los Angeles, California. After earning his degree in mathematics from UCLA, he worked in a variety of industries before leaving to pursue creative efforts. He's a classically-trained vocalist, a multi-disciplined martial artist, and an award-winning mascot. Travis has written both screenplays and short stories; *Dilation* is his first novel.